PRAISE FOR *ISAAC'S BEACON*

"David L. Robbins takes us from Hitler's camps through the British Mandate in Palestine, onto a rocky kibbutz, and into the dangerous Irgun. A profound and pivotal novel of the birth of the State of Israel, with all its adventures and tragedies on display. This is Robbins—historian, humanist, and master novelist—at the top of his game. An epic and timeless work."

—William S. Cohen, former U.S. Senator, Congressman, and Sec. of Defense

*"*Isaac's Beacon *stands alongside the great fiction epics of Israel by Leon Uris and Herman Wouk. Robbins has written an instant classic."*

—Jeff Shaara, *New York Times* Bestselling Historical Novelist

"Robbins has written his most ambitious book yet. A beautifully paced and utterly gripping powerhouse of a book. Extremely timely."

—Alex Kershaw, *New York Times* Bestselling Author of *The Liberator* and *The Longest Winter*

ALSO BY DAVID L. ROBBINS

Souls To Keep

War of the Rats

The End of War

Scorched Earth

Last Citadel

Liberation Road

The Assassins Gallery

The Betrayal Game

Broken Jewel

The Devil's Waters

The Empty Quarter

The Devil's Horn

The Low Bird

You Are Your Own Always (collection of essays)

FOR THE STAGE

Scorched Earth (an adaptation)

The End of War (an adaptation)

Sam & Carol

The King of Crimes

ISAAC'S BEACON

BEACON

A NOVEL

DAVID L. ROBBINS

WICKED SON

A WICKED SON BOOK
An Imprint of Post Hill Press
ISBN:978-1-63758-998-4

Isaac's Beacon:
A Novel
© 2021 by David L. Robbins
All Rights Reserved
First Wicked Son Hardcover Edition: August 2021

Cover design by Matt Margolis
Interior artwork by Tiffani Shea

Post Hill Press
New York • Nashville
posthillpress.com

Published in the United States of America
1 2 3 4 5 6 7 8 9 10

For Rachel L., with thanks for being my first audience,
marvelous editor, powerful role model,
and incomparable friend.

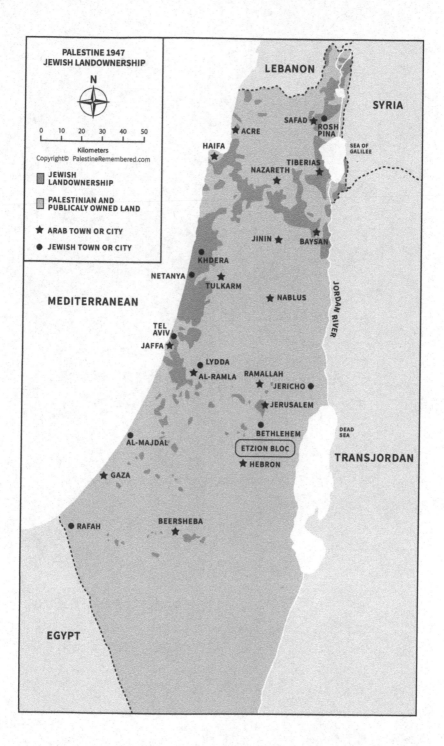

PALESTINE 1947
JEWISH LANDOWNERSHIP

N

0 10 20 30 40 50
Kilometers
Copyright© PalestineRemembered.com

JEWISH
LANDOWNERSHIP

PALESTINIAN AND
PUBLICALY OWNED LAND

ARAB TOWN OR CITY

JEWISH TOWN OR CITY

LEBANON

SYRIA

SAFAD
ROSH
PINA
ACRE
SEA OF
GALILEE
HAIFA
TIBERIAS
NAZARETH

JININ   BAYSAN

KHDERA

NETANYA
TULKARM

MEDITERRANEAN   NABLUS

JORDAN RIVER

TEL
AVIV
JAFFA

LYDDA   RAMALLAH
AL-RAMLA   JERICHO
JERUSALEM

BETHLEHEM
DEAD
SEA
AL-MAJDAL
ETZION BLOC   TRANSJORDAN
HEBRON

GAZA

BEERSHEBA
RAFAH

EGYPT

THE CHARACTERS OF ISAAC'S BEACON

(in order of appearance)

Éva, a young woman who escapes Vienna at the start of the Nazis' rise

Gabbi, the younger sister Éva left behind in Vienna

Mrs. Pappel, a Viennese woman who befriends Éva on the ship to Palestine

Emile, an Austrian boy, friend of Éva's and firebrand

Rivkah Gellerman, the name of a deceased Jewish woman Éva takes as her own

Hugo Ungar, a Jewish survivor of Buchenwald

Vince Haas, German-born American reporter for the *New York Herald Tribune*, former U.S. Marine

Capt. Beshears, U.S. Army officer in charge of Displaced Persons at Buchenwald

Gideon, the American captain of the *Berl Katznelson*, an illegal ship to Palestine

Julius, a Palmach fighter in Palestine

Mr. Pinchus, the underground leader of the Irgun, a Jewish revolutionary force in Palestine

Malik, an Arab gunrunner and poet, friend of Rivkah and Mrs. Pappel

Yakob, redheaded Palmach fighter

Dennis, news editor of the *Herald Tribune*, Vince's boss in New York

Dov Gruner Irgun, fighter captured by the British, sentenced to hang

Judge, kidnapped by the Irgun in Jerusalem and held hostage to prevent the hanging of Dov Gruner

Warden, the administrator of the Russian Compound prison near the Old City in Jerusalem

Moshe Barazani and Meir Feinstein, underground fighters captured by the British and sentenced to hang together at the Russian Compound;

Barazani fought with the Stern Gang, also known as the Lehi; Feinstein was an Irgun fighter

Bill Bernstein, American sailor, second mate aboard the illegal Jewish ship *Exodus 1947*, killed during the skirmish when the *Exodus* was boarded at sea by British marines

Judge Emil Sandström, Swedish chairman of the United Nations Special Committee on Palestine (UNSCOP)

Uzi, the commanding officer of the Palmach force at Kfar Etzion

GLOSSARY OF TERMS

The Mandate of Palestine – following World War I, the League of Nations gave Britain the mandate to administer the territories of Palestine and Transjordan, both surrendered by the Ottomans after the war

Atlit – refugee camp north of Haifa, run by the British to hold undocumented Jewish immigrants before deporting them out of Palestine

Buchenwald – complex of Nazi concentration camps built near Weimar, Germany; one of the first and largest camps to hold prisoners from across Europe and the Soviet Union

Kibbutz – a Jewish communal farm in Palestine

Gush Etzion – a bloc of four kibbutzim ten miles south of Jerusalem on the cusp of the Negev; the bloc includes Kfar Etzion, Massuot Yitzhak, Ein Tzurim, and Revadim

Displaced Persons (DPs) – United Nations term for the millions forcibly removed from their homes during World War II; many returned to their homelands while the rest emigrated elsewhere

Ma'apilim – Hebrew word for immigrants to Palestine

Haverim – Hebrew word for settlers, primarily farmers

Aliyah Bet – the Haganah's organized effort to smuggle Jewish refugees and immigrants into the Mandate of Palestine

Yishuv – the Jewish population of Mandate Palestine

Jewish Agency – the official government of the Yishuv

Haganah – the underground armed force of the Jewish Agency, originally created in 1920 to protect remote Jewish settlements

Palmach – the commandos of the Haganah

Sten gun – a small submachine gun of British design, inexpensive and simple to fabricate

Irgun – a paramilitary splinter group which left the Haganah in the belief that the Jewish Agency was too restrained in its defiance of the British occupation

Lehi – also known as the Stern Gang; broke away from both the Haganah and Irgun; the smallest of the paramilitary resistance groups, Lehi was also the most violent

Bren gun – a light, portable machine gun widely used by British armed forces

Kharda – Arabic word for scrap iron, Hugo's nickname

Acre prison – twelfth-century Crusader fortress north of Haifa, used as a prison first by the Turks, then the British

Russian Compound – in the mid-nineteenth century, Russia built a complex near Jerusalem's Old City to accommodate Russian pilgrims to Jerusalem; the compound included a women's hospice which the British Mandate government later turned into the city's main prison

Sappers – a military term for those who specialize in digging trenches, tunnels, and fortifications

UNSCOP – in 1947, the United Nations Special Committee on Palestine was charged with investigating and recommending the governance of Palestine between the Jews and Arabs

Neve Ovadia – the library in Kfar Etzion, the largest kibbutz of the Etzion bloc

Lamed Hey – Hebrew numerals for thirty-five, a reference to the Haganah platoon killed while bringing, on foot, supplies to the blockaded Etzion bloc on January 16, 1948

Spandau – a heavy machine gun widely used by the German armies in both World Wars

Sharav – a dry, hot, sandy wind occurring sporadically in the Middle East during spring and autumn

Operation Nachshon – the Haganah's plan during the 1948 Jewish-Arab War to open the road for supplies from Tel Aviv to reach beleaguered Jerusalem; Nachshon was the name of the first man to leap onto the dry ground of the parted Red Sea when the Jewish people left bondage in Egypt

Mukhtar – the leader of an Arab town or village

1940

God tested Abraham. He said to him, "Abraham!"
"Here I am," Abraham replied.
"Take your son, your only son, whom you love, Isaac, and go to the region of Moriah. Sacrifice him there as a burnt offering on a mountain I will show you."
Genesis 22:2

Restrain your voice from weeping and your eyes from shedding tears, for there is a reward for your labor; they shall return from the enemy's land. And there is hope for the future; the children will return home.
Jeremiah 31:16–17

CHAPTER 1

ÉVA

September 28
Vienna

In his blue opera coat, Éva's father rode beside her on the tram to the train station. Her mother and young sister filled the seat behind. Her father said nothing on the way; this was how he kept from shouting.

At the station, the eastbound locomotive steamed while porters' bells rang. The platform bustled with departure. Éva stood before the open door of a packed passenger car; every window held faces in profile and tears. Again, Éva told her father his decision to stay in Vienna was dangerous and foolish. He was being hardheaded. On no other day had she spoken to him like this, but she needed to be fearless at the last or carry away with her the burden of holding her own tongue.

Her father lowered his head until his long grey goatee touched his starched collar. Gabbi broke from her mother to hug Éva's waist; Éva crooked an arm around her sister.

Her father spoke in a reined voice.

"You chose to go."

"I want us all to go."

"Edvard." Her mother stroked his arm from behind because she wanted him to speak gently. With effort, he did.

"We will be alright."

"You believe this? The Germans? You believe this?"

"There are a quarter million Jews in Vienna. What can they do?"

Éva could imagine, and so could he. Why say it aloud if he would not?

"You're sending me away."

"We are *not* sending you away." His tone rose; her mother touched his arm again. "You asked for this."

"I want us to be safe. I'm afraid."

"So you leave your home. You leave my protection."

"I leave so you'll come behind me."

"You don't believe I can protect you. Say it. Say you don't."

"I don't. Not from the Germans."

"Good. You have that much courage, at least."

She indicated the many cars packed with Jews. "These people don't feel safe here either."

"I'm not their father. I want my family to stay here. You want us to go. You make me say the hardest thing a father can say. So go."

"Follow me. I'll have everything waiting for you in Palestine."

"Will you have your grandfather's shop there?"

"Papa."

"If I leave, the Germans will take it. And our home. They'll empty my bank accounts. We'll have nothing. Nothing to come back to. This is what I have. This is what my family built. And I should leave it? Stand here quietly while you tear everything to pieces?"

"You can have a shop in Palestine."

"It wouldn't be my father's."

"But it would. You see, it would."

The locomotive screeched. Ghosts of steam riffled past. Éva cupped her small sister's head.

"Let me take Gabbi."

Her father had said all he was going to. He gestured for Éva's mother to pull the younger girl away.

Her mother bussed Éva's cheek.

"My child."

"*Mutti*. Make him come."

Her mother blinked above a final smile. "Make him? Did the two of you just meet?"

"Come before it gets too late. Promise."

"We'll be alright."

Éva embraced her. She found nothing to whisper into the soft curtain of her mother's hair. She couldn't beg or argue more—or say goodbye. Éva kissed her cheek.

Her father took a backwards step. With hands that she had never before seen shake, he unbuttoned his blue opera coat. He smiled, too. He wanted to be remembered smiling. He held the long coat out for her to step into. Éva turned her back for him to drape the coat across her shoulders.

He patted her arms from behind. With a kiss on the crown of her head, her father pushed Éva gently to the train.

CHAPTER 2
ÉVA

November 24
The Mediterranean Sea

Éva hung a sheet between two bunk frames, then squatted in a basin of
seawater. She splashed her calves and thighs and poured a tin cup of cool
water down her back. With no soap or washcloth, she rubbed the water
into her armpits.

Outside the screen, in the warren of laundry and bunks, a late sleeper
snored. A man wept softly, a woman prayed, and the ship's spinning shaft
thrummed in the hull. During the nights, the ship's salon-turned-dormito-
ry brimmed with every noise and odor eight hundred people could make.
All the Jews in their wooden bunks were as stale as she. Another eight
hundred had been stuffed into the *Atlantic*'s few cabins.

Each passenger was allotted one kettle of fresh bathing water per
day. Éva drizzled the last of her kettle over her hair to knead out the
salt. Finished, she pulled the sheet around herself for a towel. One of the
clothespins jumped at her like a grasshopper.

She dressed inside the white tube of linen as if she were on the summer banks of the Danube. Éva tugged on her third and last pair of clean
underpants, one for each week at sea. She slithered into a cotton blouse,
then stepped into a wool skirt. She pulled on knee socks, laced up her

mother's shoes, and covered her hair with her mother's yellow scarf. Buttoning on her father's opera coat, Éva hurried up to the passenger deck.

The fog of last night's storm had melted away. Éva trailed fingertips along the rail through traces of the rain. The blue Mediterranean stretched as vastly as yesterday.

At the bow, she called good morning to the regulars. In the whetted light, the women chirped replies, men touched the brims of their fedoras and caps.

Mrs. Pappel made room at the rail. Éva nestled between her and a small Russian woman who could stand on her tiptoes for hours.

The air nipped here at the leading edge of the liner. The people who came every dawn wore beards and greatcoats, or dark smocks, headscarves, and brocade shawls against the November chill. Children chased each other or climbed on the anchor chain. No one knew where they were on the sea, none had a map or could navigate by the stars. No one had talked with the *Atlantic*'s French-speaking crew. After fourteen days on the Mediterranean, how much farther could they go? With the regulars on the bow, Éva leaned over the rail, trying to be the first to see Palestine.

✳ ✳ ✳

The sighting happened in the middle of the afternoon.

"*Země!*"

A murmur rippled around the bow. Men slapped their palms against the rails. Mrs. Pappel stamped a foot.

"Not fair."

The lone voice went up again, "*Země!*"

The starboard crowd clotted around the man. He stood tall, hatless, not well-fed or groomed, in need of a shave and new shoes. He thrust one arm out; those closest to him sighted down his sleeve.

"*Tamhle, tamhle!*" he hollered, "*Přistát!*"

"Who is that?" Éva asked.

Mrs. Pappel crossed her arms. "A Czech. He only comes up here to sell cigarettes. It's not fair."

A babel went up as more gazed where the Czech pointed. Éva pressed Mrs. Pappel's wrist to say she was sorry but too excited, then ran to starboard. One happy man in her way flung his cap in the air. He was lucky when the wind blew it back toward her, and she returned it to him. He beamed. "Did you see?"

"Not yet."

"Here, here." The man, stumpy and broad, towed Éva through elbows and pockets.

Éva grabbed the rail, not to be jostled or pushed off the spot. It took only a moment to pick out a faint rumple on the turquoise rim of the sea.

The awe of arrival made tongues buzz; the elders muttered grateful praise, the rest raised a cheer for the Carmel Mountains of Palestine. When Éva backed away from the rail, her place was filled immediately. She moved to an open spot on the broad deck, behind the exulting people.

Éva lifted her hands high and snapped her fingers. She snapped slowly, to dance deliberately. Step, step, step then kick, she began the hora. Mrs. Pappel emerged from the crowded rail; the rotund woman clasped hands over her own head and, nimble with joy, sidestepped into the dance. She crooned "*Ay yi yah yi.*" Linking arms with Éva, Mrs. Pappel lifted her face to the unsullied sky.

Their dancing pulled more people from the rail, until all the regulars on the bow joined arms and voices. Two circles formed, a smaller ring inside the larger. The outer line danced to the left; the inner, with Éva and Mrs. Pappel, to the right. Other passengers rushed to the bow; a third ring formed, a hundred more revelers. Young people came, younger than Éva, lean and bright as candles. They joined the dancing circles, moving, singing, crying.

Joy spread around the ship. Éva slipped away from the bow to go see it. In the narrow companionways, families embraced across two and three generations. A man handed Éva a glass of schnapps; he shouted to all who might hear that he'd saved the bottle for this moment. She raised the glass in toast, then gulped. Éva returned the glass, gasping and laughing at herself. Two tall boys, twins, ran by and kissed her on top of the head. A group of black-hatted Hasidim in spectacles and beards, all soft cheeked, read from the Talmud. Women stood near, a whispering flock of linen and covered hair.

The celebration carried on into the afternoon. The temperature climbed enough for greatcoats to come off; the flushed immigrants rejoiced hatless and in vests, bare-armed and windblown.

At dusk, Éva returned to the bow. Mrs. Pappel and a dozen regulars kept their vigil over the Holy Land on the dimming horizon. She pointed to a twist of smoke far off on the water.

"You have young eyes. What is that?"

Éva said, "A ship."

"What ship?"

"I don't know."

Mrs. Pappel nodded at the far-off wisp.

"I'm sorry." She faced Éva. "I haven't asked. No one asks. We don't know each other so well, you and me. It seems improper."

"What is it?"

The woman patted the air with her palms.

"I have my son and his wife with me. We have what we have. Family."

"That's good."

"And you. I think you're by yourself."

"I am."

"So." Mrs. Pappel crossed her palms over her breast to impart that she spoke from the heart, and that Éva could stop her. When Éva said nothing, the woman continued. "Your family?"

"In Vienna."

"Mother, father?"

"And my little sister. They'll follow before it gets too bad."

"Of course they will."

Éva planted a peck on the woman's cheek. Mrs. Pappel remained dry-eyed, though there was much to cry over. On the horizon, Palestine drew closer. Both looked there.

Ahead on the cobalt water, the coil of smoke grew and blackened. The *Atlantic* surged on, making the mountains solid on the horizon. Mrs. Pappel lapped a protective arm around Éva's waist.

A warship powered into view, bristling with guns. The ship flew the white, blue, and red standard of a Royal Navy corvette. Around Éva the men chewed their beards, women pulled the little ones closer.

The corvette pulled broadside to the *Atlantic*, a hundred meters off. A loudspeaker blared from the bridge.

"Passenger ship. You are in British waters illegally. You will follow us to port."

The *Atlantic* acknowledged by blasting its horn twice.

"What does this mean?"

Mrs. Pappel spit on the steel deck. A man might strike something with his fist; this was an old woman's way.

"It means what it means. We don't have entry certificates."

"But we bought passage. It was all arranged."

"Arranged?" Mrs. Pappel wagged a finger. "God's been trying to arrange it for two thousand years."

"But we're supposed to be let in. There's a quota. That's the rule."

"Listen, darling. I know the British, I lived in London a long time. There's no great love for Jews there, trust me. Britain's in a war right now. They're going to side with the Arabs and the oil. The Arabs don't want more Jews in Palestine. So the British don't want more Jews. God doesn't run Palestine."

Mrs. Pappel swept a hand toward the warship.

"They do."

CHAPTER 3

ÉVA

Past sunset, Éva stayed on the bow with Mrs. Pappel and two hundred others; the *Atlantic* dropped anchor in Haifa harbor with a racket that Éva wanted to believe was final. Here we stay. Only one of the *Atlantic*'s smokestacks vented as the ship's boilers banked. The liner fell still, the water lapped at her sides.

No instructions came down from the *Atlantic*'s crew. The British Navy ship that had herded them to the mouth of the port left.

Haifa lay tantalizingly close. Storehouses crowded the wharf, narrow streets and boxy buildings, cranes, and silos lined the harbor. An oil refinery spurted flame.

Near Éva, a boy with waves of black hair peered down at the water, like he was measuring the distance. She didn't know his name. On the voyage, she'd kept to herself; a girl alone had to be prudent. She walked over to him.

"I'm Éva."

"I'm Emile."

"You look like you're ready to jump."

"I could do it," he said. "I could swim that."

Mrs. Pappel arrived between them. "No jumping. And lower your voices. Look there."

She pointed across Haifa harbor, at another anchored ship, painted white, bigger than the *Atlantic*. Gathered along her rail, bunched on her stairs and terraces, a thousand passengers gazed back at Éva and the *Atlantic*.

"Éva, read me the name."

"*Patria*."

Mrs. Pappel repeated it, as if learning the name of an evil. She walked away.

✳ ✳ ✳

November 25

In the morning, Éva slipped into her mother's shoes and her father's coat. She wended through the maze of bunks, away from the waking hundreds, to the staircase and the deck above.

Across the harbor, the passengers on the *Patria* were awake with the sun, too. They lined the white ship's rails in the chilly light. Éva waved but no one answered; she lowered her arm as if she'd done something unfitting.

An announcement burst from the *Atlantic*'s loudspeakers. The captain spoke first in German, then in Czech and English:

"All passengers are to pack and be prepared to be ferried to the *Patria* in one hour."

Éva found Emile on the bow, gazing again down the anchor chain.

He said, "They're not going to let us ashore."

"It's not right."

"We can jump."

"No."

"They're going to send us away." The boy bared his teeth as though something had just jabbed him. "Do you want me to tell you what I went through to get here?"

Éva gently squeezed his wrist. "No."

Emile turned to walk off. She held his arm and asked, "How old are you?"

"Sixteen."

"I'm nineteen. We have time. We can make it back to Palestine."

"I won't go. I'll jump."

"The British will shoot you or catch you and send you to jail."

"You're just scared."

The boy yanked to free himself. Éva hung on.

"If you want to be selfish, you should have stayed home." She let go of his arm. "If you're going to risk your life, do it for more than yourself."

The boy put his back to Éva. A crowd began to arrive from below-decks, many already with luggage in hand. Emile shouldered his way against the flow.

The Jews milled about in their wooly clothes, directionless, a darker and colder people than those dancing in the sun yesterday. Éva had nothing to pack, just underclothes. Some of the grey people reached out, touching her, smiling sadly. They'd reached Palestine, even briefly. They might never see this land again. But young Éva could.

She moved toward the stern. The people she passed shuffled in downcast steps. At midship, the *Atlantic*'s long gangway was being lowered. Two motor launches waited to tie up to the floating platform. British sailors at the helms of the launches smoked cigarettes.

"Éva."

Mrs. Pappel struggled down a staircase, hauling a heavy valise. She teeter-tottered until she set the case beside Éva's shoes.

"I want to be in the first boat. I don't like the idea of getting the dregs for living quarters on that other ship." She toed her luggage. "Can you carry this? My son has his hands full. His wife has a bag twice this size."

Éva hefted the valise. "Where are they?"

"They'll come when they come. He's a grown man. I can make it on my own. With a little help. Drag it over here. Let's start the line."

✳ ✳ ✳

Mrs. Pappel led the way, the first in the queue. Her son and daughter-in-law did not appear before she started down the gangway. British sailors stopped Éva from joining her; the rules were that the first four launches would be loaded with those carrying luggage or small children.

Éva would be squeezed in later with others who had no baggage. Éva kissed Mrs. Pappel, then watched her wrangle the valise down the long incline. All the way, Mrs. Pappel carped and hindered the line.

The two British skiffs shuttled back and forth across the glassy harbor to the *Patria*. Jews clomped down the gangway, shoulders sloped.

In the eighth shuttle, Emile and Éva's turn came to load in. They clambered down the gangway to cram in. The passengers carried only handbags and briefcases. She and Emile were the youngest in the boat.

They took a bench in the center. The tall hull of the *Atlantic* that had brought them across the Mediterranean seemed giant.

Éva's motorboat passed the launch returning empty from the *Patria*. The pilot waved to the sailor steering Éva's craft, like they were doing nothing of note. Closing in on the white *Patria*, Emile's breathing quickened. Éva, afraid the boy might commandeer the launch or roll out of it, rested a hand on his knee.

The *Patria* loomed higher even than the *Atlantic*. How had Mrs. Pappel made it up the gangway? Had some impatient Jew lent a hand or thrown her bag into the water?

None of the old passengers on the *Patria* waved or greeted Éva's approaching skiff, like prisoners watching the arrival of more.

The pilot coasted to the platform. He gathered his painter to throw to the seaman waiting there, a young British sailor in shorts and tall socks.

An explosion erupted.

The great clap made the platform buck and tip the sailor into the water. The launch's pilot stood in confusion; the white hull of the *Patria* shuddered and made a great ripple that almost toppled him, too.

Near the stern, a froth welled in the water, churning into a boiling pool. The water rose in geysers, rocking Éva's launch.

The blast was not a thunder crack or a cannon, but a blast from inside the *Patria*, below the waterline. The harbor rushed into the ship's ribs; air gushed out. The pilot of Éva's launch revved his motor to speed away from the wounded liner.

Emile shouted, "What happened?" The sailor who'd fallen in clambered back onto the platform and waved for the launch to return and fetch him. The skiff's pilot came about, but he refused to get any closer to the ship.

The *Patria*'s alarms tanged. Those people crowding the rail scrambled away. Crewmen stripped the canvas covers off dozens of lifeboats swaying from davits. Éva's launch retreated more to avoid falling debris, casks and things spilled from the tipping deck.

Quickly the suspended lifeboats filled with screeching people climbing over each other. Crewmen lowered the crafts by hand cranks. In the panic, a few lifeboats lost their oars. One woman toppled out of a swaying boat and fell pinwheeling to the water.

A suitcase splashed close. A man plummeted after it, flapping his arms, losing his hat. Another piece of luggage landed, followed by a woman holding her dress down as she plunged.

"What do we do?" Emile asked.

Éva clutched at Emile to stand. They were both children, the others in the lifeboat were adults. Who were they to be on their feet?

Éva unbuttoned her father's opera coat and kicked off her mother's shoes; she left all she had of her parents on the bottom of the launch. Emile doffed his jacket; the sailor and the others in the boat kept their seats.

While the *Patria*'s sirens shredded the air, the gigantic liner staggered onto its side; panicked people leapt and fell a long way, yelling on the way down. Twenty yards from the launch, a woman in a life vest surfaced, thrashing.

Éva dove in, Emile behind her. He surfaced in the cold water at her shoulder and they swam to the woman.

Éva tried to calm her while Emile towed her to the launch where two men hauled her in. The woman wailed about her mother still onboard the *Patria* as if there were something that could be done. Éva told one of the men to take the life vest off the woman and toss it to Emile.

Shouts and splashes spread on the water. The listing liner lowered more rafts, but a thousand Jews still clung to the rails, afraid to jump even as their ship dipped them lower, soon to drag them under.

Éva and Emile became separated. Several times, people almost landed on her. She swam in front of lifeboats, pulled herself over the gunwales up to her armpits and begged those who'd been saved to toss their vests to the ones in the water without them. Someone persuaded her to put one on herself.

The *Patria* took on more water and continued to roll. Gouts of air bubbled from the stern. Éva swam in the froth of the *Patria*'s flooding; she reached dazed people and got them into vests, then lifeboats. The liner tipped more every minute. Another bellow sounded deep inside the ship. The three smokestacks belched steam; the waters had snuffed the *Patria*'s boilers.

The harbor was more frigid than she'd realized; Éva's limbs began to lock. A man with no life vest cried out, but she could not reach him before he sank.

Éva dogpaddled in a slow circle. Fleeing lifeboats surrounded her. Some part of the *Patria* split; the rending made a terrible vibration, the final drowning of the colossus. She became lost in the immenseness of the calamity, floating among people drowning. Her legs and hands stopped moving, the vest alone held Éva up. The dreadful scene became sluggish and the screams grew muted. The liner moaned again, a toll for those still onboard. Two hundred Jews jumped all at once, plummeting around Éva. The lifeboats, already filled, didn't know what to do. Some turned back to help, most sped their oars away from the *Patria* and the sputtering passengers in winter clothes that weighed them down.

CHAPTER 4
ÉVA

Éva could barely keep her chin above the cold water. Thousands of steel rivets popped as the *Patria*'s white hull slid under.

Éva didn't know how long she'd been floating. The ocean liner was nearly gone, groping for the bottom of the bay, swallowing all the water it could take. Loose luggage drifted by, bodies too, facedown as if watching the *Patria* disappear. The buckling ship groaned in the murky depths of the harbor. All else was silent. The klaxons had been submerged, the lifeboats rowed to safety, the calls for help had stopped.

Éva's teeth chattered, her arms and legs felt muddled. She'd been forgotten in the vast field of flotsam, foam, and the drowned.

The cold made panic feel like sleepiness. She had much to do, promises to keep to her father. She'd made it to Palestine, then nothing more. The dead bobbed around her, they'd broken their promises, too. The dying liner exhaled again, like the sound of her name.

Her name had not come from beneath the water, not sighed by the *Patria*, but skipped across the surface.

"Éva!"

She couldn't paddle to turn herself in the water, to face shore and the sun over Haifa, or the sound of a motor.

Someone hooked her by the life vest and snatched her into the empty motor launch. He hefted Éva onto the floor of the craft, then wrapped her in a blanket. At her feet, Emile set her mother's shoes.

Éva's teeth clacked too hard for her to speak. The pilot, a policeman, nodded, then turned his attention to his tiller.

Emile brought his face close.

"Found you."

For the first time, Éva became aware of alarms ringing in the city; clamor streaked over the water. Huddled on the skiff's floor, she dripped and struggled to find warmth. The launch motored among the bodies and baggage, looking for survivors. Emile went to stand in the bow.

The launch was one of many smaller boats scouring the flotsam. Éva hadn't seen or heard any of the craft, she'd been so numb. Jews, British, and Arabs from the city crisscrossed in fishing dinghies, work boats, pleasure craft; they plucked corpses out of the harbor and rescued others who, like Éva, could do nothing to save themselves but float.

The boy hauled eight more of the living from the water. They slumped around Éva, shivering wild-eyed and crying the names of family members, begging the launch pilot to go find them in the water. A few had strength enough to yell, point, and demand. Emile told them to stop, the little boat could hold no more.

The skiff motored to shore. Vessels of many sizes hurried from the docks; the whole harbor and city clanged with bells and horns. Emile collapsed beside Éva.

"Who did this?"

She extended the blanket around him like a wing, to add his warmth to hers on the fast ride to shore.

✳ ✳ ✳

Under the eyes of British soldiers, Éva and Emile stepped onto the dock. The guards herded them into the customs house.

Survivors from the *Patria*'s lifeboats crowded the three-story receiving hall; also, the processing of the hundreds who'd not left the *Atlantic* had begun. Women from the Jewish community in Haifa, the Yishuv, handed out donated fresh clothes; Éva took a dry blouse from a woman who touched her shoulder kindly. Éva moved along barefoot, carrying her shoes. Emile stayed at her side and accepted no charity.

In lines, the Jews handed over their identification booklets in exchange for receipts. A British woman put hands on Éva to feel her shivering. She disappeared, to return with a blanket. Éva put on her mother's shoes.

Emile gave up his ID booklet, pocketing a thin receipt. Éva explained to a soldier that her booklet was in her father's coat which she had lost. The soldier understood enough German to hold up his hands to stop her and scribble her name on his ledger.

The soldier asked, "*Atlantic* or *Patria*?"

Éva and Emile both answered, "*Atlantic*." They hadn't yet boarded the doomed liner.

The soldier pointed at the left of two doors in the rear of the customs hall. There, the *Atlantic* passengers queued. The two thousand survivors of the *Patria* filed through the righthand door. Most had no luggage; they'd lost their bags. The soldier waved Éva and Emile on.

"*Viel Glück*," he said. Good luck.

A hundred at a time, the immigrants were grouped by which ship they'd been on, then ushered out of the customs house into a bright morning. Éva and Emile joined a cluster from the *Atlantic* in a gravel lot, surrounded by warehouses and armed guards. Two buses idled, waiting for them. The Jews, still in shock, turned slow circles. Many kneeled; Éva, too. Under her knees the ground was hard. She shrugged off the blanket to let Palestine's sun warm her.

✳ ✳ ✳

The bus carried the immigrants not far, to a limestone blockhouse. The guards told them to leave their bags on the buses. Inside, the Jews were divided into men and women. Éva's clothes were collected by more Yishuv women and taken away to be treated. Nurses checked the naked people, probed private areas, and asked questions about health. Before sending each woman on, the nurses poured a stinging fluid over every head to treat for lice. Finally came a hot shower, the first for Éva in weeks. She grew flush in the flowing water, all the women did; they lathered soap bars over their skins and let themselves sigh and steam.

Their returned clothes smelled of the delousing liquid. Outside in the sun, surrounded by a dozen police, Emile waited with the men. He bore the same stink of pesticide, but his black hair was combed.

"They're treating us like cattle."

Éva said, "Clean cattle."

The buses carried them out of Haifa on good, paved roads. A truckload of British police led the way; another trailed. New construction dotted the foothills, all the street signs were in Hebrew, Arabic, and English. Scrub brush filled the crevices between the stone houses; much of the vegetation flowered. The light was rich on everything.

The buses drove north, keeping the sea on the left. Beside the road, Arab boys led mules or rode them barebacked. Jewish children played in a schoolyard. Green and golden minarets rose above a few Arab towns. Several ruined, burnt houses sulked near the road.

The rolling landscape stayed stony and monotonous for a half hour, until the bus turned off the paved road, to bounce down a short dirt lane between the posts of a barbed wire fence. Policemen swung the gates open. The Jews pressed to the windows for their first looks at rows of peaked roofs and clapboard walls. Dozens of single-story barracks were pressed close together, connected by weedy ground and blue gravel pathways. Smoke curled from chimneys in the shade of eucalyptus trees.

The buses stopped at a building marked Refugee Center. The Jews from the *Atlantic* stepped off the two buses, some with valises. Emile whispered he was sorry for the loss of her father's coat. Someone must have taken it out of the lifeboat at the quay in Haifa.

"I have my mother." Éva rose to the toes of her shoes. Emile spread his own waistcoat across her shoulders.

The pair of buses drove off through the gates. Inside the wire, armed guards paced in watchtowers every fifty meters. Scrubby hills blocked the view to the sea, but Éva could smell the water. In the other direction, the land ran sandy and pebbly until it rumpled into hills that hid the distance.

Éva and Emile waited with the Jews in the sun. Faces appeared in many cabin windows. No one wandered outside the barracks.

More British policemen emerged from the Refugee Center. They made announcements in English, German, and Polish about cleaning and cooking; the Jews were responsible for their own upkeep. After all thirty-four hundred from the *Patria* and *Atlantic* were transferred to the camp, ration booklets would be distributed.

Each cabin held thirty. The Jews were instructed to separate by families, then by gender, and choose their own shelters. They should get to it because more were on the way.

The policeman making the announcements from the porch stood tall under a stiff beige cap. He tightened his lips between statements, pouting at troubles to be borne. Before the crowd turned away to start inhabiting the camp, an elderly gent called out, "Where are we?"

"You, sir, are in the Atlit Detainee Camp."

"How long will we stay here?"

"Longer than you'll like. And not as long as you'd like."

"What does that mean?"

"You're not aware?"

"Aware of what?"

The policeman rose on polished boots and clasped hands behind his back. Clearly, he did not relish what he had to say next.

"Starting last week, I suppose while you were at sea, it has been ordered that all illegal Jews are to be deported to a refugee camp on the island of Mauritius in the Indian Ocean. You will be detained there for the duration of the war. Afterwards, you will be found suitable homes. Not in Palestine."

The commander strutted away to his office. In his wake on the porch he left a dozen police, nicely turned-out in khaki. One repeated the commander's words in English.

Emile walked off without Éva; several youths followed him into the camp.

CHAPTER 5

ÉVA

December 8
Atlit Refugee Camp

For two weeks, rumors in Atlit became like bread; each person hungrily tore off his piece then passed along the rest. Those concerned with food sought whispers about rations. Others wanted news of the war in Europe and the German occupations. Notes and letters from relatives in Palestine were smuggled in by locals who brought supplies to the camp. When the letters contained news, they set off firestorms of gossip and debate. Speculation over who sank the *Patria* fueled arguments into the nights: the Arabs, the British, German provocateurs, even the Yishuv? The Jewish Agency was reportedly working to convince Britain to let the *Patria* and *Atlantic* passengers stay. Word was that America was weighing in on the Jews' behalf. Some said the people of Haifa were planning to raid the camp, there was going to be a jailbreak, a battle. Others said the people of Haifa had abandoned the Jews in Atlit.

Emile grew thinner inside the wire. He became overly passionate and difficult company for Éva. He cursed too much for a boy. She carried bits of food in her father's opera coat to help feed him.

Mrs. Pappel had returned that coat on the second day of their internment. She'd taken it off a Polish woman she found wearing it in the camp. *Gonif*, Mrs. Pappel spat in Yiddish. Thief. Éva's identification card was still in the pocket. Mrs. Pappel told her to keep this to herself. The less the British knew about any of them, the better.

Mrs. Pappel was housed in a bloc of barracks set aside for the sixteen hundred *Patria* survivors; she'd been onboard when the white liner sank. Like Éva, her son and daughter-in-law were quartered with the *Atlantic* passengers. Mrs. Pappel rarely saw them. When she did, her daughter-in-law made a show of a fresh smock or undented hat. Somehow, the young bride had not lost her immense suitcase; Mrs. Pappel believed this was accomplished at great risk to her son. She felt scorned in their presence and avoided them.

Mrs. Pappel stood in the doorway to Éva's barracks, in silhouette against the morning sun. Éva ushered her inside.

"It's always nice in here." Mrs. Pappel nodded at the thirty girls in the barracks. "Young." From colored paper, the girls had cut flowers and daisy chains and peeled off the pretty labels from food tins to paste them on the walls. The barracks smelled of washed wood; the girls had elected a leader who gave them chores. Some had just returned from their showers before breakfast, scenting the barracks with damp hair. Some said good morning to Mrs. Pappel to show they were pleasant.

Mrs. Pappel sat on Éva's cot. "Your mattress is nicer than mine. You have springs. Mine is on slats."

"You can move in here with me. I'll make room, we can sleep together."

"It's alright. I'm stuck with all the *alt veyber*." Old women. "It's where I belong. Half are older than me. The woman beside me has typhus or something, I don't know, she won't stop coughing. They wash everything, all day. Trust me, darling, the older you get, the more things need washing out."

Mrs. Pappel rose off the cot. She pinched the shoulder of Éva's sweater to lift her, too.

"There's a shipment of hand-me-downs from the Yishuv coming in. Let's go."

Outside Éva's barrack, children played on ground dusty from lack of rain. This time of year in Austria, the earth would be snow-covered or muddy; in Palestine the December air felt cool and arid. A week ago, Éva had let one of the girls crop her hair short.

The white gravel pathways were swept and maintained by the internees. On the walk to the main gate, Mrs. Pappel said that the Jews were a clean people.

"And we're not drinkers. Can you imagine, being locked up in here like this with no liquor? Who else could do this but Jews? Not the British."

"Tell me about London."

"Back in the twenties, Mr. Pappel worked there in the movie business. He was an accountant. We stayed for twenty years. We had a son."

"What happened?"

"Morrie died during an air raid. Heart attack. I got a call from his secretary."

"I'm so sorry."

"Morrie died and I got a call from a secretary. This is the English."

Near the kitchens, old men gathered around a pile of firewood, sitting on upturned logs. They had no tobacco or newspapers, but they had their concerns, enemies, and friends, so they argued.

Walking past, Mrs. Pappel tapped fingertips on her breastbone.

"Morrie, *alav ha-shalom*, would have been right there. He would debate with those gray heads for hours, then come home and say nothing. He had a joke, a favorite. A boy comes home to tell his father he's gotten a part in the school play. His father asks what part? The boy says a Jewish husband. The father makes him go back to tell the teacher he wants a speaking role."

Mrs. Pappel and Éva were not the first at the main gate; dozens of women milled about. A few girls told Éva they liked her short hair; others gave her sideways glances. Mrs. Pappel dove into the many conversations, hands to her cheeks while some scandal was related, then palms over her breast at surprising news.

After an hour of waiting and mingling, a canvas-covered truck arrived. The police tugged the gates open. The driver halted in front of the camp offices, then a woman swung down from the cab. A lean man came from the passenger side, cigarette on his lips. Éva had never seen a woman driving a truck. She wore trousers and suspenders, a brown wool cap, shirtsleeves rolled up, and hair shorter than Éva's. She and her helper set to unloading. Mrs. Pappel and the others dug into the boxes of donated clothing. They tried on items, passed along the pieces they didn't want, and draped the bits they would keep over their arms. Once all the boxes were off the truck, the driver handed down a dozen chairs and small tables, each grabbed as fast as it was set down.

Éva wanted to speak with the driver. Before she had the chance, the woman and her helper bounded into the cab and roared off in the same rapidity with which they'd arrived.

The women traded clothes until the commandant emerged from his office. He stood on the porch and cleared his throat, but none paid him mind. One of his men strode forth to bellow.

"May we have your attention?"

The women looked up in mid-swap. Mockingly, the policeman said, "Thank you."

The commandant moved to the railing, hands behind his back. "There will be an announcement shortly over the camp public address. Please go back to your barracks."

The statement accelerated the pace of their bargaining, to finish and go. Clothing over her arm, Mrs. Pappel stepped out of the crowd toward the commandant.

"What kind of announcement are you talking about?"

The commandant arched an eyebrow. "Your English is excellent."

"It's not my fault."

"Were you onboard the *Patria* or the *Atlantic*?"

"The *Patria*."

"His Majesty's government has seen fit, for humanitarian reasons, to allow all passengers on the *Patria* to remain in Palestine. It has been deemed that by surviving the sinking, you have suffered enough. Those who were still onboard the *Atlantic* will be deported tomorrow at sunrise. Congratulations, I suppose, are in order to you."

The commandant made a shooing motion at the women.

Mrs. Pappel gripped Éva's wrists. "We're staying. My God. We're staying."

She hopped foot to foot; the secondhand clothes fell off her arm. Éva pulled out of her grasp.

"I'm happy for you. *Mazel tov*."

"What? What's wrong? We're going to stay in Palestine."

"I'm not."

"You are. You weren't on the *Atlantic*."

"I wasn't on the *Patria*."

"But you were on the way. You were in a boat. That's not right. I'll speak to them. I'll speak to the police."

Mrs. Pappel covered her mouth and spoke through her fingers.

"*Oy* no. And my son."

Éva took Mrs. Pappel in her arms. "You've been very kind to me."

"You're a good girl."

"I'll see you again." Éva pushed out of the embrace. "I will."

"Here." Mrs. Pappel scooped up the spilled clothes. "Take these."

Éva retreated as Mrs. Pappel held out the clothes. The other women in the yard clustered around Mrs. Pappel. What did the policeman say in English?

The commandant's announcement boomed from loudspeakers. The *Patria* would stay. The *Atlantic* must leave. The old men by the kitchen dropped their heads. Women collected their children out of the open spaces to hustle them inside. Those with cause to rejoice did not, not openly.

Éva walked past her quarters. The girls inside cried and tore up their paper flowers. Éva went to find Emile.

CHAPTER 6
ÉVA

That evening, Emile came to Éva's barrack. The girls wanted to moon over him. They paid attention to his ashen grey eyes and his plan.

"It's hard to say the people on the *Patria* were lucky. Two hundred drowned. Maybe some of you lost friends. I'm sorry. But sixteen hundred Jews get to stay in Palestine. I don't know about you, but I wish I'd been on that ship. I wish I'd had the chance."

The boy moved among the cots and the sitting girls.

"You're all like me. You're alone. And you'll stay alone if they throw us out. You might think you've got people around you right now, you think these are your sisters and I'm your brother. In Palestine, you're right, we are. But if we're put in another camp on some island off Africa, you're alone again. There, we're all just people looking out for ourselves. We'll live one at a time, no matter how many of us there are. The only place you'll ever have a real home is here. The only place you'll have a family again is here. In Palestine, we're a tribe. I am your brother, and these are your sisters. Here, we can work and die for each other. Anywhere else, we're alone."

Some of the girls joined hands. Emile walked to Éva's cot, took her hand, and let go.

"Tomorrow morning at five, the guards will come for you. They want you ready, packed and dressed. They'll put you on buses and take you to Haifa. You'll be on boats by sunrise and out of Palestine before the Yishuv can find out you're gone. So when the guards come in the morning, you won't be ready. Hundreds of us are going to bed naked tonight. We won't be packed. and we won't be dressed. We won't get out of bed when they try to make us. And they will try. You understand?"

A few girls answered yes. Emile repeated, "You understand?", to make the others answer yes.

"A message has been smuggled to Haifa. We're letting them know what's going on. We'll stall as long as we can, to give them a chance to stop the British. Maybe they'll talk them out of it in London, maybe they'll do something here, I don't know. But at five tomorrow morning, we resist."

The girls bit their lips. A few were convinced and said so. One, the oldest, was their leader. She might have been a wife in another place, but no one talked of their past. She rose.

"Won't we be making it worse for ourselves if we start trouble?"

Emile cocked his head. "Worse?"

"Yes. Worse."

"You sound like my parents."

Éva stood. "Emile, thank you. We'll be ready."

The boy left. When the door closed, Éva remained standing.

With all eyes on her, she stepped out of her mother's shoes and set them beside the cot. Éva tugged down her skirt and pulled her sweater over her head. She let these fall on the shoes, untidy. Last, she pushed down her underpants to stand naked and wait. One by one, the girls stood and disrobed, even the older one, the leader. None folded their clothes; some opened their suitcases, mussed them about and left them in disarray.

Together, they climbed into their cots. The leader walked about the barrack nude, blowing out the lanterns before she got under her covers.

✳ ✳ ✳

Éva slept like a skipping stone, touching rest only briefly. She awoke in darkness to a pair of policemen coming through the door.

"Wake up, Jews. Wake up!"

Flashlight beams knifed across the cots. The police knocked batons against bed frames. One stood over Éva, flashlight in her face. The cot rocked when he kicked it.

"Up."

When she made no move, he played his light across her bare shoulders above the blanket. The policeman slipped his truncheon under the edge in an attempt to peel back the blanket. Éva clutched the hem.

"*Raus*," she said. Get out.

He winked, then turned into the barrack to shout. "Up, you bloody Jews, get packed. Get moving. Up!"

"*Nein*," one of the girls yelled. Others took up her call, shouting "*Nein, nein.*" The police bellowed back, "Jews, get up!"

The leader of the girls was the first to be struck by a truncheon, on her hip through the blanket and another on her shoulder. The girl in the cot beside her screamed, "*Nein*," and took a shot on the arm for it.

Both police were young men, fair and slender, neither was impressive. Their willingness to do violence was what made them powerful. The pair leveled nightsticks at the girls, daring the next one to shout *nein*.

"Right," said one when no one answered.

He pulled back the blanket of the leader, exposing her naked on the cot. The policeman was too angry to be lewd, he only waggled the tip of his baton under her nose to ask wordlessly if she wanted another taste of it. Slowly and sore, the girl got to her bare feet. With the other girls watching and the two British boys tapping batons against their palms, she dressed.

✳ ✳ ✳

December 9

Éva sat on her cot in underpants and blouse. An orange sun crested the hills and glowed inside the barrack like the light of a fireplace. The girls packed slowly, singly, without talk. Each was locked inside the camp of herself, in her own expulsion.

Two more policemen came to hurry them along, as threatening as the first. In Britain these were shoemakers and barkeeps; in Palestine they wielded batons.

The girls took their bags and blankets to shuffle outdoors. A few lagged behind, staying on their cots. Éva stayed with them. The police lifted two girls by the collars of their coats, dragged them to the door and cast them out. The other girls grabbed up the luggage of the evicted pair and left the barrack on their own. Éva waited until a policeman stood over her, buying another minute. He tapped his truncheon on her shoulder.

"Move. Now."

She rose. He stood menacingly close. Éva took her time gathering her skirt off the cool floor, then her mother's shoes and father's coat. The policeman's thin patience snapped. He balled a fist in her hair. Éva tried to resist but he towed her to the door then heaved her out. She stumbled down the steps, barefoot in underpants and a sky-blue blouse.

The policeman stood in the doorway, barring Éva's return back to her clothes. He pointed his baton to say, You'll go to Africa like that.

On the unpaved lane in a breezeless sunrise, people emerged only from half the camp. The other barracks, fifty of them, housed the passengers of the *Patria*. They kept behind windows and closed doors.

Hundreds filed past Éva, herded by the bats and jeers of the guards. She was not the only Jew partially clothed; dozens who'd held out even longer than she, young and old alike, men and women, trudged barefoot to the main gate and the buses, some naked beneath blankets. Blood stained some heads. Éva left behind her mother's shoes and her father's coat and joined the procession.

She treaded on her hope, feeling it grow shorter with each stride to the gate and the line of buses. A hundred British troopers waited with rifles, bayonets fixed, against any intervention from outside Atlit.

A commotion swelled on the path. Two boys, the twins who'd kissed her on the head aboard the *Atlantic*, galloped past. They ran stark naked, all ribcages and knees, penises swinging as they stayed ahead of a half-dozen police. The boys yelled, "Don't go! Wait! Wait for the Yishuv!" The two disappeared into an alley, British cops in close pursuit.

The Jews ground to a halt. This confounded the guards, who couldn't beat all of them. More yelling came from the crowd; another round of naked boys, eight of them, pinker than the dawn, sprinted ahead of red-faced police; the boys flew past calling for rebellion, patience. The cops trapped one of the boys between barracks and beat him while he cowered in the dirt. The crowd raised no sound in the boy's defense, but they did not walk on.

Then naked Emile ran past. No one chased him. He might have been the fastest, he might have outfoxed his pursuers. Emile skidded to a halt near the beating to throw a stone at the khaki backs of the cops. He threw another rock and curses. All three police left the bloodied boy to light out after Emile, who challenged the people in the street to hold out before he dashed away. People hurried to the battered boy.

Éva stood motionless. A wizened old woman with a bent spine approached. If this woman boarded another ship, she'd never see Palestine again. She gazed quizzically at Éva, as if wondering what she would do right now if she had Éva's youth.

The shouts of the British trying to catch Emile and his boys bounded around the camp. With batons the guards prodded the Jews of the *Atlantic* to get moving to the buses. Éva peeled off her blouse and handed it to the old woman. She slid down her underpants and left them in the dirt street.

Éva raised her white arms to catch the attention of the hundreds around her.

"We have to wait. Someone will come, something will happen! Don't go. People! Don't go!"

The old woman pressed a hand to Éva's naked belly. She pushed Éva away. "Run, girl."

Two policemen jogged forward. One was a fat boy, the other shorter than Éva. She let them get close, shouting until she almost shouted in their faces. Before bolting, Éva danced four steps of the hora and snapped her fingers at the guards.

She left them clutching at air. Éva ran through Jews who stepped aside to let her tear by, then closed behind her to hinder the police. With every other breath she called to the people, "Don't go!" Éva hurtled down the street, into the slender spaces between barracks. She searched for Emile, for him to see her running, too.

Éva collected five cops chasing her. The fat one fell away, but the others had stamina and scarlet, irate faces. She vaulted back into the street, past the main gate and the buses, then led her pursuers into the rows of barracks filled with the people of the *Patria*.

The soles of her feet hurt, but she pumped her arms harder. The guards would spot her only briefly, scamper to corner her, then watch her run another way.

Éva kept this up for long minutes. The guards grew closer, her escapes narrower. The *Patria* people pressed to their windows to see her loping past. Ahead, two policemen came around a corner, then two more behind to block her in. She was done, her legs and lungs finished.

Éva slowed to a walk; the policemen broke into a trot, raising batons and voices. Another voice, a woman's, came from the barracks beside her.

"Rivkah!"

Mrs. Pappel came out, holding a blanket.

"Rivkah, come here!"

Éva stopped. The agony in her feet groped up her legs; she was close to buckling. Mrs. Pappel broke into a waddling run, still calling, "Rivkah."

She reached Éva moments before the guards, wrapped her in the blanket, then surrounded her with a heavy arm. The other arm she held up to the approaching guards.

"No! No!"

The policemen came up, huffing. One tried to grab Éva away. Mrs. Pappel protected her with a scolding tone and a firm hand that did not come down until she'd pushed one of the guards aside. She guided Éva away, tugging the blanket tight. The muttering cops let them go, so long as Éva was off the street.

Mrs. Pappel clucked her tongue over the blood between Éva's toes. She led Éva to her barrack; the door was held open for them.

Mrs. Pappel spun Éva to face her. The thirty others in the cabin, all elderly women, gathered around.

"Listen to me, girl. Do you want to stay in Palestine?"

Éva fought to catch her breath and her senses. She'd been moments away from a pummeling. Now she was being told she might stay in Palestine.

"I wasn't on the *Patria*. I'm not in the ship's manifest. You are."

"Again. Do you want to stay?" Mrs. Pappel gave her a quick shove. "Éva."

"Yes. Yes."

Mrs. Pappel gripped her by the shoulders. "You are Rivkah. Do you understand? Rivkah. From this point on."

Mrs. Pappel took away the blanket and left her naked again. Mrs. Pappel carried the blanket to a cot where an old woman lay, eyes shut. A white sheet covered her to the folds of her neck, her face and hair were as pallid as the pillow. Mrs. Pappel spread Éva's blanket to cover all of her.

"Her name was Rivkah Gellerman."

1945

As we walked out into the courtyard, a man fell dead. Two others, they must have been over sixty, were crawling toward the latrine. I saw it but will not describe it.

I walked down to the end of the barracks. There was applause from the men too weak to get out of bed. It sounded like the hand-clapping of babies; they were so weak....

I pray you to believe what I have said about Buchenwald. I have reported what I saw and heard, but only part of it. For most of it I have no words. If I've offended you by this rather mild account...I'm not in the least sorry.

Edward R. Murrow
April 1945

CHAPTER 7

HUGO

April 11
Buchenwald

Hugo awoke. He did not know why.

When he'd closed his eyes, he'd believed it would be for the last time. His strength had ebbed away; he lay behind his eyelids trapped with his pulse, listening to it tap like a prisoner in a cell. He slept, or did he faint? He had no idea how long he'd been on his pallet. What use was time when it measured only the living? Then his eyes opened.

He sensed first his aloneness. Licking unwatered lips, Hugo gazed up into the grey slats of the pallet above him. No one moved there, no one crowded him left or right. His shaved head lay on the pillow of his overturned food pot. He cast his hearing out into the barracks. Only a creak returned and a scratch, perhaps a rat leaping between rafters. Or maybe the big room was full, thirty to a pallet, and all the coughing, twitching, and doomed men were blocked out because he lacked the life to hear them.

Hugo's fingers traced the hem of his prisoner's coat, the spike of his emaciated hip, the corduroy of his ribs. These touches restored an awareness of himself, the thing he'd lost.

Hugo sniffed. The smoke was there; the ovens still blazed. He would take this stench to his death no matter when it arrived. He pivoted on his hard skull, left and right. No one else occupied the bunks. Far away, as though at the wrong end of a telescope, the sun glowed in the open door, golden today.

A rumble swelled until it trembled the walls. Voices climbed in volume and excitement. These were not at all like the sounds of Hugo's time in the camps, when only exhaustion, grief, and the ovens had voices. Outside, men cried welcome.

✳ ✳ ✳

Hands fluttered around him like pigeons. Pearly teeth gave off the scent of tobacco.

One held him upright on the pallet. Another rested on his shoulder, a third on his gaunt calf. A fourth man dashed away. A fleshy soldier talked loudly, close to his face as though Hugo were deaf as well as starving. The soldier said 'American,' similar enough to *Amerikaner* for Hugo to understand who they were.

For some reason, they put Hugo on his feet. Two soldiers supported him, urged him to walk. Hugo tried, though he was confounded as to why he ought to. He managed one good step in his canvas shoes, then his lagging leg buckled. Another American, a lanky one, caught him before he could collapse. The man cradled Hugo like a child to carry him out through the door.

The sudden sun was a shock to Hugo's eyes. Sitting on the ground in the glaring light, he was forced to look at himself. His hands were bundles of sticks, wrists and ankles the joints of a skeleton. The pitying looks of the Americans showed him to be an unforgiving sight. Hugo marveled at the resilience of life, even his own, how hard it must be to snuff, that it could live on inside him like this.

He sat in a circle of soldiers, some standing, some kneeling. To a man they were decked in metal: their weapons, grenades, canteens, knives, bullets, helmets, wedding rings, buckles. Hugo wore nothing but skin and tattered cloth. The soldiers spoke to him and to each other, but their voices were like birdsong, distant and meaningless.

Too weary to lift his eyes, Hugo studied the world at his level. American soldiers strode everywhere, pants tucked inside muddy boots. The prisoners of Buchenwald dragged along in their striped garb on ragged shoes. Some ran, but even their running seemed hobbled next to the long strides of the soldiers. A great tank idled beside Hugo's barrack, the thunder which had shaken the walls.

All well and good. The Americans had come. Prayers had been answered.

The stink of the smoke was stronger out here than it was inside the barrack. The Americans seemed very intent on their amazement in the camp.

Hugo didn't want this hunger that made him a pile of bones on the ground, didn't want to die. This was all he could muster, what he didn't want, too weak to recall anything more, even with Americans running about all of a sudden. Minutes ago, he lay on the brink and was done resisting. Hugo had seen a hundred thousand go to their deaths, up the chimney. His turn had come, one more. He tried to lie back to see if he might continue dying; he could do it in the sun just as well.

Before his spine could touch the dirt, hands raised him upright. Hugo wasn't annoyed or relieved. If not yesterday or now, death would come tomorrow, or on its own day. That was Buchenwald.

"Easy, friend, easy."

Others in the ring of soldiers retreated. The man on his knees seemed to have taken control. He had a fair-complexioned face and blue eyes. He smelled as dirty as the rest. He wore a "P" armband.

"You're going to be alright. Just stay with me. No more dying today, friend."

The soldier spoke German. Hugo's hands came up on their own, recoiling. The Nazis had left the camp; now one was among the Americans?

"*Nein, nein, nein.*" Hugo pushed at him. The soldier did nothing to fend off Hugo but endured the pushes, small things. Even with Hugo's useless mitts on him, the German-speaker said crisply, "I'm going to get you a medic. Stay calm. It's over, friend. We're here now."

The soldier yelled in English into the crowd of inmates and soldiers, past the growling tank. He waved at one soldier who changed directions and hustled over.

Hugo dropped his resistance and sat sun-warmed. He didn't know his fate, swerving as it was between living and dying. The short panic had shifted him toward life for a moment. He'd linger to see what life held. Death was busy with the chimney; it would bide its time and wait him.

Hugo whispered, marshalling all the voice he could. The soldier leaned closer. A yellow pencil was tucked behind the man's ear. He carried no rifle, no grenades or bandoleers, only a sidearm. His waist-coat was blank, without insignia or patches. He was long-limbed, scrunched beside Hugo.

Hugo rasped, "Why do you speak German?"

"My family's German. I grew up speaking it."

The beckoned soldier arrived. A red cross on his helmet showed him to be medical. He held a canteen to Hugo's mouth for one sweet swallow. A handful of pills came out of a bag with a tin of milk. The German-speaker said the pills were vitamins. When a passing American offered a chocolate bar, the medical man pushed it away, then had his words translated.

"Don't eat anything these men offer you. No rations, no candy. Your stomach won't tolerate it. Tell someone to get you soup, fluids. We're bringing up a hospital and a field kitchen. Finish the milk. Hang in there. You're going to make it."

Hugo needed help to tip the condensed milk to his lips. Emptying the can bloated his gut. He belched, a pain that made him clutch his chest. The thin soldier rubbed his back, making Hugo conscious of his own knobby spine.

The Americans around him, the ones who'd lifted him into the sunny yard, faded into the hurly-burly of the liberation. The medical man jogged off to other cries. More vehicles roared into the camp, and urgency charged the legs churning past Hugo on the ground.

The soldier remained kneeling at his side. Hugo didn't ask why, slightly miffed that the others had wandered off. He was pitiable and deserved some attention. Wasn't he dying? Apparently not. Hugo asked the German-speaker's name.

"Vincenz Haas."

The milk had loosened Hugo's throat enough to where his voice began to resemble his own.

"Why do you have a pencil behind your ear?"

Vincenz Haas grinned, pleased with Hugo's curiosity.

"I'm a reporter." He tapped the armband. "Press."

"Lift me off the ground. I feel like an abandoned pet."

Once Hugo was put on his unsteady feet, tall Haas had to stoop to support him. They found a chair against a wall in the sunlight. Camp guards had sat in this chair.

Haas walked off, leaving him alone again. Hugo drew a breath that he sampled in his lungs as though deciding whether to take another. Life had returned with the milk and the Americans. Healthy prisoners walked past in their stripes, jubilant, and they, too, ignored Hugo. A thousand starved men and women like him stumbled around, many shirtless and without shame, to show the Americans what had been done to them. Buchenwald's production shacks and barracks, stucco barns and black watchtowers, furnace building and command offices, all were emptied of their guardians. The Nazis had deserted the camp days ago and taken twenty thousand Jews with them, surely to eliminate them.

The afternoon sun peaked. The day was aging, but the world was new. The notion of death returned to Hugo. His life had been rekindled, but only barely. He rested his head against the wall and stared blankly ahead as if he knew the path death would take. Hugo sat in plain sight, brightly lit, no one addressed him; he might just as well be a ghost. He could believe he was dead. Some small comfort crept alongside that. There was company in death. And life? Was it going to be like this—a can of milk, a Nazi's chair, and little else?

Hugo didn't see the reporter until he strode out of the river of soldiers and prisoners. Haas carried a second chair straight for Hugo. High above, the chimney breathed no more smoke. Near the main gate, under the clock tower and the iron sign that declared *Jedem das Seine*, To Each as He Deserves, inmates hoisted two Americans onto their shoulders.

Haas placed his chair next to Hugo. He held out a lukewarm tin cup. Hugo held the aroma of coffee to his nose a long time before drinking.

✳ ✳ ✳

Vincenz Haas asked to be called Vince, the American version of his name. This struck Hugo well, the man's embrace of America. It spoke of change.

Hugo expected to be interviewed, but the reporter didn't take the pencil from behind his ear. Vince propped his elbows on his long legs and asked not about Hugo's time in the camps but his life before. This seemed a way to get Hugo talking, to ask first about his life before he became a victim, before he became the same as millions.

"You'll understand," Hugo said, "if I'm slow to talk about my past."

Vince Haas said he would go first. He was thirty-five, three years younger than Hugo. His family had left Munich in 1927 when he was seventeen, landing in New York City. Vince did a youthful turn in the Marine Corps, served two years in Cuba at a base where he did guard duty and sunbathed. After the Marines, he went home to New York where he took a college degree in journalism, then a job at a big news-paper, the *Herald Tribune*. He worked his way up from night court to crime, to sports, then local politics. When the chance arose to cover the last months of the war in Europe, he grabbed it, a step up from covering the city desk. Vince flew to Paris, hooked a ride on a truck out of France, crossed the Rhine, and caught up with the U.S. Third Army just in time.

Hugo asked, "Just in time? For what?" He was aware of how he himself must look, eyes sunk in grey sockets, camp eyes. "This?"

The American tossed away his cigarette to gaze beyond the wire to the easy hills, brilliant in spring light. A train track cut through the rolling Weimar forests to a platform, then to a road that entered the gates of Buchenwald. That was where Vince's understanding must stop, at the gates. He could not go further on into the filthy barracks that held thirty thousand where there was room for five thousand, or into the workhous-es, into the ovens for those who collapsed or were chosen, to the labs for experiments, then up the chimney. Vince the reporter had hurried here, in time for this, because he could not imagine it from America.

Vince linked his fingers. He spit into the dirt through the ring of his arms.

Hugo finished the coffee and tossed away the cup. He wanted a beer, the first one he'd thought of in a long time, though he knew a beer might kill him.

Hugo ran his fingers, thin as tinder, over his own scalp.

"So, your parents spirited their boy out of Germany before the Nazis could get him."

The American reporter did not lift his gaze out of the circle made by his arms, elbows on bony knees, and his long, joined hands.

"The Nazis wouldn't have gotten me."

"No?"

Hugo lay a hand, fingers thin as tinder, on Vince's arm.

"We have no idea, none of us, what we are capable of."

Vince focused, somewhat unnaturally, on his spit in Buchenwald's dirt.

Hugo said, "Help me to my feet."

Vince lifted him by one arm. Hugo wavered, but before the American could right him he steadied himself.

"You've told me your story. Now you believe I should tell you mine."

"I suppose."

"If you want to know something, ask. I'll tell you if I care to. I'm not a child to be tricked or traded with."

"Alright."

"I think I can walk a bit. Follow me."

✳✳✳

The Americans covered their nostrils with sleeves and kerchiefs. The smell seemed to trouble them more than the sight. None of the inmates who guided the soldiers here disrespected the dead like this.

Hugo pushed closer into the stench so Vince would have to come with him. Vince screwed up his face but did not cover his nose.

None of the observers stayed long; they got their fill and turned away.

The pile extended forty meters down a hill. Every corpse was naked and face up, stacked as neatly as could be done. The bottom row lay oriented north-south, the next east-west, and so on in six layers. The eight hundred starved bodies had been stripped of belongings and identification. Their clothes had been cleaned, stored, then given to German citizens who'd suffered in the bombings. The collection and cleaning detail had been Hugo's work. A haunted face in the growing crowd was a man who'd done this with him.

Vince would not walk off until Hugo did. Hugo had no intention of being cruel. He turned away slowly, not to unbalance himself.

The distance to the furnaces was short, as it needed to be. The stink faded enough for Vince to take a fuller breath. He was a reporter but knew well enough to leave his pencil untouched.

Barn doors stood open at opposite sides of the two-story furnace building. The brick structure had nothing striking about it, a bland face. A chimney climbed high out of its midsection, but someone had shut the fires down.

At the entrance, Vince stopped walking. He clamped his lips, visibly closing something inside. He breathed fast, grasping to stop himself from what? Throwing up, screaming, tears? He walked in before Hugo. Vince reached for his pencil and slipped a notebook out of his jacket. He did not write but sketched. Hugo followed, the first time he'd come inside the furnace building without pushing a wheelbarrow.

The brick wall rose two stories high. Thirty iron doors a meter wide and tall studded it. The tops of the openings were arched in decorative brickwork, like a bakery. A few doors stood open; the metal trays had been pulled out by the curious. Ash heaps covered all the platters, save one where a burnt corpse lay. The fire had exposed the skull, ribs, and arm bones, melted away all hair, boiled out the blood. No other colors hinted that this mound had ever been more than white and black. The ovens could handle a hundred bodies an hour; even so, the Nazis couldn't keep pace.

Vince scratched rough images. Hugo left him and walked to the wall, to flatten a palm against the bricks. Warmth lingered in them. Pressing his spindly hand to the bricks, he damned the wall. If he could push this place down, he would willingly die under it; here was where he'd been intended to die. He did push, despising his futility.

Hugo came close to exhausting himself, and when he turned, he was foggy. Vince was gone outside, smoking in the sun. Other touring soldiers entered the barn doors with their prisoner guides. As Hugo left the crematorium, a spring gust drifted past. A whorl of ash twirled off a tray to filter over him.

Hugo's canvas soles dragged on the floor. Of all the noises in Buchenwald, the shouts and wails, vehicles and whispers, the shuffle of his own feet struck loudest, an almost weightless tread.

Vince didn't turn when Hugo approached. He ground a cigarette under his heel. The American couldn't lift his eyes. Hugo stepped close, into his gaze. Vince had shed no tears. Good. His sketches would be of more use.

"I'm afraid you're out of luck."

A cluster of inmate boys walked past, vigorous and looking for some advantage, something more than food, perhaps vengeance. Vince watched them go, and this seemed to animate him to answer, "How so?"

"I have no story for you."

"What do you mean?"

"A story must have a character. And a character must have a past."

Hugo pointed at the boys walking away.

"See them. See all of us. Every one, tens of thousands, we were all different before the Nazis. We had stories, the kind you want to know. Families and homes. Now there are no families. No homes. No work. No friends. No secrets, every one of us has blurted out everything. All of it was thrown into a bonfire the Nazis lit. Our lives, the things that made us individuals, everything is in ashes now. Indistinguishable. We're all identical, reduced to one new and terrible thing. None of us has a past, just our own portion of the powder. There's nothing you can sift out."

Vince was likely the tallest man in the camp. When he looked beyond Hugo, he seemed able to see a great distance. He may have been a very good reporter.

Hugo rubbed his palms together. He patted Vince's jacket, a drunken sort of gesture.

"I need to rest." He would head back to his pallet. "Meet me here tomorrow morning."

CHAPTER 8

HUGO

April 12

On a pallet with no cushion, in a body with no fat, Hugo slept well. Everyone in the barrack did, the first night in years that they were certain they would not be murdered the next day.

No one shared Hugo's pallet, no one mumbled or whimpered beside him. He arose, blanket across his shoulders in a cape. He padded outside; the morning sun peeked over the farmland and hills, too early to lift the dew. The camp at sunrise had already begun to quicken; Americans sipped steaming coffee, scooped eggs off tin plates, hunkered against the chill.

Hugo's legs felt surer. One of the first inmates awake, he moved among the soldiers at half their clip. With an appetite, he passed a field kitchen, then a truck from which soldiers uncrated food and supplies for the camp's remaining ten thousand. He'd return later to ask for soup and perhaps something to chew, like white bread. Hugo felt nothing of the cold.

The noise of a big engine drew him through the camp. He shambled along a row of barracks, a hundred meters to the furnace building. Hugo followed the motor noise around back of the brick walls, to a small field at the bottom of a slope.

A bulldozer had dug a fresh pit and was busy shoving hundreds of
naked bodies into it. The machine spit exhaust as black as the task. The
American at the controls worked alone. No one but Hugo had come at
first light to see what he and his earthmover were doing. Could this soldier not sleep? The sorrow on his face touched Hugo, who hadn't wept
in a long while. When the driver noticed Hugo, he stopped working and
let his bulldozer growl. The man's jowls were dark; he needed a shave.
He nodded at Hugo, then shifted into gear and continued. Hugo dragged
back to the barracks.

By the time Vince caught up with him, Hugo had eaten a boiled egg
and a warm bowl of gruel, followed by a tin of condensed milk. He'd visited the latrine for the first time in two weeks; his released bowels pained
him. Other prisoners were sick in the toilets, in worse agony than him.

The Americans who'd flooded Buchenwald yesterday had put up
posters today with their own rules: no one but them could carry weapons,
curfew at sundown. Medical help and food were available in the camp only.

A handful of journalists walked the grounds searching out inmates
who could speak English for interviews and photos.

Vince waved at first sight of Hugo. He bore the gift of an Army
jacket. Hugo dropped his blanket to put it on; he could get as many blankets as he wanted.

He pointed at Vince's "P" armband. "Take that off."

Vince did without question.

"Give me your pencil."

Vince handed it over. "Okay. Why?"

"Because if you want to report, put on your armband and go report.
If you want to try to understand, come with me."

Hugo led the way, stopping every few minutes to catch his breath.
He spoke little passing the fifty barracks, dozen workhouses, and storage
sheds. They crossed open yards where inmates had assembled for roll
calls and a wooded area where guards had tied the arms of prisoners behind their backs to hang them by their wrists, which the inmates named
the Singing Forest. In a dark cement building, doctors had conducted
experiments and autopsies. Hugo said only, "The labs."

Vince was smart and stayed quiet. As they walked, the questioning looks on his face came less frequently, his shrugs of disgust quit. He stopped trying to figure Buchenwald out piece by piece, a step at a time. Buchenwald could not be encompassed by a tour, gathered by the senses, or expressed in words. The camp was not a collection of buildings and guards, days and years, trains and trucks, scraps and smoke, Jews, Russians, Roma, homosexuals, communists, criminals, despair, acceptance. No part of it could be considered separate from the rest. Buchenwald was a totality, a monolith, an inseverable thing. Buchenwald was not the story of any life or death, place, or moment, but all of it, and only someone who'd lived it could fathom it completely.

At the main gate sat an American vehicle, a small open two-seater. No one seemed interested in it, and the key was in the ignition. Aching at the hips, Hugo climbed into the passenger seat. When no one told him to get out, Vince got in behind the wheel. Quickly they drove through the main gate, beneath the clock tower.

Not far beyond the wire and the SS barracks, blossoming trees bracketed the road. In the open car, Hugo pulled tight the Army jacket.

Vince asked, "Where to?"

"Town."

※ ※ ※

The destruction of Weimar was not complete. Hugo and Vince drove past intact homes and businesses, yards fletched with tulips and flowering shrubbery, bright laundry on sagging lines. In bombed lots, gardeners under sunhats troweled in the dirt. Bicyclists avoided craters in the road, children chased a dog across a field of bare chimneys. A church and steeple were somehow untouched. Perhaps if the war had gone another month, this place would be more ruined.

In the sunny late morning, Hugo guided Vince to the town center. The reporter drove carefully; he and the Army vehicle were the only American presence in sight. Townspeople walked or biked; there was no gas for vehicles, and the horses could no longer be fed so they'd been eaten. The car's noise drew attention as they rolled into the market square.

"Stop here."

Vince pulled up to a fountain. The marble pool was dry, a naked Neptune at its center ruined by shrapnel. In February, an air raid had obliterated half the square; camp guards had ferried Hugo and a hundred others here every day for a month to sift through the carnage, salvage what remained, and dig graves.

The U.S. Army had torn down all of Weimar's swastika banners, chased out the last fighters, and killed who they had to. The townsfolk in the square kept their distance from Vince and Hugo. Young women walked without young men, the elderly picked through the debris for bits they could use. In the ruins, people chipped mortar from bricks, then stacked them neatly for the rebuilding of Germany.

Hugo peeled off the army jacket. "Stay in the car."

He climbed out in his striped prisoner's clothing. A woman walking a child pivoted to take a different path across the square.

Hugo walked a lap around the fountain, then widened his orbit. He strolled past the centuries-old *Rathaus* town hall, empty shops with shuttered windows, a field of rubble where an apothecary once stood. A nurse on a bicycle rang her bell for him to get out of the way. Old men in vests and ladies in clean dresses halted to let him go by. Schoolgirls were unable to hide their distaste.

Hugo circled back to the car. He gestured to the pistol at Vince's waist. "Is that loaded?"

"It is."

"Do you know how to use it?"

"What are you going to do?"

Hugo unbuttoned his coat to show his ribs. His gut was shrunken, a sinkhole. He advanced on the people, lurched into their paths, shook the coat as if emptying himself, made them sidestep or turn away. Women covered their mouths and the children's eyes, men froze to stare. Hugo tired and returned to the car.

Vince drove out of the square. He waited until they were well away from the bomb damage and into the fields on the outskirts of town to ask, "What was that?"

Hugo laughed at the question. "Come now. Do you have to ask?"

CHAPTER 9

VINCE

Hugo said no more in the rolling jeep. The little man leaned back his shaved head and closed his eyes to the sun and wind. Vince couldn't read a mind like his, couldn't make guesses after what Hugo had lived through, but imagined he was simply returning to life.

Five kilometers outside Weimar on the shoulder of the road, a dozen inmates in prisoners' garb walked in a tight ring. None of them were as thin as Hugo.

Hugo said, "Stop the car."

Vince halted. The inmates paid no mind. The young man they surrounded wore a brown civilian suit.

"I recognize him," Hugo said. "He's one of the camp guards. They must have found him hiding. Follow them."

Vince crept the jeep behind the walkers. The prisoners kept close ranks around their quarry, who made no attempt to bolt. They traveled a kilometer in this formation, ignoring the jeep inching along behind.

The road led past an abandoned farmhouse. The gang of inmates and their prisoner entered the yard.

"Pull over."

Vince stopped. Hugo stepped out and without a word slid into the midst of the inmates. Together, they moved beneath a great oak just beginning to bud.

Two of the inmates disappeared into a barn. They rummaged about until they emerged; one rolled a wooden cask, the other carried a coil of rope. Beneath the old tree, they set the barrel upright and lay the rope on top.

With Hugo, the inmates made a circle around the guard and the tree. One old inmate moved into the center. He'd rolled up his striped sleeves as if there was work to do, but he touched nothing, only spoke to the captured young man. The guard listened wide-eyed, then lifted the rope off the cask. The old man who'd whispered to him faded back into the ring.

Another stepped forward. Like the first, he spoke low. The guard was a fair-skinned young man, hair cropped short to leave a mop of corn-silk yellow on the crown. His clothes ill-fit him, plainly borrowed or stolen. He faced the inmates, scared and compliant, eyes fixed on whomever was speaking. He nodded like a schoolboy. The inmate, a swarthy man, made guiding gestures with a finger, instructions.

The guard fashioned the rope as he was told. He made a loop, then took wraps around it. In his quivering hands, it took on the shape of a noose.

Vince did not need his pencil or notebook. Here was nothing he would forget.

Once the rope had thirteen turns and was a proper hangman's tool, another inmate moved into the circle. He directed the guard to toss the noose over a branch two meters above his head. Another stepped forward to have him to tie the loose end of the rope around the tree trunk. The guard's movements looked automatic, not his own. Two more inmates strode forth, to hold the cask while the guard climbed up on it where the circlet of rope dangled in front of his face. The guard went stock still, a statue of a young deserter on a pedestal.

Hugo moved into the center of the ring. Peering up at the guard, he spoke quietly. The youth shook his head once. Hugo spoke again, the boy nodded. He slipped the noose around his neck, then pulled it snug.

Hugo spoke again. The guard stepped off the barrel. Hugo retreated to avoid being kicked. The guard tried wildly to grab the rope above him but failed, swinging harder. His heels struck the side of the barrel, he took one crazed shot at getting back on top of it but kicked it over. He choked out croaks until his mad arms and legs faded to twitches. When his fingers lost their clutch, he swung and the branch creaked. Vince turned for the car and waited for Hugo.

Vince drove off the instant he climbed in.

"You killed him."

"Did we?"

"You know damn well you did."

"What did we touch? Did we throw the rope over the tree? Tie the noose? Kick out the barrel?"

"That's fucking clever."

"Perhaps. It was many things."

Vince drove until they'd gone beneath the camp's tower and black sign. He parked near the main gate, left the key in the ignition, and climbed out. No one paid notice; the camp swarmed with the same activity it had an hour ago.

Hugo strode close to Vince, to speak evenly, the way he had to the guard.

"You killed him, too, you know."

"I did not."

"You have a gun. You're in uniform. You could have stopped it. You didn't. Why not? Was it for the story you'll write about it?"

Hugo patted him on the arm. "It's alright. You didn't come to Germany to be a murderer."

"I'm not."

"Of course not. That Nazi boy hanged himself by his own hand. You're innocent. So are we. That's what the sophists among us will tell ourselves. May I ask a question?"

"I'm not sure."

"I'm not setting traps for you."

"What."

"Why do you think that guard stepped off that barrel? What do you think I said to him?"

"I can't imagine."

"I told him he could walk away if he wanted. We wouldn't stop him. But one day he would hang, and he knew it. Either he'd do it in a thousand nightmares until he hanged himself in some basement. Or the Allies would catch him and do it for him. I asked him to kill himself where we could see him. If some day he slipped a noose around his own neck in private or he was executed in a prison yard, it would be a waste. Doing it in front of us was his one chance."

"Chance at what?"

"To do something that mattered. Something of note."

"This is crazy."

"Is it? I asked if he hated us. He said he did not. I told him that was a shame. If he hated the Jews, then at least what he'd done in the camps would have been some work of accomplishment. If he didn't hate us, then everything he'd done, every crime, had been the act of a stupid mindless follower. His life had meant nothing. But, I told him, he still had a chance at significance."

"How?"

"He could do what we did. At first, when the Nazis came for us, we fell back into our magnitude, our millions across Europe. We mattered for our works, our art and money and influence. Our covenant with God. All very important, yes? Then in the end, when we were proven wrong, we took solace in our victimization. We went to the pits and chimneys indignantly and bravely. We did it believing to the last that the only noble act left was to die wronged, to cast our blood on those who did this to us. Our only way to be avenged was to brand the Nazis our killers. That is what I told the guard. If the Allies strung him up, he'd die as he lived, a drone. If he committed suicide alone, he'd be just a murderer and a coward. But if the Jews hanged him, well then, you see, we'd be damned as his killers. He'd be dead, which was inevitable, but we would bear the shame and crime of his death. Hanging at our hands was the only act of meaning he had left. In this way, he was no different from a Jew."

Again, Hugo patted Vince's arm.

"Except he was wrong, of course. We didn't hang him." Hugo returned Vince his pencil. "Write this down."

Once Vince pulled out his notebook, Hugo stuck a chalky fingertip onto the blank page.

"My past. Record it and take it. I have no need for it anymore."

Vince scribbled.

"I was a plumber in Leipzig. I had a mother, father, and a sister, all teachers. One night the truck came for me. Just for me. I told my family to go from Leipzig. But where, they asked? I had no more time. At the train station, I stole a pair of pliers from a toolbox. With three hundred others I was shackled into a cattle car. Leaving Leipzig, I pried off my leg chains. I pulled down a board from the wall. The others begged me to leave the pliers behind so they could free themselves, but I needed them to take off my own handcuffs. Every minute was another kilometer from the city. I leaped into the night. I forced open my manacles and made my way to my home. It took me a week of hiding. When I got back to the city my family was gone."

"Do you know what happened to them?"

"I found a neighbor I could trust. He told me they'd been sent to the Riga ghetto."

"Do you think they're alright?"

"No. I do not. After two more days, I was captured. The Nazis deported me east to Treblinka. I survived there for three years. Only a few did. I was the Nazis' plumber, you see. When the Russians began to close in, I was transported to Buchenwald, where I survived again."

"What are you going to do now?"

"You saw the people in Weimar. The hatred. Mine for them. I can't stay in Germany."

"Where will you go?"

Hugo trickled knotty fingers over his striped coat. "Many will want to become Americans."

"Probably."

"I won't."

"Why not?"

"In America I'd be a plumber. At the moment it's my only skill. But I'm through with it. I was a plumber for the Nazis. I want other significance."

"What else will you do?"

"It doesn't matter. So long as I'm safe."

"You'd be safe in the U.S."

"I can't have my safety in someone else's hands. My own particular terror demands that it be in my own. What do you know about Palestine?"

"They're trying to make a new nation. It's a violent place."

"Birth is often that way."

"Are you going?"

"I believe I will. And I believe you should come with me."

Vince couldn't go to Palestine. He'd promised the newspaper he'd be away only a few months. He was close to having what he needed for a series of articles on the last stages of the war and the liberation of Buchenwald. He could stay overseas only a few more weeks.

"I can't."

"You can't? I see. And what of the things I can't do? I cannot go home. Keep solid food in my fucking stomach. Speak with my family. Please make me a list of what you can't do."

Hugo retreated on his disintegrating shoes. Before he'd gotten out of earshot, he stopped.

"Here is the point, Vincenz Haas, where you have two paths. Remain the American reporter and watch me walk away. Spend a few more days in Buchenwald, then write your newspaper articles. Whatever that says about you, it says. Or have faith that I will live a new and purposeful life in Palestine. Come with me and see. You may even live one of your own."

Hugo strolled off.

CHAPTER 10

RIVKAH

June 30
Kibbutz Kfar Etzion
Palestine

The barn door let in a morning breeze that stirred the smells of manure and straw. All the kibbutz's eight Baladi cows stamped, urging to be milked. On her stool, Rivkah set a bucket beneath the first one.

An unexpected boy entered the barn. He stood on the fresh chaff holding a red hen to his chest.

"Hello," Rivkah said in English.

This was Shmuel, one of ten orphan teens who'd arrived in Kfar Etzion last week from Hungary. Shmuel nodded to Rivkah. He hadn't learned Hebrew or English yet, and was not a German speaker.

"What are you doing here?"

Shmuel stood stiffly, confused. The chicken clucked in his arms.

"Why do you have a chicken?" Rivkah mimicked his hold on the bird.

Another boy and three girls strolled in. Each wore khaki pants and a white work shirt. They took positions flanking Shmuel and his chicken, gazing at Rivkah for instruction. One girl broke ranks to pet the flank of a cow; the animal stamped a hoof.

Rivkah had no idea why the children were in the barn. She continued milking the impatient cows. The teens took turns stroking Shmuel's chicken.

Five more youths entered, all in khakis. Mrs. Pappel arrived, shooing more young ones ahead of her with the backs of her hands.

"Go, go, go."

Four cows struck hooves on the straw; with so many people in the barn, each believed it should be milked next.

Mrs. Pappel wasted no time seating the children in a semicircle. She wore a sleeveless denim smock, one long grey braided ponytail hung down her back like a whip. Her tanned arms resembled a farmer's.

Rivkah asked, "What are you doing?"

"Can you stop milking and come over here, please?"

"No. Why?"

"I'm teaching class in the barn this morning. I want you to join us."

Mrs. Pappel had never taught in the barn. Rivkah stood in curiosity; the milking could wait, though the cows were used to their schedule. The children sat cross-legged in a circle around Mrs. Pappel.

Rivkah asked, "Why does Shmuel have a chicken?"

"It reminds him of his father. The man was a butcher in Budapest. Leave it alone. Sit."

"I don't need to study English. I live with you."

Mrs. Pappel pointed at the straw. "Sit."

Rivkah took a spot in the semicircle. The cows mooed for her return.

Mrs. Pappel began by having the class sing a traditional English ditty, "Dig a Ditch and Go Whoo!" Shmuel's chicken remained serene. Mrs. Pappel pointed out many things in the barn, putting them into sentences, making the children repeat. The cows eat *grass*. We drink *milk*. The *straw* smells nice. Rivkah chanted along with the ten orphans. The girls eyed her admiringly.

With pantomimes and silly faces, Mrs. Pappel drew laughter and English from the young teens. Rivkah clapped with them during the lesson.

A knock came on the open door of the dairy barn.

Five British soldiers filled the broad doorway. Under the rafters strode a craggy officer; he removed his khaki cap. Mrs. Pappel stepped toward him. Rivkah rose.

"Ladies."

Mrs. Pappel tilted her head without losing her smile. "May I help you?"

"You speak English."

"I do. I am teaching it to these children. And you are interrupting my class."

"I beg pardon. My purpose can be disposed of quickly enough."

"I'm sure. It is?"

"We're looking for illegal Haganah weapons."

"In our kibbutz?"

"Everywhere, madam."

"Are you looking in the Arab villages, too? I see Arabs carrying guns everywhere."

"I'm not a politician, madam. I have no say in that."

"Does that make it proper?"

"It makes it my job."

"You want to look in my classroom?"

"I wish to look in this barn. I didn't know it was a classroom."

"As I said, with respect, you are disturbing my class. And your guns are scaring my students."

"Where are these children from?"

"Hungary."

"Then I'm sure they've seen guns. Why does that boy have a chicken?"

"Even our pets have jobs. This one lays eggs."

The officer eyed the barn, the seated teenagers, the standing Baladis, Rivkah's full pail, and another half-empty. The cows lowed in complaint.

"Those cows need to be milked. Don't they disturb your class?"

"The children also need to learn the word for 'moo.' So, you grew up on a farm?"

Rivkah smiled at the five soldiers in the door; she slipped past them to go outside. Six British gun trucks waited in the unpaved road leading up to Kfar Etzion. Soldiers filtered throughout the settlement, in and out of buildings, accompanied by residents.

Rivkah re-entered the barn. Mrs. Pappel had one hand on her hip, the other on the officer's wrist.

"I was born in Austria, but I lived in Mayfair for years. My husband was in the movie business."

"And what brings you to this godawful place?"

"My husband died."

"My regrets."

"He left me all his money. I used some of it to come to this godawful place. The rest I donated to the relief fund. Now, Captain, you're welcome to return when class is over in three hours. We can talk then, if you like. I'll tell you all the movies Morrie worked on."

"Three hours is a long class."

"English is a very difficult language. And this young lady is going to give milking lessons. There are so many words to learn about cows."

"We'll be gone by then."

"A shame."

The officer bowed shallowly, donned his cap, and left.

Rivkah whispered, "You and I will talk about this."

None of the students or the chicken had made a peep while the soldiers were present.

Mrs. Pappel widened her stance on the straw, pretending to hold a rifle. "British soldier. Who can say 'British soldier'?"

All the young Hungarians shouted it out.

CHAPTER 11

RIVKAH

"Here."

Mrs. Pappel pointed at a spot on the ground no less rocky than any other patch. She made it plain she was tired of walking and sat with a wheezy sigh.

Rivkah handed down her canteen. The western horizon dipped and rose, mistless and sharp in the light. The landscape tumbled into sere gulches and climbed to stubby white heights. Scrub did little to color the hills. Patriarchs and prophets had walked this way out of the Negev, north from Be'er Sheva, through Hebron to Jerusalem. It was easy to see why they'd kept walking.

A kilometer away, beyond a wadi, a broad knoll cast a humpbacked shadow. Boulders made the crest look jagged and forsaken, nothing but stone and hard earth.

Rivkah said, "They say there's a spring running down the hillside."

"A life can be built around a spring."

"It's not good land."

Mrs. Pappel swallowed from the canteen. "Not like this garden spot." Mrs. Pappel patted her thigh. "Sit, *Liebling*. Put your head in my lap."

Rivkah stretched out on the pebbles to rest her head against Mrs. Pappel. The silence of the wastes wafted by.

"Go ahead. Ask me."

"The soldiers today."

"Yes, dear. The soldiers."

"Why were they looking for weapons in the barn?"

"Because they'd already found some under the chicken coop. Shmuel grabbed one of the hens before it could get away. Good boy."

"There are guns in Kfar Etzion?"

"There are guns everywhere. We need to make sure we have ours."

"Are they in the dairy barn?"

"Under the floorboards. You were sitting on them."

"How do you know this?"

"It's fairly obvious at this point. I'm in the Haganah."

"That's incredible."

"Not so much. There's only some kinds of work I can do. I'm too old to push rocks or pick olives. I can't build Palestine. So I do what I can to defend it."

"Are you a fighter?"

"Heavens, no. I hide guns."

"You're a spy."

"I'm an agent."

"Do you report on me?"

"Hardly, dear. Only on the Arabs and the British."

"How did this happen?"

"A month ago. Remember, right after I got here, there was a Bedouin attack. A platoon of Palmach came to stay for a week."

"I remember the commander. A major."

"Ari."

"I remember you flirting. With Ari."

"Goodness, the man was gorgeous. Like Errol Flynn. He asked if I would be the Haganah's eyes in Kfar Etzion. I said I would be glad to be more."

"Please tell me you're joking."

"What joke? I swore an oath by a candle, with my hand on a pistol. All very exotic."

"Who else knows?"

"A few who need to. Someone had to dig the holes. Now you."

"Are there more guns in the kibbutz?"

"No. The British found the smaller stockpile. The bigger one is still in the barn." Mrs. Pappel combed through Rivkah's hair. "Don't go looking for them."

"I have no intention."

"The weapons are going to be needed."

"Are you in danger?"

"No more than you."

Rivkah lay under Mrs. Pappel's hands. "Can you tell me more about Morrie?"

"What's to tell? Those kids from Hungary. Nothing that happened to me compares."

"Tell me anyway."

Mrs. Pappel waved at the air.

"I met Morrie back in the early twenties. He was young, good looking, trying to make movies in Vienna. We married, we moved to London, and Morrie caught on there. We started living good, Morrie and me. We could buy whatever we wanted. We had comfort; we had a boy. And this is what we did for two decades; even during the war years we were comfortable. But there's something about comfort, darling, it tends to be because you're inside something. So, there I am, inside this life. And all along, I'm reading about Palestine in the papers. The British, the Arabs, oil, gardens growing out of rocks. It seemed such a life. Mine was hosting dinners and making sure Morrie got his messages. Who could find time to go live in a tent and plant trees? After enough years and enough money, we got too old for Palestine."

One of Mrs. Pappel's hands lifted off Rivkah's shoulders, to quiet a sniffle.

"The Germans bombed London, and they bombed Morrie. He had a heart attack, so, like the movies say, exit Morrie. I figured, when the war is done, go home to Vienna. Grow old there. Get your son out of London before he becomes English permanently. But I kept watching Palestine, reading the papers about Palestine. Riots one day, a new kibbutz the next. Jews spreading over the countryside, settlements in the middle of nowhere, like a gold rush. An adventure. And everywhere, children. The Nazis had spoiled Austria; the bastards set something loose wherever they went. I couldn't trust being a Jew in Vienna again. I asked myself what good was Morrie's money if I'm still despised? So…Palestine."

"What about your son?"

"What was the little *pisher* going to do without my money? I told him and his pretty English wife, I'm going to Palestine. Come with me or stay in London broke. They had a choice? So, I bribed a few little nothings in the British government, got our immigration papers and some boat tickets. The rest of Morrie's money I gave to the Jewish Agency. My son doesn't know this." Mrs. Pappel climbed to her feet. "*Oy.*"

Rivkah joined her standing. "You're not too old for Palestine."

"That officer didn't think so either." Mrs. Pappel pointed west, shading her eyes. "Is that it? That hilltop there?"

"Yes."

"Oh my. That is one more sad-looking spot."

Both turned to face the fruit groves and terraced fields of Kfar Etzion, small homes and big storage sheds, stacked stone walls, the slow greening of the desert.

"This place wasn't such a winner at first."

Rivkah said, "Did you hear? They picked a name for the new settlement. *Massuot Yitzhak.* Isaac's Beacon."

"It's beautiful."

"A beacon for the survivors in Europe."

Mrs. Pappel lapped an arm across Rivkah's shoulders. They stood like this gazing at the white windswept knoll soon to be the next settlement in the Kfar Etzion bloc.

Mrs. Pappel pulled Rivkah into her arms. "I'm never leaving Palestine."

"I'm not either."

"Good. Now I have to ask you something hard. When was the last time you heard from your family?"

Rivkah drew a deep breath as if struck. Mrs. Pappel held on.

"I got a letter from my mother. She said the family was being sent to Terezin in Czechia."

"How long ago?"

"Three years."

Mrs. Pappel whispered, "Three years."

Standing, holding Rivkah, Mrs. Pappel rocked her. The sun pressed on Rivkah's back as if to break in on a dance. She dried her swollen eyes against Mrs. Pappel's shoulder.

"I'm sorry about Morrie."

"Me too. But honestly, he'd be useless here."

Rivkah laughed haltingly, snagging on her unfinished tears.

Mrs. Pappel said, "You have me."

"I do."

"Liebling."

"Yes."

"They're starting to gather supplies for the new kibbutz. They'll be ready in October. I was thinking it might be good for us both to start over. Together. Let's go be pioneers. Let's go to Isaac's Beacon."

"Alright."

"You can move rocks. I'll hide more guns."

A kilometer away on the crest of the chosen hill, a point of silver sparkled like a mirror.

Rivkah said, "I can see the spring."

CHAPTER 12

VINCE

September 10
Weimar

Maps papered Captain Beshears's walls. Reports and requisitions mounted on his desk; outside his door, secretaries and signal corpsmen typed more pages to dump on him and the other inexperienced administrators in their quickly-set-up headquarters. Beyond his windows, clean soldiers armed with folders strode into Weimar's City Hall to deliver more orders, communiques, and complaints.

Great forces were piling up around Beshears. The present and future of a sundered nation collided on his desk. Beshears tapped a newspaper on his desk, the international version of the *Herald Tribune*. "You write a nice column, Mister Haas."

"Thank you."

"It seems you're pretty plugged in at Buchenwald."

Vince needed a shave and bath. His tunic crackled from long-dried sweat. Most nights he slept in his boots. The "P" armband had been lost two months ago.

Behind the desk, Beshears's starched uniform showed little wear. Only his careworn face, more than a twenty-five-year-old's ought to be, hinted at the load.

"What can I help you with, Captain?"

"I asked you to drop by because I could use some advice. Maybe some help."

"I'm going to take notes. You okay with that?"

"Fair trade."

"Shoot."

"I've been given orders for the inmates at the camp." Beshears laid a hand on one of the stacks on his desk. "For the Italians. Belgians. Frenchmen. Dutch. Germans. Czechs. Poles. Russians." The captain tapped a different pile. "Criminals, communists, gypsies, homosexuals; you name it, I got orders to send all of them somewhere. I'm lining up transportation and food. That's what I do. All day. Except for one big group."

"The Jews."

"I don't have orders for them."

"Why not?"

"Because when we ask the Greeks where they're from, they say Greece. The Estonians say Estonia. But when we ask the Jews, they just say Jews. Not Poland or Latvia or fucking Germany. I've got no country called Jews."

"Yes you do."

"I can't send them there."

"You can't ask them to go back to the places that tried to kill them."

Captain Beshears leaned across his desk, among the canyon of papers.

"This war tore the world a new asshole. All over Europe, there's twenty million displaced persons. There's survivors from Nazi concentration camps, Soviet labor camps, prisoner-of-war camps, a couple million refugees afraid to go home because the Reds run their countries now. Between the Army and the UN, we've got to find places for all of them. I've got five thousand DPs left in Buchenwald. A thousand are Jews. I've got to send them somewhere. They can't keep eating off Uncle Sam."

"Have you been to the camp yourself?"

"A couple weeks ago."

"What'd you see?"

"Honest? The Jews were demanding and uncooperative. They spoke half a dozen languages, which made it hard to understand. They bitched about the canned food because it wasn't kosher. They insisted on bread that wasn't cooked in lard. We gave them sardines, that seemed to make them happy. Not much else did."

"What can I do for you, Captain?"

Beshears laid a hand on a tower of yellow, white, blue, and pink pages.

"I've got offers. I want to know what you think."

"Alright."

"Seven different countries in South and Central America will take them in. The whole thousand of them can be on a boat next week. New homes. New lives."

"What about the States? Any takers?"

"Limited availability. Washington figures we've done enough by winning the goddam war. We're feeding them. We don't have to make them Americans, too."

"That seems fair to you? Considering how little we did for them during the war."

"I don't do fair. I do doable. Here's what I want to know. If I take these offers to the Jews, how many do you think will sign up?"

"Half. Maybe less."

"Seriously?" Beshears withdrew behind the peaks on his desk. "I've got no plan B."

Vince put away his notebook. "Let them go to Palestine."

"The British don't want them there."

"Why do you care?"

"Beg pardon?"

"You said you don't have orders for the Jews."

"I don't."

"So why lose sleep over where they go? You said it yourself, you just want them gone."

"Make your point, Mister Haas."

"You have no orders. That means you're on your own; you're expected to solve this.

Why fight them?"

Leaning back in his chair, Beshears spread his arms.

"Because it's illegal. Fifteen hundred a month, that's all the British let in. Everyone else they catch and stick in detention camps in Cyprus. It's my ass if I send them to Palestine."

"I didn't say send them. I said let them worry about where they go. Where are you from, Captain?"

Beshears settled his chair on all four legs. He clasped hands under his chin, as if wishing to be back home. "Teaneck. Jersey."

"I'm from Brooklyn. Let me put something to you. When they ask you back home what you did in the war, what are you going to say? You helped out the British? Or are you going to say you helped out the Jews? Who do you think in Teaneck is going to be asking that question? You got a lot of Englishmen back there, drinking tea in fucking Teaneck?"

Beshears's lower lip disappeared behind his teeth.

"So what happens if I tell the Jews, alright, go? What are they going to do? Walk to Palestine?"

"You line up transportation. You said that's what you do."

"I do it for legal immigration."

"It's not illegal to send them to Italy or France."

"That's not fair."

"But it'll work. I promise you, a couple hundred will risk it and be out of your hair. Can you get a train?"

"A train." Beshears exhaled a long, troubled breath. "Yeah, I can get a train. And if I do. If. Where will it go?"

"I'll get back to you. Some port on the Mediterranean. There's recruiters from Palestine in the camp. They'll arrange a ship across the Med. You just take care of the train."

"You mean it, don't you."

"Think about it."

Beshears stood, extending a hand to conclude the meeting. Vince shook.

"You mind if I ask, Mister Haas, what do you get out of this? You asked me why I should care. Why do you?"

"I'm a reporter."

"And?"

"I'm going with them."

CHAPTER 13

HUGO

October 7
Fulda train station

Hugo stood in the front rank of the Buchenwald Jews. Vince kept to the back, taller than everyone.

An Aliyah Bet recruiter stepped onto a crate, to be seen and heard by all on the Fulda platform. The pink scar running under the young man's ear said he'd been in the war not long ago.

"*Ma'apilim.*" He called them the Hebrew word for *illegals*. "Your odds are good."

A woman shouted back, "That's a first."

Another woman asked, "What's Palestine like?"

"I've not been. I'll make it soon. You go first."

No train idled behind him, but he pointed at the tracks where it would appear. Nothing about the Aliyah Bet man exuded doubt.

"The train will take you to a refugee center in Leipheim. You'll cross through the American sector of Austria, over the Swiss frontier into France. In Marseille, we will have a ship waiting for you."

Hugo imagined the young man standing on a pier in Marseille, pointing down at the water, conjuring up a boat and making others see it, too.

Many of the men and women on the platform were garbed like Hugo, in cheap charity clothes. The rest were dressed to be farmers in Palestine.

The Aliyah Bet had found them white work tunics and suspenders, kha-kis and field boots. These Jews appeared earnest, they'd lived through the camps on prayer and immense luck. They'd never stolen anything, by the looks of them, and they'd never done the Nazis' bidding. In Palestine they would be good farmers, they'd plant their grief, cut it year after year, and never let it grow too high.

In the green distance, a locomotive chugged into view; the train's whistle slipped across the rolling Hessian hills. Hugo cringed, surprising himself. A German train was coming for him. He inched away from the tracks while the train screeched to a halt.

Vince stepped up beside Hugo. The Aliyah Bet man shouted good luck to them all. Vince, rangy and not hounded by recollections, jumped up onto the train car to help the women clamber aboard. Two hundred Jews stared out at hills they hoped never to see again. Vince, eager to pitch in, had no real notion of the moment, to leave Germany alive, to reach for Palestine, not just for an American's hand. The reporter had in his pocket papers that would let him in or out of Palestine, on or off this train. He had in his chest only the desire to make a name for himself. Hugo didn't begrudge Vince this. He'd take what help he could, and Vince's strong grasp lifted him onto the train.

When all were loaded in three separate cargo cars, the locomotive whistled again and the train jerked forward. The ma'apilim found places to sit on the hay-strewn floor. Vince tried to slide the door shut on them, but Hugo did not let him close them in.

✳ ✳ ✳

Hugo kept his distance from Vince. He didn't want his own trepi-dations recorded. Let Vince pick at the others for a while. They'd worn shackles, too, and could describe them just as well.

Hugo sat on the straw to hang his legs out above the clacking wheels. Hunger gnawed at him, but Hugo knew how to push that aside.

Germany looked freshly deceased. Hugo had seen corpses like this, flush and supple. Germany lay green in forests and hillocks, glowing a healthy jade, streams and rivers unhindered; then the train rolled through villages and towns. Most had been bombarded into grisly ruin, macabre friezes of life interrupted like insects in amber. Explosions had knocked down most buildings, cut others in half; bathtubs hung dizzily by their plumbing, kitchens carved down the middle showed calendars tacked to walls and dishes on shelves. Bared wood frames stripped of their clapboard or bricks suggested bones. Townsfolk moved through the wreckage as if nothing were awry. They carried sacks and tools and held children's hands, bicycled through cleared lanes, held parasols against the end-of-summer sun, old men took their ease on benches near the ruins of their favorite shops.

CHAPTER 14

VINCE

"*Nein*," the young woman said, then added in English, "Thank you." She got to her small feet to join a quiet group near the open door.

The train clattered past another nameless hamlet. Thatched huts lined a square where farmers sold vegetables from wagons without horses. Then the village was gone, receded among fields ungrazed by cattle or goats, just old men threshing to clear the scrub.

Vince tucked his journal into his pack, the pencil into his coat, and rested against the wall. Hugo hadn't spoken to him or moved from the car's doorway since the train left Fulda. Vince had approached a dozen Jews. Not one was impolite, but none would speak to him. Some began, but the instant he put pencil to paper they shook their heads and stopped; the survivors didn't want to become whatever his pencil would make them, as small as words.

The afternoon wore on, the landscape shifted between lush vistas and ruined towns. Vince kept his seat on the straw and considered that he, too, was on his way to Palestine.

He awoke from a rocking doze as the brakes of the locomotive wailed. The Jews shifted about for their luggage and coats, still wordless. In his notebook, Vince scribbled that if he'd ever been as sad as these people had been for so long, he might be as silent as them.

The train shunted to a stop. Hugo jumped down first; some of the men jumped off with him.

Vince waited to be the last out of the car. The locomotive took on water from a tower while the conductor walked the short length of his engine and couplings. The refugees stretched their legs around the platform and station house; a mile away, a spire without a cross presided over an undamaged town. The immigrants dug into paper sacks for their evening meal or scuttled off to a weedy patch to relieve themselves. Several disappeared between the cars, going to the other side of their train, where Hugo had gone. Vince followed.

On a parallel track, a second train idled. The locomotive panted steam, pointed north. American soldiers guarded five passenger cars that had iron bars welded across the windows. Chains and locks sealed every door. Stubbly faces peered out.

Hugo walked at the head of thirty who'd followed him. They closed in on the train. A trooper told them to stay back. Vince hurried to the refugees to translate. He assured the GI that everything was okay.

"I'm an American, private. Who's on the train? Who're you guarding?"

"We got a hundred krauts. Taking them to Nuremberg for trial."

Hugo asked, "What did he say?"

"It's a train of war criminals."

Hugo backed away. Four more GIs stepped into a line. Twenty paces back, the Jews clotted around Hugo, who picked up the first rock.

The stone sailed high over Vince. In moments, all the Jews flung rocks, concrete and busted bricks, anything they could find on the ground to heave. Windows on the train broke behind the bars, making the Nazis recoil. One of the five GIs readied his rifle. In the din, with debris sailing over his head, Vince rushed between the Jews and the raised gun. "They're Jews from the camps! Don't hurt them!"

The soldier lowered his gun. Vince ran at Hugo. "Stop, stop!"

Hugo cocked a stone.

Vince yelled again, "Stop!"

Hugo lowered the rock; the others did the same. Inside the train, some of the SS men cursed the Jews loud enough to be heard.

Hugo held his rock out to Vince. "You throw it."

"No."

Hugo urged the rock at Vince. "Don't write it down. Don't report. Just throw it."

"No. Why?"

"Because what those animals did will last in the world for a thousand years. You think this isn't your rock to throw. You're wrong."

Hugo pushed the stone into Vince's side.

"Why did you come, Vince? Just to watch what the Jews do, listen to what we say? Is that all? You can follow us until we drop. Talk to us until we're hoarse. Write it all down. And still, you'll never know."

Hugo held out the stone as if he might drop it.

"If you're afraid, I won't blame you."

Vince's palm was up before he'd fully thought it through. Hugo released the stone into his hand. "Throw it."

Vince took a long stride; the stone flew past a broken window, into the car to make the war criminals scatter. The same soldier lifted his gun again, at Vince.

Walking away, crossing the couplings to their own train, the Jews patted, not Vince, on the back but Hugo for making him do it.

CHAPTER 15

RIVKAH

October 9
Kibbutz Massuot Yitzhak
Palestine

Rivkah pulled hard on the bar, but the knee-high boulder refused to pry loose. Ben Joseph added his small muscles to the lever to no avail. Rivkah quit trying and let the bar drop, missing Ben Joseph's toes.

Ben Joseph sat on the rock and kicked his heels against it. At fifteen, the boy needed his first shave. Posed against the windswept view, his features hinted at a handsome but small man one day. Ben Joseph had been an orphan in Budapest, both parents were lost to Auschwitz. A wealthy couple scooped him out of the ghetto without knowing his name; they had money and no children of their own. They hadn't tried to make him their child, just saved him, sent him to Palestine, and left it at that. He arrived three months ago.

All sixty pioneers did the same work; in teams, they wrestled limestone chunks out of the bleak ground to build a wall around themselves. A mule trudged before a cart to haul the dislodged rocks downhill to where the biggest boys stacked them. Mrs. Pappel held the mule's halter, walking it back and forth.

✳ ✳ ✳

The longer Mrs. Pappel lived in Palestine, the more ancient she became and the younger. Her hair had lengthened into a twined cord down her back, her shape pared down; she moved with a queenly grace among the young kibbutzniks. In the light of campfires, she told stories in English of the great heroines from the Old Testament: beautiful Ester who saved the Jews from Haman, Judith who cut off the head of Holofernes, Deborah standing against a horde of Canaanites. Whatever work she did for the Haganah, she continued in secret. She loved the settlement's children and the land, taking on the characters of both.

At the end of their first tiring day of Massuot Yitzhak, Rivkah and Mrs. Pappel sat outside the completed stone barrier. Inside the ring, in the middle of six teepees, the young pioneers assembled around a bonfire. A rabbi from Jerusalem had brought a Torah scroll for the new settlement. He was younger than Mrs. Pappel but had a face of furrows. He'd brought tallits for the men; they sat around him draped in snowy cloth and fringes while he intoned from the scroll. The girls stood apart, close enough to listen and be tinged by the fire.

The rabbi called for responses in his reading; the *haverim*, the settlers, lifted their voices into the night along with the glitter of rising sparks. All the youths inside the stone wall had survived the camps and pogroms. Rivkah was an elder among them at twenty-four.

The first pinpoints of stars winked on the horizon. The rabbi ran a finger across the scroll by the fire's glow while the Jews sat on the hard ground. The tents flickered on the rim of the light and the wall was built of stones; the scene could have been two thousand years old.

Palestine turned vast under the stars. Kfar Etzion to the south glimmered; several Arab villages cast only patchy light. The rabbi told the gathered of Massuot Yitzhak, this was once the land of Israelite kings and the Maccabees, these were the hills where David hid from Saul. Thick forests once shaded these slopes, dark soil made them fertile. God denied Moses entry, telling him you shall see the land at a distance but you shall not go there. During the long exile of the Jews, the trees were cut, the soil weathered off the hills; this became an abandoned place, a land with no people. In the center of the bonfire, a log shifted and a shower of embers leaped to join the stars.

Out in the gloom, a sound shuffled, like a broom. Then came another. The rabbi and his young congregation seemed unaware. Mrs. Pappel freed her hand from Rivkah's.

"Did you hear that?"

"Yes."

Mrs. Pappel shot to her feet. Rivkah joined her. Out past the shadows of the bonfire, a camel grunted.

Slowly the beast ambled into the flickering light, head high. A large Arab rider filled the saddle.

The sixty young Jews spun on the intruder, with no notion what to do. The rabbi held out both arms, calling for everyone to be still.

The camel took a few more ambling strides, then pulled up at the foot of the new wall.

The Arab and the rabbi seemed fearless, locked on each other like old enemies. Both were bearded. The Arab rode taller than the flames. He wore a flowing white headdress banded by a black cord. An ebon cape framed his dark loose robes. Moving their heads as one, the rider and camel surveyed the wall, the young people, and the hilltop that yesterday was bare. This, too, could have been thousands of years old, the gulf between peoples.

The Arab drew from his saddle a rifle.

The settlers recoiled. They'd left their own weapons beside the tents; some boys ran for their guns. Ben Joseph surged in front of the rabbi to protect him. Mrs. Pappel stepped between Rivkah and the armed rider.

The Arab aimed the gun up into the night and fired a round. The crack lingered in the hills. He seemed not to have ridden up the hill for any lethal purpose, just to create this moment, to remind the Jews that this was not a land without a people. Coolly, he watched from his high seat, rifle raised beside his head like a shepherd's crook.

Before any of the settlers could rush back to the wall with their own weapons, the caped rider clicked his tongue. His camel wheeled into the night, slapping its wide feet down the rocky hillside.

CHAPTER 16

VINCE

October 10
UN Relief and Rehabilitation Center
Leipheim

Vince had many pencils. He gave one to a Jew who flung himself at the long hallway wall.

Finding a spot of blank plaster, the Jew printed his name and today's date, his hometown, and his destination: Palestine. Others from the Buchenwald train pressed behind him, putting their hands to his shoulders and back, lobbying to be next for the pencil.

Top to bottom, the wall had been scrawled over by thousands of refugees passing through the UN displaced persons center in Leipheim, on the hope that some loved one might see or that they themselves might spot a name. Handwriting covered the staircases, too, for there were multitudes adrift.

Hugo stood in line beneath a sign that read *DP Registration*. Vince stepped out of the clogged hall to join him. Vince asked, "Did you look?"

"No."

"I didn't see anyone have any luck."

"We've used up our luck."

In line behind Vince, a man tapped him on the shoulder. He was dressed like Hugo, in plain shirt, loose trousers, scuffed shoes, wool cap, and suspenders.

"Pardon," he said in English, "you are the American?"

"What can I do for you?"

From a back pocket the man dug a grubby notebook; he did this with haste, to show Vince he would be quick about his need and not wasteful of an American's time. Vince raised a palm to say it was alright.

The booklet was filled with scratches, like the hallway. "Do you know someone." The Jew paused, then uttered a name, a relative in Chicago. Vince shook his head. The man found more in his booklet to ask after, in California and "Neff York." Vince repeated a gentle "No" to each.

With the man out of earshot, Hugo said, "Thank you."

"For what?"

"For not telling him he was a fool."

"He wasn't."

"You're sounding less like a reporter all the time."

The line led to stairs that descended to a crowded basement. Some rooms served as trade schools for sewing and shoe repair. In other spaces, nurses took quick temperatures and asked perfunctory questions about diseases and medical conditions.

At the end of the line, U.S. soldiers with clipboards staffed three card tables. In German, Polish, and English, the GIs inquired of each refugee his or her name, then "last permanent residence as of January 1, 1938," "desired destination," "usual occupation or profession," "languages spoken in order of fluency," and "claimed nationality."

Hugo's turn came. Suddenly, he whirled around, grinning. "*Bitte. Geh du zuerst.*" Please. You go first.

Hugo slipped behind Vince while the GI, with hundreds to process, tapped his pen on the clipboard. Vince stepped up to let the GI survey him in his olive drab jacket, tunic, and pants. He asked in English, "Why're you dressed like an American soldier?"

Vince affected a German accent. "I vass giffen by Americans." The GI had no time for suspicion. Vince gave his real name, Vincenz Haas.

He even claimed his 1938 residence as "Neff York" and his profession as "*Schriftsteller*," writer.

At the question of "claimed nationality," he got a poke in the back from Hugo. Vince answered the way Hugo dared him.

"Jew."

The soldier presented Vince a travel visa and flimsy ID booklet filled in with his name, answers, and a refugee number. Vince stepped out of the room, back to the stairwell. He trudged up the steps with a cluster of immigrants who held their new documents like gifts. Tonight, when their train crossed out of Germany into the American sector of Austria, into Switzerland, then France, they would present their documents at every border. The survivors left the building, past the wall of ten thousand names, moved to tears. This was their first time in years, after being homeless and stateless, tattooed and anonymous, that they saw the return of their identity, even at its merest beginning.

In the courtyard, spotlights turned away the dark. The Buchenwald refugees meandered in a slight chill; food was brought out to them so they could continue on their way.

Hugo emerged from the processing center. He held out his booklet to Vince and reached for Vince's. "Let me see yours."

Vince handed over the little folder. Examining it, Hugo lifted his chin proudly. He returned the booklet to Vince.

"Less and less like a reporter."

CHAPTER 17

HUGO

The train barreled through the valleys of Austria; a three-quarters moon dodged among mountain peaks, lighting the Jews in pearlescent flashes. They said little to each other, still emotional over their ID booklets, showing their papers in the uneven light.

Around midnight, nearing the Swiss border, the locomotive blew its lonely whistle. The moon brightened a landscape of fir trees and slopes so sheer they blocked the stars.

At the border, the train edged to a halt. No one jumped down; Swiss guards in berets and ponchos waited on the platform. The guards entered the cargo cars to check documents by lantern light. Hugo showed his visa and refugee booklet. The Swiss soldier smiled in the yellow warmth of his lamp, as he did for each of the Jews, and said *Willkommen*. More guards brought baskets of crescent rolls; the refugees tucked the breads into their pockets.

The train hurried along the northern floor of the snow-capped Alps, across the free face of Switzerland. Hugo asked Vince to slide the big door shut against the cold. With the icy light gone and the clatter of the wheels muted, the refugees settled down to sleep for the first time since leaving Buchenwald that morning. Vince stayed apart, while Hugo spooned with the Jews. For years, he and these people had lain like this on pallets in the camps, on the ground during forced marches, and in train cars on straw as they did tonight.

✳✳✳

November 20
Onboard the *Berl Katznelson*
Mediterranean Sea

Hugo made sure the narrow hall remained clear, then tapped a knuckle lightly on the cabin door. She called him in.

She sat on a narrow foam mattress in her tiny stateroom. She might have made the bed, neatened the sheets and tucked in the hoary blanket, but she hadn't. She waited for him with legs crossed, casual in her green dress. The dress had become a topic of gossip on the *Berl Katznelson*. Sea green cotton, it was plain and a bit too big, but appealing because it showed her arms and legs, and it may have been the only dress onboard. Some said without charity that the dress had been a gift from one of the Buchenwald guards. Others wondered how she managed to land one of the ship's five passenger staterooms divided among the thirty female passengers.

A bright porthole framed her head, a halo. Hugo clicked the door shut and locked it. She didn't stand to greet him.

"Take off your boots."

He unlaced them and pushed them under the bed. In his socks, Hugo sat beside her. "I'm glad you decided to come."

"Did you think I wasn't?"

"You made me wait."

Hugo didn't think he'd done that. He'd let her leave the deck first before following five minutes after, so no one would put them together. How long was enough to wait, how long was too much? Already he was being made to worry over what were the proper things to do.

"Do you want to kiss me?"

She made her face available, eyes closed, looking practiced in these things. Hugo leaned close but hovered. He touched her cheek to see if he might find some fondness for the girl. He sensed the regret in her skin and suspected the other refugees, the unkind ones, might be right about a Nazi guard. Hugo didn't judge her for that, or for being in her locked little room with him. Maybe she'd been a wanton in the ghetto, maybe in the camp, and had survived. How was she different from Hugo?

He took the kiss. His hand slipped into hers without willing it. Behind his closed eyes, Hugo recalled the face of a girl from Leipzig, then another, a village girl from Markkleeberg on a lake. In the next moment, with the speed of memory, both girls were dead. Hugo pulled away.

She began to unbutton her green dress. Her bosom emerged as the cotton peeled back, revealing her prominent clavicle and sternum, then her pink nipples and ribs. Hugo became erect. In the camps, nightly in the barracks, men masturbated. After a while, this became an animalistic behavior; no one hid it, for no one was it *shonda*, a shame.

He stood from the mattress and brought the girl to her feet to stand partly naked. She wasn't pitiful or beautiful, just another version of himself, dressed and undressed. She touched Hugo's cheek as lightly as he'd done hers. Hugo searched for a difference between them, to see them as man and woman, so he might act as if this was kindness they were sharing, but there wasn't enough difference for affection.

He buttoned her green dress, and she left her arms to hang. Clothed again, she lay on the narrow mattress. Hugo climbed in beside her. The bed afforded little room, framed by cabinets.

She lay her cheek on his suspenders. Hugo squeezed her lightly. "We don't have to be what we are."

She drummed fingers on his chest, close to her face, like playing a horn. Hugo pulled the blanket over them both and held her with nothing more to say. She fell asleep first in the light through the porthole, then Hugo.

CHAPTER 18

VINCE

November 23
Sidna Ali
Palestine

Vince scanned the black shore through binoculars. The Jews crowded every inch of the rails and stairs, eyeing the grey beach, too, but with naked eyes.

The *Berl Katznelson* floated two hundred meters offshore, outside sets of small breakers. Every few minutes, the ship's helmsman goosed the props to hold her in place against the swelling tide. The shore was an undeveloped stretch of sand and brush; a cliff blocked it from sight of inland. Midnight surf made the only sounds.

Gideon, the captain, had ordered a complete blackout and silence; not a cigarette lit, no light turned on. He scowled if someone coughed. Six miles south glowed Tel Aviv, but none of the city's lights glinted on the waters off the beach of Sidna Ali.

"I've enjoyed your company." Gideon kept his voice low, barely above the susurrus of the waves. "You don't have to do this. You're a brave man."

On the ten-day sail out of Marseille, Vince had gotten to know Gideon. He and his six Haganah mates were all younger than thirty. They were *sabra*, native-born Palestinian Jews; the word meant cactus, prickly on the outside, sweet within. The *Katznelson* was their second Aliyah Bet blockade runner.

Vince lowered the binoculars to rest his eyes from scanning only blackness. "If you get caught, you get deported to Cyprus, or jail. I'm not that kind of brave."

"We'll see if we can't find something to scare you, then."

The *Katznelson*'s engines grumbled to keep her away from shore, from Palestine. Gideon spit into the water on a night so quiet Vince heard it hit.

Toward the bow, someone hissed. "There!" Others shushed the voice. The *Katznelson*'s engines shifted to idle. From the beach of Sidna Ali came a tiny wink, a white flash.

The whispers along the rail began to mount. Gideon raised an arm; in the dark, others took up the signal, lifting their hands and shushing each other in a ripple. The immigrants quieted, and the waves breathed for them.

Gideon blinked a flashlight twice at the shore. The pinprick of light answered with three more flashes. Gideon whispered, "Palmach."

One of the captain's mates appeared beside him, a brawny sabra named Kippy.

"Lower the boats."

Kippy shoved his way through the Jews. Gideon shook Vince's hand. "You'll be in the last boat."

The *Katznelson*'s gangway was lowered; two planks hinged by ropes wobbled down to the black water. The immigrants formed a hasty line while Kippy and his mates dropped three inflatable rafts overboard. Three of the crew with oars hustled down the swinging planks to man the rafts. Kippy patted the shoulder of the first man in line.

"*Zei gezunt.*" Go in health.

Vince went down the line to find Hugo. He might have walked past him in the dark had Hugo not laid a hand on his shoulder.

Hugo said, "These people don't know what they owe you. You made this happen."

"All I did was talk with some Army folks. They were glad to get rid of you."

"I suspect it was to get rid of you. You lifted me out of my barracks. You poured milk down my throat. You're persistent. A very Jewish trait."

"I'll keep an eye on that."

"I'll see you in Palestine."

✳ ✳ ✳

The Jews raised a ruckus leaving the *Katznelson*. Gideon and Kippy tried to keep order, but the immigrants couldn't check their eagerness. The Palmach had brought four rowboats; their oars added to the racket in the darkness off Sidna Ali.

Vince stayed out of the way. The offloading of two hundred and twenty refugees would take most of an hour. Vince moved to the bow to look seaward and await word from Gideon.

He sat under a canopy of stars and grew excited to have his turn down the gangway, to a raft. Something about the firmament over Palestine hinted that the stars had shined here longer than anywhere on earth.

From a hundred meters off the bow, a powerful spotlight switched on, blitzing the *Katznelson*, so bright the beam heated Vince's face. A warship appeared out of the nothingness. She'd pulled a smugglers' trick, steaming full speed for shore with her running lights out. Neither Vince nor the Jews had heard her coming over the hubbub of arrival at Sidna Ali.

The destroyer's engines revved, rushing alongside the *Katznelson*. Once her long girth had lumbered near enough, all her lights flicked on, a sudden dragon on the water.

A bullhorn commanded: "Cease all operations immediately. You are an illegal ship in British Mandate waters. Prepare to be boarded."

The *Katznelson* became a frenzy. Half the Jews had disembarked, a hundred were still on the ship. Gideon threw valises overboard and yelled at the ma'apilim to hurry down to the waiting rafts. Crowd in, crowd in. Go, go.

Vince hurried back to the bow. The destroyer loomed closer, an incredible sight, such a massive ship. The spotlight found him.

"You there," the loudspeaker demanded, "show your hands."

Vince raised both arms and had to shut his eyes until the light slid off him.

The warship powered alongside. A squad of armed marines queued at midship. Quickly, expertly, the huge vessel narrowed the gap, a steel wall closing in. The light found Vince again, and the voice called, "Keep your hands where we can see them, mate." This time, Vince didn't stand still or shut his eyes.

He dashed away from the bow. The spotlight followed him running down the rail to the two dozen Jews bunched near the gangplank, the final ones waiting for the rafts and rowboats to return. Gideon and Kippy threw luggage into the night.

"Gideon," Vince grabbed the young captain's arm, "you're running out of time."

Among the last Jews crammed at the rail, Hugo held out his arms to Vince. What do I do?

Vince yelled, "Hugo, jump! Now!"

CHAPTER 19

HUGO

Feet first, Hugo struck the black water. Others leaping off the *Katznelson* made him swim away from the hull.

He wasn't a strong swimmer; the wool pants and leather boots bogged him down. Hugo could only dogpaddle, and the beach was far. Behind him, the destroyer's siren added to the chaos and its spotlight slashed across the *Katznelson*. None of the other twenty refugees in the water swam for land but waved to be picked up by the Palmach rowboats. Hugo paddled in a circle.

Quickly, a rower found him. Powerful hands hauled Hugo over the gunnel; he came up coughing. Dripping and chilled, Hugo sputtered thanks. No one but him and the Palmachnik were in the boat. The fighter said nothing but put his back to the oars. The rest of the Jews were snatched up by other skiffs.

Hugo's Palmachnik was a hardy young man in grey coveralls. He sported a thin black moustache and his skin was olive, even at night. With each stroke of the oars, he grunted, holding nothing back, a determined man.

From around the stern of the destroyer sped a pair of motor launches, coming on fast and sweeping the water with lights. One boat fired warning shots. All the Palmach rowers dug in furiously. Hugo had no way to help except to utter again, "Thank you."

With each surge of the oars, the beach drew closer. Hugo fixed on the murky sand ahead. He gritted his teeth in sympathy with the effort of his Palmachnik. Pull, man, pull hard.

The Navy launches rushed closer over the dark ripples. The eight rowboats and rafts weren't going to reach shore in time; the launches were too speedy. Hugo's Palmachnik shouted to the rower in the boat nearest him.

"Julius!"

The hulls of both rowboats bumped. Julius grabbed hold to keep them close.

The rower of Hugo's boat said to Hugo, "*Geh*." Go.

Wasting no time, Hugo clambered overboard, into the laps of three soaked Jews. Stumbling into the bow, he nodded at the wet passengers and another strong young rower. Julius beat the water with his oars while the boat Hugo left spun around to row straight for the oncoming British. A second rowboat emptied its passengers, then joined him.

Within moments, both Palmach skiffs were speared by spotlights. The marines slowed and shouted orders. The pair of rowers released their oars, hands high. While they surrendered, the remaining six boats dug for shore.

Once they reached the shallows, the rowers leaped into the surf to pull them onto the sand. Twenty immigrants jumped into knee-deep water and ran for Palestine.

The Palmachniks gathered them and gave hurried instructions in English and German.

"There's paths up through the cliff. Find one. Across the road at the top, there's a kibbutz. Shefayim. Go there as fast as you can. They're waiting."

Hugo asked his young rower, "Then what?"

"You'll blend into the Yishuv. They'll get you papers and homes. You disappear."

"I don't want to be on a kibbutz."

The rest of the immigrants and rowers took off. Hugo and Julius were the last on the Sidna Ali beach. Offshore, two patrol boats swooped in with searchlights.

"Friend, what do you want to do?"

Hugo speared a finger into the young man's chest.

"What you do."

CHAPTER 20

VINCE

Eleven Jews didn't jump. The destroyer's searchlight turned them into ghostly figures at the rail. The destroyer eased alongside the *Katznelson*. The loudspeaker barked, "Stay where you are."

Before the boarding party could leap onboard, Vince put a hand to Gideon's chest.

"You've got to go."

The captain rattled his head. He pulled Kippy, his first mate, into a quick embrace. Kippy shot Vince a smiling thumbs up. "Tell it all." The sabra bounded over the rail.

Gideon said, "He's a fish," as Kippy swam away.

"Why didn't you jump?"

Gideon gestured at the frightened immigrants.

"I don't leave until they do."

The British ship settled alongside to lower a gangplank. The loudspeaker declared, "You have been boarded. Do not move." The siren quit; armed marines flooded plank onto the *Katznelson*.

Vince dug out the little identification booklet he'd been given at Leipheim, for Vincenz Haas, a displaced German Jew. He tossed it overboard.

He readied his American passport and press credentials. With Gideon and the immigrants, Vince raised both arms when told to at the end of a rifle.

CHAPTER 21

RIVKAH

Massuot Yitzhak

The winds on the Judean plain whipped away the dust trail of the approaching car.

The coupe stopped in front of the stone cottage Rivkah and Mrs. Pappel shared. The driver climbed out first to hold the door open for Mrs. Pappel, then both came onto the porch where Rivkah waited.

Mrs. Pappel introduced the man as Mr. Pinchus, from Jerusalem.

Mr. Pinchus said to Rivkah, "*Hanukkah Sameakh*." Happy Hanukkah.

Mrs. Pappel said, "He wants to speak to the kibbutz."

Mr. Pinchus extended a hand to Rivkah, not for a shake but to ask for something.

"But first, young lady." Pinchus adjusted his round, black glasses. Beneath a clipped moustache, his smile revealed a gap in his front teeth. He wore a long coat with a scarf and leather gloves. "Mrs. Pappel has sung your praises, and I should like a tour. Would you indulge me?"

Mrs. Pappel hugged her then hurried out of the blowing chill.

She guided him first to Mrs. Pappel's schoolhouse. They strolled along a path lined with white-painted rocks, past one-story flat-roofed homes and workshops with more going up. On the way, Rivkah did not ask who he was; Mrs. Pappel was Haganah and the mystery of Mr. Pinchus was surely entwined with that. In the orchards he knew the genera of the sapling trees, the olives, pecans, ficus, and jacarandas. He understood the basalt-laden soil of the Hebron hills, the need and ways to irrigate and reclaim more land for fields of tall grasses to feed the cows and the single mule of Massuot Yitzhak.

They strolled by a dormitory and the foundations laid for a children's rest home and a guest house. The first electric poles had been stood up to spread power from the kibbutz's generators. In the gusty afternoon, stonemasons gouged slabs of limestone and pale dolomite from the quarry to build a settlement hard as the hills themselves. Mr. Pinchus clapped his gloves and asked if they might conclude.

Inside their small house, Mrs. Pappel let Pinchus nap in her bed. She, too, did not explain where she'd been or why, or who this man was. Rivkah sat alone on the porch while Mr. Pinchus slept and Mrs. Pappel left to arrange the meeting of the kibbutz.

✳ ✳ ✳

Massuot Yitzhak had no completed space large enough to accommodate all seventy haverim. They met inside the unfinished dining hall. Carpenters nailed sheets across the windows and everyone brought their own chair for the dirt floor.

The pioneers settled with some anxiousness. Most were young Czech or Hungarian survivors who had learned English from Mrs. Pappel, Hebrew from Ben Joseph, and work from the land. They squirmed in their seats as if they might somehow be in trouble. The wind beat against the walls and billowed the linens while Mr. Pinchus took the front without introduction.

"I am a Pole. I will speak English, yes? You will understand me?"

Heads bobbed. Mr. Pinchus paced as he spoke.

"There is going to be a Jewish state, I have no hesitation to say this. It will be born in bitterness and battle. Settlements like yours, isolated in Arab territories, may prove to have the most difficult tasks, may be the most difficult to defend. However, by what I've seen on my short visit, I am confident Massuot Yitzhak is strong and getting stronger."

Mr. Pinchus pulled off his leather gloves. During their walk, Rivkah had not seen his hands. They were not slender like a scholar's, nor thick as a farmer's, but Mr. Pinchus's large knuckles had known some sort of struggle.

"Gush Etzion is ten miles south of Jerusalem, in the hills of Judea. These hills are where the Maccabees fought. You came to Palestine not to be fighters but farmers. That is what you were promised. I've come to tell you that until there is a Jewish nation, you must be one hundred percent farmers and one hundred percent soldiers. I understand. It is not fair."

Pinchus lay a hand on the shoulder of a young woman.

"I'm the lucky one, you see. I have only to be a soldier."

He touched the next in the row, brave Ben Joseph, who seemed to want to jump up. Pinchus laid his hand on several, even Mrs. Pappel, until he slipped on the gloves and clapped again.

Pinchus took on a different energy, a martial bearing, marching back and forth. He became the soldier.

"This is your land. Your promised land. Everything is yours. The British cannot wipe away your history in this place. Because your roots are deep here, the Arabs cannot pull them up. The wind, the work, the hills, all of it is yours. I came to warm your hearts. I came to recruit you. But your buildings and trees tell me you lack nothing for spirit. You need only help. So, I will tell you the one thing you must take with you to-night, and into every day and night until a Jewish flag flies over Massuot Yitzhak. You must be armed. You must be trained."

Pinchus pointed outside the stone walls where the wind howled. "The fight will come to you. Not tomorrow, but soon enough. I know this be-cause I am going to force it. I am going to bring it to you. And I am sorry."

Mr. Pinchus seemed to have upset himself. Sweeping aside the sheet nailed over the door, he left the incomplete, cold hall.

✵ ✵ ✵

At dusk in their winter coats, Mr. Pinchus sat on the porch with Rivkah and Mrs. Pappel. Jerusalem's glow on the horizon blotted out the lowest stars. The day's light passed on calmly and the sky began to sparkle. Mr. Pinchus handed Rivkah his empty teacup and stood. He thanked her for the hospitality. Rather than take his leave, Pinchus said to Rivkah, "I am told you are trustworthy. Is this true?"

"I try to be."

"Then will you walk with me one more time? A short distance."

Pinchus led them off the porch. He linked arms with Rivkah without asking and walked without explaining himself. The three of them took the quarry path down the long hill; passing the saplings, Pinchus said this would become a great orchard and, in time, he should like to come back to rest under the trees and eat their fruit.

When they reached the bottom of the slope, night had fallen. Pinchus led them off the path to a depression in the rocky terrain. Here, the spring emerged in a small, chuckling pool. Pinchus removed a glove and knelt to sip from his cupped palm, then stayed on his knees to gaze into the dark valley. Not a soul was visible, just the glows of Massuot Yitzhak and the Arab villages on their own hillcrests.

"Rivkah, I know you are from Vienna. I pray your family is alive."

He continued without facing her, speaking over the gurgle of the spring.

"Palestine can give new life. It cannot restore the old. Everything here, every breath, bone and rock, is meant for tomorrow, not yesterday. I wish it were different."

"So do I."

"Please don't make the mistake of thinking Palestine is for you. It's not. It's for the millions right now who have nowhere else they can live as Jews. For those millions who will come and those who will be born here. We are simply the first, you and me, the planters and politicians and soldiers. We're building Palestine to give it, not to keep it for ourselves."

Pinchus rose from his crouch.

"Do you understand me? Be honest."

"The young people of the kibbutz. Can you know what they've been through?"

"No. And I won't ask them."

"They didn't volunteer for your war. I didn't either. You brought it with you. I think it goes wherever you go."

"Perhaps."

"You do this without permission. You're no different than the British."

Behind his glasses, Mr. Pinchus' eyes crinkled. Perhaps he'd not thought of this. It seemed to sadden him.

"Perhaps." Gently, he took Rivkah by the wrist. "As you say, I won't ask your permission."

"Why not?"

"Because I don't believe any Jew has the right to withhold it."

Pinchus didn't release her; she did not tug away.

"I want you to trust me, Rivkah. In return, I will trust you. I have for you a gift. A secret."

Whoever Pinchus was, he was held together by secrets. For him to pluck one out and hand it over must have been precious.

"I know who sank the *Patria*."

"Who?"

"We did. The Jews."

Rivkah stepped back, almost stumbling. She fought to keep her hands off Pinchus. Mrs. Pappel didn't react. She already knew.

"Why? Why on earth?"

"It was an accident. A Haganah operation. The bomb was meant to disable the ship, to stall until a way could be found to keep every-one in Palestine."

"Two hundred people drowned."

"The *Patria* was an old ship. The charge was set too near a worn-out pressure plate. Our sappers miscalculated the proper amount of explo-sives. A hole was blown below the waterline."

Rivkah swiped at a tear. "You'll say this was war."

"Yes."

"And these were casualties."

"Yes."

"And because of it, twelve hundred of us got to stay in Palestine. Were you satisfied with the trade, Mr. Pinchus?"

"Yes."

Mrs. Pappel reached for her, but Rivkah pulled away.

From his overcoat, Pinchus produced a small flashlight. Facing the open night, he blinked the torch once, twice.

"I prefer your world, Rivkah. I want to live in it. When we are done with mine, I wish to be your neighbor there."

Out in the parched, cloaked valley, surprisingly close, a camel fussed.

The beast padded across strewn rocks toward the sounds of the spring. As it came, Mr. Pinchus retreated.

"He and I will not meet. You will not discuss or describe me to him. Understood?"

Mrs. Pappel said her first words since the porch. "Good night. Be careful."

With a sweep of his coattails, Pinchus was gone up the hill.

✳ ✳ ✳

The camel brayed as it crossed the plain with dragging steps. The rider and his mount materialized spookily.

The camel ambled close enough to smell. The caped Arab in the saddle was the same who'd entered Massuot Yitzhak two months ago on the camp's first evening and fired his rifle into the night.

Mrs. Pappel raised a hand to the stars. "*As-salāmu 'alayka.*"

The camel took one more laden stride before the Arab tapped its neck with a stick. The beast folded to lay its belly down.

The Arab's saddle was a confusion of blankets, ropes, woven bags, pommel horns, and a rifle holster. His ebony cape flowed down the camel's flanks. A pistol stuck out of his cloth belt, and a curved knife and scabbard hung about his neck.

He swung his boots to the ground, then bowed from the waist. "*Wa 'alaykuna al-salām.*"

Mrs. Pappel returned the bow, prodding Rivkah to do the same.

The bearded Arab laughed, a deeper burble than the stream. He stood a head taller than Rivkah and Mrs. Pappel. His cape made him appear very broad. The guns and knife, the way his peevish camel obeyed his hand, spoke of how this big man moved through the world.

"This," he said in English. The Arab walked toward Rivkah and Mrs. Pappel, pointing to the earth. "This used to belong to God. For thousands of years."

Rivkah had to step aside to let the Arab stride past. She came no higher than his shoulder. His robe kicked up behind him. He moved with the smells of sand and salt, and like the moon if the moon had a smell, musty and ancient. The Arab gazed down on the little stream.

"I am told it belongs to you these days."

His fists came off his hips; the robes deflated a little to make him more man-sized.

Mrs. Pappel said, "Your English is excellent."

He dipped his brow. "One picks things up."

"I'm…"

"I know who you are. You are the teacher. I asked for you. I am glad you have been delivered."

Mrs. Pappel tapped fingertips over her chest, trying not to be ruffled. "Before we determine what has or has not been delivered, this is my friend Rivkah."

The Arab pushed his right palm to his forehead, then to his heart. Again, he bowed slightly. "*Marhaba*, Rivkah."

Mrs. Pappel asked, "And you are?"

The Arab spread his hands. "I am Malik Mahmoud Akbar al Saneá. Of the Tarabin."

"What shall we call you?"

"Malik. But you must not call me late for a meal."

The Arab laughed, hands clapped over his belly as if part of him might spill. He chortled alone and was slow to give it up.

"Ah. I have known others who thought this funny."

"Likely they were British."

"Yes. They are a funnier people than you."

"What? Wait." Mrs. Pappel whirled on Rivkah for support, who wagged her head to leave the Arab's odd remark alone. Mrs. Pappel spun on him.

"Why would you try to tell a joke at a moment like this? We've barely met you."

"To put you at ease."

"I don't need you to put me at ease, thank you. The thought of it."

Rivkah inserted herself with a hand dividing them. "Keep your voices down."

With Rivkah between them, Mrs. Pappel drew a deep breath and the big Arab shrugged, causing his cape to shiver down his length.

Malik flattened a palm at his throat above his curved knife. "If I have given offense, I apologize."

Mrs. Pappel mirrored the gesture. "As do I."

Undisguised, Malik gave Mrs. Pappel a look of appraisal, as if she were a boulder, one of the things in the world which would not move out of his way.

Mrs. Pappel asked, "You've been hired to bring us guns, yes?"

"Yes. I will bring them one or two at a time."

"Where will you get them?"

"The last two wars have come through Palestine. Germans, Turks, they left behind many weapons. Also, the British have a hundred thousand troops here. Mostly young men, and young men can be careless. Sometimes their weapons fall into the hands of traders."

"You steal guns?"

"Of course. There is no better way to make a profit."

Rivkah asked, "You rode into our camp and shot into the air. Why?"

"If not me, someone else. Someone who might not have fired straight up."

"How do we know you can be trusted?"

"It matters not. I am being paid regardless."

Mrs. Pappel stepped forward to take control of the exchange. "Why are you doing this? Bringing guns to Jews is dangerous for an Arab."

Malik hoisted an arm to the south, making a black curtain of his cape. He pointed to the sallow glow on the horizon, Hebron ten miles away, the same distance as Jerusalem to the north, half as bright.

"In the time of your book, Abraham settled in Hebron. Your David was made a king out of Hebron. For thousands of years, Arabs and Jews have lived together. In my lifetime, as a child, I recall the Jews in Pales-

tine. My mother got good cloth and my father healthy goats. I gave the
Jews coins in the market for halvah. You were good merchants."

Malik turned his attention to the little stream.

"Then you began to grow in number. You bought some lands, took
others that appeared empty to your eyes. You built a village here, a settlement there, planted a tree and a field of grass. Now you claim a spring
that Abraham drank from."

Malik shook a finger at Mrs. Pappel.

"Surely something can be worked out. *Masha'Allah*, there is
enough for us all."

"If you accuse us of taking your lands, why do you give us guns?"

"I am not one who believes there must be war. Perhaps if you have
enough of your own rifles, you will not have to use them. Then our
peoples may talk."

Malik aimed his bearded chin at the top of the hill, at dim little
Massuot Yitzhak.

"Listen to me. If the Jew stays up there." He flung his old face at the
dark valley. "If the Arab stays there. We will know nothing of each other.
I believe it is our destiny to live together, even if that seems the most
unreasonable thing. We are all sons of Abraham."

Malik pressed both hands to his waist beneath his curved knife and
made another shallow bow. "I know I am an unlikely bridge. But where
there is nothing, any crossing may suffice."

The big Arab regarded Mrs. Pappel as a curiosity, then extended a
ring-bedecked hand.

"We have a saying. My brother and I against my cousin. My cousin
and I against my friend. My friend and I against the stranger."

Mrs. Pappel took the Arab's hand. "Then we must not be strangers."

"That is my hope."

"Why did you request me?"

"You are the teacher for this settlement."

"I am."

"I require a reason to come here. I cannot, as you say, merely explain
that I am bringing you guns. I am a poet. I cannot write. You will put my
poems on paper for me. In English."

"What do you want me to do with them?"

"I will claim to sell them in the bazaar. Privately, I wish you to give them to your Jews. It may help them believe the Arab is not a barbarian."

Malik presented himself as he had when he stepped off his camel, arms spread, holding his cape out from his sides. He made himself vast, performing some grand version of himself.

"I am known in the Tarabin for my poems. I will not be questioned if this is why I come here." He said to Rivkah, "You. Go to my camel. Bring my rifle."

Before Rivkah could tell him no, Mrs. Pappel gestured for her to comply.

Malik's camel followed her approach with a scornful cool. Rivkah slid the long rifle from the holster. Returning, she held it out to the Arab. He took it, then presented it back to Rivkah.

"You may not trust me, but you may trust this. I have many times, and here I am to tell of it."

Rivkah accepted the rifle as a weapon for the kibbutz. She strapped it across her back. Malik liked this.

"I will return in four days. I will not have guns, only poems." Malik covered his heart. "*Ma'al-salāmah*. With peace. Good night."

His raven robe swished around him. With an adept flourish, Malik swept across the saddle and the camel rose with a herky-jerky grace. Mrs. Pappel and Rivkah stayed in place by the whispering stream, until the camel's slapping soles faded into the night.

CHAPTER 22

HUGO

November 25
Zarnuqa

Hugo raised a hand for order, but the Arab lads kept shouting and jostling. "*Ya, kharda*," they pleaded as if it were his name. "*Kharda!*"

He chose a stocky lad. The others kicked the dirt before turning away.

Hugo paid the husky boy an advance of a hundred Palestinian mil, with the second hundred to come at the end of the job. The lad stepped between the traces of Hugo's cart, lifted, and followed Hugo into the village.

"Kharda," Hugo called the Arabic word for scrap metal into the crisp morning, to the tight-packed houses. "Kharda!"

The two thousand Arabs of Zarnuqa were beginning their day. Workers strode off to the citrus groves, women in hijab veils balanced clay pots on their heads and averted their eyes. Hard, dark men dug troughs in the bleached ground for foundations, and lean boys ferried water from the well in buckets hung on shouldered yokes. Hugo, the boy, and the cart shared the lane with school children in bandanas and riders on donkeys.

Women swept straw brooms over the approaches to their small homes, an endless task on a dirt road. At Hugo's shout of "kharda," a woman beckoned him. She disappeared inside, then bustled out holding a dented brass teapot. Hugo gave her two ten-mil coins, then another five mil when she looked at him imploringly. She thanked him and called him "Kharda." His assistant tossed the kettle into the cart and tugged on.

Within two hours, Hugo and the boy had collected fifteen kilograms of scrap: an old bicycle frame, household items, broken knives, dulled drill bits, empty food tins, an antique pistol. The boy slogged and sweated behind Hugo, complaining in Arabic. For the morning's lot, Hugo doled out three Palestinian pounds to the villagers. He'd collected enough scrap to make two guns.

✳✳✳

Rehovot

Hugo slid the soldering iron into the forge and churned the hand crank to fan the embers to a lava-like glow. Once the tip of the rod turned crimson, he laid down a bead of molten tin and lead in the seam between the tubular steel stock and the breech block. Hugo flipped the rifle over to finish the joint.

He worked quickly before the iron cooled, to solder in place the trigger guard, the final touch.

Hugo slid open a window; the shed heated by the afternoon and the furnace. Julius strode from his house, down the garden path through spindly red anemones and yellow marigolds, purple clover and dense blue lupine. Big Julius fabricated wind vanes and chimes for the gift shops in Rehovot and the Arabs in nearby Ramla and Zarnuqa. Twice this year, the police had raided the metalworking shed behind his house; each time they found nothing but a forge, anvil, tongs and hammer, sheet metal, and cartons of handmade knick-knacks for sale.

Julius entered the shed. "I looked in the cart. Good haul."

Hugo lifted the freshly completed gun, all silver steel. "Finished."

The weapon was a copy of the British Sten submachine gun, made of unburnished metal, so illegal that the possession of it by a Jew meant a life sentence in a Mandate prison. Julius admired Hugo's finishing touches, perfect seams of solder. He gave the Sten a shake, snapped it into firing position, then dropped it on the work bench. Nothing broke off.

Julius hefted a few wooden boxes filled with wind vanes and his poor attempts at metal sculpture. The last crate had a false bottom; from it, he grabbed a 9mm magazine. He jammed it into the side slot of the submachinegun, a snug and proper fit.

He swung the weapon left and right. The Sten could fire five hundred rounds a minute, with a killing distance of one hundred meters. At close range the gun was lethal, but too inaccurate and weak for longer-range combat. The Palmach guerillas found it ideal for their hit-and-run missions.

The guns Julius fabricated usually went into a sack, then under a trap door in the flower-covered garden. This one he left on the table. Julius took a chair and leaned back on the hind legs. "You're a quick study."

"I was an excellent plumber."

"If this tests, I'll take it with me tomorrow night."

Julius possessed the hard façade of the sabra, like all things left in the sun. Beneath his toughness ran a streak of kindness and artistry. He desired most to create a Jewish nation, free of the British, at peace with the Arabs. He had the casual manner of someone living a double life, careful not to overperform his role as a trinket maker. Because Palestine was a land without mountains and forests, Palmach commandos like Julius had to hide in plain sight.

Hugo took the Sten off the table and held it as if he meant to fire it. "I want to go."

"You waited one whole day before asking me that."

"I'm asking."

"It's a bad idea."

"Why?"

"Because you're not a fighter. I plucked you out of the water two nights ago. You've got no training."

"You made me a promise."

"Not for that, I didn't."

"On the beach. I told you I wanted to do what you do. You agreed."

"I had to get you off the beach, Hugo."

"Did you lie?"

"You're doing what I do. I'm teaching you to make guns."

"I didn't come to Palestine to buy scrap from Arabs." Hugo shook the cooled soldering iron at Julius. "Or to fix your mistakes."

"Hugo, listen. Before you got here, I could make two guns a week. With you, we can make four. Do you have any idea how important that is?"

"I don't want to weld, and I don't want to collect trash."

"I'll say it again. You're not a fighter."

"Don't tell me what I'm capable of. You have no fucking idea."

"The mission's already planned."

"Do you have a driver?"

"Yes."

"Is he Palmach?"

"He is."

"Then I'll drive. That'll free up one more fighter. Julius."

"What?"

"I won't say you owe me because you don't. You saved me. But I want to do this."

Big Julius considered for long moments. Hugo prodded him. "Please ask."

"You can ask them yourself."

"Thank you."

"But if you go, you stay in the truck." Julius grabbed the Sten. "And no gun."

CHAPTER 23

HUGO

Kibbutz Shefayim

Eight Palmachniks sat around the lunch table with tea, pita, and hummus. Five were dark sabras like Julius; the other three had emigrated from Europe, lighter-skinned men, former Polish partisans.

They complained that Hugo knew their faces now; all had been anonymous. Hugo had seen the anonymous before in piles. He told them not to be so proud, it wasn't an accomplishment.

Hugo stayed on his feet while they lobbed questions. What fighting experience did he have? What if he was in danger, could he kill? Could he follow orders?

He told no lies and embellished nothing. Ten years older than Julius, he was the most senior at the table. He had no military training; he was just going to drive them to and from the target. No one survived the camps without taking orders. Yes, he could kill, and he left it at that.

Julius said nothing on Hugo's behalf, left him to testify for himself. Hugo reminded the Palmachniks of the penalties he had already faced from the police. He reminded them, too, that their mission was a reprisal raid against the Royal Navy for the interception of the Aliyah Bet ship *Berl Katznelson* just days ago. He'd been onboard that boat. He could be trusted, he knew how to drive, he had courage, and they should allow him to come on the raid.

Hugo pulled out the last chair at the table and asked one of the commandos to pass the bread. He got the pita from one, the hummus from another. Alone, he broke the bread and dipped, then ate. Something ceremonial and unspoken turned his way. Hugo stayed at the table.

Into the meal, the talk among the Palmachniks ran to previous operations. They bragged like immortals and let Hugo be their audience. These young men were living secret lives of danger and they alone knew each other's exploits. Julius had not told Hugo of his missions. Hugo knew better than to ask.

In October four of them were in on an assault at the Atlit internment camp. Two hundred refugees from Europe were liberated before the British could deport them. They told of cutting the wires, entering the camp in platoon strength while the guards slept. One policeman saw them, identified himself as a Jew, and walked on. In silence, the Palmachniks gathered the immigrants for their escape. One carried a refugee boy on his shoulders, a boy so frightened he pissed down the Palmachnik's back.

Three weeks ago, all were part of an assault across Palestine; in a single night, the Palmach sank three British patrol boats and bombed one hundred and fifty-three railroad bridges.

Last week, Julius and seventy others derailed the Haifa-Jerusalem passenger train. They robbed it of £35,000 in railroad staff salaries, then spread buckets of pepper behind them to hide their scent from English bloodhounds.

These operations seemed the work of an army. "How many of you are there?"

Yakob, a sinewy redhead, said, "Two thousand. A hundred kibbutzim host twenty Palmach in each. They give us salaries and a place to live, we give them a security force." Red Yakob motioned to himself and four others around the table. "We live here in Shefayim."

Hugo went outside the safe house with the Palmachniks to kick around a football. Hugo had spent years without play. He hadn't noticed the lack of it until these young men cheered his few good kicks. Hugo began to laugh too hard at his nervous joy of the game; he felt manic and deficient and had to reel himself in. When he became overfull, Hugo raised his hands and walked away.

He sat on the small lawn, admiring how these boys had elected to lay down their lives for each other. For five years, Hugo had known every day amongst whom and where he would die, and for what single reason. The idea that he might choose for himself how and why to expend his own life made him stand. The fighters noticed and stopped, as if Hugo meant to say something to them. He sat again quickly and let them play on.

CHAPTER 24

HUGO

Sidna Ali

Without headlamps, Hugo sped down the coast road. He'd driven the narrow road twice that afternoon, noting every bend. Just two days ago, Hugo had sprinted down this same pavement away from the captured *Katznelson*.

In the last shreds of grey light he pulled the truck off the shoulder, into the brush and sand. Nine Palmachniks jumped out, each loaded with weapons, wire cutters, gelignite sticks, detonators, and cord. One commando handed Hugo a Luger pistol, despite Julius' order. Hugo left this on the seat of the cab while he leaned against the truck's grill. He listened into the deepening darkness, beyond the No Trespassing sign on the fence where the Palmachniks had cut a hole.

Hugo had overstated his bravery when he'd talked his way into the mission. Minutes after the Palmachniks filtered into the night, his teeth chattered. He walked circles around the truck.

Hugo imagined them cutting more fences on their way into the coast guard station, creeping behind cover. Then he ran out of imagery, for he knew nothing about setting explosives.

A bright orange flash and a deep crump through the trees startled him; the time for imagination was done, the raid was underway. Hugo climbed inside the truck and cranked the engine.

He idled, lights off. Three more explosions clapped in succession. With each, Hugo tightened his grip on the wheel. Submachine gun fire crackled; the Palmachniks were battling their way back to him. Hugo revved the truck's engine to let them know he was here and ready.

Stens spurted on the other side of the fence; the Palmachniks were in a running battle. Hugo crouched in fear of stray bullets.

The combat worsened, peaked, then became potshots. Hushed voices neared the hole in the fence. The first of the Palmachniks ducked through the cut links.

Julius swung his silver Sten over his back to free his hands and help the next fighter through. Yakob had trouble making it out; he dragged his bloodied leg toward the truck. Hugo jumped down; together, he and Julius lifted Yakob over the gate onto the truck bed. The others flowed through the fence, panting and wordless, stinking of cordite. Julius said, "Drive."

Hugo leaped back into the cab; Julius took the passenger side. Hugo bolted away from the fence. With headlamps still off, he knocked over several saplings, bashed through the bushes, and careened onto the pavement. He trusted his memory of the road and gunned the engine. Julius found the Luger on the seat between them and stuffed it in his own belt.

A quarter mile from the fence, Hugo pulled off to the shoulder. Three fighters leaped out to lay mines in the road. They climbed back in, pounded on the fender, and Hugo shot away. He left the headlights off for longer and drove so fast that Julius clung to the dashboard.

Hugo barreled past fields of reeds and sawgrass, isolated houses, and trees nipped short by the seacoast winds. He flew past the kibbutz of Rishpon, then slowed and cut on the headlights. Shefayim came next, three miles from Sidna Ali. The drive took five minutes. Julius told him, "Good work."

Hugo found the safe house, a wood structure behind a storehouse for farm chemicals. He jumped out before Julius; Yakob was handed down to him. A tourniquet wrapped Yakob's thigh.

Everyone hurried inside. Hugo drove to another block, abandoned the truck and jogged to the safe house. The commandos were stripping out of their black clothing, stacking weapons, shedding their remaining ammunition. Red Yakob lay on the table sucking his teeth, a bullet hole above his right knee.

Julius and Hugo grabbed up the weapons, nine Stens and several handguns, and carried them into the yard, to a trap door beneath a barrel; they stowed the guns in a shallow pit. Hugo returned to the house to gather up the clothes then tossed them into the hole. The Palmachniks changed into white shirts and khaki slacks. In the kitchen, Julius packed Yakob's wound.

The fighters sat around Yakob, who smoked, propped on an elbow. The assault had ended ten minutes ago; they'd all had a chance to calm down. Hugo was the only one breathing hard. He pulled up a chair.

Julius finished wrapping Yakob's leg. He left to bring back one of Shefayim's doctors.

The men said nothing about the mission, only encouragement to Yakob. They spoke in Hebrew, not German, Polish, or English that Hugo could follow. The Palmachniks put hands on each other briefly; their circle included Hugo.

※ ※ ※

November 26

Lying on the front seat of the truck, Hugo awoke to a cloudless dawn and a bullhorn.

A passionless voice commanded the people of Shefayim to remain inside their homes. The police were going to conduct a search.

Hugo leaped out, intensely awake. He slammed the truck door and walked away. Halfway to the safe house, he stopped; that was the last place he should go, nothing to do there but get caught. A growing crowd had begun to fill Shefayim's lanes. Hugo joined the flow, headed for the schoolyard at the center.

The people of the kibbutz didn't consider obeying the voice. Four hundred young men and women, almost as strapping as the Palmachniks, streamed from their houses. Three hundred British police and soldiers awaited them. Tracking dogs strained at their leashes.

A woman conferred in the open with representatives of the police. They explained their positions to each other; some decision was taken quickly. The woman turned away from the parlay to join the crowd in the schoolyard, all of them shouting for the British to go away. The policeman with the megaphone announced that they were going to search every building and screen every male resident. The nearby coast guard station had been bombed last night and the kibbutz of Shefayim was suspected of harboring the criminals. The people bellowed back, but the megaphone could not be drowned out.

The kibbutz was a small place. The settlers here hadn't spread out but packed themselves tightly together to leave all the land they could for crops and fruit trees. Shefayim was not difficult for the British to surround.

On the outskirts, a thousand soldiers had taken up positions. They'd set up roadblocks and patrolled the citrus groves and lanes between the winter wheat fields. Armored trucks were stationed where Shefayim could see them.

The first hour of the morning passed in a noisy stalemate. Word of the police action spread to neighboring settlements; hundreds of kibbutzniks in overalls, wool skirts, white shirts and ties, straw hats and yarmulkes hurried into Shefayim, trebling the number of Jews inside the kibbutz and swelling the tension. Fifty bearded orthodox in tallits and fedoras ran across a field out of nearby Beit Yehoshua. Two hundred Poles from Beit Yitzhak left their cars on the road to rush straight into a blockade; they swamped the soldiers there and broke through, then galloped into Shefayim shouting the name of their own kibbutz. Others sprinted through the orchards, ducking the guards.

Once the sun climbed well clear of the rooftops and orchards, the cops formed a skirmish line of three hundred. Every hand held a truncheon. The Jews scrambled to face them; they seemed to materialize out of nowhere, from between the houses, out of the bushes; Jews seemed to drop from the trees. They carried axe handles, cricket bats, and other clubs. They formed a human barricade, barring the police from searching the homes of Shefayim.

Outside the kibbutz, another thousand supporters tried to swarm the British perimeter but were held back by fixed bayonets and shots fired into the air.

The police formed a fighting wedge, fifty men wide, six deep. The policeman with the loudspeaker issued one more demand for the settlers to disperse and go back to their homes, to respect the rule of law. The Jews shrieked their answers, shook fists, and rattled bats.

The first rocks were thrown. The man with the loudspeaker said, "Right, then."

In unison, the first wave of police surged forward with trained brutality, scattering the first rank of a hundred kibbutzniks. The cops swung batons at heads and legs, battering the settlers aside or to the ground. They kept their formation, protecting each other's flanks, disciplined and dealing force like professionals. These police were young men and mature toughs, some whippet thin, others beefy. A few were fresh-faced, perhaps taking part in their first violence. The old hands among them called encouragement.

The second file of police entered the fray. They advanced abreast, calling again for the thousand settlers to go back to their homes or suffer the consequences.

"Jews, get back," they cried, tramping forward.

Hugo had room to escape. He could bolt for the orchards and hide or hole up in one of the storehouses or find some home to hunker in and tell lies when the family returned and the police came.

The Britons thrashed anyone they could reach. They chopped through the crowd, especially focusing on those who challenged them with clubs or heaved bricks and rocks. On every side of Hugo, people fled. Many reeled past with bloodied ears or cradled arms. In the schoolyard, Hugo held his ground as forty police stomped directly at him. A pair of young farmers who'd been beside him bolted. Hugo stepped back, ready to run away, and the police closed in.

That moment, Julius and his Palmachniks barreled into the British cops from behind. They tackled eight, grabbed their batons, gave them a good kick, then ran on for more, calling for the settlers to hold their ground. The Jews retreating around Hugo stopped to reconsider. Someone sent up a yell.

After the havoc caused by Julius and his boys, the forty cops in the schoolyard lost their formation; some had lost their clubs. Clashes became one-on-one, Briton against Jew. Some settlers were carted or dragged off, bloodied and arrested. A short, robust cop focused on Hugo and advanced. He stopped five meters away and patted his truncheon into his palm. He wore a billed hat, knee socks, and a tan uniform, cheeks ruddy, looking for all the world like a bully on the playground.

"Make your choice, boyo."

Hugo lowered his shoulder and charged. He rammed the policeman in the midriff and took a clout on the back for it. He slammed the cop backward to the ground, knocking off the man's cap. Hugo jumped to his feet away from the kicking, cursing policeman and snatched the cap. Screwing it on his head, he ran to find Julius.

✳ ✳ ✳

The haverim firmed up and would not be moved. Hugo trotted alongside Julius and the Palmachniks. Each carried a baton; Hugo held one too but hadn't swung it. He'd done his one courageous act and spent the rest of the melee taunting and avoiding getting smacked. Once the British withdrew to the outskirts of Shefayim, Hugo gave his baton to someone else. He set the hat on Julius's head.

Julius said, "They'll be back."

During the morning brawl, another thousand from surrounding settlements and villages had rushed to Shefayim. The thousand soldiers stopped them from entering the fray in the kibbutz. A ringleader among the Jews on a black horse galloped back and forth, urging the mob to push past the police. The soldiers answered with rifles leveled.

A shot rang out; the rider fell. His horse galloped on into a wheat field. The stunned throng stopped pressing at the soldiers. The police may have been thrown out of Shefayim, but British soldiers would not cede their ground.

Before the crowd could choose to stand down or dare the guns more, a volley of shots cracked. Suddenly under fire, the Jews ran. They dragged with them a dozen wounded and left behind five bodies in the road and the trampled field.

Three hundred soldiers marched into Shefayim. Behind them, again, came the police.

✳ ✳ ✳

One more time, bullhorns told the people of the kibbutz to go to their homes. Every person not a resident of the settlement was to stand in the open with ID papers in hand.

Not one Jew complied. They linked arms, sang "Hatikvah," and chanted slogans of resistance. The British fired tear gas grenades. A Hassid rushed forward to hurl one of the fuming canisters back at the police. The crowd erupted over this; several were needed to lift the burly man off the ground and lead him away.

Hugo wasn't going to be a Palmach, but this he could manage. Julius must have noticed Hugo steeling himself, for he grabbed Hugo's arm.

"Take off your shirt. Wrap it around your face. Hold your breath."

Hugo did as he was told. Bare chested, with tumult on all sides, he dashed over open ground into a spewing cloud of pepper spray. He flung the canister as far as he could at the soldiers and police. Hugo dropped to his knees, almost blinded, but popped up before anyone needed to come help him. Blinking and in pain, he staggered back to the cheers of hundreds. Julius guided him to a water cistern to wipe his stinging eyes.

"Kharda. That's your name."

"What are you talking about?"

"Fighters have nicknames. Battle names. You're Kharda. Scrap iron. Come with me."

Together they hurried to the safe house. Yakob slumped in a kitchen chair, looking wan, his shot leg propped on the table. Julius and Hugo guided him outside; no one could be found in the safe house, and the bullet in Yakob's calf was going to be difficult to explain.

They set him in the schoolyard on the merry-go-round. Hugo volunteered to stay with him. When the police approached, Hugo explained that some cop had shot Yakob, and he'd wrapped the man's leg. He and Yakob said they didn't know each other. Hugo was asked for his name; he answered Kharda. The cops moved in to arrest Yakob; Hugo got in their way. One of the police shook a truncheon in his face.

"You a troublemaker? You want to go with us, too?"

Yakob brought the attention to himself by struggling. He took a crack from a baton for it, then was hauled off.

※ ※ ※

The British left Shefayim at noon. Three hundred settlers were arrested, forty wounded, six killed. The police suffered minor injuries.

Drawn by Yakob's blood, the British bloodhounds found the truck. Somehow the safe house escaped notice. The Palmachniks filtered back to their homes in Shefayim and Rishpon. In the afternoon, Hugo drove Julius in a borrowed pickup back to Rehovot.

Julius said, "You don't have to worry about Yakob. He won't say a word."

"I'm not."

"So, Kharda."

Hugo wanted to smile, but the day had been somber. Jews had been killed. A wounded comrade was being questioned.

Julius extended an arm out the window, letting the wind lift and lower his opened hand, a childlike thing. Julius was still a young man, to have fought as long as he had.

"You don't want to make guns anymore. No more collecting junk in Zarnuqa."

"No, I don't."

"Just so you understand. You've got no military background. No training. You're not going to be Palmach."

"I can learn."

"You can't."

Julius said nothing more until Hugo pulled into the drive of his small house in Rehovot. "I'll do what I can."

"And what is that?"

"I'll make a call."

A Soldier's Will

A British soldier lay dying
And on his bed he lay,
To friends around him sighing,
These dying words he did say.

A Jewish boy had got me at last, lads,
I haven't much longer to live,
But before I hand my checks in,
These last words of advice I do give.

Put a bomb in the Agency building,
Wipe the synagogues all off the earth,
Make every damned son of Zion,
Regret the day of his birth.

A popular poem among British troops in Palestine

CHAPTER 25

HUGO

May 11
Tel Aviv

The basement seemed a scene from a film, though Hugo hadn't been to a cinema in eight years. He sat in the only chair on a concrete floor, surrounded by four windowless basement walls. A bare lightbulb hung on a cord above a drain. His role in the movie would be the innocent fellow caught up in a dangerous business. Then the bulb went out.

The knob turned, the door eased open, and someone fixed a flashlight beam in his face.

"Kharda?"

The man in the doorway used his nickname as a question, as if unsure he had the right room. Hugo winced into the light.

"Perhaps he's down the hall."

The flashlight stilled, considering. "A joke?"

"An attempt."

The light advanced. A second chair scraped across the hard floor. The man carrying the light shut the door, then lowered into the chair he'd brought with him.

"I have some questions."

Hugo raised a finger to signal an interruption. "Before we start."

"Yes?"

"Can we do without the flashlight?"

"It's for our mutual protection."

"That may be. But it's uncomfortable."

"Is your comfort that important?"

"Not unduly so, no. But it will make it harder to concentrate."

"Perhaps that's the point."

"Yes, of course. May I ask?"

"Yes."

"If I wanted to get up and leave right now, would you stop me?"

"I think not."

"What if I turned on the light and came back in?"

"I see."

"What I'm saying is that a flashlight in my face isn't much protection."

"I take your point."

"May we just chat, please? I waited six months for this interview. I didn't imagine squinting through it."

"I was told about you, Kharda."

"Told what?"

"That you are clever."

The flashlight slipped off Hugo and the man took it from the room; again, this plunged Hugo into darkness.

He waited until the dangling lightbulb flicked on.

A short man returned. He wore a vested brown suit and black tie, thick glasses; he was narrow-shouldered with a trim moustache. He smiled as he sat and crossed his legs, casual.

"My name is Mr. Pinchus."

✳ ✳ ✳

In the blank cellar with the drain between them, Hugo asked as many questions as he was asked.

Pinchus was a Pole. He'd served in Poland's military before the war. He'd had brushes with the Soviets as a failed communist, the Turks as a Zionist, the British as a revolutionary, and he had been imprisoned by all, including his own country as a deserter. At the start of the war with Germany, he made his way to Palestine by stowing away on a train out of Ankara.

Hugo told of his early life in Germany, the son of teachers. Talented with his hands, he'd become a tradesman, a plumber making a fine living in old Leipzig, a city riddled with turn-of-the-century plumbing.

"Any military training? Any familiarity with weapons beyond making them?"

"None."

"What are your skills, Kharda?"

"I can weld. Drive a truck. I can problem solve."

"Problem solve?"

"The things that can stop up a pipe would amaze you."

"Of course. Why did you come to Palestine?"

"I want to be able to defend myself the next time the sonsofbitches come."

"Do you also believe in the Scripture, that God promised the Jews this land?"

"No. And if He did, He did it three thousand years ago. A lot has happened since. Do you believe it?"

"I do. But there's room for both. We all have the same goal."

"Good."

"So you are not an observant Jew."

"No. But Hitler didn't make that distinction."

"He did not."

"I ended up in Treblinka. Then Buchenwald."

Pinchus inquired nothing more about the camps, only nodded in a way that said I know, and I do not know.

"How old are you?"

"Thirty-eight."

"Let me be clear. You will not be a fighter."

"Why do I keep hearing that? Do you have so many men that you can afford to let one slip by?"

"The opposite. We're so few that the loss of one is like the loss of ten. Each of our fighters is experienced and well trained. When they go into action, they defend each other like brothers. Our men will lay down their lives for Palestine and each other. But we count on them to come back alive with missions accomplished, ready to go again. There isn't time to make you one of them."

"I'm younger than you."

"I'm not a fighter. Kharda?"

"Yes."

"Who do you think you're talking to? I don't mean me, but who I represent."

"The Haganah."

Pinchus shook his head.

A frost of concern tingled in Hugo's hands and feet. "Palmach?"

Pinchus chuckled again. He tapped his fingertips together, in and out of a little steeple. "No."

"Who are you?"

"I'm with the Irgun."

Hugo caught his breath. Julius never did say who he'd called, only that a meeting had been arranged.

"You're the bombers."

Pinchus nodded above his joined hands. "Correct."

"The terrorists."

"Some say. How do you feel now?"

"Foolish."

"I imagine. When you asked me to turn off the flashlight, to speak to me in the open, were you aware of the risk? To yourself? I'm not here alone, you may have guessed."

"No."

"Do you wish to leave now that you know? Because, to be frank, you can't. Not just yet."

"Let's continue."

"Alright."

"Why did you turn on the light?"

"Because I have confidence in you." Pinchus scooted forward on his seat, leaving his hands pressed beneath his chin. "For the six months you waited, we've been watching. Watched you make guns, drive the

Palmach to and fro, walk the Arab neighborhoods. You're loyal, hard-working, and smart."

"Thank you."

"And you have a gift, Kharda."

"What is that?"

"You are not a person anyone will remember."

"This is a compliment?"

"This is how the Irgun exists. We have to live in secret. We're not eye-catching like your Palmach friends. Look at me, for an example."

Pinchus was nothing conspicuous. He could be an accountant, a rabbi, a notary, a farmer in his Sabbath suit.

"We are hunted by the British, every day. We live double lives and hide in the open from everyone but each other. We've even been hunted by the Haganah itself."

"Difficult to imagine."

"Not so much. The Irgun takes a different view from the Haganah of how to convince the British to leave Palestine. And how to defend it from the Arabs."

"How so?"

"Let us say we are more direct."

"Are you still hunted?"

"By the British, yes, of course. But by other Jews, no longer."

"What made them stop?"

"The people of the Yishuv approved of us. They protested on our behalf. Rallies were held, even in America and England. The Irgun may be bombers. But we appear to be popular."

"Were you caught?"

"I was not. I am either unimportant or too wily. No one will tell me which."

Hugo said to bespectacled, mysterious Pinchus, "I want to join."

"It's not so simple as that."

"Alright."

"We are fighting the British. There will be no surrender. No retreat. Liberty or death. Are you afraid to die, Kharda?"

"I've died in every way a man can and still be alive. I'm afraid only of dying for nothing."

"What about torture?"

"Have you been tortured, Pinchus?"

"Yes."

"Did you break?"

"No."

"Were you afraid?"

"Of course."

"Then, yes, I'm afraid of torture."

Pinchus piled his small hands in his lap. "We have no room for adventurers or romantics. We're revolutionaries. Every member of Irgun has a heart made of steel for the cause and for his comrades. Is yours a heart of steel? I need to know."

Hugo wanted to answer quickly but Pinchus sat back to wait, signaling him to take his time.

What kind of reply did Pinchus want? A simple yes, an explanation, some eloquent oath?

"Scrap iron turns into steel. If you beat it enough."

Pinchus liked this. He leaned across the open concrete space, past the drain, to shake Hugo's hand.

"Let's see if we can find where you belong in the Irgun."

The underground group was divided into four divisions. The first was the combat corps. Pinchus repeated that Hugo would not be among the fighters; he held up a palm to prevent Hugo from protesting.

"The second is our planning division. You have no military background, so that isn't the place for you, either."

One of the last two corps needed to be a match, or the best result Hugo could hope for would be a return to Julius' gun shop. The worst would be up to Pinchus.

The third corps, the propaganda wing, handled the Irgun's publicity. They wrote, printed, and distributed flyers, posters, and messages; they pasted up pages of *Herut*, Irgun's wall newspaper; they even issued quiet warnings to the Yishuv about when to avoid a particular train, office building, or restaurant.

"I'm not much of a writer."

"It can be difficult," Pinchus lifted a finger, "yet more important than any bomb. The effect of an action goes no further than the site. Words travel the world."

Pinchus took off his glasses, to clean the lenses with the end of his tie.

"So, that's not for you either."

"No."

"The last, Kharda." Pinchus slid the glasses over his nose. His eyes did not smile with his lips. "The last, we call *Delek*. Gasoline."

Delek gathered intelligence for Irgun's operations. They developed informants and infiltrators, kept a keen eye not only on British but Arab military movements, and infiltrated both in any way they could. The division was called Gasoline because intelligence was the fuel that drove all of Irgun's decisions.

Hugo was a plumber, a welder, a survivor. What did he know about intelligence gathering?

"Is that all you've got?"

"We can always use a trusted driver. But I suspect you're looking for a deeper involvement."

Pinchus cocked his head, wondering what to do with Hugo. "There is one more thing. It may not be a help, either."

"What is it?"

"Delek makes contact with local and foreign journalists."

Hugo spread his arms wide, as if stepping onto a stage.

CHAPTER 26

VINCE

June 8
New York

"You're in my chair."

The reporter held up one finger to finish typing. He smacked the carriage return; Vince waited though the bell.

Vince's old desk looked just as he'd left it, except the mess wasn't his. The backside in his squeaky chair wasn't his. Everything else about the newsroom stayed the same: morning light in the east windows, dust motes and purls of cigarette smoke in the sunbeams. The Empire State Building was still king of Manhattan's skyline. Typewriters dinged and telephones clanged in the *Tribune*'s reporter pool.

All summer, the windows of the *Tribune* stayed open. Twenty stories above the street, the temperature in the newsroom could soar ten degrees hotter than down on the sidewalks. The vertical miles of New York's skyscrapers sopped up the day's heat and clutched it past sundown. In the morning, when the reporters and secretaries arrived, the *Tribune* was already roasting.

"Pal."

"Hang on."

Vince plastered a hand over the page so the keys struck the back of his hand.

"You need to pack up."

The reporter held his arms wide in a what-the-hell query.

"I said you need to pack up."

"No, I don't. This is my desk."

"How long have you been sitting here?"

"A little over a year."

"Surprise. I've been gone a little over a year."

"You're Vincent Haas."

"And this is Vincent Haas's desk."

The reporter plucked at his suspenders, sitting back in Vince's chair. He considered what to do. "Give me a minute."

"Take your time."

Wiping the ink off his knuckles, Vince moved to the westside windows, where long shadows ran toward the Hudson. Cars, trucks, cabs, limos, horse drawn carts, all competed for too little room in the city's streets. The haze from exhaust, the open-cook fires of vendors, the heat mirages off the roofs, all made the city steamy. Vince touched the windowpane; New York was hotter than Palestine.

He greeted old comrades. No one asked much about his thirteen months overseas; they were unconcerned, or they already knew; he'd written a lot of dispatches.

The reporter who'd squatted at his desk approached. "Dennis wants to see you in his office."

Vince didn't knock on the glass door. Three floor fans and a ceiling fan worked to cool the sunny corner office of the editor-in-chief.

Behind his desk, Dennis hooked thumbs into his belt. His bowtie spread beneath a big Adam's apple; Dennis was thin and blonde, a vulgar Midwesterner who'd made his career in news like a plainsman—through hard work, most of it digging.

"You're back."

"You sound surprised."

"The last time I got surprised was the amount of my alimony. I got wind you might be in town."

"How?"

"I'll get to that. For now, what are you doing here?"

"You told me to come home, Dennis."

"Where did you get that idea?"

"Ten telegrams. One a month."

"Did you get one the last three months?"

"No."

"Then what are you doing here?"

"Good to see you, too."

"When'd you get home?"

"Three days ago."

"Okay trip?"

"If you like ships."

"I don't. I need you to go back."

"No."

Dennis indicated an empty chair for Vince to sit. His desk was always the cleanest in the newsroom. As editor-in-chief, he was good at delegating and managing, and keeping work out of his office.

Vince asked, "I just did thirteen months. Send someone else."

"I can't."

"Why not?"

On Dennis's desk lay issues of the *Boston Globe*, *San Francisco Examiner*, *Miami Herald*, and *Chicago Tribune*. Every morning, he scanned competing newspapers; it was his job to know what they were up to and to beat them at it.

"These papers. You know what's in all of them?"

"News."

"Yes, dickhead. News. Specific to our argument, news about Palestine. And do you know who wrote their articles about Palestine?"

"Just tell me."

"You. Thirty papers, nationwide. All the heavyweights have been grabbing your datelines since the start of the year. Vincent Haas from Palestine for the *Herald Tribune*. That's what it says. Nobody has anybody on the ground there like you. Look." Dennis tossed him the Miami paper. "Second page, top."

Vince opened to his article about Haifa's superintendent of police barely escaping an Irgun car bombing. Dennis tossed him the San Francisco daily.

"A3, top. A train in Tel Aviv got derailed and robbed."

Vince didn't bother to open the paper. Dennis skidded the *Globe* across his desk. "Front page. Two British officers get gunned down in some place I can't pronounce."

"Stop. Okay, stop."

"Let me ask you something. How many Jews are there in Jerusalem?"

"A couple hundred thousand."

"Do you know who has more?"

"I don't know."

"You goddam do know. New York. I got two million in Manhattan and the Bronx alone. And they need news from Palestine. The Jews buy newspapers. *This* paper. Why?"

Vince let him say it.

"Because I have Vincent Haas reporting from Palestine. Go back."

"No."

"I can fire you."

"That doesn't solve your problem."

"I'll pay you more."

"You're going to do that anyway. I've done my time overseas. I've earned my shot at the national desk. Send someone else to Palestine."

"Is that why you went? To get a promotion?"

"Don't talk like I did something bad, Dennis. When I left I was covering city council meetings. I did a year and now I'm home. I want that guy out of my chair. I want the national beat. You said people are reading me. They can read me here."

Dennis rose behind his desk. "Why? Why don't you want to go back?"

"It's complex."

Dennis shot a finger toward his window at his hot city.

"What fucking isn't complex? We just came out of a world war. The Russians are staring us down in Berlin. Mao's making moves in China. Ten months ago we dropped two nuclear bombs on Japan. India's screaming for independence. America's rebuilding the whole goddam world, and the Nazis are designing our rockets for us. So tell me, Vince, please. Where the fuck can I send you that isn't complex? Sweet Jesus."

Dennis flattened both hands on his clean desk. "Why don't you want to go back?"

"To be honest, I got tired."

"I'm sure, Vince."

"It's a lot. It's a lot to watch up close."

"I bet it's every day."

"It is."

"I mean, just reading your columns. Cafés getting blown up. Murders. Bombings. Like I said, I get it. But you know what else is every day?" Dennis stood, the focus of three fans. "The news."

He came around to sit on a corner of his desk and look down on Vince.

"Let me tell you something my Irish grandpa used to say when he was drunk, which was the only time he ever said anything worthwhile. You'd think he would've said more. Anyway, he told me when a man wants to learn, he goes. When he wants to understand, he stays. I'm sorry it's hard, and I'm sorry you're tired. But I can't send a happy guy to cover Palestine. You're unhappy, but you understand the place. Vince. I got a paper to run. And alimony."

Dennis returned to his chair. He took from a drawer two Western Union pages.

"These came in yesterday. It's how I knew you were coming. Who's this?"

Vince read the yellow telegrams. Both originated from Jerusalem.

LOOKING FOR VINCE HAAS STOP DON'T KNOW IF YOU ARE BACK IN AMERICA STOP IF YOU ARE COME BACK STOP I AM ON IN- SIDE STOP YOU HAVE ACCESS THROUGH ME STOP STORY IS HERE VINCE STOP

"It's Hugo."

"Who's that?"

"The guy I wrote about last year. I never used his real name."

"The Buchenwald Jew."

"I lost track of him. Haven't heard from him in six months. He's a bit of a bastard."

The second telegram read:

1130AM YMCA JERUSALEM STOP

Vince returned the telegrams to Dennis' fan-swept desk. The editor tucked them into a drawer before one of the fans could blow them out a window. "He wants you to meet him at the Jerusalem Y."

"I'm not going."

"You got your own private Jew."

"Don't piss me off."

"Something's going to happen and Hugo wants you there. He says he's on the inside. I have no idea what that means. Do you?"

"I don't."

"I can't think of any way to find out sitting in that chair in this god-dam heat. Is it this hot in Jerusalem?"

"No."

"Another reason to get the hell out of here. Look, he's telling you he's gonna keep an eye on that Y every day, at eleven thirty. If you show up, it's a signal to meet. This is cloak-and-dagger shit. It's big. Don't make me beg. I have an idea."

"What."

"I don't need you to report on the day-to-day stuff. I'll get that from the wire services, maybe I'll send someone else. What I want from you is a column."

"I'm a reporter."

"A reporter who wants a promotion. Okay, here's your bump. I'm making you a regular columnist. I want your insights on Palestine, all of it, from every angle. Go back. And when you come home, you can have the national desk. You can have my fucking job. Vince, listen to me. We want the same thing."

"What would that be?"

"You want your work to matter, right?"

"You don't?"

"Fuck you, of course I do. This matters. Forget my alimony. To a lot of people, this matters. But let me give you some advice. You're never going to be Hugo. Don't try to be. He's a guy who survived a death camp. Use your own understanding, not his. Let me ask, you believe in past lives?"

"No."

"Me neither. But my ex-wife did. She used to say the two of us knew each other way back. She was a queen and I was some warrior prince. Anyway, I told her that if she was ever a queen and if I was ever within ten feet of her, I know for a fact I was no prince. I died in the mud, face-down with her fucking boot in my back. And if I did have other lives, I died in every one of them with a spear in my chest on a plain in the middle of nowhere. Or from the blisters on my hands from rowing some asshole around the Mediterranean. Or in a dungeon or a factory or a cottonfield. Or begging for drachmas or doubloons or whatever the fuck. I've always been a peon, a plebeian, a nothing. You, too."

Dennis swept a hand around his warm, windy office.

"This life, Vince. This is the one we'll brag about, you and me. This is where I get to be an editor and you get to be a columnist. This is the life, Vince, where you're not Hugo."

Dennis strode to his office door. He spoke with one hand on the doorknob.

"Go back to Palestine. Have lunch at the Y. Find Hugo. Go do what matters. Just while you're at it, wire me eight hundred words twice a week. Can you do that?"

Dennis didn't wait for an answer but swung open the door.

"Take two weeks off, paid leave. Take a rest. Walk around the city and think seriously about your job. Think about a free and independent press. You want to help the world understand its complexities? In two weeks, I'll give you a raise and a ticket back to Palestine. And I'm letting that shithead keep your desk."

Vince stepped into the newsroom, accosted by swelter and the noise of tapping keys, ringing phones, and the cacophony of the city. Another reporter with another problem brushed past into Dennis's office.

CHAPTER 27

RIVKAH

July 10
Massuot Yitzhak

The news spread through the orchards, the warehouse, down to the quarry, and out to the field where Rivkah rolled a stone. She tossed her gloves on top of the little boulder she'd prised out of the ground.

Aharon shut down the belching old tractor. He held out a hand for him and Rivkah to run together. The birth of the first child in the kibbutz, a girl, had emboldened him, proof that this hard land would give way to life. In the two months since Aharon's arrival from Hungary, he'd only mooned at Rivkah through the flames of a bonfire or contrived to be near her when Massuot Yitzhak danced the hora.

She told him, "Go on ahead." Aharon was a good-looking boy and quiet. Mrs. Pappel had encouraged her to pay attention to him. "I'll catch up."

Aharon galloped off with the rest. Rivkah stayed behind on the terrace. She'd spent weeks clearing and leveling this ground on the eastern slope of the hill. The bigger stones had been cemented into a retaining wall, the smaller stones tossed into a pile to line a cistern. Once the terrace was finished, the soil would be washed for months to clean away the salt. Then Massuot Yitzhak would plant. The pioneers would then carve out another terrace and shape the land more. If the covenant was true, their children would do the same for a thousand years.

Rivkah drew a breath of the ancient view. No one in history had ever stood where she did, because she had created this spot. Even so, no wall or terrace could match the baby, the Jewish girl who'd not had to climb this hill but arrived on top of it.

Rivkah hurried up the path to stand with Aharon outside the clinic to greet her.

✳ ✳ ✳

The news had spread to the Arab villages. On the afternoon of the birth, they came to Massuot Yitzhak.

A hundred Arabs flocked to the bottom of the slope. They were same number as all of Massuot Yitzhak. The boys tied black and white *keffiyehs* around their necks and hid their faces like bandits. They arrived on foot and in mule-drawn carts. In Arabic and Hebrew, they shouted for the Jews to stop stealing their land, to go away, and to be damned.

Dozens of Jews formed their own mob on top of the hill. The Arabs climbed far enough to fling rocks at them. Some showed talent with slings, sailing pebbles almost to where Rivkah stood on the crest.

The two sides kept this distance in the July heat. A few Arabs and settlers got hit, each yelped, then came up yelling louder. No one got badly hurt, but the risk was high. Tempers might flare, the confrontation could grow into a brawl.

Several kibbutz girls stood with their boys. Mrs. Pappel appeared beside Rivkah in the shade of an olive tree. She'd been with the new mother and child. Mrs. Pappel clucked her tongue.

Rivkah asked, "How is the baby?"

"The baby's fine. I'm not going to put up with this a lot longer."

Mrs. Pappel mopped her brow, then reached to the small of her back and filled her hand with a pistol.

"Put that away."

"If one rock goes in that baby's window."

"You'll make things worse."

"I'll make it stop."

"Put it away. Right now."

Mrs. Pappel sat under the tree and set the gun where no one might see it.

The fracas on the hillside stayed at an even pitch, a stalemate of anger. The Arabs at the bottom of the hill had the greater number, but the settlers held the high ground. Both sides reveled in chasing after the same stones that had been thrown at them to heave them back; it became a test to see who could grab them off the ground first. In ones and twos, boys in scarves and boys in sun hats surged forward to launch their stones, then skip backward, taunting.

After an hour, Mrs. Pappel gathered her handgun and left to check on the child. She had no more fear that the squabble would escalate and invoke her.

The clash wore on as if it were the day's work. Arabs and settlers bellowed with an inexhaustible dislike of each other, in a perfectly balanced fear that kept them apart and near enough. The violence slacked only at sunset. Both sides raised their arms at their opponents to skirl their last curses and stones. Calls for prayer rose from nearby Surif and Jab'a. The bell rang at Massuot Yitzhak's dining hall. All the boys and girls withdrew, dutiful and hungry.

Rivkah filled a tray for Mrs. Pappel and the newborn's mother and delivered it to the clinic. She returned to the plum trees overlooking the Wadi Shahid, the valley at the foot of Massuot Yitzhak. Rivkah sat with the opening stars and restored quiet. She thought of her family and her promise to build Palestine for them. Behind her the young settlement settled down to sleep. Rivkah stayed late under a spangling sky, hoping for a better country than what she'd seen that day.

CHAPTER 28

VINCE

July 22
Jerusalem

In the back of the YMCA's patio restaurant full of white linen tables and umbrellas, Hugo waited behind a beer.

He stood at Vince's approach. Vince didn't extend a hand. Hugo looked rested, fed, even prosperous. He was on the inside now and appeared to take to it. His beer was half full.

"Hugo."

"Vince. It's been a while."

"Eight months without a word from you. Yeah. A while."

"I'm sorry. Did you stop believing we are friends?"

"I don't know."

"Then pretend to be happy to see me. We'll go from there."

Hugo sat, Vince followed.

"I figure you owe me for three more weeks at sea and another four days of waiting for you to show up here."

"I'm sorry about all that. The four days I can explain." Hugo motioned across the sunny patio for a waiter to bring Vince a beer. "Let's eat."

A beer for Vince came immediately. He ordered an American hamburger, Hugo the same.

"I regret having lost touch. But I always knew what you were doing; you've been easy to keep track of in the newspapers. You're getting to be famous. It turns out you're a wonderful writer."

"Thank you."

"Actually, I've been wanting to thank you. I've had time to think about all you've done for me. Gave me hope, perhaps even life. Gave me Palestine."

Hugo lifted his beer to tap against Vince's glass. Vince complied, then both drank. Customers began to fill the restaurant. Many were British military from their headquarters in the seven-story King David Hotel across the street, and others were hotel guests drawn to the Y's sunny deck and lower prices.

"You look well, Hugo."

"As do you. I'm glad you're back. Why did you come? It's not because I asked."

"I got a promotion. This was part of the deal."

"Ah. Ambition. Perhaps of all the things that came back to me," Hugo held up his hands, once rail thin, strong again now as they once were, a plumber's hands, "I was most glad to see the return of ambition. A corpse is nothing a man should want to be."

"What have you been doing? Since you jumped."

"Things I haven't been able to share with you. I apologize. But I can share them now. They will explain my absence."

"What are you on the inside of? Palmach?"

Hugo laid a palm to his filled-out chest. "You flatter me. No, it seems I'm not Palmach material."

"Then what?"

"Let's leave that for last."

"Whatever it is you're doing, a lot of Jews are going to jail for it."

"I've already had my share of imprisonment; I'm not jealous."

"Why are you doing this?"

Hugo leaned back. The waiters kept their distance and seated no one near them.

Vince said, "I came a long way to have this conversation. I'm not guaranteeing I'll stay. It's got to be worth my while."

"It will be." Hugo checked his watch before signaling for another beer. Vince had barely touched his own. "Are you going to take notes?"

"No. Where have you been for four days?"

"Waiting for word that I could make contact. Following you."

"I don't like being followed."

"Nor do I. I suspect it will happen again to us both."

"Waiting for word of what?"

"Again, let's save that for the end. The food will be here in a moment. I need to explain a few ground rules between us."

"Go ahead."

"You will report no real names. No exact locations. You'll develop no other underground contacts in Palestine. When you want to meet, you'll take a table on this patio, at this time. I'll be informed and you will hear from me, only me. When I want to see you, I'll know where you are and send word where to meet."

"If I can't use names, what do I call you?"

"Kharda. It's Arabic for scrap metal."

"Why?"

"Another time. Do we agree on the terms?"

"For now."

Hugo leaned on his elbows, conspiratorial. "I'll show you things, Vince."

The waiter appeared with the hamburgers and Hugo's beer.

Before he tucked in, Hugo rubbed his palms with delight. A year ago, this was something Vince couldn't imagine he'd witness. Hugo checked his watch again.

"Are you a terrorist now, Hugo?"

"As I've been saying, I'd like to keep that for the end."

"We're at the end." Vince pushed back his chair.

"Yes, Vince. I'm a revolutionary now."

Vince didn't rise but stayed clear of the table, to show Hugo he would walk if answers weren't forthcoming.

"I guess that's what you have to call yourselves. Why do you keep looking at your watch?"

Hugo pushed back his own chair. Some pretense of affa-
bility was broken.

"You can sit and wait, or you can go."

"Who are you with, Hugo?"

"The Irgun."

"What do you do for them?"

"They've assigned me to you. I've convinced them you can be an ally."

"I'm not an ally. I'm a journalist."

"The truth is a weapon."

"What's going to happen?"

"Wait."

"Why can't you tell me?"

"Because you're not Irgun."

The two sat like this, drawn back from the table. Hugo had promised
to show something remarkable; Vince promised to leave if he didn't.

Lunch patrons began to stand from their tables and move in bunches
to the front of the patio, to peer across the street at the King David. On
instinct, Vince rose too.

"Don't leave the patio, Vince. No matter what happens."

Hugo remained seated with fingers laced. Vince pushed into the
crowd. Across the street, Julian's Way, military police poured out of the
hotel's main entrance. Ten khakied officers veered left, racing for the
sunken driveway and service dock at the rear of the King David. The first
cop vanished behind a limestone brick wall. Shots rang out.

Hidden from view in the sunken drive, a gun battle erupted as the
police rushed to the service driveway. The shots were single rounds until
one long burp ripped, then another, fired from semi-automatic weapons.

Hugo appeared beside Vince. He lay a hand on Vince's shoulder, to
remind him to stay in place.

The gunplay grew louder. Five men dressed as Arab laborers rounded the berm that hid the sunken driveway and sprinted into the gardens
in front of the King David's entrance. The pursuing police took cover in
the hotel's landscaped bushes and trees.

The fighting spilled into Julian's Way. Two more Arabs arrived on
the road to pull Sten guns from under their robes; they let loose at the
British cops among the bushes.

The seven Arabs ran off, east to the Old City. The British dashed after them on the road, taking only potshots in the populated area. Far-off tires squealed, ending the shooting. The Arabs had made good their getaway.

The echoes and smoke cleared quickly. The police faded back toward the hotel.

The lunch patrons, agog, traipsed back to their tables.

Vince turned on Hugo. "Tell me. Right now."

The answer almost knocked Vince off his feet.

A blast swept across the face of the YMCA. On the patio, the concussion toppled umbrellas, shoved tables and customers over. Vince dropped to his knees, protecting his head. Hugo was blown onto his back.

Debris rained, a dust cloud swept over the patio. Slowly, the haze cleared. A bomb had blown outside an Arab souvenir shop next to the YMCA. The store's façade was smashed to busted glass and strewn rubble. No bodies lay in the wreckage. An Arab stumbled out of the gaping hole in the storefront.

Across Jerusalem, klaxons blared. Hugo climbed to his feet, holding the back of his head. No one else on the patio appeared hurt. The staff dusted themselves off, then righted tables, umbrellas, and chairs.

In the street, traffic had stopped when the first gunshots were heard. A bus had halted directly in front of the souvenir shop; the blast had shattered all its windows. Passengers, all Arabs, tumbled out. Some sat in Julian's Way clutching arms or stanching their bleeding faces with scarves. Drivers left their own cars to give aid. Police directed the wounded who could walk into the King David to be cared for. Many remained inside the bus, too injured or traumatized to come out.

With the bombing over, Hugo had disappeared.

Vince hurried down the patio steps to the bus. The carnage stunned him. Victims limped past, blood dotted the hot road and spattered the broken glass. An elderly Arab spread an arm across Vince's shoulders and hobbled, bringing Vince with him to the hotel.

The wounded collected in the King David's lobby. Vince kept an arm around the old man's waist while British police patted down the Arab. Moving through the grand lobby, the old man admired the upholsteries, Oriental carpets, polished woods. His grey eyes fixed on the high, decorated ceiling.

The lobby swarmed with wounded, frightened passengers, police, and hotel staff scurrying to be of help. More Arabs from the bus flowed into the lobby; sirens continued to shriek across Jerusalem. Vince deposited the old man in an empty chair.

Vince was grabbed from behind.

He spun on dusty Hugo, who immediately said, "I told you to stay on the patio."

"You knew about that bomb."

"I did."

"You're a bomber now?"

"Let's go back across the street. I'll tell you everything."

"No. Right here."

Hugo backed away. The old Arab in the chair hadn't lowered his gaze from marveling at the ceiling.

"Do you remember lifting me out of that barrack? Do you remember telling me to jump off the ship?"

"What's that got to do with this?"

"I trusted you, and I'm alive because of it. Trust me now."

"What's going to happen?"

Hugo retreated more. "Come with me now. Or we won't talk again." He walked away.

Hugo didn't look back leaving the lobby. Vince didn't follow.

Around him, people bustled, the hurt, their helpers, and the curious. He turned a circle in their midst, searching for evidence, a clue, anything to tell him what to do next. He could shout the alarm, maybe start a panic, maybe save lives, or maybe be ignored and arrested. He might die here shouting; he had no way to know what the moments might bring. Vince had only one fact: Hugo's warning. Everything else was a guess.

Hugo was Irgun. Vince couldn't trust him. But could he believe him?

He leaned down to the Arab he'd helped into the hotel. "Get out of here."

The old man was comfortable in the leather chair, and he had a glass of water.

"No."

Vince headed for the King David's entrance; notions of the inconceivable chased him out the door. He hurried past faces he would not look at.

Outside, Vince crossed Julian's Way. A cop blew his whistle, but Vince dodged through the back-up-and-moving traffic, stepping again over broken, bloody glass. He leaped up the steps to the YMCA patio, thinking he might punch Hugo in the nose. Hugo was nowhere to be found.

Alone, Vince watched the King David. The other patrons had left or gone back to their tables. Waiters swept up dust and served tea to return the restaurant to normal. Policemen probed the souvenir shop, taking notes, measurements, and samples. Vince didn't know what he was waiting for; he supposed this was how it must have been for Hugo in Buchenwald.

The thickness of the King David's pink limestone muffled the first blast. The explosion boomed out of the basement. One corner of the seven-story façade facing Julian's Way expanded, as if inflated. For seconds, nothing more happened.

Then, the entire south wing of the hotel began to melt. The walls and windows of the upper tiers lost their balance and tottered top over bottom into open air. The lower half of the hotel's corner dissolved straight down, sliding into a cumulus of dust in an ordered collapse. The rumble became a quake, a horror in the earth.

Boiling haze blinded the boulevard and the YMCA patio. Vince shielded his eyes from pelting dust and blast-blown bits. When he could see and breathe again, the damage to the hotel tripped him backwards, and he fell.

A slope of debris, stone and masonry, climbed up the mangled hotel and entombed the street. Vehicles were crushed or turned over; the Arab bus was consumed in the mound. The King David stood severed and in shock like an amputee. Tangled in the vast spill were tables, chairs, desks, plaster, doors, floorboards, pipes, linens, curtains, and bodies.

Vince wiped powder off his lips. An eerie, quashed silence settled over the scene so deeply the dust fell with the patter of snow.

CHAPTER 29

RIVKAH

August 6
Massuot Yitzhak

Rivkah lay on her belly, cradling the long rifle Malik had given her last year.

Malik towered over her, dusty boots near her head. He spoke through the ringing in her ears. "We've been over this many times. You must hold the rifle like what it is. The one thing in the world that may save your life when nothing else can. Breathe out. Pull the trigger naturally, as if it is simply the next thing you will do."

The target was a fifty-gallon drum at seventy yards, the size of a man's torso. With the late sun stretched across her back, Rivkah shot through several magazines. Since the lessons began weeks ago, her aim had improved too slowly for Malik's patience. She had no love of guns. Malik toed Rivkah's ribcage with every miss. "Can you smell it? The burning of your fields?"

Malik kept her practicing until sunset, when Mrs. Pappel came to stop them. Malik bowed, whistled for his camel, which came grunting, then disappeared into the darkening land.

Paper lanterns had been strung between plum trees in the center of the kibbutz. With sundown came the end of fasting for Tisha B'av, the day of mourning to mark the destruction of the First and Second Temples.

Dinner was a banquet for those who'd worked on empty stomachs in the fields planting, watering, plowing, or hammering in the quarry.

Once the meal was done and baths taken, the pioneers came under the flickering candles to rest on blankets and talk. Malik returned to sit with Mrs. Pappel at the perimeter of the candlelight. Malik was the lone Arab who visited Massuot Yitzhak. His twice-a-month appearances had become exotic events; his snooty camel even allowed itself to be petted by the young Jews, but never ridden. Malik, too, kept a distance about himself, though not from Mrs. Pappel. His robes swirled when he moved among the trees, on the smoothed earth—something stormy about him.

His gunrunning was an open secret among the kibbutzniks. Aharon and Ben Joseph had tunneled out a small underground chamber beside the schoolroom, a hiding place for weapons and ammunition. The ventilation shaft to the little underground armory, a steel tube poking out of the ground, was disguised as the fulcrum to a children's seesaw.

Malik smoked a pipe, cool in his robes and headdress. Mrs. Pappel sat on a blanket with him outside the ring of pioneers, wreathed in his smoke.

For the past several days, the radio from Jerusalem had been filled with little else than news of the King David Hotel bombing. The death toll was in: ninety-one people killed, seventy injured. The victims included Arabs, British, Jews, Armenians, Russians, a Greek, and an Egyptian. Most of the casualties were civilian clerks and typists for the military office, hotel staff, and passersby on the street. The Irgun claimed responsibility.

Twenty minutes before the explosion, a smaller bomb had blown up an Arab souvenir shop across the road. The Irgun phoned the King David to tell them the first blast was a warning and to evacuate the building. The British military determined the call was a hoax. An official was quoted as saying he didn't jump when Jews told him to.

The young settlers regretted the loss of innocent lives. A few said the British brought this on themselves. Malik and Mrs. Pappel sat off to the side in a silence which looked like wisdom.

A shooting star striped the night sky. Rivkah was eager for the conversation to veer away from bombs.

"May we ask Malik for a poem?"

The big Arab tapped his pipe on the ground to empty it, a short ritual of reluctance before rising. Other than the mule, Malik was the largest living thing in Massuot Yitzhak.

He held no notes; he carried all his poems in his head.

"I am sorry. The war has come a step closer. While I listened to your talk, I composed this."

Malik spread his hands and turned a full circle under the candles, to see all the young settlers. When he stopped turning, with both hands over his heart, he faced Mrs. Pappel.

"The desert is not empty nor still.
Like the ocean it is vast.
It rolls at the pace of years.
The desert is not for the eyes or ears
But for the heart.
If a man's heart is empty
The desert is not the place for him.
If a man is full, the desert is an intent listener.
The desert keeps a still tongue.
When it does speak
It comes for your life."

Malik remained in the hush he'd made. He turned his creviced face to Rivkah to say that was for her, as well. Another falling star fired across the firmament.

To the south, a car's headlights left Kfar Etzion. The road between the two kibbutzim was an unpaved track, rutted by the occasional rains and not an easy thing to travel after dark.

Mrs. Pappel stood to watch the car bounce out of Kfar Etzion, Malik beside her. For no reason she could name, Rivkah joined them. The rest of the haverim ignored the headlamps working through the wadi; their hard day was done, and the lanterns made them sleepy.

The car, a taxi, climbed the slope; it stopped on the rim of the light. A tall girl with a small suitcase got out. The cab paused, but she waved it on.

The girl wore a skirt, her blonde hair fell past her shoulders. This was not a farmer. Approaching the lanterns with unsure strides, she gripped her valise with both hands.

The girl trod into the sallow candleglow. With all eyes on her, she set down the suitcase. She addressed all the settlers of Massuot Yitzhak.

"I'm looking for Éva."

CHAPTER 30

RIVKAH

Rivkah fell to her knees. Gabbi ran to her and buckled, and they embraced. The pioneers surrounded them.

Mrs. Pappel and Malik raised both girls to their feet, then walked them out of the crowd. Beneath the lanterns, Mrs. Pappel whispered, "Let's get you two home, you can talk there.' Malik brought the girl's suitcase.

Clutching Gabbi, unsteady, Rivkah said her first words to her sister. "Papa? Mama?"

Gabbi shook her head, a small gesture, not so dreadful for her; she'd known for years. But Rivkah needed her sister's arms to keep from collapsing again.

On the short walk to the house, every step felt new in the world. So much more to know, even the pain of knowing. The touch of Gabbi's hand made the answers, whatever they might be, bearable. What could Gabbi say beyond her arrival in Massuot Yitzhak, out of her own grave?

On the porch, Rivkah took a spot on the floor, knees pulled in tight. Mrs. Pappel sat in the chair behind her, to rest hands on Rivkah's shoulder. Gabbi took the other chair while Malik stood off under the stars.

Mrs. Pappel spoke first. "Dear, how on earth did you find us?"

"Actually, I found you."

"Tell us."

Gabbi said to Rivkah, "A year after you left Vienna, we were made to sew yellow stars on our clothes. Living like that was awful. People stopped doing business with Papa, others forced us off of trains and buses. Papa kept saying it was temporary. The next year, the trucks came into the Jewish neighborhoods. Papa was taken away by German police. The last thing he said was for us to find a way to go. Leave Vienna. He told me to find you."

Mrs. Pappel's hand tightened on Rivkah's shoulder.

"It was too late. I never forgot you said that. Come before it's too late. We'd given up all our travel papers. Mama and I were sent to Ravensbrück."

Mrs. Pappel reached for Gabbi, who did not take the offered hand. Mrs. Pappel didn't pull back. "What happened to your mother, child?"

Gabbi chose her words. The girl was sixteen now, the same age as many of the haverim of Massuot Yitzhak. Most had been in the camps, all had lost families. Gabbi seemed younger than them, paler and softer; she'd not had the years in Palestine to scour her. But in her sadness, she was the same as Rivkah, Mrs. Pappel, any of them; no one was older.

In the spring of last year, the war was collapsing around the Nazis. After surviving two years in Ravensbrück, Gabbi, their mother, and twenty-five thousand women were forced from the camp. Guards marched them north, away from the advancing Red Army, to keep them from bearing witness to what they'd endured. The women walked for a month without enough food, clothing, or shelter. Many died of malnutrition and exposure.

The girl dabbed her eyes on the backs of her wrists.

"Mama."

Rivkah smeared her own cheeks dry. Mama and Papa were buried for tonight, for the arrival of Gabbi, and for the first moment of forever in Rivkah's heart.

Gabbi said, "I couldn't go back to Vienna. For a year I stayed in a displaced persons camp at Dachau in Munich, looking for a way to come here, to find you. I joined a Youth Aliyah group, then took a train with them to Italy. In La Spezia, I got passage on an Aliyah Bet ship, the *Dov Hoz*. Before we could sail, the British blockaded us. The Italians in the town contacted the press. Newspapers from all over the world got involved. There were a thousand of us on the *Dov Hoz*; we staged a hunger strike for three days. After that, the British let us leave for Palestine."

Mrs. Pappel asked, "How did you find me?"

"We got to Haifa in May. In Éva's letters, she said she'd come on the *Atlantic*. I went to the Atlit camp to check the records, to see if I could find where she'd gone after she left the camp. They told me about the *Patria*, how it sank. I got scared that you'd drowned. But you weren't on the *Patria*'s manifest."

"No."

Gabbi dug into a pocket of her skirt, to hand Rivkah a small, creased paper.

"You were dead."

Rivkah unfolded her old identification card, left in the Atlit barrack the morning the guards rousted everyone to board the *Patria*. She'd left Éva's card inside papa's opera coat, on her cot when the guard threw her out.

For the first time since she'd walked into the lantern light, Gabbi smiled.

"I asked to see the record of your death. You were found in the wrong barrack, you had no identification papers, and you died of old age." Gabbi tapped Rivkah's old card. "The British had a body with no identification. And an identification card with no body. So, they matched the body with your card and balanced their books."

Before Gabbi left Atlit, she copied the names of the others in the barrack where Éva's corpse was found. One of them lived in Haifa, running a hostel. The old woman said Gabbi would surely find her sister if she found Mrs. Pappel, recalling how the two had become inseparable. Gabbi's search for Mrs. Pappel took her from Atlit to Haifa to Kfar Etzion, then a short truck ride over bumpy ground to Massuot Yitzhak.

Gabbi held both hands out to Mrs. Pappel. "And there you are. Hello, Mrs. Pappel."

She leaned down to nuzzle her cheek against Rivkah's. She whispered, "Hello, Rivkah Gellerman."

Rivkah pressed a hand behind her sister's head. "I'm so sorry."

In the dark, off the porch, a patch of blackness eddied. Malik headed for his mewling camel and called over his shoulder.

"When I return, I will bring a poem for this. And I will teach the girl to shoot."

CHAPTER 31

OCTOBER 5
KIBBUTZ SHOVAL
BRITISH MANDATE OF PALESTINE
By Vincent Haas
Herald Tribune News Service

YOM KIPPUR, the day of atonement, ended tonight at dusk.

I am in the Negev, holding on in the rear of a ten-wheeler truck, bouncing over rocks and sand. I sit on a stack of poles that shift as we bounce, threatening to pinch me.

My truck is the lead vehicle of five, all piled with construction tools, prefabricated walls, bags of concrete and gravel, water barrels, shingles, crossbeams, and two-by-fours.

Yom Kippur's sunset saw ten more convoys like ours, secretly dispatched from Jerusalem to establish, before dawn, eleven tower-and-stockade settlements in the most remote part of Mandate Palestine: the desert.

British officials recently announced a map that will permanently divide Palestine into three sections: forty-three percent of the Mandate's land, including Jerusalem, will remain with Britain; forty percent goes to the Arabs, and the rest, just seventeen percent, will belong to the Jews. All three areas will remain under British rule.

The Jews are not happy.

In response, the Jewish Agency is racing across the face of Palestine, even into the Negev, to create as many settlements as it can outside the area the British propose to allot them. When statehood comes, and the

Jews are resolute that it will, these overnight colonies will anchor their case for different boundaries.

We're headed for a windswept hill seven miles north of the Arab city of Be'er Sheva. The Jews will call the new settlement Shoval, after the son of the son of somebody in the Bible.

My thirty comrades are a rowdy bunch of survivors from a ship that sank six years ago in Haifa, the *Patria*. They're young men and women, mostly teenagers, who've been training and waiting for two years for this first night in the desert.

After an hour of bouncing in burnished light through a bleak land, our convoy climbs a slight hill. We stop, jump down, and immediately begin building a three-story watchtower. Holes are dug while strong backs unload the supplies, all in the trucks' headlights. I take a turn on a post hole digger. The ground fights me. But even as I hack at it while others roll away stones, I know this hardness is how the land makes you prove yourself. I quit digging before I get blisters.

The pioneers finish by sunrise. There's an old Ottoman law that still holds sway in the Negev: any structure with a roof can remain. The Arabs respect this and the Jews take advantage.

After the watchtower stands on four legs, the Jews erect sheds at its feet and nail down their vital roofs. A perimeter stockade goes up next, six foot high, surrounding the settlement. Shoval now covers a single dunam, another Turkish holdover, that area which can be plowed by a team of oxen in a single day. About a quarter acre.

After my short shift digging holes, I only watch and take notes. The pioneers don't mind; I was slowing them down. They're friendly, high spirited, and on an adventure.

A red dawn paints the faces of the young Jews even ruddier. Exhausted, they drink cool wine and dance the hora inside their new wall. Shoval and ten sister settlements like her have been birthed on the same desert night.

An hour after sunrise, the Arabs arrive, camel-riding Bedouin from the village of Rahat. Settlers scramble for their guns. Emissaries go outside the wall to talk while armed farmers man the watchtower. Together, the Jews and Arabs strike a deal, that they will try to live side-by-side.

I've seen too few of these handshakes. But they must be happening. They must. No one in Palestine can ignore where all this is headed if Arab and Jew can't share the land. Maybe, just maybe, that handshake was repeated ten more times in the same morning sun, out in the white wastes of the Negev.

It's not enough to give me hope. It does, however, let me sleep. Reporting from Shoval, Palestine.

CHAPTER 32

VINCE

December 27
Jerusalem

The police captain settled his bulk behind a desk in his small office. Vince slid into a hard-backed chair. The captain removed his billed khaki cap and set it in a spot on the desk that seemed reserved for it. Medals coated one side of his starched tunic, on the other hung a badge and a whistle on a chain. A gold clip held his tie. He smoothed a speckled hand over strands of carrot hair. The man was a Scot; he seemed a wall.

"Mister Haas, is it?" The captain's watchband made a click when he flattened both palms on his desk.

"Yes, sir."

"New York paper, right?"

The man's hair was not matted; he'd not sweated. He lay ten finger-tips lightly on the table, though he had heavy hands. Nothing about him hinted that he'd just come from a flogging.

"That's right."

"What can I do for you, Mister Haas?"

"I understand you were a witness to the beating."

"The caning. I was there."

"You whipped the boy on the Sabbath."

"That was not a concern for the government."

"Was it eighteen strokes?"

The policeman answered in the trained manner of a press release.

"Abraham Kimchin was taken from his cell this morning to the courtyard of the Jerusalem Central Prison. He was stripped to the waist and tied by the arms to a post. Two policemen administered punishment with bamboo rods, eighteen strokes as ordered by the Mandate court. What else?"

"How did he take it?"

"Defiant."

"He's sixteen."

"He'll see seventeen."

"You think he got off light?"

The policeman tapped one finger on the table, the sole display of his impatience.

"Kimchin is Irgun. He was found guilty of three capital offenses. Possession of an illegal firearm. Five rounds of ammunition. He discharged a firearm in the robbery of a bank in Jaffa. Eighteen years in jail and eighteen strokes with a cane are better than one rope. Yes, Mr. Haas, the lad got off light."

Vince dug out of his pocket a flyer he'd snared off a wall two days prior. He unfolded the blue page to lay it out before the captain.

"You've seen this?"

In Hebrew and English across the top, the poster declared: *Warning!*

> *A Hebrew soldier taken prisoner by the enemy was sentenced by an illegal British Military Court to the humiliating punishment of flogging. We warn the occupation government not to carry out this punishment which is contrary to the laws of soldiers' honor. If it is put into effect, every officer of the British occupation army will be liable to be punished in the same way, to get eighteen whips.*

The captain slid the page back to Vince. "I've seen it."

"Would you care to comment?"

Beneath the freckles, the Scotsman turned one shade redder. "The Jews need to understand we mean business."

"I think they're saying the same to you."

The captain pulled his hands off the desk, to knit husky fingers in his lap. Every focused movement seemed to help him contain some heat building within him.

"We know you have dealings with the Irgun, Mister Haas."

"Is that so?"

"It's rather clear from your writings."

"And?"

"It would be helpful. It might save lives, if you would let them know that British restraint, while practiced over centuries, has limits."

"I'm not your go-between."

The policeman ignored this. "Tell them what is on the other side of our limits."

"And what is that?"

"The noose."

"Captain?"

"In this decade, not one Jewish terrorist on death row in Palestine has gone to the gallows. Over the past year alone, eighty-three Jews have been jailed for capital crimes. None have been executed. I am informing you that word has come down, from very high up, that our policy of leniency will be reconsidered. If things do not change."

"Understood."

"Do you know the name Dov Gruner?"

"No."

"Keep it in mind."

The policeman rested both palms again softly on the tabletop beside his neat hat. This called an end to the meeting.

"I know how to contact you. Anything else, Mister Haas?"

Vince stood while the cop kept his seat. The Irgun were going to retaliate for Kimchin; the cop knew it. Who was Dov Gruner? Was he the Jew already chosen to pay for whatever action the Irgun was going to take?

Outside the police station in the brightness of Jerusalem, Vince checked his watch. Ten minutes before eleven. He had time to make it to the YMCA patio.

CHAPTER 33

HUGO

December 29
Tel Aviv

Hugo finished a supper of brown bread and fig jam, white cheese, and a Jaffa orange. He stepped out onto his third-floor balcony to smoke. On days of wilder weather, the crashing of the sea and a trace of salt drifted to his open windows. Tonight, a gentle night, Hugo dropped ashes to the lawn. Below, after the shops closed, Arabs and Jews walked to their homes.

The Irgun didn't pay Hugo enough to keep his own flat. For the rest of his rent, Hugo did small jobs in the building for his landlord, an old Czech. The man had offered Hugo work the day he'd rented the apartment, without Hugo mentioning anything about his skills. The money the old Czech gave him on Fridays was always a little more than Hugo's invoice; that was the secret Irgun share. He did some carpentry, some patching of mortar, and no plumbing. A Škoda parked beneath his balcony at the curb belonged to the Irgun, left there for tonight. The key had been slipped under his door during the day while he'd been out.

Hugo tossed the nub of his last cigarette off the veranda. The old Czech hired a deaf Arab boy to sweep the grounds every morning. A young couple strolled beneath a streetlamp. The man was Hassidic in black hat and suit; the woman hid her head and arms under a wrap. She carried two mesh sacks of groceries. The man spoke too faintly for Hugo to catch his words in the cool night, but he seemed to be lecturing in Hebrew while his wife carried the groceries.

Hugo plucked the car key from his pocket and left the veranda.

✳ ✳ ✳

Vince waited at the corner on Rothschild Boulevard. Hugo drove past twice, checking to see that no one was following Vince. On the third pass, he pulled over across the street.

Hugo rested his arm on the windowsill of the Škoda. On the sidewalk, Vince stood taller than anyone; he looked plainly foreign. Hugo whistled.

Vince crossed the street and got in. A sour mien seemed to get in with him. Hugo patted Vince's shoulder, cheery as he drove off.

"You look worried."

"I'm not sure this is a good idea."

"Of course it is. A warm winter night, a breeze off the sea. A pleasant drive."

"I know what's going to happen. That makes me complicit."

Vince still clung to fairness and rules. Hugo found it outmoded. In a small way, it made him sad for old Leipzig and the time in the world when those notions were not dead.

Hugo peeled back the hem of his coat. "I have a gun. Does that make you feel better?"

"Why would it?"

"You can say I'm making you come along. You had no choice. Would you like a blindfold?"

"I brought my own."

"Oh, stop worrying. Everyone in Palestine knows what's going to happen."

They'd not seen each other in two weeks. Hanukah had come and gone, and Christmas. Neither mentioned the holidays; they didn't speak of gifts or their time apart. They weren't friends, a relief for Hugo because he was unsure how he might handle such an overture from Vince, to share a meal, talk between missions. Vince as a friend would keep playing the American, the moralist and caretaker. Hugo had no need for someone else's morals or their morsels of concern.

He motored south from the city, skirting the minarets and alleys of Arab Jaffa. Four miles from Tel Aviv, in an open swath of scrub and sand-hills, Hugo pulled into the parking lot of a ruined gas station. Two miles away lay the Jewish towns of Holon and Bat Yam. The gas station had been demolished in the riots of 1929, the fighting that once flared out of Jaffa. Hugo shut down his headlights. Vince didn't fidget or look around, not nervous or frightened.

Hugo peered into the darkness between the two Jewish towns, beyond the lights of Jaffa to the stars over the sea. Dunes and weedy grasses seasoned the night with a briny smell, the oily odors of the old gas station leeched from the busted concrete.

From behind an aboveground fuel tank, three shadows came unstaked from the ground. They came to the Škoda, to crowd into the backseat. Hugo didn't turn to greet them, the Irgun practice of anonymity.

✳ ✳ ✳

Six miles south of Tel Aviv, Rishon LeZion was the second old-est Jewish farming settlement in Palestine, with seven thousand residents. The citrus orchards and vineyards had been established for half a century. Hugo drove through the long-cultivated plots, past clusters of fruit-blooming branches and rows of grape arbors.

Rishon LeZion had its own main street of office buildings, shops, cafes, a British police station, and a military headquarters. In the heart of the commercial blocks, Hugo pulled to the curb outside a well-lit café, the Theresa. The evening had grown late; few patrons filled the tables. Traffic on the sidewalks and street was thin.

Inside the dark Škoda, Hugo, Vince, and the three Irgun waited. The watches on every man's wrist ticked audibly.

After ten minutes, a policeman exited the café. He trod the sidewalk toward the precinct building.

Hugo hadn't spoken since the three fighters entered the car. He asked, "Why not that one?"

The trio in the back were all young sabras, dark and bunched like crows. They wore waistcoats, caps, and pleated pants; these were city men. A pistol butt bulged in each waistband. The middle fighter, a pock-faced boy not long out of his teens, had the brittle look of confinement, as if he'd been in jail. He said, "Too skinny. We're trying not to kill him."

Not long after the first cop left the Café Theresa, a sergeant with a beamy build ambled down the steps. A black-holstered pistol rode at his belt, and no other visible weapons.

Someone patted Hugo's shoulder. He started the Škoda. One of the Irgun exited the car and zipped up his waistcoat. Beside Hugo, Vince patted a fist quietly on his own thigh. Hugo laid a hand on Vince's wrist to ask him to be still.

Hugo drove two blocks past the soldier and the Irgunist tailing him. Stopping in the broad shadows of an alley, he let the other two out; both zipped up their jackets and tugged down the bills of their caps. They headed the direction of the oncoming soldier. Hugo cut off the Škoda's lights to idle and wait.

The kidnapping went quickly. The two approaching from the front stepped in the sergeant's path, guns drawn. The Irgunist behind closed in. Hugo wheeled the Škoda fluidly into the street next to them. The soldier was relieved of his sidearm, then the fighters bundled him into the Škoda's backseat, leaving not enough room, so the smaller of the Irgun sat in the pock-faced one's lap. Hugo drove off without hurry.

The sergeant asked, "What are you going to do with me?"

"I'll knock you out," the pock-faced one said, "if you don't shut up."

Hugo drove out of Rishon LeZion, north to the sand flats. The short ride ended when Hugo cut off the lights, drove across the lot of the abandoned gas station, and shut down the engine in the moonless night.

Hugo got out first. The four in the back had to disentangle themselves. Vince got out, too, and stayed close to the Škoda. Hugo opened the trunk; with fast hands, he spun the nut holding down the spare tire. He reached beneath the tire for the whip. It was a real rawhide lash, something from an American cowboy movie, two meters long.

The Irgunists pushed the sergeant to a pillar of the gas station. The pockmarked fighter kept his pistol trained while the others stripped the soldier of his tunic. The man had a wide chest and overhanging belly which pressed to the column when the Irgunists bound his arms around it. The sergeant's exposed back was hirsute.

One of the fighters walked around to face him. "Do you want a gag?"

"Why are you doing this to me? What did I do to you?"

The pockmarked fighter took the whip from Hugo. "Do you know Abraham Kimchin?"

"No."

"He's sixteen years old. He was arrested for bank robbery. Your bunch flogged him, eighteen strokes with a cane."

"He's a boy. Right, I get it. That's barmy; he shouldn't be whipped. But your lot shouldn't be sending a kid to rob banks neither."

"His age isn't the point." The fighter held up the lash. "We won't be whipped."

"Look, I agree, alright?" The sergeant nodded against the column. "Alright? I agree with you lads. I do. What do you want me to say?"

"You weren't brought here to talk."

"Ah, Jesus. Come on, mate. I'm just a bloke doing a job."

"Do it somewhere else."

With his big arms, the sergeant bearhugged the column to shove his barrel chest into it and ready himself.

"Right. Just so you know. I'm sorry, right?"

"You'll get eighteen. Same as Kimchin. Do you want me to stuff your mouth? If you start screaming."

"Did they gag the boy?"

"No."

"Well, then. Sauce for the goose, I reckon. Get to it."

The pockmarked fighter struck the first blow. He didn't know how to handle a whip; he stood too close, not enough distance for the lash to uncoil. The stroke landed too soon, with little power. The sergeant stiffened against the pillar and kept his mouth clamped. The young Irgunist backed away two steps. This did the trick. The whip played out to its full length. The next two blows landed with a crack of the lash. The sergeant whimpered but, to his word, did not cry out.

The sergeant took five more strokes with lip-bitten grunts. The pockmarked Irgunist paused to catch his breath. The sergeant's back was crosshatched, welted and bleeding. His knees hadn't bent, and his head didn't drop.

Vince asked Hugo, "Can this be stopped?"

"Millions have asked that question."

"Say something."

"Alright." Hugo walked to the pockmarked fighter. "Give it to me."

"Why?"

"Give it to me."

Hugo would not explain himself. This said enough to the young Irgunist, and he handed over the lash.

Vince stepped forward. A fighter blocked him.

Hugo measured the distance to the pillar. He practiced once with the whip to make a proper snap. He reared back and put the ninth stripe on the soldier, then the tenth, and the eleventh. Hugo made each stroke harder than the last but could not bring the Briton to his knees.

CHAPTER 34

RIVKAH

December 31
Massuot Yitzhak

Rivkah looked into her sister's soft palms.

"You're not a Palmach."

"You don't know who I am. I don't even know who I am."

Mrs. Pappel set her teacup on the kitchen table. "You understand what it means. Any Jew caught with a gun will be sentenced to death. Palmach train to kill."

Rivkah could see none of this in her sister's hands.

Gabbi said, "I understand."

Mrs. Pappel asked, "When do you leave?"

"On the bus tomorrow morning."

"Where will you go?"

"Beit Zera on the Galilee."

"How many are going with you?"

"Three from Massuot Yitzhak, eight from Kfar Etzion."

"When will you come back?"

"I don't know."

Rivkah grabbed her shawl off the back of a chair and carried it to the porch to sit in the dark with Malik. The old Arab smoked his pipe.

The winding road from Jerusalem remained empty among the sable hills. Nothing came to Massuot Yitzhak, yet tomorrow Gabbi would leave. This felt unfair.

Mrs. Pappel stepped out on the porch, teacup steaming. Gabbi stayed inside to pack. Mrs. Pappel settled in the chair Malik abandoned for her; the old Arab carried his pipe off the porch to stand darkly in the open. As ever, when Malik moved, somewhere in the night his camel brayed.

Mrs. Pappel spoke across the brim of her teacup.

"That girl has spent half her lifetime letting go. She's used to it. Don't be hurt."

Malik puffed his pipe; Mrs. Pappel sipped. They made an odd team, intuiting that the other had more to say. They both waited, polite, until Rivkah insisted, "Pick one of you."

Malik offered an open hand to Mrs. Pappel, who returned the gesture. Before Rivkah could rise, Malik squatted, puddling his black robes.

"Do you know what is a *hadith*?"

"No."

"A saying of the Prophet. A tradition."

"Are you going to tell me one?"

"May I?"

"Fine."

Malik paused for a draw of the pipe, perhaps to let Rivkah alter her manner. She repeated, more kindly, "Fine."

"If a man will address an injustice, let him do it with his hand. If he cannot, then with his tongue. If he cannot, then with his heart, but that is the weakest faith."

"What does that mean?"

"Your sister has chosen an act of the hand. That is the strongest. It is hers to choose."

"I want to stop her."

"And that is your choice." Malik put his pipe to his lips.

On the porch, Mrs. Pappel crossed her legs. Should Rivkah stomp off, Mrs. Pappel would not follow.

"You can do one of two things, Liebling. Turn yourself into someone who stops feeling and stop your heartache. Or mourn your hurt but still love."

Malik exhaled smoke on his voice. "The silencing of the heart will make you strong. But what is the purpose of such strength?"

Rivkah could not guess Malik's age. The Negev had scored his face beyond what years could do. He might be younger than he looked; hardened by the sun, he might be much older.

She asked, "What do you do? When you hurt?"

"I write poems."

"Mrs. Pappel?"

"I cry at night, dear."

Malik opened a hand to Mrs. Pappel. He didn't feel she'd spoken well enough of herself.

"You are a warrior. And a teacher."

Gabbi emerged from the house wearing a coat. "I'd like to go say goodbye to some friends."

When no one answered quickly, Gabbi stepped off the porch.

Rivkah stood. "Stay. Please."

Malik rose to his full, black height. "I will write a poem. I will do it now."

Mrs. Pappel uncrossed her legs. "I think I've got the makings for a cake."

Gabbi let the three of them stare at her. Malik threw back his shoulders to begin reciting. Gabbi lifted a finger to shush him.

"Cake."

1947

They are a people, and they lack the props of a people. They are a disembodied ghost. There they are with a great many typical characteristics, many strong characteristics which have not disappeared through-out centuries, thousands of years of martyrdom and wandering, and at the same time they lack the props which characterize every nation.

We ask today: "What are the Poles? What are the French? What are the Swiss?" When that is asked, everyone points to a country, to certain institutions, to parliamentary institutions, and the man in the street will know exactly what it is. He has a passport.

If you ask what a Jew is—well, he is a man who has to offer a long explanation for his existence, and any person who has to offer an explanation as to what he is, is always suspect—and from suspicion there is only one step to hatred or contempt.

Dr. Chaim Weizmann

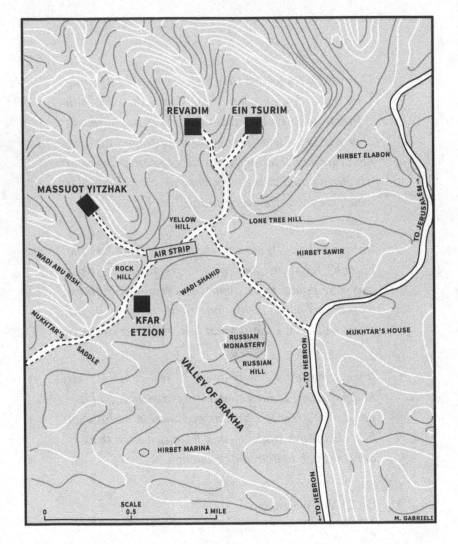

REVADIM
EIN TSURIM
HIRBET ELABON
MASSUOT YITZHAK
YELLOW HILL
LONE TREE HILL
TO JERUSALEM →
AIR STRIP
WADI ABU RISH
ROCK HILL
HIRBET SAWIR
WADI SHAHID
KFAR ETZION
MUKHTAR'S
RUSSIAN MONASTERY
← TO HEBRON
MUKHTAR'S HOUSE
SADDLE
RUSSIAN HILL
VALLEY OF BRAKHA
HIRBET MARINA
SCALE
0   0.5   1 MILE
← TO HEBRON
M. GABRIELI

THE ETZION BLOC

CHAPTER 35

VINCE

January 2
Jerusalem

Scaffolding, cranes, wheelbarrows, and mule-driven dumbwaiters raised the King David Hotel up from ruin. Hammers chinked and Arab laborers shouted from overhead, while on Julian's Way traffic honked at the congestion.

On the YMCA patio, Vince finished his juice and coffee. He signed the bill to his room, then went down to the street to wait on the chalk-dusty sidewalk.

He had no idea who would come for him. The note, slid under his door this morning, had read:

> Our mutual friend cannot contact you. We will pick you up at 0930 in front of the YMCA.
>
> P

Vince had no idea who "P" was. He assumed the mutual friend was Hugo. Why couldn't Hugo make contact? Was he in trouble?

On time, a black police car stopped in front of Vince. A cop, alone in the car, told him to get in.

The driver, a young brown-skinned officer, perhaps a Gurkha, didn't let Vince ride in the front. Vince climbed in the back of the squad car, inside the cage.

The cop pulled away with needless speed, wheeling in and out of the morning traffic. The crosshatch wire separating him from Vince, plus the cop's speeding, dissuaded Vince from asking questions. They headed west out of Jerusalem.

✳ ✳ ✳

Twenty minutes into the drive, the policeman began to talk. He made no mention of where they were going, but they were on the Tel Aviv road. He said nothing of who'd sent him. He was Nepalese, had served with the British in North Africa; he'd come to Palestine with the occupation, then joined the police force. He asked Vince about New York and America. Vince told him about Broadway, the Statue of Liberty, and the Dodgers; he tossed in the Grand Canyon and Hollywood. The policeman had seen New York and the Empire State Building in a make-believe movie about a giant ape.

Several miles shy of Tel Aviv, the car turned off the main road. A chain-link fence bore signs reading No Trespassing. A guarded gate appeared ahead. The policeman slowed and told Vince to say nothing.

At the gate, the policeman handed a soldier his credentials. He flicked a thumb behind him at Vince inside the wire. "Another one." None of the armed guards leaned in to look. They opened the gate.

The cop drove past rows of olive drab barracks built to face a manicured drill yard. British Army trucks, jeeps, and a half-dozen police cars lined the edge of the grass field. A hundred soldiers jumped down from truck beds to stride across the open ground. A dozen police in khaki shorts, high stockings, and stiff hats tromped with them. Each cop carried a baton. On the far side of the drill field, two buses waited in the camp road.

Vince's policeman parked in line with the other police vehicles. He got out, then said to Vince, "I'm a Jew. Don't write that. Don't write anything until you leave here. Stay in the car."

The cop opened the trunk, then slammed the lid. Striding across the grass, he carried a black truncheon.

Vince called after him, "What's happening?"

Without turning, the policeman raised one finger, to show the back of it. Wait, the cop was saying. Not long.

CHAPTER 36

HUGO

Tel Aviv

Hugo understood the pre-dawn pounding on his door. He'd heard it once in his life and would never forget. He didn't think to leap out a window, too high up, and his flat had no backdoor. Someone shouted his name, and "Open up!" Hugo called back, "Coming," so they wouldn't break down the door.

He knew enough to dress in whatever he could find, to not be dragged away in his bed clothes. He called to the door every few seconds as if keeping calm some beast. He dressed in under a minute and opened up to the police.

Two cops filled the threshold. One said, "Come with us." The other laid hands on him.

✳ ✳ ✳

Fifty Jews packed the cell with Hugo. Another fifty crammed the cell across the concrete hall.

No one professed to know why the British had snatched them out of their beds, but each knew. They said to each other only their names and where they were from, Netanya, Petah Tikvah, Rishon LeZion, Ramat Gan, Rehovot, and Tel Aviv. All were known hotbeds of support for the resistance.

Hugo listened to lies and didn't bother to add his own. Every man grousing about a bump or bruise the police gave him in his arrest knew an Irgunist or three and supported them with silence or money. The whippings of four British soldiers in return for the caning of young Abraham Kimchin had taken place in their districts, but none of them knew anything.

✳ ✳ ✳

Hugo smelled no worse than the man sitting next to him. No one on the bus had showered or shaved or eaten more than the soup and water pushed into their cells at sunup. When the man beside him leaned across Hugo to the window to see the drill field, Hugo shrugged him back in his place.

The pair of buses idled in the road. The Jews mumbled to each other what they feared was going to happen on the bright drill field. Four British paratroopers in the aisles shouted at them to shut up.

Pinchus had told Hugo he was a man no one would remember, so Hugo kept his face to the window. He was certain he'd been swept up in a random search, another door-banging exercise from the British to coerce the Yishuv into cooperating, giving up names. The Mandate government was swinging blindly, for if they knew who Hugo was, he'd be somewhere worse.

The buses lurched forward. One of the men was missing a leg below the knee and relied on a crutch. He called out, "Hear, O Israel." A soldier threatened to strike him; the one-legged man thrust out his chin.

The buses stopped beside the drill field. Sun drenched the grass; not a shadow broke the expanse. On the grass, two lines had been formed of soldiers and police facing each other, the phalanx spanned the length of the field. Some of the Jews on the bus took the hands of others.

An army officer boarded. "Everybody off."

The hundred men filed off the two buses and by instinct packed themselves tight to each other's shoulders. In the drill field, truncheons shifted in every hand like waves of black wheat. The officer clutched his hands behind his back.

"You are not here because you have done something. You are here because you have not."

The Briton looked no one in the eye as he strode but spoke to the ground before his boots.

"The Mandate government has garrisoned one hundred thousand troops in Palestine. This equates to one fully equipped soldier for every adult Jewish male in the land. Still you will not cooperate. You refuse to report illegal activities in your midst. You refuse to help us shut down the terrorists among you. British wives are left widowed. British mothers lose their sons. His Majesty's Government will no longer tolerate this insult."

Both buses rumbled off to the far side of the drill field. They halted at the opposite end of the formation.

"You may get back on the buses and return to your homes. Please, in your communities, engage your neighbors in a more productive dialogue. I expect you will reference your experiences of this morning."

The officer opened a hand to usher the hundred into the gauntlet. "Gentlemen."

The one-legged man was the first to move. Propped on his crutch, he shouted down the twin rows, "I lost this leg fighting alongside you lot in Italy. Let's see if you bastards have gotten any tougher since Alfonsine."

The first few soldiers did not touch him. Perhaps that was to lure the next man in, for after the Jews started to make their way between the lines, a soldier snatched the legless man's crutch. He balanced as best he could; the crutch was tossed down the line, away from him toward the waiting buses.

A soldier said, "Start hopping."

The legless man did, until a policeman tripped him. He caught himself on strong arms. With a push from his stump, the one-legged man popped up. He turned to the Jews.

Only five had entered the gauntlet. The rest hesitated; they'd seen the first ones get punched and the one-legged man knocked over.

"Coming, lads?"

Hugo pushed his way to the front and took a bat in the hip for it. He glared at the soldier who'd struck him, something he'd never dared do to at a Nazi.

He paid no attention to anyone behind him, cared nothing if the others followed or what their treatment might be. Hugo leaped past the few Jews before him, all with arms protecting their heads. He shot to the front before the one-legged man could be upended again.

Hugo slipped a shoulder under the man's arm. Their first strides together drew wallops to their ribs and arms from batons and fists, kicks at their feet to bring the one-legged man down again. Hugo safeguarded him from thumps and would not let him fall. The British vented themselves on Hugo, and many times he was the one held upright from falling.

Not every soldier and policeman hit them hard, some swung lightly. Curses mingled with the blows. Hugo took a fist to the temple, another to the neck, a smash on his back that two years ago would have left him begging a guard to stop. He kept his eyes on the buses ahead and his arms around the one-legged Jew.

CHAPTER 37

VINCE

January 6
Jerusalem

The year's first chill had crept into Jerusalem. Vince stepped onto the YMCA patio on a crystal-clear morning and buttoned his sweater. On Julian's Way, the British traffic cops still wore shorts and knee socks.

Hugo waited at a table, hunkered in a blue woolen coat, a black scarf about his neck. The puffiness hadn't left his face, nor the shadows of bruises. The cold snap and the beating made him appear a larger, darker man.

Vince motioned to a waiter for coffee. Hugo already had a beer. Vince circled a finger in the air at Hugo's swollen face. "I was there. I saw it all."

"I read your column."

"It's been a week since we talked. I've been waiting to hear from you."

Vince took a seat. The nip in the air kept most patrons away. Vince and Hugo didn't need to whisper; the waiters had come to know they required privacy.

Vince said, "You don't look so bad."

"You've seen worse."

The coffee arrived speedily; the waiter left.

"I'm sorry that happened to you."

"You wrote a beautiful piece about it." When Hugo smiled, his lips held a lingering fatness. "Careful you don't start picking a side, Vince."

"The British aren't too happy with me right now."

"Things balance out. The Irgun is very pleased with you. That's why they arranged to have you there."

"I don't know who 'P' is."

"My commander."

"What's his name?"

Hugo rattled his head. He finished his beer, then raised an arm for another.

"Where have you been, Hugo?"

"Resting. Enjoying myself."

"Really."

"Did you know that in Jerusalem, if a Jew walks around with a swollen face, everybody assumes the British did it. I haven't paid for a meal or a drink since it happened."

"What you did for that man with one leg. That was brave."

"Not at all."

"What was it, then?"

"I wasn't going to let a Jew crawl. That's not brave."

A steak arrived with Hugo's second beer. Vince ordered nothing; Hugo dug in. His discolored knuckles looked like purpled eggs on straw. Hugo cut a piece of meat and spoke with it in his mouth.

"Britain's losing its grip. Their economy is falling through the floor."

He stabbed another bit of meat, put it past thickened lips, then twirled his fork in little circles while he chewed.

"London just had its fourth record snowfall in a row. There's rolling blackouts. They're rationing bread."

He chased the steak with beer, then set down his fork. Hugo left the meal half eaten. This was Hugo, who flung himself at everything until he'd had his fill.

He asked, "What does a man do when he's losing his grip?"

"What."

"He grips harder."

Vince warmed his hands around his coffee cup. "Who's Dov Gruner?"

"Irgun. Why?"

"His death sentence was confirmed by the government yesterday."

"We know this."

"The execution's four weeks from now."

"It's just for show. They're not going to hang Dov Gruner."

"Yes, they are."

"Did you hear something?"

"Yes."

"Who said it?"

"It's high up."

"Is it going to happen?"

"I think you need to take it seriously."

Standing, Hugo lay a sore-looking hand on Vince's shoulder. "You're a friend to me. Thank you."

"What are you going to do?"

"We won't let it happen."

Before rounding a neighboring table, Hugo turned.

"Don't worry about the bill. The waiter said it was free."

CHAPTER 38

HUGO

January 27
Tel Aviv

Hugo turned to the pair of Irgunists in the back seat. This broke a protocol, to face them when he was just the driver. He didn't know their names and had not heard their voices.

"Let me go through the window."

Neither answered. Both were bigger than Hugo, one particularly beefy, an intimidator, the other hairy with tufts on his knuckles.

"Look at the three of us, for God's sake. I'm half your size. Let me do it."

The hairy one said, "No."

The big Irgunist added, "Pinchus said you drive."

"Pinchus told you to complete the mission." He indicated the hairy one. "What if you get stuck? What if he can't lift you out?" Hugo faced front. "I'll fit better than you. He can lift me out easy. I know my way around basements. And I can cut a fucking wire."

Hugo kept his eyes away from the rearview mirror. A pair of wire cutters was laid on his shoulder.

He said, "I want a gun."

Both Irgunists said, "No."

✳ ✳ ✳

Hugo snipped every white phone wire running up the walls and through the ceiling joists, in and out of junction boxes. The job took a frantic minute, because one minute had been allotted.

He hurried through the basement, back to the half-window. Two pairs of shoes and the backs of pantlegs blocked the window, hiding the busted pane. Hugo hissed to signal he was waiting below. The big Irgunist's arm came through; Hugo latched on and scrambled against the wall to be lifted out into the alley.

The two Irgunists patted him on the back, then disappeared to the front of the courthouse to stand watch. The long hems of their overcoats kicked as they walked, as if dogs ran at their sides. Hugo hustled the other direction through the alley, to where he'd left the beat-up Škoda.

Hugo started the engine, timed out two minutes, then pulled into the street. His timing was perfect; in front of the courthouse, eight Irgunists burst down the steps. They encircled a judge in crimson robe and jurist's wig. The two watchmen pulled their Sten submachineguns from under their coats; the sidewalk crowd recoiled just as Hugo screeched to a halt. The car's rear door was flung open; one Irgunist leaped in, pistol drawn. Behind him, the judge was shoved in and the door slammed. The judge was long-legged, his robe fouled in the abduction. He did not resist the pistol in his ribs. A second Irgunist, a tough in a cap and waistcoat, yanked open the passenger front door; his landing on the seat shook the Škoda. Hugo snapped back all their heads accelerating away from the scene. The other six fighters scattered on foot, pell-mell in different directions.

Beside Hugo, the heavy Irgunist whirled around to shove his pistol in the judge's face.

"If Dov Gruner hangs, you hang. Understand?"

Hugo stole glimpses in the mirror. The judge straightened his white wig.

"Let us hope Mr. Gruner has a good lawyer."

Hugo drove quickly through traffic. Sirens wailed around the city. He needed to get out of Tel Aviv before the roadblocks went up.

CHAPTER 39

VINCE

Jerusalem

January in Jerusalem was far warmer than in New York.

On the YMCA's patio, Vince sat in the sun beneath no umbrella. He sipped black coffee and held his *Palestine Post* high and spread wide. The paper blocked the sight of the King David's resurrection but not the noise of jackhammers and pulleys.

"Mister Haas."

His name was said loud enough to be heard over the construction din, but not from close by. Vince lowered the paper, on alarm. Someone had come looking for him, someone who couldn't have known who was behind the newspaper.

A small fellow stood with arms at his side, gazing from three tables away. He wore a brown suit, vest and tie, and black-frame glasses. He cut the figure of a teacher, weak-eyed and wintry pale. Something about him said immigrant, something said prison.

"Can I help you?"

"I'd like a word."

"Who are you?"

"We have a friend in common."

"You sent the note."

"I did. Would you buy me a cup of coffee?"

Vince beckoned him forward. The two said no more until a waiter had been summoned and sent away.

"My name is Pinchus."

"What can I do for you?"

Pinchus pushed up his glasses, looking baffled, as if he'd not anticipated the question.

"Nothing, actually. Nothing more than you're doing."

Vince waited through the arrival of the coffee and Pinchus's first sip. Pinchus was not dainty with the cup as it seemed he might be, but held it wholly in both hands, like a man gathering warmth.

"I don't want to talk to you."

"Why not, exactly?"

"Because I don't want to know any more."

"Of what are we speaking, Mister Haas?"

"I don't want to be told things before they happen. Not by you, not Hugo, not by the government. If Dov Gruner's going to get hanged or not, I shouldn't have anything to do with it."

"You feel badly. About the kidnappings of the police."

"I feel badly, Mister Pinchus, about being used. About you sending me to go watch Hugo get beat up. Having me watch whippings." Vince pointed at the savaged King David. "And that."

Pinchus set down his coffee. He pressed his palms together to absorb the last of the heat.

"It has not been my intent to compromise you."

"I'm a journalist. Nothing else."

"What Kharda says is you are a man trying to learn something about himself by understanding the Jews. I must be honest; in all the world's history, I've never heard of anyone who held that view. It's not a responsibility we're accustomed to. All our time is spent trying to understand ourselves."

"What are you doing here, Mister Pinchus? My guess is you don't come out in the open very often. Why this morning, why to me?"

"I may owe you an apology."

"I'm listening."

"Perhaps you feel responsible for the kidnappings? Your warning about Gruner's execution was very much appreciated. You must have known we would take some preventative action."

"I did."

"Yet you told Kharda anyway."

"I won't do it again. It's getting hard to have sympathy for you."

"I understand. But sympathy is not what we ask. A free man has no need of it. We are a nation without a land, Mister Haas, you know this. Over two thousand years, the Jews have had no single place in the world to display what we are, what we have done, or what we will do. We need Palestine in order to gather ourselves, to relearn what it is to be a people. The world thinks it is witnessing the rise of the Jew as warrior and farmer. It is not. The world is witnessing our return. I believe you might be someone who could help us along. Someone who would tell us what you see of us, a fair appraisal. For over a year, you have done us this service, and marvelously so. But we may have overburdened you. I'm sorry if this is the case."

From Pinchus, this was not a rebuke. He was a man who wasted nothing, like the heat of the coffee. If Vince would not do one thing, he might do another.

"Allow me to make it up to you."

"You can try."

Pinchus removed his glasses to clean them on the tip of his tie. He left the glasses on the table. A simple gesture, it had the quality of an unmasking, perhaps candor.

"Dov Gruner will not hang, at least not for now."

"What happened?"

"A clash of wills. The government threatened to impose martial law unless we released the judge we kidnapped. The Jewish Agency has determined that martial law would be a ruinous thing, it would mean a strict curfew, the stoppage of all business and social activities. Myself, I believe it would be ineffective, but I am one voice. Private appeals have been made to us. We agreed to release the judge, in return for a stay of execution. The government has granted that stay. Everyone got what they wanted."

"And in the process you humiliated the British."

"That was always the point."

"The judge?"

"Tomorrow, he will be set free. And Gruner lives. So, you see, Mister Haas, you are off the hook."

Pinchus slid the glasses back over his nose. The lenses greatly magnified his eyes. Vince imagined him in a cell, deprived of his spectacles, unable to focus on the outer world so he was left locked inside his head, plotting.

"I appreciate the visit."

"You were owed this."

"Tell Hugo I'm out. I don't want any more insider information."

"Won't you miss your friend? He speaks very well of you."

Vince should have risen and walked off, but this was his table; the tab for the meal and Pinchus's coffee was his. Pinchus needed to go.

"Tell me something, honestly."

"Of course."

"You're a dangerous man. Am I safe from you?"

"Why would you ask that?" Pinchus didn't refute the accusation. That explained why Vince would ask. "Yes, Mister Haas. You are safe."

"I'll be glad to pay for your coffee."

Pinchus stood, tugging his vest into place. "May I make one request?"

"What."

"A Jewish state is coming. The British will leave. Not much longer can they explain to the world their reasons for sending the survivors of Europe's death camps to internment in Cyprus. Once Britain is gone, the Arabs and Jews will stay behind. Others will draw lines to limit where we may live. Before that happens, we are spreading out. Jews are settling in every corner of the land, even into harm's way. They are not terrorists but pioneers. The story of the Jew in Palestine is in their hands no less than it is in mine or Kharda's. Why not tell their story?"

"I'll consider it."

"A suggestion, if I may."

"Go ahead."

"There is a small alliance of kibbutzim in the Judean hills. The Etzion bloc. I have a favorite place there. A green hilltop in a white expanse. Everything you are looking for is there. The fighter and the farmer. The sabra and the survivor. The rock and the flower. All our hopes for Palestine are there, Mister Haas. Please go."

"What's the name of the place?"

"Massuot Yitzhak. In English, you would call it Isaac's Beacon."

Pinchus turned away. Before he'd gone many strides, he snapped his fingers. He whirled among the tables, looking younger for that moment.

"Do ask for Missus Pappel."

CHAPTER 40

HUGO

January 28
Petah Tikvah

Hugo lifted the latch on the outhouse. He jerked the door open to surprise the man inside. Hugo said, "Boo."

The judge gazed up from the *Palestine Post*, giving Hugo none of the reaction he'd hoped for. The judge's folded black robe and gray wig lay neatly beside him on the latrine's two-hole bench. He looked relaxed, even after a night locked in here. Orange peels and cracker wrappers littered the wooden floor. He wore cufflinks and suspenders. The judge folded the newspaper.

"Are you my executioner?"

"No."

The judge didn't rise from the privy seat; Hugo had given him no instruction yet. A confused moment hovered between them, until the judge asked, "Yes?"

"Get up."

The judge rose to his full height, far taller than Hugo. He filled the doorway and waited, palms out, for the next order. The judge's compliance felt like mockery.

"Let's go."

"Where?"

Hugo had lobbied long into the night, then into this afternoon, to be given a pistol. If he had a gun, he argued, no one else would have to go along. Hugo pulled back his jacket to show it stuck in his belt.

"Don't ask questions."

The judge gathered up his robe and wig. Hugo stepped aside to have him walk in front.

The outhouse stood in the small courtyard of an abandoned factory. The distance to Hugo's Škoda was short, and the judge took long, eager strides.

Hugo put him in the front passenger seat with a crisp warning for no false moves. The judge shook his head to tell Hugo there would be no reason to worry.

The judge waited to speak until Hugo had the car away from the factory and on the road, with night falling. "May I ask a question now?"

Hugo kept one hand near the butt of his pistol. "Go ahead."

"Has Dov Gruner been hung?"

"No."

"So I am to be returned?"

"Yes."

"I say. That is a relief."

Hugo motored west toward Ramat Gan. He eyed the judge and kept a hand close to the pistol. Both men were lit up, then faded, by the headlights of oncoming traffic.

Minutes from Ramat Gan, the judge turned to Hugo. He loomed large in the car, a broad man. "I assume you are Irgun."

Hugo tried to hint at menace. "I am."

"You're not wearing a mask. The eight boys who snatched me out of my courtroom, they did nothing to hide their faces, either. I admire the courage, if not the wisdom of that."

The judge rolled his wide frame around to face front again.

"I hear a German accent. Am I correct?"

"Yes."

"Were you there for the war? I realize, that is an awful question."

"I was."

The judge paused. When Hugo turned, the judge had his eyes fixed on him.

"I'm sorry. But listen to me. That does not excuse you."

Hugo pulled to the shoulder aggressively, skidding in the gravel. He said, "Your country needs Arab oil. Does that excuse you? Don't start a debate with me."

He leaned across the seat to open the passenger door. Hugo pointed into the dark.

"Get out."

The judge turned his back to leave. He spoke over his shoulder.

"I promise if I ever see you again, I will sentence you to death and personally watch you hang. I hope that cheers you."

Hugo snatched the wig from the judge's hands, then shoved him out. He mashed the accelerator to spray pebbles behind him.

CHAPTER 41
RIVKAH

February 23
Kibbutz Massuot Yitzhak

Rivkah touched Gabbi's short sun-bleached hair, then the coarsened skin at the back of her neck. Gabbi had been gone eight weeks, a sliver of her life, and these were Palestine's first marks on her. The land would not stop asking its Jews to remake themselves.

Gabbi wore slacks and suspenders, white sleeves rolled up. Her gaze across the pale hills was not that of a stranger.

Rivkah wanted to talk about Mama and Papa. She had no one else in the world to recall them with, and if she and Gabbi did not recall, their parents were gone. The past beckoned, but tomorrow had a strong voice, too. Mama and Papa were not in tomorrow, never again would be. Rivkah rose from the porch. She would not pull Gabbi backwards tonight.

"I'll check on dinner."

Gabbi, sitting on the step, didn't look away from the western rim of Judea. The sun seemed to pause. For moments, Rivkah stayed silent behind her sister to watch the balance tip between day and night, orange bleed into red. Then she went in to Mrs. Pappel.

Rivkah sat at the kitchen table. Mrs. Pappel stirred a bowl of rice.

Rivkah said, "I don't like it."

"What don't you like, Liebling?"

"She's been training for two months. That's not enough."

"Not enough for what?"

Mrs. Pappel spooned rice onto plates. Two more pots boiled, the stew and vegetables; she stirred them, too. Mrs. Pappel looked competent, wiry and perfect, and this made Rivkah more afraid for her sister.

"To go off on her own."

"With thirty others."

"Thirty teenagers who trained for two months. Why so fast?"

"The decision's been made."

"What does she know?"

Mrs. Pappel brought the plates to the table. "Palestine doesn't care what you know. Just what you're willing to do."

Mrs. Pappel fetched Gabbi in from the porch. They ate with a strain on their conversation.

When the meal was over, Gabbi kissed them and excused herself to Rivkah's room.

Wrapped in a shawl, Rivkah sat on the porch with the flung, faint glows of Arabs and Jews on their hills. She missed Malik, the spark that came even in the dark with his testy camel. She would like a poem, some wisdom not her own, and not Mrs. Pappel's, who came out on the porch to ask if she wanted tea to keep her warm. Rivkah did not accept and did not invite Mrs. Pappel to stay.

Rivkah rocked. If she were granted a wish of the possible, she would have much to ask for. Gabbi was leaving to make her own hilltop home, a new kibbutz called Revadim only a mile away, but a mile. Rivkah knew no one who didn't live within sight of where she sat, even Malik. She hadn't left the Etzion bloc since she came here a year and a half ago.

From where she sat, Palestine was a vale of wind and stone. The mood and the chill also felt like loneliness.

CHAPTER 42

HUGO

March 1
Jerusalem

Hugo braked for a mother and two children crossing King George Avenue. They waved to Hugo; in the uniform of a British soldier, he waved back. He couldn't warn the woman to walk her children faster, to run.

He played a finger over the pistol stuck in his waistband. Pinchus had finally let him keep a gun.

Smoothly, Hugo shifted gears, not to draw attention to the stolen army truck or jostle the three bombers riding in the back. Traffic in the Rehavia neighborhood ran light on a Saturday, a young spring day, the first to shrug off winter. Jerusalem had come out for a stroll. Never before had the Irgun attacked on a Saturday. Pinchus declared that no longer would the Sabbath be a day off from the revolt.

Two cars ahead of Hugo, a taxi carried three more fighters, in military uniforms, too. He drove his second circuit around Goldschmidt House. The British officer's club was a four-story mansion of bland masonry, fat pillars, iron porches, and stone windowsills.

Barbed wire and guards surrounded the place, allowing no approach from the street or rear. The one weak spot was the parking lot. There, two armed guards manned a sentry post; a single long coil of wire ran from it.

The taxi approached the turn into the parking lot. Hugo lagged. If the taxi stopped, then drove on, that meant the way was clear, the operation was a go. The taxi didn't slow because four trucks blocked the entry while their drivers' papers were being checked. Hugo drove on.

He and the taxi circled Goldschmidt House twice more, past sunny lawns, Sabbath-shuttered shops and offices. After each circuit, the taxi failed to slow at the lot.

On the next circle, Pinchus stepped out of a synagogue across the leafy street from the officers' club; he hailed the taxi. After exchanging quick words with the driver, Pinchus waved Hugo forward.

"We can't wait any more. Go through the wire." He patted Hugo's arm. "Good luck, Kharda."

Hugo drove a last time around the block, careful not to let his excitement push his speed.

He rounded the final corner onto King George Street, beneath the twin steeples of a monastery beside the synagogue. He eased past the broad face of the officers' club. Two soldiers smoked and enjoyed the Saturday balm in the brick courtyard. Four guards strolled the perimeter of barbed wire. Hugo told the three in the truck bed, "Get ready."

The last truck still clogged the parking lot road. Hugo tapped his brakes a final time to signal that he was ready.

The guard shack in the parking lot came under fire. From a roof beside the synagogue, a Bren gun sparked. The guard hut spewed splinters and fell over; both sentries and the truck drivers dove for the pavement. Behind Hugo, brakes screeched; the taxi skidded sideways to block the road at his back, and three Irgun fighters leaped out to engage the soldiers in front of the officers' club.

One of the bombers in the back of the van yelled, "Go!" as if Hugo might hesitate.

With gunfire nipping on every side, he gunned out of the street, jumping the curb into the lot. Hugo gripped the steering wheel hard and floored the gas.

He rammed the row of barbed wire in the middle. Razor-sharp barbs twisted around the grille, wire scraped the pavement and the sides of the van. A confusion of strands boiled up in front of Hugo, but he didn't back off, adding speed across the lot, dragging the wire and the keeled-over shack with it. A bullet hole spider-webbed the windshield; the van leaped the curb out of the lot, onto the sidewalk, then onto the grass. Hugo tore up the lawn, surging to the front doors of Goldschmidt House.

Ensnared in the barbed wire, he slammed the brakes. Satchels on their backs, Stens in hand, the three fighters flung open the van door. They leaped over the sentry shack, moving fast under the cover of hundreds of rounds from the Bren and the three Irgunists in the street firing from behind their taxi. A British guard already lay face down in the grass, another limped away. The three running bombers sprayed their Stens left and right, then rushed through the front doors, tugging the satchels off their backs as they disappeared.

Soldiers traded shots with the rooftop machine gunner across the street and the fighters behind the taxi. Soldiers who found themselves in the open without weapons flung themselves to the ground. Another soldier in the courtyard crumpled, a waiter got hit and collapsed screaming. On the sidewalks of King George Street, pedestrians ran away.

A bullet pierced the door close to Hugo's leg and another hole in the windshield goaded him out of the van. He tumbled onto the brick courtyard, hunkered behind the open door, and drew his pistol.

Bullets sizzled over his head and all around the truck. Two rounds zinged off the bricks near his boots. Hugo was dressed like a British soldier, but cowering beside the van, he was Irgun.

He wasn't sure what to do next. He wasn't supposed to be out of the vehicle, but where could he drive? The jumbled wire might pop the tires if he rolled over them, could wrap around the axles. The windshield took two more ugly holes. The whole truck was getting pelted; Hugo wouldn't get far in a bullet-riddled van even if he made a getaway. He couldn't drive off, and he couldn't hide here much longer.

The backup plan was to escape on foot to the monastery behind the synagogue. Any moment now the bombers were going to emerge. They'd have just seconds to get away from the courtyard or be caught in the blast of a hundred kilos of gelignite. Hugo and the bombers were going to have to fight their way back to the parking lot, under cover from the Bren and the taxi fighters battling the guards, then cross King George Street.

Another bullet beat at the truck door but didn't punch through. Hugo was in someone's sights.

He peeked over the sill. Twenty meters away, near the Club's front doors, a blue-hatted cop hid behind a robust oak. He caught Hugo peering at him and squeezed off another round from a snub-nosed revolver. The cop aimed at Hugo's legs below the van's door. The bullet skipped off the bricks, making Hugo jump. If Hugo took a hit in the legs, he'd die in the gunfight, or in the blast, or be hanged later.

He waved to grab the attention of the three Irgunists firing and ducking behind the taxi. One stayed above the taxi's hood long enough for Hugo to point out the policeman. The Irgunist turned his Sten on the oak tree; the short burst shaved some bark and make the cop shrink back.

The bombers had been inside more than twenty seconds. They were going to dash out, and when they did, the policeman behind the tree would have an angle on them. He could take down one or more before they knew he was there.

The Bren on the roof riveted the attention of the guards in the parking lot; the taxi gunners in King George Street dueled with the three remaining soldiers on the lawn. The cop belonged to Hugo.

The Irgunist behind the taxi pointed urgently at the policeman. Go, go, the fighter motioned, go take care of him. Now.

The Irgunist raised his Sten to unleash another volley at the oak tree. The cop made himself small behind the blistering trunk. Hugo touched the barrel of the pistol to his forehead; he didn't know why but sensed the need for some rite, perhaps to wake the gun. He flashed out from behind the van's door.

Hugo sprinted down the length of the wire; barbs snagged his trousers making him lurch to free himself. Bullets buzzing, he jumped over the sentry post and headed for the tree. Hugo held the pistol at arm's length and fired once into the oak to keep the cop's head down. The gun leaped in his hand; the recoil threw him off his gait. He fought off a stumble and pressed on, gaining ground. Hugo fired again at the profile of the cop's face and blue hat.

The Irgunist behind the taxi fired one more salvo at the oak tree. Hugo tore off the last few running strides; the cop kept his back to the tree, safe against it, blind to Hugo.

The policeman's pistol was close to his chest when Hugo cleared the trunk. The man believed he was hiding, and in the instant he learned he was not, Hugo skidded on the grass before him, holding the gun two-handed. He shot the cop first in the gut which did not stop the cop from extending his own pistol. Hugo pulled the trigger more times than he had rounds. Each bullet slammed the man into the tree. The life leaving him fought to stay, shook him like a doll, before slumping him dead against the trunk.

Hugo lowered the gun. All four bullets had struck the cop's chest; the blood hadn't risen yet through the rips in his tunic.

The bombers burst out of the club. They didn't see Hugo behind the tree; he could have shot them all. He stepped out, hands up to show them it was him, the driver.

"We have to run for it!"

On the rooftop across the street, the Bren fired without stop. The perforated van was engulfed in barbed wire. The fighters in the street jumped into their taxi and took off.

Hugo dashed with the bombers for the parking lot. They galloped behind their barking Stens, firing carelessly, only to get away.

The pistol weighed down Hugo as he ran. It was empty in his hand and he should have thrown it away, but he did not.

CHAPTER 43

RIVKAH

April 5
Massuot Yitzhak

At dusk, with the evening meal finished, the haverim took to their porches to talk of planting and blossoms. For many, this was their first spring in Palestine, and it seemed a miracle.

A car descended the white hills out of the north. It didn't turn for Kfar Etzion but made straight for little Massuot Yitzhak, motored up the slope, and parked close to Rivkah's stone house.

Two men got out. A tall, thin one wore a beat-up fedora, the shorter a wool cap. The lanky man, fair-haired, needed a shave on his long face and an iron to his clothes. The other presented neatly; he seemed urban. They approached the porch where Mrs. Pappel took Rivkah's hand. The tall man cast his gaze around the kibbutz, enquiring of the place in the purpling light. He took off his hat. The smaller man spoke first.

"Missus Pappel?"

"Yes?"

"I am Kharda. Mr. Pinchus sent me."

"I've been expecting you."

Mrs. Pappel squeezed Rivkah's hand to tell her all was okay. The quick exchange reminded Rivkah that Mrs. Pappel had secrets. And if Pinchus sent only him, who was the one with the fedora in his hands?

Kharda did not introduce his companion but referenced him with an open hand. The man stepped up to speak for himself.

"Hi. My name is Vince Haas."

"Do I hear an American accent?"

He nodded. "You?"

"I am Austrian, Mr. Haas. But I lived in England. This is Rivkah Gellerman. Please come in."

Rivkah held the door to let them pass. Kharda did not take off his cap until he was seated at the kitchen table. When he sat, Vince Haas stuck his felt fedora on his knee. Rivkah moved to the sink while Mrs. Pappel sat with the men.

Filling the teapot, Rivkah asked, "What sort of tea would you like?"

Kharda requested black. Vince Haas said whatever she had handy, the answer of a man not looking to be pleased.

She set the pot to heat and did not join them at the table. Mrs. Pappel and the one who called himself by an Arab name leaned toward each other, to their business. Vince Haas watched Rivkah.

"Mister Haas, we should let them discuss in private. Before the sun goes down, would you like a tour of Massuot Yitzhak?"

He plucked the hat off his knee and swung his legs from under the table. "Thank you."

Vince Haas rose without comment from Kharda. The two had traveled together, but they seemed separate. He followed Rivkah out the door.

"There is the apple orchard. We'll expand it next year when we terrace more of the hill. Those are plum trees, too young to pick. The saplings are eucalyptus and pine for shade. In that building we've started a carpentry shop. We have rooms for welding, a tannery, and a bakery. That's the pumphouse for our water pipes. There is Missus Pappel's school room."

Rivkah felt she was racing something, not just the falling day. Vince Haas noticed it, too.

He said, "You can slow down."

"I'm sorry."

"You don't have to apologize."

"May I ask why you're here? Pinchus didn't send you."

"Actually, he did, three months ago. He wanted me to see this place. Pinchus has a fondness for it."

"I believe his fondness is for Missus Pappel."

"He made it sound like I needed a vacation. Like this was where I should come put my feet up."

"No one puts their feet up in Massuot Yitzhak, Mister Haas."

"I see that. And please. Vince."

"I agree with Pinchus. You look like you need a rest. And a shave. And a laundry."

"Kharda showed up and grabbed me out of my room. I didn't have time."

"Are you a gun runner like him?"

"What? No. I write for an American newspaper."

"Did Kharda bring guns?"

"For the new kibbutz. Revadim."

"My sister is there."

Vince spread his hands. "That's great. You have family."

Quickly, keenly, he reversed himself. "I didn't mean it to sound like that." He lowered his eyes to the cinder path and the painted rocks that marked it.

"You assume that I lost someone."

"Yes. Sorry."

"I did. My mother and father."

Vince Haas said no more. He had yet to put his hat back on.

The sun doused in the orange horizon. The dry season had begun, and the clear night twinkled early. Rivkah didn't turn back for the house but led Vince to the trickling stream, to the quarry, the terraces she'd helped build, and a starlit view of the Valley of Brakha where the prophets had walked.

"How do you know Kharda?"

"I was with the U.S. Army when we entered Buchenwald. I met him there. Three months after that, I sailed with him on an Aliyah Bet ship from France. I didn't see him for most of a year, went home to New York, then turned around and came back when he telegrammed me."

"What did he say?"

"That he could tell me the story of Palestine."

"Is that what he's doing?"

"I think I've learned just as much in the last ten minutes. My boss told me if I didn't come back, he'd fire me."

With a shared laugh they walked the rows of a young citrus grove. Vince plucked leaves. Their boots crunched on the moon-bright ground, and she said, "Tell me about your own work."

"It's too peaceful out here to talk about it." He pinched another leaf.

Rivkah walked him to the place where a year ago she'd danced around Massuot Yitzhak's first bonfire and watched Arabs and Jews throw stones at each other. She'd worked this spot with hoe and pick to make space for the orchard's roots. Vince sat with her on the ground; he folded in a funny way, like Malik's camel. He didn't look comfortable, knees up to his chin. Rivkah stayed quiet, leaving him to the dark hills and the scents of the first fruit, to the stars and rawness of the land, the things that would have kept her company tonight had Vince Haas not come.

CHAPTER 44

HUGO

Waiting for Vince and the girl to return, Mrs. Pappel asked, "Would you like to see my guns?"

"I would."

They went first to the Škoda. Hugo opened the truck to heft three sacks, in each a pair of silver Stens made in Irgun shops. Mrs. Pappel grabbed another bag containing four Lee-Enfield rifles captured in raids on the British.

Mrs. Pappel's hiding place was ingenious. A secret door inside the closet of her schoolroom led down earthen steps to a small armory. An electric lamp and a fan stood on a workbench beside tools spread over a cloth. Twenty small arms hung on hooks: British and Dutch rifles, American pistols, ten crates of ammo stacked against a wall. Hugo stood straight in the cave, though Vince would need to crouch.

"Where did you get all these?"

"A friend."

Back at Mrs. Pappel's stone house, she went inside to brew tea. Hugo had barely settled into a porch chair when an immense Arab rode a camel up the quarry road. Hugo got to his feet should he need to dash for the Škoda and the pistol in the glove box.

Mrs. Pappel came out to see the new arrival. "And here is my friend."

"Him? An Arab brings you guns?"

"Magnificent, isn't he?"

The Arab dismounted from a camel he did not tie up. The beast harrumphed before lumbering off. The Arab bowed to Mrs. Pappel, then introduced himself to Hugo by pronouncing a long family name. He took Hugo's hand into an enveloping grasp and said, Hugo may call him Malik.

Mrs. Pappel introduced Hugo as Kharda.

Malik asked, "Why are you called Scrap Iron?"

"Because I have turned Arab scrap into Jewish weapons."

Malik liked this. He asked if Hugo might make him one.

"No."

Robes shrouded the big, bearded Arab; a bronze scabbard and knife dangled about his neck. Mrs. Pappel told Malik another guest, an American, was out on a stroll with Rivkah. With familiarity, the Arab entered the house to bring out a kitchen chair so he, too, might wait for Vince and Rivkah. Unbidden, Malik recited a poem. Hugo's thoughts wandered while the Arab intoned about the sun and barren ground; Hugo cared little for the lessons of the desert.

On the porch, Malik and Mrs. Pappel talked as familiars. Hugo sat through banter about weather and bland topics that excluded him and told him he was not liked. Neither asked Hugo about himself. Had they inquired, he would have waved his story off as Irgun secrets; had they asked about the camps, he would say that was too much to talk about. He'd killed a policeman, but the girl had paid him no attention. Vince fell over himself to accept her offer of a tour. Hugo looked to the glow of Jerusalem.

Out in the murk, Malik's camel hooted. Vince and Rivkah arrived, chatting as they came.

CHAPTER 45

VINCE

Vince hesitated before stepping onto the porch. A great, dark Arab sat there with Hugo and Mrs. Pappel. Rivkah pressed her hand against his back to tell him he should walk on. She hadn't touched him before.

"Malik, I'm glad to see you."

In a swirl of robes, the Arab stood. His head rose level with Vince's. He offered Rivkah the seat he'd vacated. She motioned for Vince to sit instead.

"This is Vince Haas. He's a newspaperman. From New York."

Malik dipped his forehead as he covered his heart. "*Effendi.*"

Vince sat between Hugo and Mrs. Pappel. The shuffling on the small porch was accompanied by a grunt out in the night. Vince asked, "Was that a camel?"

The Arab said, "Yes."

Rivkah asked if Vince wanted tea. He accepted and she went inside, though neither Hugo nor the Arab had tea, and she didn't offer to them.

Standing off the porch, Malik propped one boot on the step. "I saw your car in the dusk. When you stopped at this house, I thought it might be Pinchus."

The Arab's voice came from deep in his chest, a laden voice that had traveled. He had little accent to his English. Malik made slow movements when he spoke, languorous as if he were always in the sun.

"Pinchus owes me money. Of course, I am an Arab and he is a Jew. One of us will always owe the other money."

Mrs. Pappel spoke to Vince across the lip of her teacup. "Hugo tells me you saved his life."

"I didn't do anything."

Hugo scooted forward in his seat. "He saved me twice. Once in Buchenwald, again on a ship. I've only managed to save him once."

Hugo waggled one finger in the air to symbolize the King David.

"Did you know he's famous? He's read around the world. Vincent Haas."

Off the porch, Malik ruffled, though there was no wind. "Perhaps Vincent Haas would like to hear some of my poems."

Behind her teacup, by the light spilling through the window, Mrs. Pappel said, "Perhaps he would. Some time."

Rivkah returned with the tea. Vince stood to accept the cup; she touched him again, to settle him back into the chair.

Malik pressed his large hands together. "You are *misafir* in this house. A guest. In Islam, there is no greater status."

Hugo said, "This is a Jewish house."

The Arab's weathered features did not change. He opened his hands and presented them together to Hugo like a book.

"That is why we must learn each other's ways." Malik shut his palms as if closing the book. "Or we will remain strangers."

Mrs. Pappel set her teacup beside her feet. Vince couldn't guess the Arab's age, but the woman seemed the elder on the porch. She tugged her braided ponytail across her shoulder.

"Tell me, Mister Haas. As an American. What do you think?"

"About?"

"Let's start small. Massuot Yitzhak."

Vince glanced quickly at Rivkah, then away.

"Beautiful."

CHAPTER 46

HUGO

Vince's gift of saying little played well on the porch. When Rivkah came out with tea for Vince, she had no cup for Hugo. Vince was a visitor to Palestine, an observer on their lives. Hugo was a survivor, Irgun, and they knew it. These were farmers, an American, an Arab.

The talk ran long, about land and seed, blossoms and labor. Mrs. Pappel called the people of the kibbutzim "pioneers." Hugo sniffed at this.

"That is a luxury."

Mrs. Pappel engaged him, unafraid or unaware. "Aren't you a pioneer, in your way?"

"No."

"Then what are you?"

"A fighter."

"How are we different? Aren't we all fighting for the same thing?"

Hugo's ire rose, he paused it in his throat. Every person in this bloc, every Jew in Palestine, had lost someone. He should respect that; they all shared the tragedy of it. But the similarity ended there, with loss. Hugo was no farmer, and they were not warriors. He chose to speak his mind, and the trees and fields be damned.

"You plant, you build. You milk cows. You plow and irrigate. That's a day's work for you. It's not what I do."

Vince said, "Hugo."

"I fight the idea of the Jew ever again being at the mercy of others. I fight the old claims on Palestine, the British, and yes, the Arabs. I destroy things. I kill people. I'm hidden inside the revolt. I can't use my name, and my face can get me hanged. You live in the sun. He writes poems about it. Vince writes stories about me."

The old Arab nodded, a small gesture, hidden from the rest but not from Hugo. This Arab had done violence, understood it and, like Hugo, saw the truth that Palestine was not the green of a field or the moonlit fruit of a tree.

Mrs. Pappel folded her hands. Vince remained ever the witness. Rivkah answered.

"How can you do to others what was done to you? Was there not enough horror for you?"

"What do you know?"

"Don't you dare ask me that."

Vince raised both palms, for Hugo to stop. Was Vince going to defend the girl now? She didn't seem to require it. She pressed on.

"For you, Kharda. Tell me. Has the gun become *Zur Israel*?" One of God's names.

"It has."

"Then why do you keep a newspaperman from America with you? It's to have him watch what you do. This is how you forgive yourself. Vince won't judge your violence. He can't. He reports from a distance, and that distance cleanses you. The people cheer your bombs and your murders; they clap hands that have no blood on them. They know it's wrong, what you do, but they let you be damned instead of them. You, your Irgun, your killers, you're the kind of evil the rest of us call necessary. But you've forgotten what Palestine will be when you're done." Rivkah pointed into the night. "Come look at Massuot Yitzhak in the sun. We will remind you."

Without hurry, Hugo stood from his seat; it may have looked like anger because Vince braced himself on the arms of his own chair. The Arab remained motionless on the edge of the porch, wrapped in the night and his robes when Hugo moved past.

He walked the short distance to the Škoda where he popped open the glove box. Making no effort to conceal the pistol, Hug carried it back to the porch, feeling all the more powerful for the fact that he should not have it. Malik shifted only slightly; his hands disappeared inside his robes where he surely carried his own weapon.

Hugo lifted the gun for them to see, aimed at no one.

"This. This is why we are not victims anymore. If you think you're safe without it, if you believe the British will leave Palestine without us using this, you're ignorant. And the Arabs, including your friend here. Are they going to turn the land over to us out of pity, out of friendship? Or because of this? Where are you from, girl?"

"Vienna."

"Vienna happened to you." He tapped the gun to his chest. "Leipzig happened to me. Are your sun and crops going to stop it from happening again here? Will your schoolhouse, your little village on a hill, your fucking teacups, stop it because we're in Palestine? If the Jews don't fight, we stay victims. The Germans win."

"If we make others our victims, the Germans win."

Hugo became aware of Vince standing near him only when he took Hugo's arm.

"Come on."

Vince positioned himself between Hugo and the women on the porch. Hugo groped for something to say across Vince pressing him backwards, something searing. Vince wrapped Hugo's wrist to push the pistol down, perhaps to take the gun away. Hugo tore his hand away and kept the gun.

His momentum took him off the porch, beside the big Arab. Hugo expected a shove from Malik, a hiss, or some contempt. The Arab's hands had come out of his robes empty. He whispered, "I'm sorry."

Mrs. Pappel came to the edge of the porch. "Listen to me. You are welcome in this house. But the next time you bring a gun up my step, you'll leave it with me. Good night."

Hugo backpedaled, inclining his head to Mrs. Pappel as he headed for the car. He would not come back to a house where he was compared to the Germans.

"Vince?"

Vince didn't step off the porch. "I think I'll stay here tonight."

Hugo didn't ask if Vince had an invitation or a ride home. He had no curiosity; his desire for company was gone. In the dark, Hugo turned away.

Putting the stone house behind him, he shoved the pistol into the glovebox. Vince's staying would break no bond between them. Hugo had said nothing that wasn't true; Vince, in typical fashion, had said nothing.

CHAPTER 47

RIVKAH

No one moved until Hugo's taillights blinked out among the Judean hills.

Malik stepped onto the porch to take the open chair. Mrs. Pappel patted Rivkah's knee. Vince watched the Jerusalem road, then turned to them with palms up.

"Sorry."

Mrs. Pappel knitted her fingers. "Sorry for what, dear?"

"I didn't think before I said that."

Mrs. Pappel tapped her thumbs together. "I suspect that's the case."

"I'll sleep out here, okay?"

"You can stay on the couch. It's short and you won't like it. You'll freeze out here."

Malik twirled a large finger. "The winds."

"Tea." Mrs. Pappel pushed herself to her feet. "Malik. Join me."

The two left Rivkah alone with Vince. He held his stance, still without his hat on his head. Rivkah asked him to sit. She named for him the visible lights in the hills: the two newest settlements, Ein Tzurim and Revadim; further north, Nahalin; to the west, Arab Jab'a on very high ground; and glowing behind them all, Jerusalem.

The windows of Massuot Yitzhak blinked from white to buttery; the diesel generators shut down every night at 9:00 p.m. and the homes still awake switched to lanterns and candles. Inside Rivkah's house, Mrs. Pappel laughed.

Rivkah said, "They like you."

He seemed to waken from the landscape. "Oh."

"Your friend Kharda."

"I'm not sure we're friends at this point."

"I'm sorry to hear that. He and I have very different views. One of those rifles he brought might wind up in my sister's hands. The thought terrifies me. May I ask what you think?"

"The world just came out of a pretty brutal war. I don't blame him."

"How can you not?"

"He's been through the worst of it. Violence is what the world has gotten used to."

"May I change the conversation?"

Vince rubbed his unshaven chin. "Uh-oh."

"You said I was beautiful."

"Did I say that?"

"In a way." In the measly light she could not read his face.

"I wasn't trying to be forward."

"You're not in trouble. I was flattered, if that's what you meant."

"I did. I mean." Finally, he put on his hat. "You are. If that's okay. Look, we just met." His fingers drummed on the arm of his chair.

"It doesn't feel like that."

"I'm an American."

"Is that a problem?"

"Rivkah." He'd not said her name before this. "I'm not Jewish."

She laughed quietly. "You don't have to be everything."

The brim of his hat lowered between them; Vince was staring at her hand.

"Can I take it?"

"Yes, Vince."

He gathered up her hand to hold it in his lap, asking wordlessly if he might keep it like this for a while. Rivkah sat back, not realizing she'd leaned forward.

Around the kibbutz, candles snuffed in windows one at a time, like sleep falling across the settlement. Mrs. Pappel came onto the porch, Malik behind her. Vince didn't let her go but eased his grip to tell her she could pull it back if she wished. Rivkah left her fingers meshed with his.

Malik strode off the porch; Mrs. Pappel stopped at the step. Both kept their backs turned to Vince and Rivkah. Without any call, Malik's camel shambled out of the night. The beast approached, bowed its long neck, then eased bony joints to the earth. Malik swept onto the blanket-draped saddle. With a click of his tongue, the camel stood, hoisting him into silhouette.

"Vince."

"What?"

"Nothing. I like the sound of your name."

The camel carried Malik's laughter away. Mrs. Pappel watched him vanish. She turned to the porch, arms crossed.

She lowered her brow, visibly indicating Vince's lap, where Rivkah's hand rested in his. Mrs. Pappel cleared her throat. When neither Rivkah nor Vince offered an explanation, Mrs. Pappel faced the night again where Malik had ridden off. She left her arms crossed.

"Vince."

"Yes, ma'am."

He squeezed Rivkah's hand, then let go. Mrs. Pappel spoke with her back to them.

"Would you like something before bed?"

"No, ma'am."

"Rivkah. Tea?"

"No, thank you."

"Alright. I'll put a blanket on the sofa. Vince, what time should I wake you?"

"Any time."

Rivkah asked, "Can you stay tomorrow? I can show you more."

Mrs. Pappel walked past to enter the house. She lowered a hand to Rivkah's shoulder for a quick pressure.

Rivkah took the fedora off Vince's head to stop the brim from shading his features. She tossed it into the empty chair. Elbows propped on her knees, Rivkah evened her shoulders to him. She could not say how afraid she was or how hopeful. Her first sight of Palestine had been like this, at the end of a sea so wide it might never have ended.

CHAPTER 48

VINCE

April 6

Mrs. Pappel handed Vince a plate of bread drizzled with honey. He accompanied her to the porch.

The clear spring made the horizon appear limitless. Nowhere else Vince had been in Palestine, not by the sea, in the desert, or the emerald Galilee, felt so swept clean by the sunrise as this hilltop.

The settlers left their cottages to start the day. All the labor of the commune trooped by in hoes and picks, leather aprons, rolled-up sleeves, sun hats, wheelbarrows, and buckets. Before Vince had awakened on the sofa, Rivkah had left to milk the cows and tend the mule.

Mrs. Pappel asked, "Will you spend the day? We can find you a ride back to Jerusalem this evening."

"What will I do if I stay?"

"Work. There's not much else."

"I'm not a farmer."

"We'll find something suitable."

Vince cocked an ear to the first raps of the tools of Massuot Yitzhak. Chisels rang in the quarry at the bottom of the hill, axes and hoes clashed with the salted soil, and in the carpentry shop a handsaw hewed a plank. Mrs. Pappel took Vince's finished plate.

"You're not a fool."

"No, ma'am."

"With all this going on. You and Rivkah."

"Did she say something?"

"No."

Vince stroked the back of his neck. "Yes, ma'am."

Mrs. Pappel tapped the plate in her hands. "I see the water truck coming. Can you carry a bucket?"

✳ ✳ ✳

Vince hauled the bucket back and forth from the water truck to a dozen plum trees in the center of the kibbutz. When he'd finished irrigating the little grove, Mrs. Pappel switched him to the big stand of orange trees on the western slope.

The orange blossoms' scent followed while Vince slogged up and down the hill. A wiry lad took up a pail to join the work, into and out of the orchard. The boy spoke better German than English, but Vince had little breath for conversation. It wasn't long before the boy quit tramping with Vince and passed him.

The water truck filled Massuot Yitzhak's cistern. Settlers gathered at the well to fill their buckets and lug them off to their work and homes. Vince touched the brim of his hat at the young Jews and kept working. Mrs. Pappel walked by many times.

The shadows in the orchard shortened to midmorning. The orange trees wouldn't mature for five more years; the water was needed to tempt the roots deeper, away from the dryness on the edge of the Negev. When the irrigation was done, Vince sat on his upturned bucket in a patch of shade beneath a powder-blue sky. A breeze tickled the branches on the hillside where he and Rivkah had strolled last night. The place still felt theirs, like a song danced to.

She walked through the saplings, swinging her arms in a downhill gait. Vince didn't stand for her arrival, to show how tired he was. Rivkah opened her hand. Vince took it, and she tugged him to his feet.

"I don't want you to go."

"That's good."

"The driver of the water truck will give you a ride back to Jerusalem."

"It's alright. I can go later."

"No."

"What's wrong?"

"You'll need to go."

"Did something happen?"

"The driver heard it on the radio." Rivkah blocked her mouth with both hands and spoke through her fingers. "They've hanged Dov Gruner."

CHAPTER 49

APRIL 17
RUSSIAN COMPOUND PRISON
JERUSALEM
BRITISH MANDATE OF PALESTINE
By Vincent Haas
Herald Tribune News Service

WEDNESDAYS ARE THE TRADITIONAL day for hangings in Palestine. On April 16th, the British executed Dov Gruner.

He was held at Acre Prison, a Crusader fortress outside Haifa. At 4 a.m., guards rousted Dov Gruner from his cot. They denied him a last breakfast, the comfort of a rabbi, coverage by the press, a visit from his sister who'd traveled from America, or any warning that this would be his last morning. Dov Gruner refused to stand in his cell while the order was read aloud. It took a clubbing to put him on his feet. On his way to the gallows through the damp stone halls of Acre, Dov Gruner sang *Hatikvah*.

Who was he?

A Hungarian. Dov Gruner emigrated to Palestine ten years ago, then left to fight alongside the British in Italy. He was wounded twice, twice a hero. He came back from the war to learn that his family in Hungary had been wiped out by Hitler. Dov Gruner fiercely believed in a homeland for the Jews, a place where the horrors could never again happen. He joined the Irgun; soon after, in a raid, a cop's bullet shattered his jaw. Dov Gruner was arrested and spent eight months in the hospital. Then he was sentenced to death.

He died before dawn, in the red burlap garb of the condemned, a sack over his head, a rope around his neck. Dov Gruner stood on a trapdoor which collapsed beneath him.

The Irgun are calling the hanging of Dov Gruner a war crime. They insist he was a combatant and should be treated as a prisoner of war, not a criminal. For the past decade, the British have restrained from executing the Jews they arrest. Britain has changed its mind. The Irgun have sworn revenge.

Dov Gruner died in secret and alone. That same Wednesday morning, three more Jews shared his fate.

Yehiel Drezner, Eliezer Kashani and Mordechai Alkachi were arrested in December trying to shoot their way past a roadblock outside Netanya. In the trunk of their vehicle, police found two rawhide whips. The three Irgunists were part of a plot to flog British soldiers and police in return for the caning of a sixteen-year-old Irgunist named Abraham Kimchin.

Like Dov Gruner, each of the three prisoners did nothing to contest his death sentence. They believed they could serve the Jewish revolt better as martyrs than alive in cages. At twenty-minute intervals, before the sun rose, they followed Dov Gruner to the scaffold, first Drezner, then Kashani, then Alkachi. None got breakfast, a visit, or a prayer.

In four days, two more fighters will hang for what the British call crimes and the Jews call war. They are Moshe Barazani and Meir Feinstein. Secretly, the British have scheduled the executions for a Monday instead of Wednesday, in an attempt to hide them.

Tomorrow, I intend to go to the jail at the Russian Compound in Jerusalem and refuse to leave. I will sleep in a cell, stay, and report on the executions of Barazani and Feinstein. I will see to it, this time, that the public knows the details, and the men's deaths won't be in secret. Reporting from Jerusalem, Palestine.

CHAPTER 50

HUGO

April 19
Tel Aviv

For three days, Hugo had heard nothing from Pinchus. He spent the time on his balcony where he nibbled cheese and bread, sipped beer into the sunny afternoons, and drew pictures in the rose-colored dusks.

Hugo had long had a knack for drawing. He was glad to see his little talent hadn't disappeared in the Leipzig ghetto or the camps where nothing wanted to be remembered.

He began with an elevated view of his street, the parked cars through the trees. Soon he felt the urge for company in his drawings and so penciled in people, curious if he could catch them in mid-stride or standing still, in their hats or bare headed. He tried to capture the folds of women's skirts, the beard-ringed lips of pious men. He emptied his apartment of blank paper, then walked to the market to buy a sketch pad, more food, and beer. On his only excursion out of the flat, Hugo knew no one and was known to no one.

He knew Pinchus was busy. The Irgun had retaliated with ferocity for the execution of Gruner and the others. Bombs struck targets in Rehovot, Haifa, and Jaffa, killing two policemen. In Netanya, a medical station was blown up and one British sentry shot to death. In Tel Aviv, an attack on an armored car took the lives of a cop and a Jewish bystander. In Haifa, Irgunists fired on soldiers from a commandeered taxi. In Haifa's harbor, British frogmen defused underwater bombs attached to three vessels being readied to deport a thousand more Jews to Cyprus. At the military cinema in Netanya, a bomb injured four soldiers.

On Hugo's third evening on the balcony, as the light slouched toward sunset, the blank pages of his pad asked not for something he could see from his perch but a scene from memory. Hugo drew a tree, a great straight oak. In front of the trunk, a sitting man, a heavyset figure in shorts and a dark-billed hat. The man held a pistol before his mouth as if it were a candle to blow out. Hugo left the man's eyes open and his blouse unbloodied. He'd seen a hundred thousand dead; because this would always be the first he'd killed, Hugo chose to leave the cop among the living.

Past sunset, he stopped drawing but sat with the pad and the cop in his lap. Curfew took hold and the street went vacant. A patrol walked past. The soldiers eyeballed Hugo, up on his balcony living his secret life.

He drank all his beer above the quiet, anxious street. Toward midnight, Hugo shuffled off to bed.

A note had been slipped under his door.

CHAPTER 51

HUGO

April 20
Russian Compound prison
Jerusalem

Barbed wire closed off the sidewalks; three soldiers and a candy-striped pole blocked the road. Morning sun reflected off windows of the Russian Compound to make the checkpoint a glaring hot place. Hugo waited while the sentries searched a car. They poked under the hood and trunk and used a mirror on a pole to scan the undercarriage. Beyond the checkpoint, police walked the grounds of the Jerusalem prison, past sandbag gun positions and spotlights on towers.

The guards cleared the car to move on. Hugo handed over his ID booklet. One guard took it while another, a bullnecked young Brit, pointed at the sack of fresh oranges across Hugo's shoulder.

"What's this, then?"

Hugo shrugged off the sack. Before he could set it down, the big guard put out both hands. "Give it."

The mesh bag was heavy as Hugo extended it. He said to the guard what the vendor in the souk had told him. "Don't drop it."

Hugo pocketed his returned ID booklet. The thick soldier shook the sack.

Hugo said, "They're oranges."

"I can see that, you git. We'll have a few." The other two sentries nodded.

"Of course."

The British guard untied the drawstring. He rummaged into the center of the bag before tossing three oranges to his comrades and leaving the sack on the road.

"Going to visit your friends?"

"I'm just delivering."

The big soldier leaned in. "You figure these'll be good for their health, do you, mate?"

"I don't know."

"Trust me. They won't be."

His tone was intimidating, as though he intended to remember Hugo.

The soldier peeled his orange. He separated the crescents and flipped through them like playing cards, checking for razor blades, something. When he ate, the other guards followed.

Hugo submitted to a body pat-down. Another car pulled up to the striped bar, too near; the heat of the radiator heated the checkpoint more. The burly guard sweat under his brimmed hat, he seemed to be fighting meanness and impatience. Another guard told Hugo, "Go on, now."

Hugo retied the sack and hoisted it across his shoulder. He passed the checkpoint, into the scrutiny of a dozen more police scattered around the compound. Their attention sloughed off Hugo; they saw him and looked away. He was nothing noteworthy, a Jew carrying a bag of oranges.

CHAPTER 52

VINCE

The younger prison guards, the ones who'd joined the Palestinian Police for the travel away from cold Britain, were heartbroken. They were boys who'd not fought in the world war. They held no brief that the Jews owed them anything. Their older brothers might have served with Monty or their fathers with Allenby, but these lads had not. A few were thugs, but they would've been thugs anywhere. The others, when Vince got them alone, felt Britain should leave the Jews and Arabs to figure it out between themselves. The young ones had little stomach for the killings and mayhem on all sides. They wanted to go home. A few called themselves good boys.

Among the older guards, ex-soldiers made up a majority. They'd seen the lives and places that war had lain to waste, had tasted and dealt violence. They considered themselves honorable and despised the murderous tactics of the Jews. They loved their homeland and believed that where Great Britain went, virtue followed. Some were scarred, many were grey; they worried over their empire, leaving Egypt, losing India. They would be damned on their feet if they would see the loss of Palestine. An Englishman was born on a small island, but he might die around the world under the Union Jack. History had given them the back of her hand; this wasn't the way of their fathers and grandfathers who'd controlled far greater lands with a fraction of the force.

Vince promised not to use their names, though many asked to be identified; they wanted their names read back home. A few added greetings to their mothers, wives, or children, as if Vince might write them down.

None of the guards in the Russian Compound wanted to hang terrorists in their prison; Barazani and Feinstein should be sent to Acre to be executed like Gruner. Their jail was in the middle of Jerusalem. Jew central.

Vince spent the first night in an empty cell. The prison had once been a women's hospice; the cells were roomy and white. Most of the five hundred inmates were Arabs; the seven Jewish political prisoners were held in a separate block. The Arabs were petty robbers and knife-fighters. Vince found little hatred among them for the Jews; these men had lived and worked alongside Jews. Mostly the Arabs complained that the Jews were sharp dealers.

The warden was an academic gent. On the record, he told Vince that he found the treatment of Gruner, Drezner, Kashani, and Alkachi shameful, and none of that nonsense at Acre would be repeated at his facility. The condemned men under his care would have the last comforts every human deserved.

Vince would be allowed to see Barazani and Feinstein, but only under escort. He could not speak with them; the two Jews had said their piece in court. It wasn't the prison's place to provide terrorists an additional platform. Vince mentioned the beating Gruner had taken at Acre when his executioners came for him; Vince wanted to be at the cell when the guards collected the condemned men on the morning of their hanging and to stay with them to the gallows. The warden agreed but could not imagine why anyone, even a reporter, would want to watch such a thing.

✳ ✳ ✳

In the early morning Vince awoke to splash water from the sink about his chest and armpits, then shave. The Arabs clapped when he pushed open his bars to walk out freely.

In the warden's office, Vince asked for his first look at the two condemned men. They were to be hanged after midnight, at 2:00 a.m. The warden summoned a guard to accompany Vince.

Skylights lit the long, plain plaster corridors. Arched ceilings gave the halls the look of white tunnels, like the passages people reported seeing while dead. The air was fresh and flowing. Debtors, crooks, and brawlers called messages for Vince to carry out of the prison. Tell my brother. Tell my wife. Tell my lawyer.

The Jews' block lay behind a locked gate. Seven condemned men occupied two side-by-side cells, both roomy and bright. Barred windows opened to a courtyard. The bars between Vince and the prisoners ran from floor to ceiling like a zoo.

Five Jews occupied the first cell. Two were lithe, the others stubby and strong. Their prison clothes were rough, knotty red. None came to the bars at Vince's approach. They sized him up, then returned to their writing or talking. They had a disdain about them, and a stubbornness. And something else, like they were ticking. Vince knew none of their names.

In the next cell, Moshe Barazani and Meir Feinstein stood from chairs at a table. They drifted to the bars as Vince eased toward them. The young guard shadowed Vince but remained quiet. Inside the cell, a third man, older and bespectacled in a black suit and skullcap, sat at the table. A springy beard made his face large. He stayed seated before a Bible. When the two men came close to Vince, only three hands wrapped the steel rods.

Feinstein was the younger of the two, just twenty, born in Jerusalem. He'd joined the British army at sixteen, the Irgun after the war. Seven months ago, Feinstein was arrested for driving a stolen taxi during an attack on Jerusalem's rail station. In the raid, he took a wound which cost him his left arm. The police found him by following the trail of his blood.

One year older, Barazani immigrated as a child with his family from Iraq. His rabbi father did little to support the household; Barazani went to work as a boy. When he turned sixteen, he joined the Stern Gang, pasting up propaganda leaflets. He graduated to operations and became an experienced saboteur. Two months ago, Barazani was nabbed out past curfew in Jerusalem with a grenade in his pocket, on his way to assassinate a British general.

Vince said, "Hello." The guard reminded him that no one was allowed to speak to the condemned.

Vince stayed back. Barazani and Feinstein breathed slowly, audibly, as if each breath were a sigh. The two were handsome, soft-featured, a shared dark cast to their eyes and olive skins.

Feinstein spoke in a deep voice, older than him. "We know who you are."

The bearded man arose, leaving the Bible on the table. He came to the bars; with a gesture to the young guard, he was let out of the cell. He was shorter than Vince, built like a block. Dandruff sifted his shoulders.

"You are a reporter."

"Yes, sir."

"I am a rabbi. You may hear what I say. Please recall it correctly."

The old man wrapped fingers around the bars above the hands of Barazani and Feinstein. Vince, too, stepped close enough to put a hand around the bars. The rabbi spoke to the boys.

"Each man is brought into this world for some purpose. Some men fulfill the task given them in twenty years, some in seventy, and others never at all. For those who never fulfill it and go on living, life no longer has purpose. That, too, is a kind of death. But in lives such as yours, my sons, death can get no footing. Even your death is turned into life."

Through the bars, the rabbi laid a hand on each head.

"I will be with you at the end. The last face you see will be a Jew."

The rabbi lowered his brow, making his beard fold under his chin. He muttered a Hebrew blessing, then backed away from the bars.

Barazani waved, not in farewell but to refute something.

"Rabbi. Please. Don't come tonight."

The old man hoisted a finger over his shoulder as he walked off. "I will not argue. No."

The guard walked the rabbi to the gate of death row. While the cop had his back turned, Vince reached inside the bars. First he shook Feinstein's lone hand, then Barazani's. Vince asked, "What do you need?"

The young guard returned. He laid hands on Vince, not roughly but enough to pull him away from the cell. Neither Barazani nor Feinstein answered his question. Perhaps they needed nothing.

A reply answer came from the adjoining cell. One of the terrorists came to the bars. He called to Vince, "Oranges. We'd like oranges."

✳✳✳

Vince asked to see the gallows. The guard took him on another long walk through white halls.

The execution chamber lay at the end of an empty block, out of the way so no prisoners would hear it work. The room was high-ceilinged and uncluttered. One wood beam spanned the space overhead; from it hung a rope and noose. Vince stepped onto the trapdoor, a platform of boards and hinges that creaked under his weight. A lever in the wall would make it fall away. A noose dangled in his face.

Vince grew anxious standing on the trapdoor, afraid it might fall open. He dared himself to touch the rope and made it sway.

The guard guided Vince back to the warden's office and left him there. Vince found Hugo waiting in the hallway. They greeted each other coolly.

Vince asked, "How did you know I was here?"

"I'd be remiss if I didn't know."

Hugo indicated a mesh bag stuffed with oranges at his feet. "I need you to get these to Barazani and Feinstein."

"What's inside the oranges?"

"I don't lie to you, Vince."

"You just never tell me the whole truth."

"Truth. Would you like me to be philosophic about truth? I can be. How did you enjoy Massuot Yitzhak?"

"Did I cheat you somehow? Why are we trading slights all of a sudden?"

"You didn't think it would be like this, did you? When you plucked me off my wooden slats and my pisspot for a pillow. When you set me out in the sun like a sick flower. You didn't see this."

"No."

"You thought I would always be that skeleton."

"I didn't."

"You did. You and everyone else. Give him milk, easy; he can't take too much. Give him a new set of clothes and an identification card. Feed him on pity. Give him a train and a ship, send him somewhere he can fatten up and quiet down. Let's put this ugliness behind us."

"I've tried to help you."

"Truly? Be honest. Everything has been for yourself. Your search. Your understanding. Your newspaper. And I told you, didn't I? Come to Palestine with me, Vince, see the stories we will live. That was a great truth, maybe the greatest of your life. I think you owe me for it."

Hugo lifted the sack of oranges from the floor.

"Do you know what I found in Palestine? People who don't pity me. The Jews here don't talk about anyone's deathbed in Europe. I'm not special. Palestine might be the only place in the world where the present is bigger than the past. Yet every time I look at you I feel that sun, I feel my ribs sticking out. I taste that goddam milk."

Hugo held the oranges out.

"Don't drop them."

Vince walked away. "Find someone else."

Hugo called down the white hall after him, "Stay away from Barazani and Feinstein. You will owe me for that, too."

Vince headed for his cell among the Arabs to sleep into the evening.

CHAPTER 53
VINCE
April 21

Vince sat up on his dark cot. He laced his shoes, a few minutes after midnight.

He left the cell. Around him, the Arabs knew where he was going and that he wouldn't return. They muttered to him, *"Ma'a salama."* Some reached open hands into the hall, a salutation for him or for the two who would be hanged, Vince didn't ask. A brotherhood existed here and the two Jews who would die tonight hadn't killed Arabs, so he believed the Arabs' gestures were for them.

He padded the long halls to death row. Inside the locked gate, the lights were on. The Jews were singing.

When the song broke, Vince asked to be let in. The young guard came to open up.

"You're early, sir."

"Couldn't sleep."

"Understood."

"How are they?"

"In good spirits."

"May I ask you a question?"

"Yes, sir."

"Did they get a sack of oranges today? Did someone bring them?"

"Yes."

"Did you see who it was?"

"No. When I came to check on them this afternoon, this lot handed me a good one." The guard indicated the cell of five Jews watching Vince. "It's what they asked for, yeah?"

"Yeah. It was."

The guard ushered him closer to the cells. They stopped five paces from the bars.

"Stay here, Mr. Haas. The rabbi and the warden will be here soon. You can watch, but no talking."

The guard did not stay beside Vince but paced the length of both cells. Barazani and Feinstein sat at their table. Before them lay a pack of cigarettes and the remains of a meal. Feinstein scribbled something inside the cover of the Bible. In the other cell, the prisoners sat on their cots, dark heads bowed.

Feinstein closed the Bible and brought it to the bars. He called the guard to come take it. The two exchanged delicate words Vince could not hear. The guard rested a hand on Feinstein's shoulder.

"Move back, please," Feinstein asked. "We would like our time to pray in private."

The guard moved beside Vince. Barazani motioned them further away. Vince and the guard backpedaled again, putting their backs against the wall.

Barazani and Feinstein did pray together, but not a long prayer. They finished by touching foreheads tenderly, brotherly, then Barazani lit a cigarette. He inhaled a deep drag to raise a red glow. From his own pocket, Feinstein pulled an orange.

Vince's back came off the wall, instinctively alarmed. The guard barred him from taking another step.

Barazani touched his cigarette to the top of the orange. A small shower of sparks flickered at Feinstein's breast. Barazani clutched his comrade in both arms and the two pressed the crackling fuse between their hearts.

The guard dropped the Bible and flung out his arms, screaming something. The blast knocked him backwards the short distance he'd leaped. Vince was rocked back into the wall.

The explosion boomed down the long halls. The guard scrambled up off the floor, fumbling for his keys. In the adjacent cell, the five Jews gripped the bars as if they might all pull together to free themselves.

Vince's ears buzzed and his face flashed. He didn't enter the cell with the guard where smoke cleared like hurrying specters.

He lifted the Bible the guard had dropped. Feinstein had inscribed in it:

> '*In the shadows of the gallows, April 21, 1947, to the British soldier as you stand guard, before we go to the gallows, accept this Bible as a memento and re-member that we stood in dignity and marched in dignity. It is better to die with a weapon in hand than to live with hands raised. Meir Feinstein.*'

The two had elected not to kill the kindly guard who stood too close, or Vince, or the old rabbi who couldn't be talked out of joining them on the gallows, or the executioner and the warden who surely would've been on the scaffold with them. Barazani would have asked for a final cigarette; Feinstein would request a bite of his last Jaffa orange.

Vince put the Bible on the floor where he found it. Inside the cell, the guard stood over the remains of Barazani and Feinstein. The young man could not kneel though his legs shook, and he seemed to want to. He could do nothing but set the table aright.

CHAPTER 54

RIVKAH

May 9
Massuot Yitzhak

Gush Etzion celebrated a three-day rain.

The leaders of the bloc declared a break from the soggy fields. In the constant drizzle, Rivkah hiked to Revadim to visit her sister for the first time in weeks.

Gabbi squired her around the new kibbutz. Two big tents, each covering thirty cots, served as living quarters. The young settlers shared toilets and showers. Cooking was done over outdoor fires. Barbed wire marked the borders of Revadim; sandbag gun positions protected every approach. Gabbi showed Rivkah the beginnings of a fig orchard, the kibbutz's five young goats, and a tin roof over a welding shop. They walked hand-in-hand under the dripping sky. Gabbi was lively, fed by the showers; the drops were the smallest of things. A pistol was holstered on her hip as she described the Arabs of Nahalin who sometimes fired guns in the night over Revadim.

Over tea, Rivkah told her about Vince. She showed Gabbi a column Vince had mailed, about Dov Gruner. Gabbi asked whether Vince was handsome, rich; would she go to America? Rivkah said no to all three. She folded the newspaper column away to keep it dry.

During her walk back to Massuot Yitzhak, the storm broke like a fever, with a chill and quivers of lightning. Toward dusk the sky opened to tracts of blue, with some gold in the clouds. At sunset, a car came to Massuot Yitzhak.

Mrs. Pappel met Rivkah on the porch. "It's your American."

"How can you tell?"

"Liebling. It's him."

Vince arrived in an old Chevrolet that coughed when it shut down. He stood beside the car; Rivkah stayed on the porch. Neither knew how to say hello. When Rivkah stepped off the porch, Vince sped until she pressed against him.

"You got some rain."

Rivkah laughed into his chest, pleased that this was the first thing he said, unremarkable and acquainted. She took him in to Mrs. Pappel. At the table, Vince presented Rivkah with a typed copy of his most recent column, about Barazani and Feinstein. Vince sipped hot tea while Rivkah read.

Vince had been at the cell of Barazani and Feinstein in their last minutes. He called what he'd witnessed horrible but wrote, too, of his own horror. Two Jews had died by their own hands, an act of courage, but he didn't overlook that they died plotting to kill more British. He described the kindness of the guard, the compassion of the Arab prisoners. Vince called the event what it was, a tragedy.

Pappel asked, "Will you stay the night? You've missed supper. We can scare something up."

"Thank you, I'd like to."

"We won't be watering tomorrow. I'll find something for you to do."

Before Rivkah could stop Mrs. Pappel from enlisting Vince's labor again, he spoke.

"I was wondering if, tomorrow, Rivkah would like to come with me to see what I do."

"Vince." Rivkah slid a hand across the table to bring the conversation around to her.

"Yeah?"

"You don't have to ask Mrs. Pappel. Ask me."

Quietly, Mrs. Pappel took the cups away.

"Do you like music?"

"I'm from Vienna."

"Do you know the American composer Leonard Bernstein?"

"Everyone does."

"He's conducting his *Jeremiah* symphony tomorrow at a kibbutz north of here, Ein Harod. Would you like to go?"

"Yes."

Mrs. Pappel returned with refilled teacups. "Will that old Chevy make it to Ein Harod?"

"Yes, ma'am."

She set the tea in front of Vince, then sat behind her own cup. "Will it make it back?"

Rivkah stood. "Vince, go outside. We'll find something for you to eat."

With his teacup, he left for the porch.

Mrs. Pappel pointed at Vince's column on the table, written for an American newspaper, by an American.

"You understand. He will go home."

"Don't."

Rivkah made Vince a meal of vegetables, hummus, and bread. Mrs. Pappel sat with Vince's words to read for herself.

CHAPTER 55

VINCE

May 10

Vince sat up on the sofa, in undershirt and khaki pants. The sun wasn't up yet. Mrs. Pappel presided over the stove and the pops of eggs.

"How do you take your coffee?"

"Black, please."

"Rivkah's in the shower."

Vince blinked to catch up to the pace of the morning. Mrs. Pappel brought him a mug.

"My husband Morrie took his coffee black. Come sit. I learned to make crepes when we lived in London."

Vince buttoned on his blue cotton shirt, then carried his coffee to the table. Mrs. Pappel set down a plate of eggs and pancakes. Rivkah's shower cut off. Through the window, other lights in dark Massuot Yitzhak glowed. Dawn was not the start of the day here. Mrs. Pappel sat across from Vince.

"Morrie and I lived in London for twenty years. He thought many things about the British were odd."

"Like what?"

"He was in the movie business. A lot of money changed hands. We came from Vienna, an old place for the Jews. London, not so much. The

British did business over gin, at the club, nice leather chairs, some stuffed heads on a wall."

"Good description."

"Thank you. Morrie was an Austrian Jew. He came from people who shook hands after they signed the papers, not before. He'd have a drink when a deal was finished. Morrie liked ink, he liked details. He liked a profit but only his share. He never lost his accent. Didn't shave his little moustache, never joined the club. He was always Shylock. He never understood the British."

Vince forked more into his mouth. She smiled at his appetite.

"May I say something else?"

Vince nodded.

"I should have said this last night. I'm old and maybe I've been left in the sun too long. I'm a little hardened and things don't soak in so fast like they used to. You're a good writer."

"Thank you."

"You're important to Palestine."

"Pinchus told me the same thing."

Mrs. Pappel reached across to pat one of his hands. "That makes it true. Vince."

"Yes, ma'am."

"I'll say only this. Palestine is like nothing history has seen before. It's complex."

"That's funny."

"What is?"

"I said that exact thing to my editor when I told him I didn't want to come back."

"This isn't about Palestine. It's about you. I want to say this before Rivkah comes out."

"Okay."

"This is not just a land. We're not just a people. We don't just live here. I lived in Vienna. The Jews here, we've become a new thing, us and this place. It doesn't have a name yet, but there's never been anything like it, our need for Palestine. And it seems to need us. I don't know how to explain."

Mrs. Pappel stood.

"What I'm saying is you may not, in the end, understand us. Please don't use Rivkah for that purpose."

"I won't."

"That's a glib thing to say. Have you used others?"

Vince pushed away the breakfast plate. "You don't know me."

"No. I don't."

Rivkah emerged. The smells of damp hair and freshness spilled around her. She beamed to see Mrs. Pappel and Vince together.

Mrs. Pappel pushed Vince's unfinished breakfast back to him.

CHAPTER 56

RIVKAH

Driving north through the parched hills, Vince barely spoke. Plainly he'd crossed words with Mrs. Pappel over breakfast.

She let him mull, let the sun rise with her window down and the air buffeting in. Rivkah made a wing of her hand in the wind.

The road elevated on the approach to Bethlehem. Vince skirted the city and headed west, where the land fell into green valleys. They rolled through fertile spaces, past Arab villages and minarets, Jewish settlements, mule-drawn carts in the road, fruit and vegetable vendors beside fields, long fallow stretches, bleak hills, stone homes.

Vince drove into a northern stretch Rivkah had never before traveled, up the seacoast past Rishon LeZion, Ramat Gan, Petah Tikvah. The towns were like bits of Europe; fifty thousand Jews lived in these places where offices and factories, not fields, swallowed the workers, and the avenues bustled with commerce. In Massuot Yitzhak, Rivkah could forget that all Palestine wasn't just a boulder and a pry bar.

A half hour out of Tel Aviv, the road slowed into the industrial outskirts of Netanya. Vince ran fingertips across his lips, to say something, but first he seemed to feel for the words.

"Look."

"Yes?"

"There's some things I want to tell you. Just regular things about me. And questions I want to ask about you."

"Go ahead."

Vince freed a hand from the wheel to make circling gestures, trying to summon more.

"I want to know about you. Your family. But I don't want to upset you."

"It will."

"Then we can talk about other things. That's okay."

Rivkah rested her back against the passenger door, facing him.

"I'd like us to wait. Until after we've had these few days together. Let's not put the past between us until we're strong enough to hold it."

"Sounds good."

"I like the way I just said that."

"You could be a writer."

"Good. I think you have no chance of being a farmer."

"Oh, no?" Vince laughed as if she'd challenged him. The sourness in the car disappeared, and the ride became something they did together, not apart.

North of Netanya, the highway gave them blue glimpses of the Mediterranean. Vince described the things he saw, flowers in the sunlight, boys on mules, emerald stretches of crops, as if practicing the words he'd write about this trip. He put his own hand out into the speeding wind. Rivkah matched it and, for a while, they flew over the road.

CHAPTER 57

VINCE

Ein Herod

Rivkah hurried across the grass for a spot close to the stage, leaving Vince to keep up. She carried a blanket; he handled the basket Mrs. Pappel had packed with food and water jars. Hundreds of concertgoers flowed into the meadow, hauling umbrellas, folding chairs, and baskets.

The stage was set up at the far edge of the field. A roof and canvas walls would keep the weather off the performers. Behind the stage lay a vista of barley, rows of alfalfa, and young corn. Mount Gilboa rose behind the fields with a cloud snagged on its peak like a white banner.

Several hundred concertgoers were already in place. Thirty meters from the platform, Rivkah spread her blanket. Others filled in, though Bernstein and the orchestra wouldn't arrive in Ein Harod for several more hours.

Strangers greeted one another as they set up their little sites. By the time Rivkah handed Vince a plate of chicken and slaw, she'd already been given tomatoes by neighbors and made promises of sharing Mrs. Pappel's cake and pie. Married people and young lovers gabbled about the perfect afternoon, the setting, the thrill of the event. They swept Rivkah into their talk; she became the center of their circle.

She identified Vince as an American newspaperman. Briefly, he became the focus, and he didn't mind. The neighbors introduced themselves by their professions, as teachers, businesspeople, craftsmen, and tradesmen. One couple had just gotten engaged. An older pair named places in the States they'd visited. Only Rivkah among them lived on a kibbutz. When she said she was from Gush Etzion, this drew much admiration, for they knew of it, knew it was surrounded by Arabs.

While their group ate and shared, the tide of people flooding into Ein Harod tripled. In an hour, three thousand crammed the field; behind them, hundreds reclined in truck beds and horse-drawn carts.

The sunlight began to slant; the day cooled. The crowd whiled away the remaining hours until the concert. Cigarettes and pipes came out, heads lay on pillows or laps, voices eased.

Vince reclined. He took Rivkah's hand but did not pull her down; that was for her to decide. So much of what they did together, they did for the first time. In this field of unfamiliar people, they could be their own invention, a couple.

She eased her head onto his shoulder and flattened a hand on his chest. Under her palm he felt the beating of his own heart. Rivkah fidgeted; by that, he knew she lay awake with his heartbeat, too.

✳ ✳ ✳

The crowd cheered the sight of the orchestra's buses coming into view and continued cheering while the musicians filed onto the platform. Stagehands carried in a tympani drum and a harp and got applause for it.

A hundred orchestra members—men in tuxedos, women in floor-length black—arranged themselves by instrument: strings, flutes, woodwinds, and brass, with percussion and harp to the rear. All faced a small box where Bernstein would stand.

The famous conductor stayed out of sight while his orchestra warmed and tuned. When he mounted the stage at last, he took only a few moments with the thunderous ovation; Bernstein bowed, stepped onto his podium, put his back to the crowd, and raised a baton. The audience hushed; the musicians readied. Leonard Bernstein held motionless, arms aloft in the outpouring of silence from his orchestra, from the audience, the land, as if to allow everything else to step aside before he began.

The first stanzas of *Jeremiah* opened gently, a plea from the strings and punctuating brass, but Bernstein didn't ease into the score. From the first notes, he conducted with an athletic breadth as though he were the prophet himself begging the Chosen People to remain faithful, the underlying tale of the symphony. As the movements progressed from the first to the second, "Prophesy" into "Profanation," Bernstein presided over the battles between brass and woodwind, strings and percussion, to tell the story of God's people who had strayed. The music ascended and raced along, either hopeful or clashing, with Bernstein fanning it as much as directing. In other passages the passions plunged, seemed to wander in valleys, and the conductor let them mourn until he bid the music rise, a guide star to the lost.

For the final movement, "Lamentation," a mezzo-soprano stepped to a microphone. She became the voice of Jeremiah's grief at the destruction of Jerusalem, an angry and tearless sorrow: *How doth the city sit solitary, that was full of people? She hath none to comfort her among all her lovers; all her friends have become her enemies. Jerusalem hath grievously sinned, how doth the city sit solitary, a widow.*

The thousands on blankets and on the hoods of trucks spilled their hearts when the symphony ended. They'd been welled-up during the performance, too rapt to cry. When Bernstein lowered his baton, every voice in the field erupted, Rivkah's too. She rocketed to her feet, wiping eyes on the pads of her palms.

She clapped and shouted for the orchestra, which took many bows; Vince couldn't hear her voice for the wild ovation. Then she turned to him.

Knowing she could not be heard, Rivkah mouthed the words, "Thank you." She lifted her strong arms in her rolled-up sleeves. Rivkah held them apart but did not step forward to him. She waited, beaming more than she had even at Bernstein, for Vince to come to her.

He held back, not to hesitate but to marvel at her in the sea of hurrahs and deafening applause, every person looking forward and she looking backward, only at him.

CHAPTER 58

RIVKAH

At the end of the concert an announcement was made. Something had happened in Nazareth; the British had shut down the roads. No one could leave Ein Harod tonight. All were welcome to camp in the field for the night.

The lights came on in the hundred homes of Ein Harod. Barn animals bawled to be fed. The lights of the orchestra's buses faded around a bend, but they wouldn't get far. Stagehands packed up the larger instruments. The crowd on the grass settled again on their blankets.

Rivkah patted the ground. Vince looked about as if taking stock; he seemed never to have considered sleeping outdoors before.

A nearby couple said, "We have an extra blanket."

Rivkah accepted, then rummaged inside Mrs. Pappel's basket to find two jars of water and half of a cherry pie.

"What do you think happened?" The woman who'd loaned them the blanket asked Vince.

"A bombing. A raid. Something."

Rivkah entered the talk to stop it, to spare Vince from being made the authority on violence. She offered the last of the cherry pie to anyone who wanted it. No one took it, but all saw what she was doing; the couples shifted the topic to the concert.

The stars over the Jezreel Valley were as plentiful as Massuot Yitzhak's. Rivkah tried to see patterns, though she knew no constellations. The music swirled in her head, her hands held the tingle of so much clapping. The concertgoers carpeted the field, and on the rim of the grasses a few hundred reclined in the beds of trucks and wagons. A calm descended over the throng, a warm, living silence.

Vince, all knees and elbows, lanky and confounded, mentioned sleeping in the car. Rivkah tutted at him. She rose and said as she walked away, "Silly."

From behind the stage, she plucked an armful of barley, gathered it into a sheaf, then used the stems to tie a bundle. Returning, Rivkah slipped the bale under the ground blanket for a pillow. She rested her head on the soft bulge; Vince's head settled next to hers.

For the first moments lying beside him, Rivkah thought of anything but Vince. The pinprick stars, a cushion of spring grass, a borrowed blanket, she took in everything that was not him because the instant she turned to Vince the rest would disappear. She listened to other couples say goodnight, whispers in the field, insects in the grass, snores and coughs that swept her back in time to a ship. The night would be damp and different from her dry hilltop. When she had enough of the world, when she felt brimming, like drawing a deep breath before diving, Rivkah rolled to her shoulder and kissed Vince.

CHAPTER 59

HUGO

June 22
Tel Aviv

Hugo let the screen door slam behind him and sauntered in. He let himself appear friendly and a little lost when he stepped up to a counter. "Hello?"

A heavyset man in coveralls wiped his hands on a rag. Hugo reached across the counter to shake, to show he didn't care about dirt on anyone's hands. On the wall behind the counter were calendars, carmaker signs, adverts for oil and windshield wipers.

"Are you the owner?"

"I am."

Hugo told him he was a produce merchant from Jaffa who needed a cool basement to store potatoes, to transport them to the Tel Aviv market in the mornings. Did this building have a basement?

"It does."

"May I see it?"

Hugo followed through the building, a murky, airless storehouse for auto parts. Starters, solenoids, piston rods, carburetors, and radiators lined shelves, spark plugs and all sizes of hoses filled cubbies and barrels. The gritty floor smelled of grease, iron, and rubber.

The man appraised Hugo in the way of a mechanic, measuring the little potato merchant. Hugo flattered the warehouse, claimed he could build an entire car from the contents. The owner said he lacked tires but the rest, yes, perhaps so. Hugo selected a hose from a barrel. Fuel line for a Ford? Yes.

"Your basement must be full."

"It's not. The garage is falling off. I used to do a lot of work for the police."

"Oh?"

"Their headquarters is across the street, at Citrus House. These days, with barbed wire and checkpoints everywhere, curfews, no one can drive. Now, I work on one or two cars a week."

The owner opened a door to a flight of down steps. He tugged a chain for the stairwell light and led the way.

The basement was wide open, a bare dirt floor and brick walls. Judging from the cobwebs and dust, it was dry. Overhead, stout floorboards would be soundproof. A shorter set of steps led to a storm door. Hugo pushed the door open into an alley.

"I'll need it for a few months."

Hugo followed the owner up to the storeroom. The man's heavy steps said he was not political, only tired. He might have suspected something, he might not, but he was quick to explain he rarely came to the storehouse, never went down to the basement. At the counter he drafted a bill for the first month's rent.

After the lease was signed, Hugo returned to the produce truck he'd parked in front of the garage. He drove to the alley and stopped at the storm door. The two Irgunists riding along jumped out of the cab when he did.

Hugo's porters lowered the truck's gate and set to unloading several bags of potatoes. A bag spilled and broke open in the alley; spuds rolled in every direction. Hugo loudly berated the two for their clumsiness while across the street, behind barbed wire, policemen watched.

CHAPTER 60

HUGO

June 24

At dawn, Hugo rapped on the cellar door, then waited while it was lifted by a dirt-streaked digger he didn't know. Hugo descended the steps from the alley.

Four more sappers sat with backs against the walls; shovels, short-handled picks, and rakes leaned beside them. The north wall had been punched through, bricks stacked out of the way. A lone bulb made all the sweaty men glisten. Twenty bulging burlap sacks waited to be carried out. The clods inside made the bags knobby, like they were filled with potatoes.

The filthy lad indicated the tunnel, for Hugo to have a look.

Hugo kneeled in the mouth. At the far end burned a lantern. The first night's work had broken through the wall and bored fifteen feet. At this rate, the operation would take a week, right on schedule.

Hugo crawled inside. On his knees, he touched the rounded walls of the shaft, then brought the lantern with him when he backed out.

He tried to heft one of the burlap sacks by himself but couldn't manage. The sappers waved him off the task. Kharda had his piece of the mission; they had theirs. They shouldered the bags up the steps into the truck bed.

When the vehicle was loaded, Hugo went into the basement with the sappers, to stay a minute. He gave them cigarettes and sat against the walls like them. He couldn't talk to them because he couldn't know them. They tipped up their chins, smoking with eyes closed. Their labor was done until sundown; they dug only at night and boobytrapped the tunnel while they were gone.

Hugo climbed the steps into the morning. Across the road, beside rail tracks, stood Citrus House, a modern metallic building, five stories high, shaped like a barrel. Barbed wire ringed the place; police snipers patrolled the roof. Dozens of cop cars were parked close to the building, as if afraid.

Hugo drove out of the alley, six miles east to a farm in Petah Tikvah where Irgunists would dump the dirt in the fields.

CHAPTER 61

HUGO

July 1
Ramat Gan

Hugo didn't like waking to clucking hens; someone near the safe house kept a pen and a roost. In an early and gloomy light, he made his coffee.

The drive to the basement in Tel Aviv took ten minutes. At this hour, nothing but trucks rolled with him on the road, some with headlights on. Arriving, Hugo cruised slowly past Citrus House. Even at sunrise, every pillbox and checkpoint was manned, the long barrels of sniper rifles prickled the roof, armed cops roamed the wire. Hugo rumbled into the alley behind the garage. This was his fifth trip and might be the last; yesterday, the sappers had had twenty feet to go. Tomorrow, they would be directly under Citrus House.

He jumped down, eager to congratulate the sappers. Hugo took with him a fresh pack of cigarettes to hand around. No one answered his rap on the basement door. They knew to expect him. He peered both ways in the alley, then climbed back into the produce truck.

Before he could start the engine, the basement door lifted. He reached for the glove box.

"Hugo."

With his finger on the glove box button, Hugo froze. None of the sappers knew his real name; to them he was only Kharda.

Up the basement steps climbed tall, white-shirted, broad-shouldered Julius of the Palmach.

"How have you been? I haven't seen you in a year."

Hugo kept his hands on the wheel though the engine wasn't running. "I've been well. You look the same."

"Come down. Let me get a good look at you."

Hugo wanted to flee, but there would be roadblocks set for him. He slid down out of the truck. Julius, as ever, towered over him.

Julius indicated the truck. "Are you working for a produce company now?"

"Can we get to it?"

Julius nodded and gestured to the steps for Hugo to descend first. This felt like respect, like they were equals.

In the basement, in the wan glow of the bulb, three armed men waited against the brick walls. The sappers were gone. The mouth to the tunnel had been sealed with concrete. Above the blocked opening, a message to the Irgun had been scrawled in chalk on the bricks: *The Haganah was here. We want you by force not to carry out your evil intention. Signed Haganah.*

Hugo asked, "Did you catch the others?"

"No."

"How did you know?"

"May I have a cigarette, Hugo?"

He shook one out for Julius and lit it from a match. Hugo made no offer to the other three. Julius knew Hugo well enough; he put a hand on his shoulder.

"You're a pawn."

"I am not."

Julius lowered the hand. He kicked the concreted tunnel. "This. You've been told to risk your life. To take how many other lives? For what?"

"For the same reasons you risk yours."

Beneath the chalked words, Julius squatted on his haunches. He smoked and considered the dirt floor. Hugo asked, "How long did you wait for me here?"

"Since yesterday afternoon."

"You've had me followed?"

"For a long time, Hugo."

"Why now?"

"The UN has sent a committee to Palestine. They're going to make a recommendation. This could be what we've been hoping for. A Jewish state."

"Then why stop the Irgun? We've done all the dirty work. We're the ones who've made Palestine a place the British can't govern."

"While the UN's here, the Jewish Agency wants no violence. The world needs to see we can govern ourselves. The British are the beasts, not us. But Pinchus."

"What about him?"

"He wants to put on a show. A show, Hugo. Kill a hundred, maybe more. Just to make a point that's already been made."

Julius stood, finished with the cigarette, done with Hugo standing over him. He pointed at one of his men, who disappeared up the steps.

"Are you going to turn me in?"

"I'll know in a moment."

Light from the alley flowed in the open door. One of the truck's doors was opened, then closed. Julius' man returned. At the bottom of the stairs, he handed Hugo's pistol to Julius.

"Is this yours?"

"No. It belongs to Pinchus. The man you introduced me to."

"It was found in your truck. So it's yours."

Julius returned the gun to the Haganah man. Again, Julius moved in front of the chalk message. He scraped a boot across the dirt, through a stain on the raw floor.

"His name was Zeev Weber. He was the one following you. Yesterday morning, when you left to dump the bags, after the sappers were gone, he came down here. Zeev found the tunnel. He didn't know about the boobytrap."

Julius turned his back to mount the stairs, with no hint that he might say more.

CHAPTER 62

VINCE

July 2
YMCA
Jerusalem

A year after he'd destroyed the King David, Pinchus appeared to admire it. Vince eased into the chair opposite him. Silverware and menus waited on the table.

With his focus on the hotel across the street, Pinchus said, "This is what the British do well. They rebuild from ruin better than any nation in history."

Vince said, "I didn't expect to see you this morning."

"You should never expect to see me, Vince."

"I heard about Hugo."

"Yes."

"Are you going to do something about it?"

Pinchus smiled broadly but made no reply. A waiter approached; the smile stayed fixed while Pinchus ordered eggs, toast, and coffee for himself and Vince. The waiter left, and behind his glasses Pinchus blinked as though from the strain of his grin.

"Do you judge me, Vince?"

"You're a hard man to trust."

"I don't ask to be trusted."

"What, then?"

"Believed in. A revolution is only partly politics. The rest is war. And war is belief."

Pinchus wiped a napkin across his lips. His smile disappeared; he had no more use for it.

"Did you enjoy Massuot Yitzhak?"

"Stay out of my personal life."

"Alright. What would you have me do about Kharda?"

"What can you do?"

"I can beat someone. Hang someone. Threaten. You know the responses as well as I. Are you advocating this? I thought you were done with that sort of thing in Palestine."

"You're going to let them execute him? They found him with a gun."

"For a Jew in Palestine, that is a capital offense."

"He's Irgun. He's yours."

"He is, indeed."

"You sent him to help blow up Citrus House. How many would that have killed?"

"We would have warned the British before setting the fuse."

"And what if they didn't believe you? Again."

Without raising his hand from the table, Pinchus lifted a finger at the resurrected King David where almost a hundred had died. The small gesture meant a similar number. Vince prodded, "Hugo's trial is next week."

"I will let it proceed."

"You'll let him hang?"

Pinchus smiled slightly this time, a crinkle behind his glasses. A waiter delivered their coffees. Pinchus sipped; his satisfaction seemed genuine.

"I enjoy our talks, Vince. You test my patience, you challenge my mindset. Not enough people around me do that. It's a price of the secret life. Those living it alongside me tend to agree too much."

"What are you going to do?"

"You need to understand."

"What."

"The Haganah stopped our operation. The Jewish Agency was very pleased, the British, too, of course. But a Haganah man was killed in that basement. A Jew, by the Irgun's hand. If I rescue one of the men who killed him, I insult the Jewish Agency. I insult the family of Zeev Weber. When Hugo was found with a pistol, he couldn't claim he was just a driver. At that point he became what he wanted to be: a fighter."

"And fighters die."

"Too often."

"So to avoid an insult to the Jewish Agency, you'll let Hugo hang."

"As I said, a revolt is partly politics."

"You'll do nothing."

"I'll never do nothing."

A server arrived with the eggs and toast. Pinchus appeared to pray before he raised his darkened face.

"The British are holding three more Irgunists on death sentences. They were captured in May during a raid on Acre prison. We freed two hundred and fifty-five inmates. When we speak of Habib, Nakar, and Weiss, the British will know, we are speaking of Kharda, too."

Pinchus ate ravenously. Vince had seen the same hunger in Hugo, not just appetite but avarice.

"What are you doing here."

"I very much enjoyed your column on the Bernstein concert." Pinchus washed down the eggs with coffee. "I need a favor from you."

"Do you realize everything you say sounds like a threat?"

"No." Pinchus wiped his mouth. "I apologize."

"Are you sorry for being a shit or for being caught at it?"

"Both, to be honest."

"What do you want?"

"The United Nations Special Committee on Palestine is here. In Jerusalem. You are covering them, yes?"

"I am."

"UNSCOP will decide if the British must go. Now is our time. Now is what we have fought for. Our own state."

"What do you need from me?"

"Make sure they see Palestine for what the British have made of it. A bastion of barbed wire and pillboxes. Checkpoints and sentries. I want the Committee to witness the measures Britain must resort to, the batons and nooses, just so they can claim they still have an empire, that they control us. They do not control us. They cannot. To continue to try will be a bloody lie. Show them."

"How do you expect me to do that?"

"You are Vincent Haas of the *Herald Tribune*. Don't lose sight of that. You have access. Use it. Tell them what you know, what you've seen. From Galilee to the Negev, to Massuot Yitzhak. Help them understand the cost of keeping the Jew from his homeland."

"You're that cost, Pinchus."

"I'm part of it, yes."

"I've already said I don't trust you."

Pinchus rose from the table. He glanced in every direction because he was hunted.

"I haven't told you the favor yet."

"What is it?"

"Bring the Committee to me. I'll be in touch about when and where."

"I'll see what I can do."

"One more thing." Pinchus walked away. "Thank you again for breakfast."

CHAPTER 63

VINCE

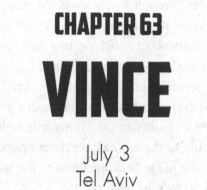

July 3
Tel Aviv

Vince rode in the front of the taxi. When the Irgun driver pulled to the curb on a dark, leafy street, he got out first to help the judge exit the rear. The two diplomats with the judge, younger men, climbed out on their own. The taxi left them on the sidewalk.

A young, well-dressed woman approached. She uttered Pinchus's password, "Homeland." The group followed her to another taxi waiting with headlamps off. She departed without a look backward. Vince offered the front seat to the judge, but again was politely refused.

The driver weaved through neighborhoods, unnecessary turns to foil anyone following.

During the forty-minute drive from Jerusalem to Tel Aviv, the diplomats asked Vince only one question: Did they have anything to fear? He said the Irgun kept their word.

The driver, a tough-looking sort, nose broken like a boxer, nodded. "Ask the British."

✳✳✳

Pinchus greeted Judge Sandström with a hearty handshake. The white-haired Swede, the chairman of UNSCOP, was of a very different type from Pinchus, an elegant and tall man who offered an indifferent handshake. Pinchus hid his disappointment.

"Thank you for coming. And your delegation."

The Judge smiled through Pinchus's blandishment. "Vincent Haas said you wished to keep our meeting secret. I chose to bring none of the other Committee members, to avoid alerting their watchdogs. Besides, Mister Pinchus. Let me introduce my delegation. Chinese envoy Victor Hoo and American political scientist Ralph Bunche."

Pinchus offered the Judge the chair at the head of the dining room table.

The others filled in, including their hosts, a Jewish poet and his wife. Pinchus spoke warmly to the woman, an Irgun operative. Vince took a seat against a wall; the judge beckoned him to the table. Pinchus sat at the far end, flanked by two lieutenants.

Sandström began with a prepared question off a notecard. "Mr. Pinchus, do you carry the rank of general?"

"I carry no rank at all."

"How do you command?"

"By agreement."

Pinchus summarized the Irgun's aims: the liberation of the country from foreign rule and the attainment of freedom for the Jewish people in Palestine.

The judge asked why the Irgun chose violence instead of diplomacy?

"Britain attempts to keep the country under control by force of arms. There's no other way to accomplish our aims than to meet force with force."

Sandström pressed the commander about what would happen if the Jews got their way. If the British left, could they live peacefully with the Arabs?

"Arab opposition to a Jewish homeland is a myth spread by the British to justify their presence, the claim that foreign troops are needed to keep the Jews and Arabs from each other's throats. I am fighting for Arab liberation, as well."

"What happens if you are wrong? What if the Arabs attack you after the British go?"

"We will smite them hip and thigh."

"How so?"

"In modern war, numbers do not decide the issue but brains and morale. As for brains, I do not feel I need to elaborate. As to fighting spirit, you have read of the men who went to the gallows."

"Was Dov Gruner a high officer in the Irgun?"

The mention of Gruner ratcheted Pinchus's volume up a notch. He hardly kept his seat. "Gruner, Barazani, Feinstein, all of them, they were not officers of Irgun, not criminals, but warriors. Their capture made them prisoners of war. Hanging them was itself a crime."

Dr. Hoo changed the subject. "If you get Palestine as a Jewish state, and you bring in several million people, how will you handle the increase in population? The country is small."

"That is why it would be absurd to set up a small Jewish state."

Dr. Bunche asked, "How confident is the Irgun in the support of the Jewish people?"

"How could we exist if we did not have their backing, in the face of the number of British police and troops? We're not professional fighters. We take no pleasure in shooting or being shot. In Europe, we lost six million. Every Jewish life is precious. The Irgun take our strength from the people. They protect us, though, yes, we bring them troubles."

"What of those troubles? Curfews, restriction, retaliations. Executions."

"Suffering cannot be separated from struggle."

While Pinchus jousted with the diplomats, the poet and his wife brought food and drink to the table.

Pinchus was never cornered. He blended invention and logic with facts and passion, threaded his remarks with cajolery and lies. Vince knew Pinchus well enough; he'd talked to the man without the smokescreen of decency. Sandström bandied with him over the Mandate's legality, the Jews' Biblical claim on the country, plus the realpolitik of the Jews' own spreading occupation. The judge and Pinchus dueled, firing questions and answers, a contest that grew exhausting and slippery.

Finally, Pinchus stood to end the interview.

"The British have announced they will stop the hangings if the Irgun quit fighting. This is blackmail. Ridiculous."

The judge asked, "Is it?"

Pinchus flattened both hands on the table, a little man, shouting.

"Go to Acre prison. Ask the three boys sentenced to death whether they are prepared to buy their lives at the price of our revolt. They sent me letters. They say, 'Whatever happens, fight on.'"

Pinchus and his men took their first strides out of the dining room. Sandström was not quick to his feet. This slowness irked Pinchus; he whirled on the judge.

"No member of Irgun asks for mercy. Ever."

Pinchus left the small house with those words. The Judge's aides gathered their notes. The Judge asked for wine. The poet fetched a glass, for his wife was outside calming Pinchus.

CHAPTER 64

HUGO

Jerusalem

As Hugo neared the defendant's table, his lawyer presented a card. Hugo, with wrists shackled, took the card two-handed. The chains on his ankles made him hobble like an old man.

"Who hired you?"

The lawyer lifted a legal pad from a briefcase. The first page was blank. "The government. Can you afford your own barrister?"

"No."

"Then, for the moment, I'm it. How are you going to plead?"

Hugo wore the white drawstring pants and tunic of a prisoner. The lawyer dressed in a summer grey suit with silver cufflinks. A receding hairline and a beaky nose made him appear the well-bred Briton. Hugo didn't like his slate eyes, they darted, taking the measure of the court-room to see who was there to see him defend the captured Irgunist: the press, the local bar, the police, the Yishuv. Though he was on the government's pay, this was a lawyer with a reputation.

"Not guilty."

The lawyer lapped an arm across the back of his chair. "Are you certain?"

Two hundred spectators filled the pews of the District Court gallery. The Union Jack and a picture of Britain's king flanked the judge's high bench. Fourteen armed policemen ringed the courtroom; six more stood within arm's reach of Hugo.

He saw no one he recognized, not Pinchus, Julius, nor even Vince. The crowd felt ready for a commotion; the starchy cops rested hands on black gunbelts and holsters.

The lawyer waited for Hugo's answer. Why shouldn't he plead innocent? He wasn't in the basement when the Haganah man was killed, wasn't in the truck when the pistol was found.

How had Gruner pled, or Barazani and Feinstein? They were caught red-handed. Did they shout Guilty when asked? Hugo didn't know, but he was no less than they, so he would like to answer as they had. That was why this lawyer had questioned him. Didn't Hugo want to be a martyr?

The bailiff, a colorless man, called, "All rise." The courtroom got to its feet. Hugo's chains jangled.

The bailiff intoned, "Silence be upstanding in court. All persons having anything to do before the lords and ladies, the King's Justices at the District Court of Palestine, draw near and give attendance. God save the King."

With long strides, the judge in a scarlet robe entered and mounted the bench. A powdered wig capped his head, a white collar crossed tabs below his throat. He stood tall, squarely above the courtroom. He lowered into his leather chair with no more than a raised eyebrow at Hugo. In the end, Dov Gruner was hanged, and this judge got a new wig.

The bailiff announced, "Be seated."

Pews creaked when the gallery sat. The clerk announced Hugo's case. The judge nodded down at Hugo to agree that this was the place they were destined for.

He said, "Hugo Ungar."

Hugo and his lawyer stood again. Hugo's handcuffs dragged across the wooden tabletop.

The judge intoned, "Mr. Ungar, you stand before the court accused of murder, conspiracy to commit murder, and the possession of a firearm and ammunition. These are capital offenses. How do you plead?"

Hugo had the sense of acceleration, a suffocating speed. The courtroom quickened, every second sliced to a sliver. How could he think at this pace? He looked over his shoulder to the crowd; was there going to be a rescue? Faces, white and blank, gazed back. He faced the judge, the police, his lawyer, and the bailiff. The judge's face was the only one in the courtroom with wonder on it. What will you do, Hugo Ungar?

Time slowed. Hugo had to catch his balance. Every choice seemed wrong or impossible, to beg or scream, weep or disappear.

He felt closer to death than when he'd been minutes from it in Buchenwald. There, death would have been a release from a weary life. Tens of thousands around him had been on the same path. In this courtroom, death had found him alone and come marching. Facing it with no company was dreadful.

The judge folded his hands in a show of patience, to demonstrate that he was better than Hugo, safer, wealthier, powerful enough to keep his word. Hugo was small, the chains hurt his wrists and made his feet drag.

He held out his arms and let the shackles drip between them, to show them to the judge, to tell him, You are not better than me. You are not more powerful. We are in Palestine.

"Guilty."

The lawyer said nothing on Hugo's behalf.

The judge surveyed the precautions in his courtroom; he seemed to find them excessive. Twenty policemen guarded the courtroom, twenty soldiers patrolled outside. The Irgun wouldn't come, Pinchus had made no threats in Hugo's name. The judge shook his head, bewigged and grand, at his many protectors. The judge knew who Hugo was, a little fellow bound and famished and defiant.

The judge left Hugo to stand in the shifting of the gallery, the creaking benches. When he spoke, his chin rested in his hand.

"Before I pronounce sentence, I'm curious."

Hugo's shackles were quiet. He was not shaking.

"Can you guess how many lives would have been lost if you'd managed to blow up Citrus House?"

"No."

"Do you know when the explosion was planned to go off, how much dynamite was to be used?"

"No."

"Do you know anything about your mission besides driving a truck?"

"No."

"As I suspected. You lack the character to even be a proper villain."

The judge paused to allow Hugo the last seconds of his old life, to say farewell to that former man.

"Hugo Ungar, for your crimes against the Mandate of Palestine, I sentence you to hang by the neck until you are dead." Because he would not, the judge added, "May God have mercy on you."

CHAPTER 65

RIVKAH

July 5
Massuot Yitzhak

The dark mule had been named Zipporah after Moses's wife. Rivkah called her Zipp because she was slow.

Rivkah led the mule by the halter up from the quarry. In the groaning cart Zipp pulled a half-ton of cut stone. She champed at her bit and foamed around the lips. The morning sun beat on Rivkah's back, on Zipp's rump, and on the stony road. Rivkah swatted the animal's flanks with a switch to keep her plodding.

Zipp's long ears flicked up to face the white hill. Someone ran their way, raising dust. Something was wrong, urgent. Rivkah took her hands off the mule to have them ready.

Vince was the runner. She opened her arms; he could barely slow on the pebbly ground. Rivkah caught him from skidding past.

"What are you doing here? Is everything alright?"

Vince nodded against her cheek. Along with his greeting, his clasp had departure in it. Rivkah asked again, "Are you alright?"

He leaned away with hands on her waist. "I can't stay long."

"I'm happy to see you." Rivkah touched his scratchy jaw. "Why are you here? Walk with me."

She slipped her hand inside Zipp's halter to move on. Vince reached to take the bridle for her, to do her chore. Rivkah patted down his wrist; it was alright if they had different lives. Vince put his hand to the small of her back, amusing Rivkah once more with how out of place he was on a farm.

"I came with UNSCOP."

"They're here?"

Walking up the hill, Vince's long legs went too fast for Zipp and the load of stone. Rivkah kept the switch pattering on the mule's flank.

"I'm covering the Committee on a tour of Palestine. Two weeks of open meetings in Jewish and Arab towns."

"How's it going?"

"The Jews talk for hours. The Arabs boycott."

At the top of the hill, the sun streamed down on the kibbutz; heat mirages wavered off the roofs and the Committee's buses. Settlers paused in the middle of their workday, with tools on their shoulders or in aprons, to gather around the Committee. Rivkah rolled down her pants legs, buttoned her tunic, and wiped her kerchief across her dusty face. Vince said, "You're fine."

He tugged Rivkah forward, Zipp behind her, and with the squeaky cart they advanced into Massuot Yitzhak. Mrs. Pappel waved them over to her conversation with a tall, pale man who shaded his eyes from the light.

✳✳✳

Mrs. Pappel did not brew tea. The judge said he'd come to be of service to Massuot Yitzhak, not the other way around. Wearing a cream linen jacket and slacks, he sat on the porch with Mrs. Pappel and Rivkah. Vince stood aside.

Judge Sandström's questions were dignified and dispassionate, a Nordic manner that cooled the noon shade. He asked Rivkah and Mrs. Pappel how they came to be in Palestine; they told their separate tales of Vienna, their losses, and the *Patria*. The judge said he was sorry for Sweden's neutrality during the war and said that was the reason he'd accepted the job from the UN.

Mrs. Pappel asked how the Committee came to be in Massuot Yitzhak? "I hope we are not an inconvenience."

"It's a small kibbutz. You're an interruption, not an inconvenience." Sandström looked Vince's way. "He convinced me."

Rivkah asked, "What did he say?"

"That everything good in Palestine was here."

Vince grinned at his shoes. The judge paid no more attention to him, fixed on Rivkah.

"Tell me about that. The good."

She told of the kibbutz's orchards and small fields, the work desalinating the soil, terracing it, turning back the desert. Animals and tractors did their share, the rest done by hand. The hilltop commanded vistas in all directions, clean breezes and deep-set stars. Massuot Yitzhak was cold and warm, everything in between. It repaid struggle and faith. If it were given a chance, it might last a thousand years.

"How many more settlers could you support here?"

Rivkah swept her arm across the vista. "You see what I see."

Mrs. Pappel patted Rivkah's knee. "If this girl can make rocks bloom, what else might she do?"

The judge, too, reached for Rivkah, pale fingertips on her wrist. "We must find a way to let her do it."

Mrs. Pappel said, "You remind me of someone."

The judge straightened, remembering to be distant. "Who might that be?"

"Mister Pinchus."

"I've met your Mister Pinchus."

Mrs. Pappel asked, "Does he look well?"

The judge let his curiosity be obvious. Mrs. Pappel did not back away and cocked her head for an answer.

"Quite well."

"What did he have to say?"

"Some things difficult to believe. Much that wasn't."

"Can you tell us?"

"Pinchus says he is also fighting to free the Arabs from the British. He meant to give the impression that you and the Arabs might live in peace if there were an independent Jewish state. Do you agree?"

Mrs. Pappel nodded.

"You do?"

"Yes. After a war."

The judge put his elbows to his knees. The mood on the porch turned secretive.

"Pinchus says if there is a war, the Jews will win. Is this so?"

"There is an Arab. He is our friend. He's a powerful man and he would be a powerful enemy. But he's part of a clan. There are six clans alone in his town, and there are a hundred Arab towns. They have no leaders in common. In the Negev, the Bedouin follow no one. This is why we will win."

"You sound confident. So did Mister Pinchus."

"I know what he knows."

The judge laid out an open hand, a request for Mrs. Pappel to give him something he might take away, that he could tell, quietly like this, to others.

"And that is?"

"We have the guns."

The judge's hand closed around that. "You do?"

"In Kfar Etzion and Massuot Yitzhak. I have over five hundred. All hidden."

"What do you mean, you have?"

"I'm Haganah."

The judge looked to Vince, who shrugged. Rivkah had not told him of Mrs. Pappel's status or her armory.

Mrs. Pappel had multiplied the number of her hidden weapons by twenty. She gestured to Rivkah.

"This girl's sister is Palmach. What I'm saying is we are ready, in ways you will not see."

The judge tapped the arm of his porch chair.

Rivkah wanted no more talk of war. She could not send the Judge away, so she excused herself; she had more stones to move. Mrs. Pappel had a way with powerful men. The judge would not mind Rivkah's departure. She left the porch. Vince followed.

He stayed in her wake through the middle of the kibbutz. On a dozen porches, Committee diplomats spoke with more young settlers, asking what do you grow, what do you make, will you fight?

Zipporah and the cart had been emptied of their load. Rivkah took the halter to lead her back down to the quarry.

Vince asked, "Are you upset with me?" When she gave no answer, he said, "I'm sorry. I have to go."

"I have to stay."

"It won't always be this way." Vince bent to the road for a smooth, white pebble. "I'll bring this back to you."

He seemed to want to kiss her, but Rivkah shook the notion off. She walked the mule downhill to do her own work in the sun.

CHAPTER 66

JULY 19
HAIFA
BRITISH MANDATE OF PALESTINE
By Vincent Haas
Herald Tribune News Service

THE NIGHT BEFORE his ship, the *Exodus 1947,* was boarded by British Marines, American sailor Billy Bernstein told his crewmates he'd had a premonition that he would die.

Billy was not a somber man. Quite the opposite. He was a carrottop, cheerful Californian, a young veteran with the rest of his life ahead of him.

For the war, he left pre-med studies at Ohio State to join the Merchant Marine. After serving, he got accepted into the Naval Academy. But Billy put his life on hold to volunteer for Aliyah Bet, the underground effort to smuggle Jewish survivors of the European Holocaust by sea past the British blockade, into Palestine.

Billy took a berth as second mate on the *President Warfield*, a luxury steamer built in 1928 to ferry passengers and packages up and down the Chesapeake Bay. The vessel had room for 400 passengers. In 1942, the *President Warfield* was acquired by the British to serve as a troop transport. Britain gave her back to the Americans for the Normandy landings; she anchored off Omaha Beach as an accommodation ship.

Last November, the Aliyah Bet found and purchased her. The *President Warfield* was a perfect fit; built for the Chesapeake with a shallow draft, she could be refitted to hold 4,498 passengers on wooden racks not unlike what the Jews had escaped in the camps. Some dark night, at the eastern terminus of the Mediterranean, she'd be run aground in the shallows of some Palestine beach. Then, the refugees could wade ashore.

On July 11, the *President Warfield* departed the south of France, loaded with displaced persons from across Europe. The Jews carried the shards of their lives in sacks and battered valises. They hoped, but didn't really expect, to reach Palestine on this try. Since the war's end, the British have interdicted over a hundred thousand like them on sixty different Aliyah Bet ships. To date, little more than ten thousand survivors of the Nazi exterminations have made it without permits into Palestine. The Jews whom the British capture are being held at internment camps in Cyprus, with no promise of ever seeing their promised land, so long as Britain controls it.

All the Yanks on the *President Warfield* were American Jews like Billy, a dozen young men who, like him, lied to their mothers about where they were going.

For a week on the Mediterranean, their ship was trailed by two, then six British cruisers and destroyers, behemoths of guns, bullhorns and spotlights. The day before landfall, the crew and passengers of the *President Warfield* unveiled the ship's new name. They unfurled a banner down her flank which read: *Exodus 1947*.

The next night, July 18, twenty miles off the sands of Bat Yam south of Gaza, the British warships made their move. They tried to cut *Exodus* off from approaching shore. They rammed her repeatedly, but the refugee ship would not be turned away. Rather than confront thousands of immigrants splashing to the beach and thousands more Palestinian Jews rushing from towns and kibbutzim to greet them, the British decided to board the Aliyah Bet ship at sea.

In darkness, two huge destroyers pulled alongside, starboard and port. They squeezed the *Exodus*, damaging her hull, while loudspeakers demanded she cut her engines. Planks were heaved into place. British Marines flooded onboard.

The Jews were prepared for a brawl. Stacks of canned goods and bags of potatoes waited on deck, even rocks from the ballast, to be flung at the boarding party. With fists and tins of beets, the refugees battled for four hours against guns, truncheons and tear gas, the longest fight yet of any Aliyah Bet ship against British Marines.

In the melee, two young Jewish passengers were killed, one shot in the head, the other in the stomach. Billy Bernstein manned the pilot house. He had nothing with which to defend it but a fire extinguisher. He sprayed and swung it at ten Marines who together bashed him with their truncheons until Billy fell, his skull crushed. He died within the hour.

The warships escorted the *Exodus* into Haifa harbor, where I stood on the pier alongside Judge Emil Sandström, chairman of the United Nations Special Committee on Palestine. We watched British police and soldiers force the survivors of Europe's concentration camps off their ship at bayonet point, watched the refugees get doused with delousing powders. Then 4,496 Jews were herded onto three prison ships. Most went quietly, spent and afraid. The few who kept up resistance took blows for it. The immigrants were not bound for detention on Cyprus but back to holding camps in Germany, to a Europe that had become, for them, a graveyard. The Judge remarked that if this was what Britain had to do to keep their rule in Palestine, it wasn't worth it.

Two soldiers carried Billy Bernstein's body on a stretcher past the judge and me, though we didn't know who lay under the blanket. I followed the bearers, showed them my press credential, and asked who it was. They knew only that it was an American. I pulled back the cover to see a bloodied young redhead, his life given over.

I don't know what Billy Bernstein's death means. Senseless death seems to be the coinage of this struggle over Palestine. I do know he was an American, and for that I mark his passing. You can think what you want about a self-determining state for the Jews. But know that people of many nations, including ours, are dying for it. More than that, they're being killed for it. Reporting from Haifa, Palestine.

CHAPTER 67

HUGO

July 20
Jerusalem

The guard held the iron door open. Hugo asked, "Is this the same cell?"

The guard motioned him in. "It is."

"I don't want to go in there."

"I can imagine. Come on, then."

The guard put gentle pressure in Hugo's back to guide him past the bars. Hugo stepped inside the white walls and black bars; behind, keys jangled to lock him into the cage where Barazani and Feinstein had blown themselves apart.

Hugo sat on the cot, then at the table, then set a chair in the barred window to see into the Russian Compound. Looking for evidence would be too macabre, but he could not stop examining spots on the floor or divots in the plaster.

The heat in the cell encased Hugo in a torpor that made him lie on the cot. Could he sleep? The adjacent cell was empty. Hugo wanted to be sent to Acre Prison, to be near Habib, Nakar, and Weiss. He didn't know the three Irgunists personally, but their names were in the news. Their sentences had been confirmed by the British government; Hugo's had not. They were scheduled to hang in two weeks. Hugo assumed they were courageous; it might be a help to be near them. He worried that he was not linked to them; being in different prisons made them even more separate.

Hugo fell into a sweaty doze. He awoke to the workings of a key into death row.

A thick-waisted guard came close. A .45 pistol rode his hip, heavier than standard issue, a man-stopper. The gut of his starched shirt halted an inch from the bars. Blue-eyed with busted capillaries in his cheeks, he said, "Get up."

Hugo didn't have to do it, had to submit to no one, but there was no point in exercising that fact at the moment. He arose. The guard backed off.

A smallish man entered the cell block. He wore a blue suit, a gold watch fob crossed his vest. He'd lost much of his hair and combed the rest over to pretend he had more.

He carried a paper sack and introduced himself as the warden. Hugo and the warden stood close enough to shake hands through the bars but did not.

"I came to tell you a few things, Mr. Ungar. To give you a few guarantees."

"Alright."

"As long as you are my responsibility, you will be treated by the rules. You will not be accosted or harmed. You will get all your meals. You may receive small gifts such as books after they've been inspected. You may receive visits from family members and your clergy."

"I have no family."

The warden seemed authentically to take this in.

"I understand."

"Perhaps you don't."

"Perhaps not. May I ask something of you?"

"What."

"In this prison. In this cell, in fact. There have been others who were brave men. They suffered no maltreatment at my hands or at the hands of my guards. Even so, they laid a plan that would have cost me my life had they followed through. I ask you, sir, to show the same respect for me that I will for you."

"You don't want to die."

"No. I suppose you don't, either. But our situations differ."

From the paper bag, the warden pulled folded garments, the scarlet tunic and pants of the condemned.

"You'll need to put these on."

The warden pushed the clothes through the bars. He said, "I am frightened, Mr. Ungar."

"Of me?"

"The Irgun have attacked Acre prison. Whipped British soldiers and policemen. Bombed hotels and British headquarters. You would have killed hundreds at Citrus House. Not a day goes by in Palestine, sir, not a day without a shot fired or an explosion from your people, without a death or injury among mine. I was almost murdered in my own prison. Yes, sir, I am frightened. Of you."

Hugo tossed the red outfit onto the cot, then sat at the table. He'd brought the oranges to Barazani and Feinstein. The warden would be more afraid if he knew.

"You're safe from me."

"I'm relieved to hear that. What of your terrorist friends?"

"They won't come for me."

"The Irgun has done awful things whenever one of you has been sentenced to hang."

"I'm not their martyr. Warden?"

"Mr. Ungar."

"I don't want to be in this cell. Can I be moved?"

"I'll consider it."

"I've only shot one policeman who was shooting at me first. I didn't set the traps in the tunnel to Citrus House. I used to make guns. I'm a driver."

The warden took the bars in hand. He seemed a bureaucratic man: a cipher and hard to read. Hugo lifted the grey prison tunic over his head, to strip down and put on the red wool suit while the warden watched and the guard stayed back. Hugo paused, bare chested, a thumb between his ribs.

"I was in the camps. I was in Treblinka and Buchenwald."

The warden retreated. Hugo sensed something, a chance, had passed.

The warden said, "You don't know."

"Know what?"

"Last night. The two sergeants."

Backing away, the warden showed his open hands, holding no reason to trust Hugo. He said no more and left death row.

The heavy guard followed. He locked the gate with a deliberate, clanking twist of the key.

CHAPTER 68

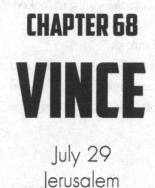

VINCE

July 29
Jerusalem

Vince ordered only tea on the YMCA patio. A dull sky did little to cut the heat; the city felt muggy and perspiring. The Arab trick of drinking something hot on a sultry day didn't work on this third morning of trying to summon Pinchus.

Vince left money on the table and walked off.

Jerusalem, a city of hills, sweated him. He labored the half-mile to the Russian Compound; half the streets were blocked by barbed wire, or sandbag bunkers and machine guns. The free avenues still bustled with shoppers and delivery trucks. Hasidim read while they walked, business-men in yarmulkes argued on corners or in stride with one another, old men and women burdened with mesh grocery bags outpaced Vince up the inclines. He stopped at a street vendor for an orange.

At the prison, Vince's press papers got him beyond a checkpoint. He wended through more twisted wire, then past the guards manning the compound's doors. He found the warden in his office. The man, small and genteel, agreed to let Vince speak privately with Hugo. This took Vince by surprise; he expected he'd have to argue.

The warden ushered Vince into the hall. "You'll let me know if you hear anything." He showed some anxiety. "About anything."

A guard escorted Vince down the arched halls of cells. Arab cheats, robbers, and scufflers remembered him from his previous stay. They called, as they had before: My friend, my friend. Can you get a message to my wife, my brother?

Half-light sieved through the skylights, failing to brighten the halls. At the end of the cell block, the guard unlocked the gate to death row. He held the bars open but did not follow.

"Shout if you need me, sir."

Vince stepped inside. The dreary day had taken hold in the small corridor with an overcast light, as if it might rain in the white walls and on Hugo, alone on his cot. Looking frail, Hugo lifted his head from his pillow.

"Vince."

"Kharda."

In red, ill-fitting prison dress, Hugo came to the bars. His pants legs and sleeves hung too long, the shoulders too wide. The clothes mocked him; Hugo wasn't big enough to fill them.

"I brought you something." Vince held the orange between the bars.

Hugo plucked it from Vince's hand. "Gallows humor." He shook it beside his ear, playacting to raise a smile from Vince.

Hugo peeled the orange and gave back half. The cell was neat, absent of anything comforting or personal. Save for the wrinkles on the cot, no one seemed to reside here.

Hugo brought a chair to sit in front of the bars. "Stay a while."

Vince folded his legs under him on the concrete floor. He looked up at Hugo, something he'd never done.

"I'm sorry you're in here."

"I promised you a story. You first. How have you been?"

Vince described his travels with UNSCOP. He told of the ugliness around the *Exodus* on the Haifa pier a week ago. The Committee had left Palestine, headed for Lebanon and Trans-Jordan, then to Europe to tour displaced persons camps. Vince made no mention of the judge's meeting with Pinchus, or Massuot Yitzhak, or the concert in Ein Harod, or Rivkah.

Hugo listened with ankles crossed. Vince had first seen him like this: bony, dwindled.

Hugo tapped his temple. "Where is your pencil? I've never seen you without it."

"I don't need it anymore. I remember everything."

"That's a very Jewish thing to say."

To cheer him, Vince said, "You don't belong in here."

Hugo sucked his teeth as if some part of him hurt. "Don't tell me that."

"Why not?"

"If I thought I didn't belong on death row, I couldn't stand it." Hugo leaned elbows to his knees, face close to the bars. "In Buchenwald, I was there because I was a Jew. We were hated in Germany, we suffered. But there was no mistake, I had to be there. I could tell myself I had no choice, no options."

Hugo indicated the empty cell around him.

"I'm here because I'm a Jew. Because I'm Irgun. Because I deserve it. If I believe anything else, if I think a mistake has been made or I haven't earned it, I'll go insane before they can hang me."

Hugo told Vince about Goldschmidt House, the policeman he'd shot to death. He'd helped kidnap the same judge who'd sentenced him to die. He'd delivered the oranges to Barazani and Feinstein. He was the potato merchant who found the warehouse for the tunnel that might have killed hundreds in Citrus House and did kill Zeev Weber.

Hugo crossed his arms and dropped his chin. He'd arrived at the end of his story outside prison; the rest of it would be lived inside. He'd tired himself. Vince stood, preparing to leave.

"The warden's afraid of you."

"I know. But thank you for saying that. Why did you come?"

"Pinchus is in a fury. This week, there's been attacks all over the country. Road mines, mortars, railroad tracks, shootings, bombings. Eight police have been killed. Eighty wounded."

"Good."

"I'm not going to argue with you over that."

"Then why are you telling me?"

"I can't get in touch with Pinchus."

"I think his calendar is full. Why do you want him?"

"The three at Acre. Habib, Nakar, and Weiss. They're going to be executed in four days. I've tried to get into Acre to interview them. The British tell me no every time."

"Pinchus can't help with that."

"No. But the Irgun kidnapped two British sergeants in Netanya. They've been missing for a couple of weeks. Pinchus has said he'll hang them if the three Irgunists hang."

"You can assume he means it."

"I want to ask him to stop. I want to speak to the sergeants."

"Why? They're dead men."

"I can put faces to their names. I can write who they are, their stories. Maybe the Yishuv will act, maybe something or someone can save them. Maybe if Pinchus promises not to kill the sergeants, the British will show some fucking mercy. I don't know. But Pinchus is political. If we can turn public opinion, he might re-think it."

"Why would Pinchus let you talk to his hostages?"

"He owes me a favor."

Hugo plucked the red garb away from his chest. "What do you think he owes me?" Hugo stood and replaced the chair at the table. "It's not like you. You're so involved. What's changed?"

"Nothing."

"Is it the girl?"

"Mind your business, Hugo."

"I don't have to mind my business. I don't have to do anything. What do you want?"

"Can you contact Pinchus for me?"

"I'm not sure. I haven't tried. Why should I?"

"Men will die if we don't."

"Men are going to die, Vince. I'll probably be one of them. Write about me."

"Will you do it?"

Hugo lay on the cot, on his back. Vince looked at the hemp soles of Hugo's prison shoes, waiting for him to say something.

After enough silence, Vince said, "I know there's an Irgun network in the jail."

"There is."

"Will you try?

"Will you come back to visit me?"

"Yes."

Hugo gazed at his white ceiling. "Will you come to my hanging?"

"Hugo."

"Will you write about it?"

"Yes."

"You'll remember everything we said today."

"I will."

Hugo rolled onto his side, knees bent, hands joined at his chest. His focus fixed on the floor as if searching it.

"I'll try."

Vince didn't say goodbye, not sure how to leave the condemned. At the gate, he called, "Guard."

CHAPTER 69

VINCE

July 31

Vince was awake when a note skidded under his door.

He leaped from his dark bed. No moon shined on Jerusalem, and he knocked his knee on a chair leg rushing for the doorknob.

Vince flung the door open. In the bright hallway, a man in a red servant's vest hurried away. Vince called after him, "Hey." The man should not have looked back because Vince recognized him, one of the black-haired waiters from the Y's patio. He scurried around a corner.

Inside the room, Vince tore into the envelope. In handwritten script, the note read: *It is done. Go to Netanya. P.*

Vince moved in front of the open window. Far below, trucks and buses were the only traffic, too early for doves to coo on the sills of the King David across the street. A half mile away in silhouette lay Jerusalem's Old City.

Habib, Nakar, and Weiss had been hanged yesterday.

Now, the sergeants.

Hugo hadn't gotten to Pinchus in time. Or Pinchus had ignored him. *It is done.*

Vince stuffed a duffel bag, then left the YMCA hotel.

The drive to Netanya would take an hour and a half, down from Jerusalem into the Bab al-Wad gorge, between bookending cliffs and overlooking Arab villages. Halfway to Tel Aviv, the sun rose on Vince; he managed to pass the city before traffic awoke.

Driving in the breaking light, the salt smell of the sea flowed in his window. Ten miles north of Tel Aviv, the roadblocks began. Vince idled in a line of trucks and taxis until his car was searched. Policemen rooted in his trunk and duffel; a young cop took his credentials, then told Vince to move along.

Closer to Netanya, the cordon grew tighter. Armored police trucks girding the road, checkpoints every mile, evidenced the government's fury over the sergeants' kidnapping. Foot patrols and motorcycle cops filtered through neighborhoods, snooped through the warehouses and back-lots of Netanya's commercial area. Two thousand police and soldiers put Netanya through a strainer, screening the ways in and out, casting open every door, kicking into the shadows to find their two missing mates.

Vince drove to the Netanya police precinct. He passed more check-points, wire, gates, and guns to get inside. The building was warm, ceiling fans roused the humid coastal air; handcuffed Jews filled every chair, bench, and corner. Vince found nowhere to sit. He and another reporter, a thin Londoner from the *Times*, wandered among the detainees and the cops guarding them. One at a time, the Jews swept up in the search were escorted behind closed doors. More were brought into the precinct every minute, all with hands bound.

With the Londoner, Vince sipped burnt coffee offered by the duty officer. The Londoner had served in the Royal Navy and talked of stalking German U-boats in the Atlantic.

He'd seen this before, what he called the death of an era. He meant change, but he called it dying. The German war machine, the British Empire, all dead. He said that he, too, was dying.

The reporter took from his coat pocket a rumpled, unopened pack of cigarettes. "Carried these bastards for four months. I thought if I stopped it might help."

He gave Vince the pack.

"Been here a while now. I'd like to see this bloody deal to the finish. String a few up here and there, ours and theirs, if that's what it takes to speed things along. I don't mind. I'd just like to know how it ends."

Vince wanted to be done with the Londoner's company. Before he could drift away, a cop beckoned them both to follow down a crowded hall. Vince slid past Jews waiting to be questioned, among them women, teenagers, and elderly. He and the Londoner were ushered into a police captain's office.

The officer was a drowsy man with a droopy face, or maybe that was the morning he was having.

"You're New York. You're London. Right?"

Vince and the reporter lifted hands like schoolmates.

"I've sent a dozen of your lot out already this morning with patrols. We're getting calls claiming to be Irgun, telling us the bodies are here and there. I've got teams watching both the sergeants' houses. Someone phoned in to say they were going to be strung up in their own front yards. Sons of bitches." The captain tapped the black phone on his desk. "I just got off the line with the precinct in Jaffa. They had a caller who was quite specific. A map coordinate."

The captain fingered a note on his mussy desk. He muttered a number—13751895—that meant nothing to Vince.

"That's a mile outside Netanya. It's in a eucalyptus grove. You two interested?"

The Londoner said, "Yes."

"The site might be mined. There might be snipers. I have no earth-ly clue what else the sons of bitches can think of. But this doesn't sound like a goose chase, not this one. Leave your cars here, you'll ride with my boys."

Outside the precinct, three squad cars idled. Vince separated from the Londoner and climbed into one. He gave the crumpled cigarette pack to the young cop beside him on the back seat. The boy, still a teen, tore it open and took a stick. He handed the rest around.

"Someone give me a light."

Pulling away from the precinct, the driver eyed his comrade in the rearview. "Laddie, you don't smoke."

The cigarette wagged on the young cop's lips, like an old hand. "I'm starting."

✳ ✳ ✳

At the curb, a soldier met Vince, the Londoner, and the ten cops loading out of the squad cars. "This way." A dozen military vehicles were already parked on the street. Vince followed into the trees.

Single file, they walked a meandering path. The eucalyptus grove felt not like a forest but an orchard, planted and peaceful. The gray branches weren't thick or leafy; the ground stayed mottled and sunny. The Londoner coughed again, a grating sound in the quiet little forest.

In the spotty shade, fifty soldiers, police, and civilians stood in a semicircle. The soldiers were Welsh Guard, in berets and high socks. Vince slipped past to see more clearly the pair of hanged corpses.

A firm hand stopped him. "Go no further, sir." A big corporal behind a brown moustache released Vince's arm. "They're sweeping for mines. Best to keep a distance."

Vince nodded thanks. The large soldier folded heavy arms and chewed on his moustache.

The bodies dangled from nooses slung over low branches; they'd been tied wrist and ankle, bare toes floated inches off the ground. Both wore khaki pants and white undershirts, tunics tied around their heads as blindfolds. Notes were pinned to their chests. No one was allowed close enough to read them.

Two sappers walked slow circles around the sergeants, skimming the flat saucers of their metal detectors over the ground. No breeze swayed the trees, birds seemed to take no liking to the place. The corporal beside Vince cursed under his breath.

"You're not a Jew, are you?"

"No."

"What, then?"

"American. Press."

"Right."

The soldier stared at the bodies as if he saw them for the first time every second.

"This is bad."

"I know."

The Welshman shook his great head. "No, sir. You don't."

The crowd was left alone with the suspended corpses while the two sappers cleared the ground. In an audible whisper, one policeman lectured a civilian near him, likely a Jew from Netanya, perhaps an official making some complaint. Within moments, every soldier and cop began to murmur, unbottling their disgust.

A captain of the Welsh Guard had waited long enough. He stepped out of the semicircle to bark at one of the sappers, to know if they'd completed their job. He was told they wanted to go over the ground one more time. The captain said, "Bollocks."

He produced a knife, then moved to the first strung-up corpse. The sappers stopped circling. The big corporal beside Vince stepped out to assist; a few policemen padded, too, toward their murdered comrades.

Before slicing the rope away from the first body, the captain unraveled the shirt from the corpse's head to make sure everyone saw the young sergeant's swollen blue face. The officer unpinned the paper from the undershirt; this he walked to one of his men who announced to the crowd it was a handwritten death sentence from the Irgun.

With one slash of his blade the captain cut the noose. He made no effort to catch the body.

The corpse collapsed into a kneel; for a moment it appeared to beg. Before the captain could cut down the second sergeant, the body on dead knees vanished in a burst of fire. Vince, the soldiers, and the cops dove for the earth.

Vince scrambled to his feet, ears ringing. The Welsh captain writhed in the dirt, scorched and alive. The boobytrapped corpse had been obliterated. The detonation had hurled the other sergeant into the weeds, still at the end of a noose tied to a broken branch.

Cops and soldiers leaped off the ground, weapons drawn, searching for threat. The corporal had been knocked facedown, and the back of his uniform was shredded.

Vince sprinted to the downed captain. The bomb had badly scored the man's arms and face. Vince pressed both hands into the officer's smoking chest, trying not to hurt him but needing to keep him down and still. The captain tried to roll over as if he were still aflame; Vince shouted that he was going to be alright. A private skidded to his knees to ask what he could do; Vince told him to run out of the grove to the street, call his headquarters and report what happened, have them send an ambulance. The boy flashed away into the trees.

The reporter from London walked up. He coughed, then turned away, taking notes.

On the ground, the captain was wild; he would not pass out. Others helped Vince pin him down. No one in the crowd had anything for his pain. Soldiers leaned in close to say, "We'll find them, sir. We'll get the bastards."

Vince left the captain to his men. The two sappers inched closer to the second corpse with metal detectors. The body's face lay exposed, wrenched and blue as the other.

The big corporal with a tattered back regained his feet, to order soldiers to locate and mark body parts. The rest of his squad he arrayed in a perimeter to protect the people in the grove.

Vince wasn't concerned. Pinchus had come and gone.

CHAPTER 70

RIVKAH

August 2
Massuot Yitzhak

On the dark porch, Malik recited a poem, the dream of a thirst-dying man. Mrs. Pappel and Rivkah would not sip their tea during his performance, wishing to be mannerly. Mrs. Pappel despised cool tea; she tapped lightly against the cup where Malik would not see it.

Malik interrupted himself, to raise a big palm. "Do you hear that?"

Mrs. Pappel said, "Yes."

Malik's camel, always on guard in the night, grumbled. Malik's hand went into his sleeve. "Someone is coming."

Mrs. Pappel stood on the porch step. "I don't see headlights."

Rivkah asked, "Who could it be this time of night?"

Mrs. Pappel entered the house to blow out the lantern in the kitchen.

Rivkah rose from her chair. Malik gripped her wrist. "Where are you going?"

"Someone's coming up the hill."

"Yes. And what will you do?" Malik blotted out much of the night. "It is dark. The someone who has come does not want to be seen. It is a car with its lights off. We do not know what they intend."

Mrs. Pappel emerged, pistol in hand. Malik pulled a handgun from his sleeve. Mrs. Pappel said to Rivkah, "Stay here."

"I'm going with you."

"Malik." Mrs. Pappel hurried off the porch.

Malik lapped a big hand on Rivkah's shoulder. He dipped his face. "If they are friends, we will bring them to you. If they are not…" Malik shrugged. "This is not for you. Stay here."

When he turned away, his robes swirled across Rivkah's legs. The camel bleated from a different place. The beast was moving with Malik.

The pale dome of Jerusalem lit the northern horizon, Arab Nahalin glowed on its hill. Stars and a half-moon glossed the ground to make inky shadows. Rivkah saw nothing on the quarry road, not Malik or Mrs. Pappel or intruders.

She moved under the open sky. No one ran among the buildings, no one called alarm, the rest of the kibbutz was unaware.

On the quarry road, the unseen car's motor revved, not skulking any longer. Rivkah hurried back to the porch; the car sped uphill, toward her.

A gunshot popped in the night, and another. The car's engine wound tighter, working up the slope, still without headlamps. Two shots answered, not from the road but the hillside, Malik and Mrs. Pappel firing back. Rivkah crouched on the darkened porch. She clutched the stones of her house with shaking hands.

The car neared the crest of the hill, invisible but roaring. Behind it another shot crackled, and Malik's strong voice sailed up the slope, bellowing the alert.

Rivkah chanced a glance from behind the porch wall. A fat car, black and grimacing, raised a rooster tail rushing along the edge of the kibbutz. The first settlers emerged from their homes, calling to each other. The car barreled at Rivkah's darkened house.

The vehicle slid on the gravel to stop. A dust cloud trailing it caught up and drifted past. In the driver's window, a pistol was leveled, too dark to see the face behind it. Rivkah dropped behind the low porch wall. She shuddered at each bullet smashing her windows and pelting the front door. The shots rang loudly but did not mask Malik's running scream of "No!"

The car fishtailed into a U-turn to run across open ground before it crashed through a fence, back to the unpaved road. Shots from Malik and Mrs. Pappel chased it downhill.

Rivkah stepped over broken glass on the porch, out to the road, into the tracks of the car. At the bottom of the hill, the vehicle cut on its lights among the empty hills. Haverim came to stand with Rivkah and watch the raiders depart. Rivkah stayed in the road until Mrs. Pappel came running out of the dark calling her name.

CHAPTER 71

RIVKAH

August 3

Rivkah sat on a broiling rock in a field of stones, mopping her brow. The distance wobbled with warped mirages. In this wincing heat, Vince arrived.

She was quick to embrace him, despite her sweat and the other settlers watching. She and Vince did not kiss or whisper greetings or news, she only closed her eyes against him to feel him searing and breathing. Vince stepped back, making a show of beholding her.

"I came as soon as I heard about the shooting."

"How did you find out?"

"I read a police report. Let's go up to the house."

Rivkah said, "I have to finish here. You go ahead. I'll be an hour. Will you stay?"

"Yes."

"How long?"

"I don't know."

"What does that mean?"

"I checked out of my room at the YMCA hotel."

"Do you mean it?"

"I'll sleep at the guest house."

"You'll sleep on our sofa."

"What'll Mrs. Pappel say?"

"Many things. But the last thing she'll say will be yes."

"Do you have any idea who shot at you?"

"No. Do you?"

"Probably the cops."

"Why?"

"You know about the hangings. The sergeants."

"Yes."

"I was there."

"How terrible. I'm sorry."

Vince only nodded. The smallness of the gesture spoke to the horrors. "Get out of this heat. I'll see you soon."

Rivkah swiped the kerchief over her face. Vince backed away up the hill, taking many steps without turning.

✳ ✳ ✳

Vince opened the door; he'd been watching for her. On the couch lay a pillow and folded blanket, a full duffel on the floor. Vince closed the perforated door; a pair of bullet holes let in light.

He said, "That wasn't in the report."

Mrs. Pappel emerged from her room. "He's staying." Mrs. Pappel threw up her hands.

Rivkah headed for her bedroom. "I'll shower. Don't exhaust him."

Once she'd toweled off and dressed, Rivkah found Vince and Mrs. Pappel on the porch sipping tea. Vince sweated; Rivkah fetched a fresh kerchief. Would he stay long enough to grow used to the extremes on the rim of the desert?

Mrs. Pappel said, "We waited for you. I didn't want Vince to have to tell it twice."

Vince spoke first about Hugo, the little Irgunist who came with him months ago to rattle a pistol in their faces. He was in Jerusalem on death row, guilty of the murder of a Haganah fighter and possession of a weapon. Mrs. Pappel and Rivkah had heard the news of Hugo Ungar's conviction, but nothing more. Mrs. Pappel said a man with Hugo's sadness was bound for such a fate. Vince offered no defense; perhaps they were no longer friends.

Mrs. Pappel leaned to touch his hand. "What of Netanya?"

Vince rubbed his palms together, hesitating. "Pinchus."

Mrs. Pappel nodded. "I expect so."

"He wanted a crowd. He made sure the cops got a bunch of false calls to whip everybody up looking for the sergeants. One call was so specific; everybody knew that was it. Pinchus played us like a violin. Cops, soldiers, the press, people from the town, everybody flocked to a eucalyptus grove in Netanya."

Vince called it a peaceful, dappled place. Already he was selecting the language for his column to America.

"A soldier in the grove warned me it was bad. He said I couldn't know how bad it was."

Rivkah asked, "What does that mean?"

"Boobytrapping the bodies of those sergeants might have been the last straw. Add that to the King David, the Goldschmidt House, all the whippings and kidnappings, bombings and violence for two solid years. This might've broken loose something in the British."

"What?"

"I think rage."

Mrs. Pappel nodded. "That's why they shot up our house."

"This sort of thing is going on all over Palestine. Vigilantes are firing into Jewish buses and taxis, beating up Jews in the street. It's bad in England, too. Synagogues are getting vandalized, shops and factories are being torched."

"I've seen this before," said Mrs. Pappel. "We all have."

"It won't be long until Pinchus answers."

Rivkah said, "He's a monster."

Mrs. Pappel asked, "Why do you say that?"

"He only creates the need for himself. Violence makes more violence."

Mrs. Pappel said, "I won't argue with you over this, Liebling. Vince, why don't you take Rivkah for a walk."

Rivkah let him lift her by the hand from the porch chair. Together they stepped out into the warm, waning dusk.

The settlers of Massuot Yitzhak filed out of the dining hall. Vince and Rivkah held hands, and without jealousy the young men dipped their heads. Many of the teen girls joined hands to swing arms in a parody of the two strolling.

CHAPTER 72

VINCE

Vince steered her onto the path to the orange orchard. They strode down the rows of young trees, under the calming wonder of the blossoms.

He said, "I'm from Brooklyn."

"I don't know what that means."

"It's a part of New York. Small yards, tight houses. My mother grows four tomato plants. My father takes ten minutes to cut the grass with a push mower. I live in an apartment in the city. I don't know how to do any of this."

He trailed a hand through the citrus branches. The leaves rustled with the swish of a dress. He'd not seen Rivkah in a dress.

"I don't know how to cut stone. I can't build anything. My father's a millwright at a shipyard. He doesn't keep tools in the house. I don't cook."

"You can carry a bucket."

"I made six trips before I sat on it."

Vince stopped walking and framed Rivkah's shoulders with his hands. The day's last rays played in the orchard's leaves; the light made Rivkah pink and the reclaimed earth rosy.

"I wired Dennis, my editor in New York. I let him know I was coming here for a while."

"A while."

"What do you want me to say?"

"What did you tell him?"

"I said the story of Palestine is here on the frontier as much as anywhere else."

"Did you mention me to Dennis the editor?"

"I did."

"And?"

From his pocket, Vince produced the smooth pebble he'd taken away when he visited with UNSCOP.

"Do you want me to make you a promise?"

She took the pebble from Vince and tossed it among the orange trees.

"No one in Palestine can make a promise and be sure of keeping it. Only Pinchus."

Rivkah pulled him by the hand.

"Let's go back. Mrs. Pappel will figure out work for you."

CHAPTER 73

HUGO

September 5
Jerusalem

Hugo laid a towel on the tile floor for his knees. His bones sometimes ached, a legacy of the camps. Kneeling, he wrestled the white porcelain toilet bowl over a new wax seal.

From the bedroom, through the open door, the warden called, "How's it going?"

"Five minutes."

Hugo caulked the edges, matched the bolts and nuts, and tightened his work. He secured the water tank, then turned the spigot to fill it. The warden left the easy chair beside his bed to stand in the doorway. Hugo gave him the honor of the first flush.

"There," the warden said to the swirling water. "Like a dream."

Hugo asked, "Do you cut your own hair?"

"I do. Why?"

"Throw the hair in the trash. Not the toilet."

Hugo gathered up the tools the warden had assembled: wrenches, a wire snake, caulk gun, hammer, and screwdrivers. The warden said to leave them.

"Guard."

The warden backed out of the small bathroom; he didn't help Hugo to his feet. The armed guard took Hugo's place to gather the tools.

Hugo followed into the den. A second guard leaned against a wall. The warden indicated a stuffed chair for Hugo to sit.

The apartment was sparsely decorated, a touch of temporariness. The tables had doilies, the walls a few framed pictures, a handful of books lined a shelf, and the windows were curtained.

"Tea?"

"With a splash of milk."

The warden sat across from Hugo in a similar chair. Without instruction, the guard entered the kitchen where he padded about, sifting through drawers and cabinets. The warden made a tsk-ing noise.

"Because of you terrorists, I do not have my wife with me. I have a clod there making my tea."

"Apologies."

"Do you play chess?"

"No. You could teach me."

"I'm afraid that would take years." The warden pressed fingers over his lips. "That was an inappropriate jest. You must think me an ass."

Hugo waved it off. "I hear the guard laughing. It wasn't a waste."

"Checkers, then."

The warden set up a game table. He let Hugo choose, red or black, fire or smoke. Hugo picked smoke and began the game.

With his corresponding move, eyeing the board, the warden said, "What an odd thing, that you turn out to be an excellent plumber."

Hugo responded with a checker, then leaned back. "Why is it odd?"

"I suppose it's convenient to think of you as a killer and little else. In any case, I'm pleased. How did you find out about my toilet clog?"

"Some of the guards make fun of you as a dandy. It was mentioned. So, I thought while I was here I would fix it for you."

The warden answered with his own move. "Why did you do it?"

"I swore I would never be a plumber again. The thought repelled me. A man swears things. He means them when he does it. I did. Now I understand no one can know what's coming. A clock can, yes, a clock. And a calendar. Not a man."

The warden winced at Hugo as if recalculating something. He sat back in his pillowy chair.

"If you could choose. We know you can't, but if you could. Would you be better off if you'd become a plumber here in Palestine?"

Hugo lifted one of his black checkers.

"I didn't know Gruner, or Barazani and Feinstein. Or any of the others. I knew men like them. When they swore they would die for the Irgun and independence, they meant it. The ones who got hanged were given chances to save their lives, at least prolong them. They all refused. For each, the Irgun mounted an incredible effort to save them, or retaliate. But I."

Hugo set down a checker on the board.

"I'm Irgun, too. I've been treated like a plumber. So I fixed your fucking toilet."

He pushed the checker to a new square.

"My actions killed a Jew. So be it. If I'd killed an Englishman, there would be a fury swirling around to free me."

The warden, a man who jailed men but did not seem to judge them, nodded.

Hugo said, "In an odd sense, we have the Nazis to thank for this. Killing a Jew has become one of the worst acts in the world. You British have done a bit of it, and look. You're being tossed out of Palestine, though we've killed many more of yours than you have of ours. I did it, killed one Jew, and here we sit."

The guard brought a tray of china cups, teapot, and a small pitcher of milk. Hugo raised both hands at the warden, surrendering his own irritability.

"Yes. Of course, I'd be a plumber."

The warden poured. "Have you considered, Mr. Ungar, that perhaps your lack of notoriety is the best thing you have going for you?"

The tea tasted better, warmer, than any he had been given on death row. The chair sat more pleasantly. The windows lacked bars and the warden, his conversation partner, wore no uniform, nor was he a ghost. Hope was being dangled. No one could predict.

"How so?"

The warden set aside his tea. It appeared he'd brought Hugo to his quarters not for the toilet, tea, or checkers, but to have this chat.

"I was not pleased to learn that my prison was going to receive you. Another Irgunist bound for the gallows." The warden gestured for the guard to stop looming and step back. "The fact that you are being ignored may cause you grief. If one must die, better to do it celebrated, avenged, and all that. But to be truthful, I am safer, my guards and your fellow inmates are safer, if you are forgotten."

"What if I don't want to be forgotten?"

"What if you may not die?"

Hugo's spine straightened off the chair. He palmed another dark checker from the board to bleed off some of his excitement. "Go on."

"I assume you are unaware that the United Nations Special Committee on Palestine has released its report."

"When did that happen?"

"Last week."

"News comes slowly to death row. What did they say?"

"The committee has concluded unanimously that the Mandate must be ended. Palestine should be granted its independence as soon as practicable."

"I should like to see that."

"Forgive me, Mister Ungar. I expected a more enthusiastic response."

"To be fair, I've never thought much about independence. I was drawn to the fight mostly because I lost my tolerance for being helpless. I simply wanted to fight. I won't expect you to understand."

"I'm trying."

"I have a friend, an American reporter. He tries to understand, as well. I don't know that he ever will. May we return to the topic of my not dying?"

"UNSCOP's report recommends the partition of Palestine into Jewish and Arab states. The Jewish land will contain half a million Jews and four hundred thousand Arabs. The Arab state will hold seven hundred thousand Arabs and ten thousand Jews. The Jews will get land in the Negev, the coast from Tel Aviv to Haifa, and the eastern Galilee. The Arabs get Gaza, western Galilee, and all the highlands of Samaria and Judea, with the exception of Jerusalem. That city will become an enclave under the UN's protection."

Hugo wagged a finger. "The Jews will not accept this."

"On the contrary. The Arabs are the ones who rejected it. Your Jewish Agency has embraced the plan. They've argued, of course, that the boundaries are not final. But they see that UNSCOP has finally proposed an independent Jewish nation. It's considered a start. You realize how that affects you."

"I will not be hanged in a Jewish nation."

"You will not. But…there is a fly in the ointment."

Hugo put the checker between his teeth. He bit lightly, then placed it back on its square.

The warden said, "The committee has advised a two-year transition period. Palestine will continue to be governed by the British, overseen by the UN. Full independence will be granted after constitutions are in place and treaties exist between both states."

"Two years."

Hugo wouldn't survive death row for two years. With no threats from Pinchus, no press from Vince, no sergeants kidnapped on his behalf, the British would have little reason not to settle their accounts before packing up for home.

Hugo rose from the chair. Both armed guards stepped his way. The warden kept his seat.

"Thank you for the update, warden. May we play another game when I'm feeling up to it?"

"Of course. A few items to consider before you go?"

"What."

"The judge who sentenced you to hang has been reassigned to Tanganyika. The Jewish Agency has their hands full politicking and grabbing all the land they can before the final boundaries are set. Your Irgun and Haganah will fight for every inch of land they wish to hold onto. We British are determined to disentangle ourselves from this country as soon as possible. What I'm saying, Mr. Ungar, is that if you will let yourself be overlooked, then perhaps you will be. Do not agitate. You may be spared. And I will not die in a blast in Palestine."

Hugo approached a window opening onto the plaza outside the compound. The warden's apartment was on the first floor. Hugo had no notion of jumping and running. He was not that kind of Irgun. He settled once more into the chair across the checkerboard from the warden.

"Do not ask me again to be a plumber. I should like to keep my word to myself at some point."

"I understand."

"I believe it is my move."

CHAPTER 74

VINCE

September 24
Massuot Yitzhak

When the meal was over, everyone took their plates, flatware, and cups to the dining hall counter. Every child old enough to walk did the same, bearing plates and cups with great care.

The hall settled, the cooks emerged untying their aprons, and the one hundred and twenty-five pioneers of Massuot Yitzhak prepared to hear Vince.

Mrs. Pappel asked him, "Ready?"

Rivkah laid a hand on his arm. She'd tied back her ebony hair, worn longer than when they'd first met, and around her shoulders a deep blue wrap. Vince had not seen her in a swath of color like this, only in white tunics and khaki pants. Her face seemed to rest on a pedestal of sapphire.

Mrs. Pappel moved to the front of the hall. Behind her stretched a wall-length mural of labor, of young women and men planting or rolling boulders; a boy and girl in the foreground held high a sheaf of wheat and a bright red apple.

Mrs. Pappel faced the haverim. She appeared quintessential, as if she belonged in the mural. She was the oldest person in the dining hall. Vince was next.

After a sweeping gaze, Mrs. Pappel said, "Vincent Haas is an American journalist. He's come to us not as a newspaperman, but as a friend. Vince has spent the past two years covering Palestine. In that time, he's seen more than any of us. I've asked him to speak. Listen to him."

Rivkah's hand slid from Vince's wrist; he rose without applause and took Mrs. Pappel's place before the painting. The Jews in the dining hall weren't like the ones in the mural, stylized people working the fields and orchards, stripping stone from the quarry. None of the painted figures strained or sweat, none looked exhausted. The real pioneers held children on their laps; they'd smoothed and cleaned their hair and clothes as best they could. They were wiry more than muscular and the wind had scored their young eyes. They were tired to the last of them.

"Massuot Yitzhak. Thank you for welcoming me."

Rivkah's blue shoulders stood out from the crowd. Vince focused away from her.

"As you know, yesterday the British rejected the United Nations plan for the partition of Palestine into separate Arab and Jewish states. Britain doesn't want to stay here two more years. They're going to leave, sometime next year. There's no date set, but there's no doubt anymore. Before they go, the UN will draw a map that will divide up what lands you get and what the Arabs get."

Among the first tables, a child of eight stood beside his father. The boy swelled his chest as though to make sure Vince knew he was a pioneer, too.

"Massuot Yitzhak is on the frontier. You're surrounded by Arabs. That's not going to change. Any map the UN draws will put the whole Etzion bloc inside Arab territory. You'll still be isolated, still surrounded. But there's going to be one important difference. Britain is done playing referee. There'll be no more soldiers or police to stand between you and the Arabs. Not the UN, not Britain or America. No one. The world is going to leave you and the Arabs to figure this out on your own."

Mrs. Pappel got to her feet.

"The Arabs are not going to let us keep our land. If we want to stay, we will have to fight. Massuot Yitzhak, Kfar Etzion, Ein Tzurim, Revadim. All of us together. Do you understand this?"

The settlers nodded and wrapped themselves in their arms. The little boy with the puffed chest nodded, too.

Mrs. Pappel lay a hand over her heart to say she was sorry, but she could not say or do anything else.

"Some of you remember Mister Pinchus's visit two years ago. He told us then that a war was coming. It's here, my friends. I have reached out to him and to the Haganah for training, reinforcements, and weapons." Mrs. Pappel indicated Vince. "Until they respond, I've asked Vince to organize the defense of Massuot Yitzhak."

Mrs. Pappel returned to her seat. In the dining hall, a hand went up to Vince, a reminder that many of these settlers were still school age.

"Yes."

"Were you in the American army?"

"I was a U.S. Marine."

"Did you fight in a war?"

"No. I was in Cuba. On guard duty."

"A guard?"

"What's your name?"

"Aharon."

"Listen to me, Aharon. There's a hundred of you in this hall old enough to fight. Maybe three hundred in the whole bloc. I don't know how many guns you've got. The Arabs will outnumber you, by a lot. But if you have a plan, if you train, if you build defenses, you've got a chance to hold out against greater odds. One defender inside a fortress is worth three attackers, maybe more. We need to make Massuot Yitzhak a fortress. I know how to get you ready. And I have an idea you'll fight well enough."

Aharon seemed satisfied with Vince's answer. Vince waited to allow the next question from the hall. None came.

"We'll also prepare an evacuation plan."

Voices raised at this. We won't leave. We stay. Vince spoke over them.

"That will depend on your government. All I'm saying is you need to be ready for whatever happens. That's the smart thing. Tomorrow, I want everyone to assemble at noon, outside the dining hall. Then we'll start."

Vince took his seat across from Mrs. Pappel and Rivkah. The meeting wrapped up; the haverim went out into the dark, back to their homes. Dozens filed past Vince to thank him. The proud boy and his father walked up last. The father shook Vince's hand, a firm squeeze, then the boy shook in the same fashion.

Once the hall had emptied, Mrs. Pappel rose. "You did very well."

"We'll see."

"Come on then, you two."

The walk to their house passed gardens and the mewls of barn animals. Because they would only work half a day tomorrow, a few machinists grinded in their shops; the generators hummed to power them. This made the early night in Massuot Yitzhak unquiet and industrious.

✳ ✳ ✳

Rivkah sat on the porch in lantern light. She wore her shawl over her head like a widow.

"Tell me the truth."

Vince said, "Always."

"Can we win?"

"Maybe."

"I'll start setting up a clinic in the guest house. We'll make bandages, find beds."

"I want you to be safe."

"Malik taught me to shoot."

"You any good?"

"I don't think so. We'll see."

"That scares me."

"Vince. What will you do?"

He came back to the porch to sit close. "What I have to."

She lay a hand in his. Vince eased back the hood of Rivkah's shawl. He pushed her black hair behind one ear, for no reason other than to show he would care for her in every way he could.

CHAPTER 75

VINCE

September 26

Scrub brush dotted the slope. Below the orchard, wildflowers grew in clumps, cyclamens and anemones.

Vince said, "From here up to the grove. Burn everything."

He hefted one gas cannister, Mrs. Pappel the other. They sprinkled fuel over the flowers and scraggly growth. Vince struck a match to ignite a line of shrubs. Twenty yards away, Mrs. Pappel did the same. Together they charred the hillside, stripped it down to pebbles, leaving nowhere to hide.

They climbed to the orchard above the burning incline. On the edge of the citrus trees, Vince indicated six spots, twenty feet apart. "Three firing lanes, two guns on each. We'll need sandbags."

They refilled their cans at the machine shop, then headed for the southern slope to scorch it clean, too. On the long decline to the wadi, Vince made a map of every rut and boulder where an attacker might conceal himself. On the far side of the wadi rose Rock Hill, commanding the valley and the access road between Kfar Etzion and Massuot Yitzhak.

Vince and Mrs. Pappel torched every bush and blossom for one hundred fifty yards, as far as the Abu Rish. He made notes of where strongpoints might be hacked into the slope and trenches dug between them for communications and support. The pioneers had already transformed this impossible land into a garden. They'd need to change again to hold it.

✳✳✳

The settlers came in from the fields, shops, tannery, barns, quarry, and kitchen. At noon, they laid aside their tools and arrived outside the dining hall in hats, bibs, gloves, and bandanas.

On a pair of blankets, Mrs. Pappel spread her arsenal: fifteen rifles, ten revolvers, five Sten submachine guns, and fourteen crates of ammunition. The farmers buzzed. They thought these were a lot of weapons. Mrs. Pappel called for their attention.

"There will be a signal." A bell hung beside the dining hall door. "When this rings, one-two-three, one-two-three, drop what you're doing. That is the alert. We are under attack."

With three quick jerks of the cord, she chimed the alarm, let it ring, then repeated. Some children came out of a nearby house and were waved back inside.

"How many of you have ever fired a gun?"

The big lad Aharon, four other boys, and Rivkah raised their hands.

Mrs. Pappel beckoned the six to come forward.

"Pick."

Rivkah stepped up first. She selected a long rifle to show to Vince. "Malik gave this to me."

"Let me see it."

She handed him the weathered rifle. Vince opened the action, looked into the barrel for scoring, and checked the trigger for tightness. The gun had been worked hard but was cared for. He returned it to Rivkah; he held it with her for a beat before letting go.

The pioneers chose until the weapons were all taken. Vince divided them into three groups—west, north, and south—for the approaches they would guard. The rest were promised guns later. Until then, they'd keep the agriculture and business of the kibbutz going as well as they could.

✳✳✳

Stonecutters loaded burlap feed sacks into the cart behind Zipporah, to fill them in the quarry with rock dust and small stones. Another team set off for the southern slope with shovels and picks to hollow out foxholes in the spots marked on Vince's map.

The rest of the seventy settlers followed him through Massuot Yitzhak. Vince assigned four-person teams to strategic houses. In each, two would shoot, a third would handle ammo and bandages, and the fourth was to run between houses to keep them coordinated. The haverim pushed tables against windows; Vince taught them to stay back when firing to hide their muzzle flashes. To waste no ammunition, they should let the enemy come close.

Vince set up a watch schedule and night patrols. He put two-person teams behind each sandbag bunker in the orchard. In case of a firefight, the settlers must stay out of wooden structures like the barns and shops and get behind stone walls. Vince crossed the orchards, fields, terraced lands, and singed slopes laying out the defense of the kibbutz.

In the late afternoon, Mrs. Pappel stepped in front of him. She announced to the settlers following Vince, "That's enough for today. She took him by the elbow to peel him away. The haverim dispersed or sat where they were.

"You're scaring them."

"They don't look scared."

"Did you know that Rivkah and I are the only two in Massuot Yitzhak who weren't in the camps?"

"No."

"Every one of those boys and girls has a horror behind their eyes that you and I can barely imagine. You won't see the fear on their faces. These children don't show it, not anymore. But the terror hasn't left them." She gestured across Massuot Yitzhak. "How else could they do this?"

She took his hand. "Vince, I'm frightened. Not for me; I'm old enough. I could keel over tomorrow and it's been a good life. For them. You are, too."

"You asked me to help."

"You've run them around the kibbutz for five hours. You're push-ing. They can see how worried you are. They've faced death be-fore. Respect that."

"How?"

"Believe in them."

"I do."

"No, you don't. You want to, but you can't. I couldn't either until I saw what they're capable of. They changed me. I made a choice to link my life to these young people. To these hills."

She kissed her fingertips, then pressed them to Vince's cheek.

"Bless you, my boy. But you're the only person in Massuot Yitzhak who hasn't picked this place to be his grave. Get them ready, but stop being afraid for them. It doesn't help. And if, God forbid, you see them fight, you'll see a marvel."

"What about Rivkah?"

"She's not going to leave Massuot Yitzhak."

"That scares me the most."

Mrs. Pappel led him back to the house. Rivkah waited on the porch. The workshops stayed silent; no one in the kibbutz would work tonight after their first day of carrying weapons and digging trenches.

Rivkah kissed Vince and Mrs. Pappel for their arrival home. She went in to shower before the evening meal, Mrs. Pappel made tea, Vince went over his hand-drawn maps.

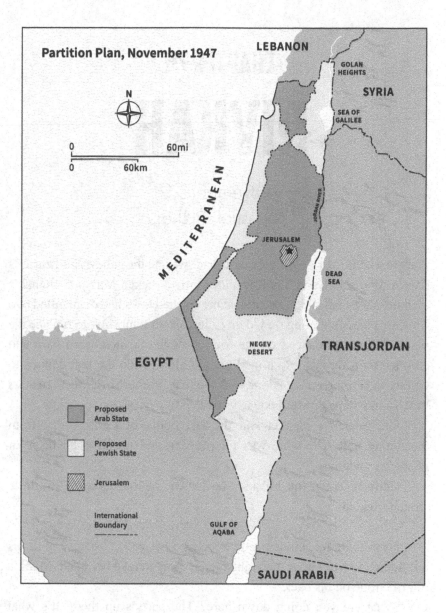

Partition Plan, November 1947

N

0 — 60mi
0 — 60km

LEBANON

GOLAN
HEIGHTS

SYRIA

SEA OF
GALILEE

JORDAN RIVER

MEDITERRANEAN

JERUSALEM

DEAD
SEA

NEGEV
DESERT

TRANSJORDAN

EGYPT

Proposed
Arab State

Proposed
Jewish State

Jerusalem

International
Boundary

GULF OF
AQABA

SAUDI ARABIA

CHAPTER 76

RIVKAH

November 29
Massuot Yitzhak

The great bonfire in Kfar Etzion cast shadows into the valley. Ein Tzurim's flames were small, and tiny Revadim's only a flicker. Massuot Yitzhak's own fire shot sparks high because some spirited boys had dismantled two walls of a barn, claiming they'd go to Jerusalem tomorrow to replace the planks. The boys danced on the rooftop of the dismembered barn and emptied their throats into a mad orange glow while the rest danced to violins and an accordion. Along with the fires, the sure brightness of stars lit Rivkah's steps down the quarry road.

She carried a blanket and the last bottle of kosher wine from the dining hall. The wine was for prayers, and prayers had been answered, so why not?

Halfway down the hillside she halted. In the darkness the little stream trickled.

"Vince?"

From foxholes, hidden settlers echoed her call, "Vince?" until his tall figure loomed out of the night and he came to take her hand. Malik's old rifle rode on his back.

"What are you doing down here? The party's up there. It's what you've all been waiting for."

She held out to him the blanket and wine. "Come on."

Vince led her to his foxhole. The hole was deep enough to cover Rivkah up to her armpits, Vince to his belly. The dirt was chilly like the night. Rivkah lay the blanket on the dirt floor.

He asked, "What was the final vote?"

"All of western Europe said yes. Then the Caribbean and South America. And Canada. Then America."

"Good."

"The big surprise was the Soviet bloc. All in favor."

"The Arabs?"

"All against."

"Britain?"

"Abstained."

"What was the final tally?"

"Thirty-three to thirteen."

"Hand me that bottle."

Rivkah had brought no glasses down the hill. With his knife Vince pried off the bottlecap. He offered her the bottle. She pushed it back.

"You first. You helped it happen."

Vince raised the wine by the neck. "To the UN." He took a good swig, then handed the bottle to her. Rivkah held it like Vince had, by the neck. She raised the wine to Massuot Yitzhak, to the bonfire there and the boys who'd stripped the barn to make it, to the hora she'd danced until she was dizzy. She took a deep swallow and kept the bottle. Rivkah kneeled in the foxhole.

"You've never asked what I've been waiting for."

A second time, Rivkah lifted the bottle to her lips. The wine was bitter, not made for happy occasions. She set it on the lip of the foxhole and pulled Vince down.

CHAPTER 77

RIVKAH

December 10

Rivkah sat alone, draped in a shawl. The pioneers had vanished indoors to wash off the day's work. Two days ago, the bonfire's ashes had been shoveled into wheelbarrows and carted to the ash pit, but Massuot Yitzhak still smelled smokey.

The scuffing of feet gladdened Rivkah. Malik arrived with the dusk; he dismounted close to the porch. The camel eyed Rivkah, then shambled away. Rivkah didn't call inside for Mrs. Pappel and Vince but kept Malik to herself for a moment.

"You've come to say goodbye."

Malik stepped onto the porch. He took a knee before her and extended a hand.

"May I?"

Rivkah nested her hand in his. Malik wore a ring on every finger and thumb. He lowered his big brow to the back of her hand. He held like this, then released her and took a chair.

"I tried to write a poem, so I could bring it to you. I rode in the desert all day. I listened to the sun and read the faces of rocks. I was given nothing. The world feels very new right now. I am better with the ancient. I am sorry."

"It's alright. We're not strangers."

"We are not."

Vince came out on the porch. Malik got to his feet; with his girth and robes he seemed a thousand blackbirds launched from a tree. He greeted Vince with a two-handed clasp.

Vince asked, "How'd you get past the perimeter?"

Malik patted Vince's hand. "I came a way only one man on a camel can come. A thousand will not do that."

"Why all the rings?"

"They are my wealth. And the old camel. I do not know what will happen. But where I go now, they are with me. Where is Mrs. Pappel?"

"Here."

She stood in the doorway. Malik opened his glinting hands. Mrs. Pappel stepped onto the porch with her palms up to admire the rings.

"They're magnificent."

"Take one."

"Truly?"

"Truly."

From his left pinky, Mrs. Pappel slid a ring, silver studded with small gems. She held it close to her eyes, turning it in the late daylight. She went inside the house, to return quickly.

"I offer you this gift, Malik of the Tarabin."

The great Arab examined the ring she handed him.

"This was Morrie's pinky ring. He had big hands, too."

Malik slid the band on, pleased at the fit. He bowed. "I am in your debt. I shall remain so."

"Sit." Mrs. Pappel pointed Vince and Malik to the open seats. She went inside for a chair. Around Massuot Yitzhak, one house after another lit candles and lanterns, hearths, stoves, and oil heaters. Rivkah took Vince's hand; Malik raised not an eyebrow. When Mrs. Pappel returned, Rivkah did not let Vince go.

Rivkah spoke first, so Mrs. Pappel would not have to ask it of Malik. "Has the war begun?"

The old Arab scratched his beard as if consulting it. "It has not."

He slid his ringed hands inside his sleeves. Malik spoke with a graven stillness, only the motion of his lips inside his great beard.

"There has been a call for an Arab boycott inside Jerusalem. Yesterday, my nephew Walid left Nahalin to join the strike. He fell in with two hundred other angry boys. Inside the Old City, they went on a rampage. They burned and looted Jewish shops. They carried only knives and clubs. The British police did nothing to stop them but joined in the ransacking. On Jaffa Street, Walid and his rabble ran into an armed band of Haganah. The Jews fired over their heads, but a few fired into the mob. Walid returned home to my sister with a bullet in his shoulder."

Rivkah said, "I'm sorry. He'll recover?"

"Yes."

She pressed. "When will it start?"

"When we stop arming ourselves with stones and knives and turn guns against you. When one violent day does not pause into the next. The killings of Arabs and Jews will mount. We will not go to war. We will awake in war."

Malik's camel, which had never been named by him, had not wandered far. Without a call from Malik, the beast mooched to the edge of the steps. He ducked his long neck to poke his nose onto the porch. The camel came close, bulging eyes and long lashes, to sniff Mrs. Pappel. She petted his dusty crown; the camel closed his eyes. With a moan, the beast withdrew. Malik stood as though summoned.

"Please, do not rise. Let me leave you all like this, together on your porch. Safe in your village." He pressed his ringed hands together. "I wish you peace. Farewell, my good friends. *Ma'a Salama.*"

The camel folded in stages, knobby knees to the dirt for Malik to climb on, then hoisted him. Rivkah let go of Vince's hand to step into the glossy light. Malik reined the camel east, to saunter down into the Wadi Shahid. A long rifle rode in the holster. He didn't circle back to give it to Rivkah or Mrs. Pappel as he had on other visits. This gun he kept.

CHAPTER 78

HUGO

December 11
Jerusalem

A jangle of keys awoke Hugo. He muttered, "No," before he'd opened his eyes and jerked up on the cot. He said again, "No," when the warden stepped out of the morning dark. The warden put a skeleton key into Hugo's barred door. Hugo shoved out a hand when the man entered his cell.

Hugo reeled in his legs to pull himself into a ball against the wall. He had nothing to grab onto and said, "*Nein*."

The warden waved both white palms. He repeated Hugo's name, but that was the name of the condemned.

Through pounding eyeballs, Hugo watched the warden backpedal from the cell. The warden did not shut the barred door but left it open. He'd come alone.

Hugo became conscious of his own untamed breathing; this helped him slow it. The warden continued to speak in English. A stack of folded clothes lay on the floor where the warden had dropped them. The clothes were not striped or gray or red. Over the back of the chair hung a pea coat. The warden wouldn't lower his hands. Through quickened breaths, Hugo asked, "What are you doing?"

"I apologize. I've surprised you."

"Are you here to hang me?"

"Heavens, no." The warden indicated the pile of clothes. "Get dressed."

"Why?"

"Have you heard nothing I've said?"

"Not much."

"I'm letting you go."

The warden eased into the cell; cautiously he pulled out a chair for himself.

"We are leaving. And before we go, there may be some settling of accounts. By the police and the army. Do you understand what I'm saying?"

"You mean to say, me."

"I do. I don't know if anyone will come looking. In any case, it's best if you're not here. Neither of us can say what your Irgun chaps would do if you did get hanged, after all. I believe I may be saving some poor soldier's life along with your own. Do you trust me?"

In the camps, there had been no need for trust. The Nazis kept their word.

"Yes."

"Then you are free. If you will get dressed."

The urge spawned in Hugo to run from the open cell. Waste not a second. Instead, he stood over the clothes on the cold floor. They were his, what he'd been wearing five months ago at his arrest.

The warden said, "The winter coat should fit. It belonged to a fellow who'll be here a bit longer."

Hugo lifted the white shirt to smell it for no reason he could fathom, some animal sense to find himself in the fabric. He pulled death row's scarlet tunic over his head and tossed it aside. Hugo had a circlet of fat at his waist, evidence that he'd been well-fed. Buttoning on the white shirt calmed him.

Hugo asked, "Will you get in trouble?"

"I'm sailing out on the first boat today. I will claim no knowledge of your disappearance, Mister Ungar. The beauty of your Irgun is that they may be blamed for many things."

Hugo tugged up his pants and suspenders.

The warden continued. "Do not stay in Jerusalem. In case someone does look for you."

"My flat is gone by now."

"Do you have any money?"

"No."

"Friends?"

Hugo sat on the cot to lace his leather shoes. "I have one."

"Where?"

The pea coat fit well.

"He may be at Massuot Yitzhak."

Hugo followed the warden out of the cell.

"In the Etzion bloc?"

"Yes."

"You realize that's in Arab territory."

"Will you pay for a taxi?"

"No taxi will take you. The road has been blockaded."

"What do you mean?"

"There's been sniping south of Jerusalem. The Arabs are trying to shut down the road."

The warden walked Hugo down the white halls, past inmates sleeping or whispering messages to him.

"May I suggest you consider somewhere else?"

Where could he go? To Julius who'd arrested him? Pinchus who'd deserted him?

"I have nowhere else."

The warden stopped at the door to his office. "Then come inside."

"What are you going to do?"

"Make a few calls."

"To who?"

"Who do you think? The Jews."

✳ ✳ ✳

Hugo waited outside the Russian Compound. A taxi arrived and asked for him by name.

The taxi took off into the Jewish Quarter. The driver, a timid Pole in thick glasses, crept along on the tight roads and would not pass horse-drawn carts or delivery lorries. The ride became an affair of patience for Hugo.

He considered making conversation; it would be his first in a while not through bars. The weather had cleared. The taxi was clean; the Pole seemed a fastidious man. He had a large nose and would need a shave before day's end. Perhaps he was a new immigrant and unsure, the way he leaned forward to grip the wheel with both hands.

Hugo said, "I was on death row."

The driver checked his rearview mirror. He couldn't look long at Hugo because the car entered a curve. When the narrow way straightened, the driver gained speed and asked nothing.

Shops and kiosks for cheeses, meats, herbs, and produce melted past. On Mamilla Street, near the bazaar, the taxi stopped; the warden had given the driver this address. Hugo stepped out of the taxi with no money nor thanks for the Pole. Not waiting for either, the taxi motored off. Hugo entered the souk.

The cobblestones of the Mamilla market bustled. Shoppers brushed past while Hugo stood still, unprepared for the flowing crowd. Bicycles and hand-pushed carts wheeled by, women shouted in the ghetto languages of Europe and in Hebrew. A child chased a cat, old men debated over newspapers, and a merchant poured figs onto a scale. In prison Hugo had existed for months without the smells and sounds of the living Jew. He jumped when a man took his arm.

"Hugo Ungar."

"Who are you?"

"Come on."

The man, redhaired, lean, and Hugo's age, led through the throng. He wasn't shy about elbowing his way. He squeezed past a pack of women in headscarves and long coats and beamed back at Hugo.

"Kharda, you don't remember me?"

Hugo wracked his brain, hearing the name Julius had given him.

"Were you Palmach?"

"The coast guard station at Sidna Ali. Two years ago. You drove us."

"You got shot in the leg."

"At the riot in Shefayim, you stayed with me. You scuffled with the cops to keep them from taking me away."

"Yakob."

Pressed between the satchels and handlebars of the market crowd, Yakob reached back for a handshake.

Hugo asked, "Are you still Palmach?"

"I spent some time in jail. Now I just come when they call."

"I was in jail, too."

"I know."

Yakob forged a path through the souk. Hugo followed the man's fiery hair, trying to take on Yakob's nimbleness; the dizziness of the bazaar faded. In two minutes Hugo had walked more than he had in half a year of prison.

Yakob led him into a crevice between shops, one selling candy, the other books. Both merchants looked elsewhere when Hugo slipped behind Yakob into a passage so narrow they had to turn their shoulders.

They emerged into an alley behind the Mamilla market, under clotheslines and archways. Gangs of men loaded four pickup trucks with foodstuffs, feed sacks, and ammo crates. Eight British policemen stood guard, armed and hawkish beside their armored car.

Hugo asked red Yakob, "What is this?"

"A convoy."

"The warden didn't say anything about this. He just said he found me a ride."

"If you want to get into Gush Etzion, this is how you go. For the last week, the Haganah's been supplying the bloc."

Hugo indicated the policemen. "Why them?"

"They go along as escort."

"Why?"

"Arabs tend not to shoot at the British. We leave in five minutes."

"Will I get a gun?"

"If you want one."

"I do."

✳ ✳ ✳

Eight policemen climbed into their armored vehicle. The Haganah men, Hugo among them, boarded the four supply trucks. The first truck was bound for Kfar Etzion, the second for Ein Tzurim, the third for Massuot Yitzhak, and the rear truck, the smallest in the convoy, had been loaded for Revadim.

Yakob and Hugo sat in the bed of the third tender in line, on a half-ton of supplies. Yakob had given him a well-worn bolt-action Dutch rifle. Hugo hadn't handled many long-barreled weapons, mostly the short Stens he'd made with Julius, and his pistol. He nested the rifle in his arms the way Yakob did.

Following their British escort, the convoy wended through the alley out of Mamilla. Sitting in the open bed, Hugo became glad of the warden's winter coat; the blue morning belonged to December. He hugged himself as the convoy left the city, the truck accelerated, and the wind rose.

Two miles south of Jerusalem, the landscape opened to olive trees and a hamlet. A tiny kibbutz had taken hold here around the tomb of Rachel, a domed building visible from the road. The people of Ramat Rachel waved at the convoy. Beyond their settlement began the Arab lands.

The police in the armored car set a quick pace. This made a cold, jostling ride for the Haganah fighters seated on boxes. A mile past Ramat Rachel, the road skirted two towns, Bethlehem on the left with eight thousand Arabs, Beth Jalla on the right, home to three thousand. Houses of cinderblock and humble stone crowded every hilltop; women walked the road's shoulder with bundled-up children; every child gave the Jewish supply trucks an unfriendly stare.

Three miles beyond Bethlehem, the convoy passed Solomon's Pools, a great reservoir from the king's time. The ruins of Roman aqueducts linked the hills in the rising landscape. Beside the winding road, many houses were abandoned.

Yakob sidled closer behind the screen of the truck cab. "We were sure you'd hang."

"The warden let me out."

"Did the Irgun get to him?"

Hugo celebrated with a little lie. "Pinchus himself." Yakob patted his shoulder. Hugo asked, "Has there been trouble for any of the convoys?"

"Not too bad. Yesterday was quiet. The day before, we swapped a few rounds with some locals on the high ground. They shoot. We shoot. They go home. We keep going. Tell me something."

"What?"

"Why are you going to Massuot Yitzhak? There are safer places."

"The fellow I'm going to see said the same thing to me in Buchenwald."

"Then why are you going?"

"The warden told me to keep a low profile. It doesn't get lower than a kibbutz on the edge of the Negev. Is this rifle loaded?"

"Yes."

With Yakob, Hugo hunkered against the cold as the landscape grew barren and gained in elevation. South of Solomon's Pools, the road wended up steepening hills. The four laden trucks strained to climb the grades and navigate the switchbacks. A limestone cliff loomed, sheer and white. On the bluff, in the wind, stood a dozen Arabs. They weren't hiding, and they had guns.

Red Yakob charged the bolt of his rifle. Hugo scrambled upright to do the same. The engine of their truck whined higher; the driver floored the gas. The last truck in line, the one behind Hugo, couldn't keep up on the incline and began to fade.

Yakob saw something menacing from the Arabs; he raised his carbine and fired at the clifftop. Suddenly the Arabs disappeared, but gunshots snapped above and around Hugo. Yakob worked his long rifle at targets high and low; Hugo brought his rifle to his cheek but in the bouncing truck could find no one to shoot at.

The Revadim truck, last in line, straggled too much. Out of the crags of the cliff, a dozen Arabs surged into the open, swooping down the windswept hillside to intercept it. Yakob scrambled to reload a fresh magazine. He screamed at Hugo, "Fire!"

Hugo brought one Arab into his sights, but his truck stopped and spoiled the shot.

Yakob leaped out and sprinted straight at the raiders.

Hugo's driver and assistant jumped out, too, rifles in hand. Hugo expected them to gallop after Yakob; he prepared to do the same, but the two Haganah men stayed with the truck and took cover behind the opened doors. A machinegun on the cliff opened up on the halted convoy. Hugo stayed on the boxes of bullets and fruit, unsure where he should run or hide.

The Revadim truck showed it was still alive. Squealing tires, the driver spun off the road onto the stony slope and dashed away, bounding downhill. Round after round punched its sides and hood, spiderweb holes blinded the windshield as it fled. The Haganah men in the back emptied their weapons at the chasing Arabs and managed to drop one. The body rolled down the incline, spilling a checked keffiyeh on the hill.

With shouts of "*Jihad! Yallah al Yahud!*" the Arabs turned on Hugo's truck, the next in line. Behind a boulder, Yakob singlehandedly held the attackers at bay. He picked off one, then another, and the rest dove to the ground. Hugo, with no one to tell him what to do, fired at the Arabs but wasted the shot high.

The Haganah driver and assistant popped up to fire from behind the truck's doors. They gave no orders or help to Hugo, too occupied on their own. Hugo twisted to look through the busted windshield at the assault on the trucks ahead, all under attack and returning fire. The British cops in the lead truck had driven beyond the skirmish.

In ones and twos, more Arabs descended on the trucks. Yakob winged another, then looked back at Hugo but shouted nothing. Hugo was supposed to know what to do.

A hammer-blow struck the driver's door of Hugo's truck; the fighter behind it grunted and fell backwards. His rifle clattered out of his hands onto the road. He lay face up, gasping and panicked. Blood spread around a hole in the chest of his white shirt. Only his hands twitched. The driver's eyes affixed straight up, past Hugo. Another bullet banged the door. Hugo flinched but watched the driver take hard breaths, slacken, quiet, then draw to a close as if he'd climbed out of his body on those breaths.

A bullet smashed into the tailgate of the truck, an ugly gong that reset Hugo's attention.

With the butt of his carbine, he smashed at one of the wooden ammo cases until it splintered open. He knew too little about the rifles he and Yakob held, but it seemed reasonable to think the guns were intended for the Etzion bloc. Probably the ammo matched them. He scooped up as many small boxes as he could carry, labeled *.303 British*. A bullet zinged behind his head to pierce the rear windshield. Shards cut his cheek, barely missing his eye. Hugo rolled out of the truck and landed beside the corpse. He gathered up the dead fighter's rifle, threw the strap of his own Dutch gun across his shoulders and, keeping the truck between himself and the cliff where the Arabs had a bead on him, took a deep breath.

The din of the fighting swelled. Shouts of Arab bravado, anger, and pain mixed with the gunshots. The assistant driver on the other side of the truck fired in two directions, at the attackers ahead and the ones behind creeping up on Yakob.

Under the truck, Hugo slid him the dead driver's rifle and two boxes of ammo. The assistant paused in surprise at what arrived had at his feet, then resumed firing.

Behind his big rock, Yakob's gun went quiet. He held up a small metal sleeve, an empty five-round clip. He dropped it, then showed Hugo another clip, meaning when this runs out, we are dead.

Hugo exhaled with puffing cheeks and bolted away from the truck. He ran a zigzag, dodging rounds that zinged off the road left and right, then he slid in behind Yakob's boulder.

Hugo flung down the ammo cartons. Urgently, Yakob broke into them. He spilled out twenty-five loaded clips. Yakob punched him in the shoulder, then grabbed at the ammunition.

"You alright?" Yakob asked. "Blood on your face."

Hugo touched the little wounds on his cheek. "I'll be very happy if these are all I get."

Firing fast, Yakob put the advancing Arabs on their bellies. He had more bullets now and let them know it. Hugo propped his own rifle next to Yakob; he'd let the redhead shoot.

He kept one carbine loaded while Yakob emptied the other. Bullets geysered the dusty ground. The shooting deafened Hugo; he couldn't hear the rest of the battle on the road and hillside. The number rushing down on them grew to a hundred.

Beside Hugo's truck, the assistant driver took a bullet in the gut. On his knees, he kept firing. His mouth hung open, but Hugo's ears were too stuffed to know if he was screaming. An emptied clip sprang from the Haganah man's magazine to bounce on the road. The fighter groped with blood on his hands for one of the ammo boxes Hugo had slid to him. Another bullet drove him back against the truck door. His head loosened on his neck, fazed and querying. A last smash rocked him off his knees to fall on his side next to his rifle.

Four boxes of ammo remained to Yakob, plenty to live a few minutes more. Hugo shouted, inches from Yakob's face, "I'm going to run for the truck."

Yakob asked nothing, again supposing Hugo knew what he was doing. He squeezed off more rounds at Arabs fifty meters away. Hugo darted from behind the cover of the rock. Snipers on the cliff tried to zero in on him.

Hugo bolted for the pickup and skidded in the road behind the open passenger door. He tugged the rifle from under the dead assistant, then tossed it into the cab. Hugo hurtled into the truck bed to lift the opened ammo crate and push it through the bullet-busted rear windshield. A bullet thudded into the sacks of cattle feed. Hugo leaped out, then as fast as he could, bounded into the driver's seat.

The truck had been left idling. Hugo dropped it into gear and floored the pedal. The pickup rocketed forward. Both bullet-punched doors slammed shut.

Yakob might think Hugo was trying to escape. Hugo wished he'd explained himself.

The next truck in line was fifty meters ahead. Hugo barreled to it, then locked the brakes. He spun the steering wheel to slew the truck sideways, smoking the tires. Three Haganah men were holding their ground; two others were splayed on the pavement, killed or too hurt to fight. Hugo wedged his truck between the defenders and the Arabs, hiding inside the burnt-rubber haze to toss out a dozen cartons of ammo. Rounds drummed on the side-panels of his pickup. A bullet stabbed through the door to nail his thigh but didn't break the skin. Hugo yelped and mashed the accelerator, cranking the steering wheel into a sharp turn; he spun the pickup on squalling tires and surged for the lead truck.

Again, Hugo sideslipped between the Haganah men and the Arabs. He threw out more ammo and tossed the three fighters the dead assistant's rifle. One boy in a wispy moustache threw down his Sten and snatched up the long-barreled gun. He broke open a carton of ammo, loaded fast, and fired through the first five-round clip. Another bullet punctured the passenger door; this one drilled a rut through the tops of both of Hugo's thighs, ripping the pants he'd been arrested in. The slug banged into the driver's door and dead-ended at Hugo's feet. He felt no pain yet, the wound happened too fast, but the grooves across his lap oozed. The young fighter reloaded and kept up a steady barrage.

Hugo wheeled the pickup around. The steering handled sluggishly; a bullet had popped the front right tire. He leaned on the gas to get all the speed the truck had left. Screeching on the metal rim, the pickup howled back toward Yakob.

Hugo drove flat-out. Downed Arabs littered the hillside and the shoulder of the road. Trailing sparks, he rushed at Yakob who cast a worried glance as Hugo closed in, again not knowing what Hugo was doing. With ten meters to go, Hugo pitched the truck sideways, careening to a halt that blocked Yakob from the battle behind him. Before the truck settled or the haze from the smoldering tires drifted away, Hugo grabbed the last ammo boxes and rolled out of the cab. Bullets drubbed the truck's hood and beat at the feed sacks. Hugo ducked behind the buffeting truck. Kneeling awoke the ache in his thighs; the wounds seared, and blood pulsed in the grooves.

Behind his rock, on the other side of the truck, Yakob bellowed, "Now!"

To the roars of Yakob's rifle, Hugo limped around the rear bumper, expecting a bullet. He hobbled until he buckled behind the boulder, just ahead of a ricochet.

Yakob handed him the spent rifle to reload. The barrel almost burned Hugo's hands.

✳ ✳ ✳

The Arabs vanished when three armored police cars and a Red Shield ambulance powered up the hill. Leading the way was the shot-up Revadim pickup that had escaped to Bethlehem for help. Fifty cops piled out of the metal-plated trucks to take control of the scene. No more shots were exchanged except for Yakob, who kept shooting as the last Arab disappeared from his sights.

Six khaki-clad cops crept around the bullet-pocked pickup. Approaching, they said to Yakob, "Easy, easy." Yakob squeezed off a final round. The policemen inched up, hands in view.

The first cop took a knee. He gestured at Hugo's blood-soaked pants, a red trench across each thigh. The policeman sucked his teeth. "These will take a few stitches." Two cops crouched beside Yakob to ask if he was hurt. He was not. His freckled skin was afire, and his hands trembled; Hugo saw how scared Yakob had been.

The cops lifted Hugo to help him limp from the boulder. The carnage of the battle clogged the road and cluttered the hillside. The Bethlehem cops collected ten bodies of the Haganah and loaded them into the Red Shield ambulance which turned for Jerusalem. On the rocky terrain, a dozen black robes flapped in the highland breeze. The Arabs would return for them.

The cops helped Hugo stumble toward their truck. Skid marks from his crazed driving scored the road. One defender staggered up on a wounded hip, two were borne away on stretchers. Only four of the seventeen Haganah had come through unscathed, one of them Yakob. None of the British escort inside their armored car had been harmed.

Yakob asked the police commander if a ride could be arranged to take him and the remaining defenders the rest of the way, four miles south to Gush Etzion. The officer agreed.

Hugo asked the cops to set him on the pavement. A medic hurried over to bandage his thighs. Yakob, still flush, came to sit beside Hugo.

Yakob started to cry. None of the cops tried to comfort him. Hugo didn't touch him, either.

CHAPTER 79

RIVKAH

Massuot Yitzhak

A cold wind whipped out of the north, carrying the clatter of gunfire from the bleak hills. Hundreds of reports hinted at a furious battle. When the shooting stopped, the silence was sudden and ominous. Something had been decided.

Standing in the quarry road, Vince lapped an arm around Rivkah's shoulders. Rivkah wore Malik's rifle across her back. Others waited, too, to find out who had been fighting.

The grinding of gears replaced the quiet. A heavy armored car turned off the Hebron road into the Gush Etzion bloc, then climbed to Massuot Yitzhak.

A kibbutz boy with a rifle stepped into the vehicle's path, one hand up. The driver motioned for the young guardian to walk around back. The boy did. A door opened; the boy peered inside. Whatever he saw made him wave the truck onward. The boy and his gun disappeared into his foxhole.

The armored car lumbered up the hill to stop in front of Rivkah's house. Mrs. Pappel came off the porch to meet it. Vince, Rivkah, and the settlers followed. The truck's rear door opened. A medic climbed down, then reached behind him to offer a hand.

Vince left Rivkah's side to help Hugo step out. Gauze wrapped both of his thighs; dried blood crosshatched his face. Unsteadily, Hugo spread an arm across Vince's shoulder.

Vince said, "Hello again."

Hugo took ginger steps, doing all he could to keep upright. Mrs. Pappel looked in the backdoor of the ambulance. She asked someone inside, "What happened?"

Rivkah helped Vince get Hugo through the crowd and into the house. They set him at the kitchen table. Hugo grunted into a chair; Rivkah set a kettle to boil, then hurried to her bedroom for fresh bandages.

Vince sat beside Hugo. He was supposed to hang, wasn't he? How had he dodged death row? What had just happened in the hills above Bethlehem? This was Rivkah's home; it was her place to ask. But Vince sat covering Hugo's smaller hand. Hugo offered no explanation yet, and Vince asked him nothing.

Vince said to Rivkah, "Bring me a wet cloth."

She soaked a towel. He dabbed clean the cuts on Hugo's cheek and temple.

Mrs. Pappel entered; behind her came a redheaded man. Though he was unhurt, he appeared, like Hugo, still in the aftermath of a battle, apprehensive and battered. He stank of gunpowder. The redhead shuffled to a chair at the table without being invited, not because he needed to sit but to come beside Hugo, with whom he'd shared something terrible.

Mrs. Pappel said, "This is Yakob."

✳ ✳ ✳

Rivkah kneeled before Hugo to unravel his hasty bandages. Hugo touched her shoulder.

"This is how Vince first found me. No home. Nothing. Wretched."

"You're safe."

"He said that to me, too."

She sucked a breath at his wounds. The bleeding had stopped; the matching channels across both thighs were pink and clean-cut. Rivkah helped Hugo remove his ruined trousers. The little Irgunist showed no shyness or humility for his thin legs or roughspun underwear. Both thighs would require stitches, and he'd need something for the pain. She wrapped his wounds, then put him in her bed.

Rivkah pulled up the blankets and sat beside him. Vince peeked in the doorway, then left again.

Hugo said, "You haven't asked me what happened. Why I'm here."

"It seemed more important to take care of you."

"We don't know each other."

"No."

"I apologize if I made a poor first impression."

"That was a while ago."

The bed quivered under Hugo's laugh. "A while."

She stood to let him rest.

He said, "I'm supposed to be dead, you know. A few times over."

"You're not."

He shrugged against the pillow, a *we'll see* gesture.

"It hurts."

"Mrs. Pappel went for the doctor."

"May I stay here? I don't want to go to a clinic."

"It's a small house."

"Until I feel well enough. Then I'll go. I've been alone a great deal lately."

"I'll speak to Mrs. Pappel."

✳✳✳

On the porch, away from Hugo and the doctor sewing him up, Yakob talked about the attack on the convoy and what Hugo had done.

He said to Mrs. Pappel, "I'd like to stay in Massuot Yitzhak. The others will, too. You need fighters. I was Palmach."

"We have a guest house. You'll be welcome there."

Vince said, "I've been in charge of the defenses. I'll be glad to turn it over to a Palmachnik."

The doctor came out to say he'd put ten stitches in each of Hugo's legs. Hugo was to rest for a week and have his bandages changed daily.

Rivkah volunteered for that. They must watch his wounds for infection. Hugo would recover with a fine set of scars. The physician left into the night for the mile walk to Kfar Etzion.

Rivkah said, "Hugo wants to stay with us until he feels better."

Yakob had no right to speak, this was not his home or decision, and lifted his hands to accept that he was out of turn, but said, "This morning, he was on death row."

The redhead offered a memory of Hugo from two years ago, when Hugo had been the driver on a mission against a British coast guard facility. He recalled a dauntless little man fresh off the boat, who pitted himself against the police during a riot in Shefayim, made off with a cop's hat, and stayed with Yakob when the police came. Yakob tugged up a pants leg to show a bullet scar below his knee, proof of the tale.

Vince told a story about Hugo, on the second day of his liberation from Buchenwald, emaciated and enraged, chasing German civilians around a Weimar fountain. Vince shook his head as if this were a pleasant remembrance.

Mrs. Pappel crossed her arms. "He was Irgun. He can't be Irgun here."

Rivkah left the porch. She entered her room to stand at the foot of the bed. Hugo lay as she'd left him, covered by the blanket, arms crossed in repose.

She asked, "Why are you here? Why did you come?"

"Because you have Palestine. You have all this. Why shouldn't I?"

She took the chair to sit beside Hugo Ungar in her home.

"Do you know what they're saying about you on the porch?"

"How could I?"

"Yakob said you were brave. Today on the road, and on some mission two years ago."

"Do you believe him?"

"It doesn't matter."

"What did Vince say?"

"He told us about Weimar."

"Ah, yes. Chasing Germans around a fountain. Did he mention a hanging?"

"No."

"Good. And your Mrs. Pappel?"

"She's decided that your past won't follow you here."

"If it's as simple as that, I should have decided it myself long ago."

The face above Rivkah's blanket was a bland face. She said, "I understand your point now."

"What point is that?"

"Why not build Palestine with a gun or a bomb? Why not use wickedness if nothing wicked sticks to you? Evil and violence are forgiven if they serve Palestine. You should hear them on the porch. You're heroic."

"I may have been. But that's not my point at the moment."

"Why not?"

"I have twenty stitches and no beer."

"Have you changed your mind?"

"Changed my mind. Let me see. After five years of waiting to go up a fucking chimney. Followed by five months of waiting for a noose and no one giving a fuck about me. Yes. I thought I'd try changing my mind."

"What about the Irgun? Everything you've done?"

"Everything I've done is a drop in the bucket to what I've lost."

Rivkah struggled to stay seated.

"You've lost? Do you know where you've come? Who we are here? We've all lost, some maybe more than you. But we don't talk about it. We don't ask the broken to carry the broken. We ask them to plant trees."

"I'll admit. You seem happier for it."

"Is that why you came to Massuot Yitzhak?"

Hugo closed his eyes. "The doctor gave me something. I need to sleep."

Rivkah stayed in the chair beside Hugo. In a minute, he began to breathe easy.

She collected clothes from her dresser; she'd spend the next week sleeping with Mrs. Pappel. Before leaving the room, Rivkah set a hand on Hugo's arm through the wool. She felt his smallness and wondered how death had not caught up with this little man somewhere along the way.

✳ ✳ ✳

December 13

The Arab shepherds of Surif and Jab'a were warned to stay out of the fields today.

Two thousand mourners were traveling from Jerusalem. The British had committed a massive force to escort a mile-long procession of vehicles on the heels of the attack on the relief convoy yesterday.

At noon, the first buses arrived in Kfar Etzion.

In the cemetery, the final depths of six graves were dug only minutes before the mass of dignitaries and rabbis descended into the Abu Rish. People in black picked their way to the fresh holes; three hundred settlers of Gush Etzion awaited, everyone in white work shirts and suspenders. Each had taken a turn with a shovel. Two hundred more settlers, on guard duty, would pay their respects tomorrow. Of the ten Jews killed in the convoy, six were from the Etzion bloc: four from Kfar Etzion, one from Ein Tzurim, one from Massuot Yitzhak. All had been Palmach. After the battle in the road, the British had taken the bodies to Jerusalem. They returned them now to the Gush.

Six caskets arrived draped in white and blue tallits, borne on the shoulders of Palmachniks. The cortege trekking down from Kfar Etzion was so long it took thirty minutes to assemble around the graves. After the coffins were set in place and the great crowd gathered, members of each kibbutz lit candles at the head of each casket.

The Sephardi chief rabbi recited Psalm 83, a prayer for the destruction of Israel's enemies. The Ashkenazi chief rabbi eulogized the martyrs, concluding with a quote from Moses: "Neither shall you weep, nor even desist from your labor." The two thousand from Jerusalem marched past to kiss the six pine boxes.

The line of mourners lasted another hour, then took the slow ascent from the wadi graveyard up to Kfar Etzion and the buses to Jerusalem. After the last griever had climbed the hill, gravediggers lowered the dead. Rivkah and Vince, Mrs. Pappel, Yakob, and all the haverim stayed behind and, in single file with the three hundred, threw shovelfuls into each grave.

At the rear of the line, the ten Palmach fighters who'd served as pallbearers, eight men plus Gabbi and another woman, tossed the last dirt into the holes. Rivkah didn't catch her sister's eye; Gabbi looked nowhere but into the graves. Rivkah and Gabbi hadn't spoken in a month, though less than a mile separated them. Rivkah was her only true family, but Gabbi had found other sisters and brothers in the Palmach. For seven years, Rivkah had Missus Pappel and a community of settlers around her. In that time, Gabbi's companions had been lost and searching. Rivkah would let her sister have whatever time and distance the girl needed to feel found again.

The immense convoy pulled away to Jerusalem; the British escorts joined them. Gabbi and her Palmachniks walked off to Revadim.

The settlers went to their homes to wash before dusk and the start of Shabbat Hanukkah. At her kitchen table, Rivkah asked Vince to light the menorah while Yakob said Kiddush for the dead. Seven days of mourning would pass alongside the days of Hanukkah.

Mrs. Pappel took tea to Hugo, whose wounds would not let him attend the funeral. Rivkah carried in the menorah to share the holiday with him. She sat with Mrs. Pappel and by the light of the candles told Hugo of the day.

Are we really soldiers, is it a dream?...Despite the heavy mourning...the bell is sounded and we respond; we eat, perform guard duty, hope and even laugh from time to time. Apparently, we are quite strong... Difficult days await us, but we will prevail, and we will yet see our children ambling among these trees, where danger now lurks behind every tree and rock.

—A letter from Massuot Yitzhak
   January 1948

CHAPTER 80

VINCE

January 5
Massuot Yitzhak

Young fathers clasped their children and made promises to their wives. Only for a few weeks, they said. Until we win.

Two British armored trucks idled on the quarry road. They'd been sent from Jerusalem to evacuate the Etzion bloc's hundred mothers and children, among them eleven children and six mothers of Massuot Yitzhak.

An army captain climbed down from the lead truck when Mrs. Pappel and Vince approached. The officer presented himself properly starched. Mrs. Pappel shook his hand while Vince stayed a step behind.

"Captain. I'm Missus Pappel."

"You're in charge?"

"For the moment."

"If your people are ready to go, please load them in. Be advised, I have a squad of soldiers inside every vehicle. I don't want to frighten your women and children."

"It's not a concern."

Vince retreated to stand with Rivkah on the shoulder of the road, to wave goodbye to their friends. The captain extended an arm to block Mrs. Pappel, a polite gesture for her to stay a moment. "Madam. If I may."

"Yes?"

"I received a rather odd order last evening. I am to make certain a Missus Pappel is on board a transport."

"Really? I was mentioned by name. How flattering."

"We're to evacuate the elderly, as well."

"Do I look elderly, Captain?"

"It's not for me to say, Madam. But why would you be singled out for evacuation? Are you the relative of a dignitary?"

"No. It was probably Pinchus."

"The Irgun's Pinchus?"

"You've heard of him, then?"

"Quite."

The officer hooked thumbs in his gun belt. "Madam, should I arrest you for something?"

She rested a hand on her own sidearm, for which she would have been sentenced to death months ago.

"Young man, you're a little late."

Mrs. Pappel scooped up one of the toddlers. She kissed the girl's cheek before handing her up to a soldier in the rear gate. She helped the little girl's mother inside. The air in the truck was dark and close; the seats were benches and the windows mere slits, gun ports.

The officer asked, "May I help you up?"

"I have no intention of leaving."

"I have orders."

"And to obey them you will have to lay hands on me. In the middle of a Jewish settlement. Are you willing to do that? No? Then safe travels."

Mrs. Pappel pivoted quickly enough for her ponytail to barely miss the officer.

The convoy lurched out of Massuot Yitzhak. The settlers lined the lane, arms raised in salute as much as farewell.

CHAPTER 81

JANUARY 10
MASSUOT YITZHAK
PALESTINE
By Vincent Haas
Herald Tribune News Service

THE CHILDREN HAVE BEEN evacuated from Massuot Yitzhak. They are gone, their laughter with them. At the end of the workdays, they do not wait in the road to greet their parents from fields and workshops. The teacher has no students, the barn workers no little ones to help in the barns and the chicken run. The children do not galivant around the gardens; they are no longer here to be shooed or shushed or comforted.

Water shipments from Jerusalem have been cancelled for the next month, following the ambush on the convoy in December where ten Haganah fighters were killed. No traffic comes to Gush Etzion. The winter rains have slackened; the cisterns are not filling. Each settler is permitted one shower per week; laundry is limited to essentials.

Diesel for the generators is reserved for nighttime to power Massuot Yitzhak's searchlights and the lights on the perimeter fence, also to operate machinery and the bakery. There's no more kerosene; homes make do with candles, early bedtimes, and extra blankets.

After the evening meal, the kibbutzniks gather around their few radios to listen to broadcasts from the Haganah's *Kol Israel* station. Reports of the world, especially the civil war with the Arabs rising in Palestine, are distorted or incomplete. Relief packages dropped by small single-engine Auster airplanes twice a week rarely include newspapers.

Over the past month, three convoys have reached Gush Etzion. The first on Christmas Day brought a platoon of fifty students from Hebrew University who pull guard duty and have thrown themselves into the work of building fortifications. Today, sixty young Haganah fighters arrived with thirty weapons. Twelve were assigned to Massuot Yitzhak, a necessary strain on the kibbutz's meager resources. I begged their driver to wait while I dashed off this column, for him to take it to Jerusalem and radio my copy editor in Tel Aviv.

One convoy of relief supplies arrived two weeks ago. Hungry settlers and fighters crammed around the vehicles. Soldiers bounced on toes for letters and packages; the few married men hoped for word from wives, but most of the settlers received no mail. Their loved ones are already around them.

Massuot Yitzhak has become a cold and wanting place. Searchlights sweep across the wadis and over the inclines of Rock Hill and Yellow Hill, past the quiet quarry and through the leafless orchard, north to dark little Revadim and Ein Tzurim. The pioneers of this hilltop swore to build Palestine, for themselves, for their dead, for the living who will one day come or be born here. But this was not what they swore to create. This is guns, spotlights, sandbags, and stone walls, an outpost without families. Reporting from Massuot Yitzhak, Palestine.

CHAPTER 82

HUGO

January 14

Hugo felt a nap coming on. The sun had risen enough to warm the white hillside and make him wish to return to his bed. He slumped to the bottom of the foxhole. Hugo might doze if Yakob would stop talking.

Yakob talked all the time. He scheduled Hugo's hours on watch to mesh with his own. Red Yakob was immune to sarcasm. Hugo threw him tidbits, got him started, then let him roll by like clouds to pass the hours, but Yakob wouldn't stop when Hugo wanted him to.

In close quarters Yakob smelled bad, even outdoors. Yakob was hungry, too. Hugo muttered he would get used to it. Yesterday's convoy with fuel and food was ambushed on the return trip to Jerusalem. Two Haganah defenders were killed. That would likely be the final shipment for a while.

Last night, Yakob had spoken on the settlement's radio with his mother in Jerusalem. She told him she was scared for him, and hungry, too. That made Yakob feel worse about being away. Hugo shifted on the floor of the foxhole to signal that he was trying to settle in.

Yakob took up the subject of constructing a runway in the valley. Supplies and reinforcements could be landed in Gush Etzion, bypassing the blocked roads; no more parachutes drifting outside the perimeter or crates crashing to earth.

Yakob said, "Can you drive a bulldozer?"

"I suppose."

"Then, see, there's work for you. Building a runway. Something you'll be good at."

This seemed a small jibe at Hugo's poor approach to soldiering.

The putter of a light plane swelled overhead, suddenly making sense of Yakob's random remarks about a landing strip.

Yakob kneed Hugo. "Come on. Get up."

Hugo slid his legs under him. The wounds in his thighs had knit, but if he took a wrong step the scars sizzled.

A Piper Cub dove toward the hillside. The plane booted out a crate. A blue parachute opened and immediately collapsed. The crate plummeted a hundred meters down the slope and crashed to splinters. The parachute had been only a bed linen. A mule cart would have to rattle down to fetch it. First, the crate had to be found, checked out, and marked.

Yakob tapped Hugo. "You go, Hugo."

"That's not funny, and no."

Yakob stuffed Hugo's rifle into his arms. "Find what's left of the crate. Stay by it. I'll send the wagon when it comes."

"Why can't you do it?"

"Because if I go, you'll fall asleep."

"I won't."

"Hugo." Yakob cocked his head, kindly. "You will."

"Alright." Hugo struggled out of the foxhole, slapping away the redhead's attempt to help him.

Hugo's gun was heavy and upset his balance on the uneven hill. His legs hadn't regained their stamina. The incline had been burned clean of life, then the winter had done the rest. With all the brush and weeds gone, the hill looked unfertile forever.

Halfway to the crate, Hugo paused behind a chest-high sandstone boulder. Arab bands had been reported in the surrounding hills. He spotted the blue sheet flapping on the bleached earth and waved back at Yakob, who motioned him to keep going.

Hugo spit, unhappy to be out here by himself. He'd already been alone as much as any man in Palestine.

He inched from behind the boulder. Both legs griped as Hugo crouched downhill where boxes and tins littered the ground, a scatter of noodle cartons, tins of fruit and kosher meat, and ammo cartons. He tiptoed through the debris to stand on a stone to signal Yakob.

A flutter caught his eye, fifty meters downhill in a dry streambed.

"Oh, damn."

In the shallow ravine, sixty Arabs squatted; Hugo had caught them hiding. Their robes and headdresses flicked on the windswept slope, but nothing else of them moved. The Arabs hunkered as if surprised or embarrassed to be seen. Hugo held his breath and his place on the stone; his legs prickled to get out of there and run shrieking to Yakob. Half the Arabs stooping in the crusty dirt were women and children. The rest were older, worn faces. These were *fellahin*, peasants. Every one held a sack; none had a gun.

Hugo jumped off the rock. Both thighs flared as he dashed up the hill. Again, the rifle put him off-kilter. Yakob's red hair stood out against the hillside.

"Arabs!" Hugo yelled. "Arabs!"

Yakob's rifle reared, pointed past Hugo but he had no one to fire at. Hugo limped to the foxhole and tumbled in. Yakob lifted him to his feet.

"What did you see?"

Between shallow breaths, Hugo told of the sixty women and children in the ravine. Yakob gave him the rifle and jumped out. Hugo had two rifles when he didn't want one. Yakob unpocketed six clips of ammo.

Hugo said, "No, no. Where are you going?"

"Those are looters. There's an attack coming."

"Wait."

"I've got to warn the kibbutz. You can't make the run."

"I suppose not. Alright. What do you want me to do?"

"Is it not fucking obvious?"

"Shit. Go."

Yakob dashed uphill. Hugo bent his eye behind one of the rifles and aimed at nothing. He'd fire at the first thing that moved on the sterile slope.

The foxhole was too big without Yakob, too quiet. He cradled the rifle stock to his cheek but the pulse in his hands and his heaving lungs ruined any chance at shooting well. He needed to find his courage and hold his ground. Hugo flung curses down the hill at the invisible Arabs, trying to stir himself.

He arrayed eight clips on the ledge and chambered a round in the old Dutch rifle. Down in the Abu Rish, outside the perimeter fence, a shadow in the cemetery came unstaked from the ground. It might be a man. Hugo shot to see if it would hide, or fall.

CHAPTER 83

RIVKAH

Rivkah flung open the door. Yakob stood huffing, hands to his knees. He raised his beet-red face.

"Arabs. On the south hill. Hugo."

Mrs. Pappel hurried to the door beside Rivkah.

"Hugo what?"

Down the quarry road, a gunshot popped. Before Yakob could answer, the same gun fired again. "That's him. Where's Vince?"

"In the orchard. How many?"

"Sixty. Women and children, but there'll be fighters. I don't know how many."

From the east, other guns crackled, rapid and nasty. Yakob straightened.

"Ring the alarm."

He whirled away and leaped off the porch. Mrs. Pappel hustled to her room to arm herself. She belted at Rivkah, "Go!"

Rivkah broke into a run. She wanted a single moment, one last peaceful tick and tock before war, but gritted her teeth and dashed for the bell.

Two girls saw her running for the dining hall; instantly, they pivoted to their own homes, shouting. Rivkah didn't slow until she braked against the hall. She yanked the bell's lanyard hard, one two three, one two three. When she stopped, she heard nothing but the clanging. In seconds, the settlement became a crossroads of streaming, shouting farmers.

Massuot Yitzhak's fifty weapons were clutched in unsure hands. The haverim upended tables in windows, teenagers lugged ammo boxes. Yakob rounded a corner ahead of a pair of Palmachniks. Spotting Rivkah, the redhead rapped a fist to his heart to bolster her. Leading the two, he disappeared down the quarry road.

She ran to the guest house which served as the clinic. Rivkah stayed outside the door, reluctant to be out of sight in case Vince came looking. The bell stopped ringing in her head, and she heard the gunplay on the southern hill: Hugo.

Mrs. Pappel hustled to her through others crisscrossing. She took Rivkah into her arms. "Be safe, child."

"I need to find Vince."

Mrs. Pappel shook her head no. "Listen to me. You can't ask him to think about anything else. Not today."

"What if we die?"

"Then we'll die the way we set out to. In Palestine."

Massuot Yitzhak flurried on all sides. The settlers ran and were changed as they ran, into soldiers. On the slope below the orchard where Vince had gone, bursts of gunfire rocketed above Massuot Yitzhak.

Mrs. Pappel pressed a hand over Rivkah's stomach. "We won't die today, Liebling. Stay with the clinic. I'll see you soon."

She walked off calmly, pistol on her hip, so much rising around her. Rounding the corner, Mrs. Pappel drew her gun, turned downhill to the sound of fighting, and hastened.

CHAPTER 84

VINCE

Up in the settlement, the alarm rang. This was no drill.

Vince stopped digging. Nothing moved on the parched western slope below the orchard.

A small dot of sound, a little pow, swept from the south. A gunshot was followed by another.

Vince tossed away his pickaxe to sprint through the saplings. He reached the top of the incline winded and took a moment before shouting at the eleven haverim arriving full-out, carrying six long rifles and two Stens. Three ammo bearers skidded in, loaded with boxes. Vince tramped along the crest of the hill, calling each into place behind the sandbag redoubts they had built a month ago.

The western approach was cleared, elevated, and commanding. In the morning light among the crouching boys, Vince stood with hands on hips. Nothing came their way through the Wadi Abu Rish. More shots crackled from the south, then in the east from Yellow Hill.

Young faces watched Vince pace, each cheek smooth and cherry-red from the chill. On the plain, beyond their rifles' range, a hundred Arabs emerged from below a rise. They advanced in a steady saunter without vehicles or camels. Vince's instinct was to run and find Rivkah, get her away somehow. In these first moments of seeing their enemy come, the young kibbutzniks around him wanted the same, to be somewhere else, live without killing, die on a different day. Vince watched each eye blink to clear a tear or a fleeting thought, then lower to a gun.

Hugo and Yakob were together on the south slope. Was that Hugo running through his ammo? Vince's nerves made him laugh; Hugo always claimed to be an awful shot. The Arabs wouldn't know that. Vince's laugh might have sounded brave; his eleven boys picked it up and laughed too.

Below in the west, the Arabs split their force in two. Half continued their approach, the rest lagged.

The attackers came within four hundred meters on the stony flats. Vince told his boys to stay hidden behind their sandbags and rocks. The Arabs wore keffiyehs, bandoliers across their chests, some in robes, others in jackets and pantaloons. They had beards and moustaches, they were villagers, a rabble, and might not fight well.

"Remember. They're out in the open, you're not. They're climbing a hill, you're not. You've got a hundred rounds each. Stay in your firing lanes. Make every bullet count."

Two hundred yards distant, at the base of the hill, the first wave reached the perimeter fence. They used wire cutters to nip the barbed strands.

"Stay down."

With the fence cut, the first rank of attackers started the long climb. A few out front gave a yell, then ran up the bare slope. Their first shots at the orchard were wild. Vince took cover.

The cleared hillside gave the Arabs nowhere to hide. Even so, a second rank lurched up the hill. Behind them in the wadi, fifty Arabs bided their turn.

"Wait."

At a hundred yards below the orchard, the first wave stopped shooting to climb faster. At their backs, the second wave did the same. Then, at the base of the hill, the reserves began their ascent. All one hundred Arabs labored up the slope, looking for cover that wasn't there.

"Wait."

The slope steepened as it neared the crest. Some Arabs stumbled as they moved within range of the six Dutch rifles and two Stens.

The fellahin in the lead closed to thirty yards from the orchard. Vince popped his head up from behind the sandbags. The Arab out front, not a young man, realized his mistake.

Vince called to him, "Turn around."

The Arab shook his head without sadness.

Before the Arab could surge the last distance, Vince shouted to his eight guns, "Now."

✳ ✳ ✳

Vince's boys kneeled behind sandbags, beneath winter-naked trees, and emptied everything into the Arabs coming up the hill.

The charge fell apart. The defenders of the western slope unleashed a final fusillade, the loudest of the day, like a firing squad. The Arabs withdrew, shouting no longer. On the hillside and in the wadi, they left ten bodies but took away their wounded. Tonight they'd return, specters on the dark slope, to carry off their dead. Vince told his boys not to fire on them.

He got to his feet, creaky from the cold. Vince sent five of his eleven boys to the dining hall to eat and bring back blankets, then send the others. He thanked none for the killing they'd done that cold morning. No one exulted, none were hurt, all had shown valor. They would stay in position through the night and he would stay with them. First, Vince went to find Rivkah.

He walked through Massuot Yitzhak, sensing the exhaustion. He entered the dining hall. Bread, eggs, and meat stew were on every table; the kitchen wasn't going to stint today. Little Hugo wasn't among the fifty haverim in the hall. At a table in the rear, Mrs. Pappel rose with Rivkah. Both waved. Vince stepped into Mrs. Pappel's outstretched arms for a strong, telling hug. He reached for Rivkah's hand, then sat holding it.

Vince asked, "You both alright?"

They nodded. Mrs. Pappel asked, "Are you?"

"Tired. Hungry."

"Will they come back?"

"I don't think so. I'll spend the night in the orchard. What have you heard?"

"A thousand Arabs attacked across the Gush. We beat them with two hundred rifles."

"How many settlers hurt?"

"We don't know yet."

Rivkah said, "Get something to eat."

In line, Vince asked for a half-portion, to leave more for the fighters and ammo runners, for Hugo still guarding the quarry road. The cooks dishing out the food felt the marvel of being alive and wouldn't hear of anyone taking less than a full share. Vince accepted two eggs, two pieces of bread, a bowl of lamb stew, and a cup of water.

Yakob entered the hall and came to the table with Vince, Rivkah, and Mrs. Pappel. Blood marred his hands.

He said, "Listen to me. That was a miracle."

Undeterred by the scarlet stains, Mrs. Pappel took Yakob's hand while he spoke.

"We had three killed on the south slope." This was where Yakob had been, laying down a corpse.

Vince asked, "Hugo?"

"He's alright. He's a terrible shot."

Rivkah said to Vince, "Come outside."

He followed through the tables. Outside, Rivkah turned to him with arms crossed. The noon sun made short shadows for them to stand on. Vince moved closer, but she didn't unfold her arms.

"It's an awful day. And a miracle. I don't know which today is."

"What's going on?"

"This isn't the way I wanted to tell you."

"Rivkah?"

"I'm pregnant."

Vince stepped back, to behold her head to toe.

"Are you happy about it?"

"It's a hard thing to say with blood on the ground. I feel guilty. But yes."

Vince stepped to her now. They held each other for uncounted time while settlers pulled tables down out of their windows and hugged others who'd come through alright.

"How long have you known?"

"A little while."

"Mrs. Pappel knows?"

"She does."

"Gabbi?"

"No one else."

Hugo trudged up from the quarry road. The barrel of his rifle rose far above his shoulders. He walked alone, dog-tired like a soldier. He stopped for a hand on Vince's shoulder. Vince didn't take his arms from around Rivkah.

Hugo said, "That's pretty. Is there food?"

Rivkah said, "Eggs, bread, and stew. And water."

Hugo shuffled to the dining hall. "Great. Prison food."

They watched him go inside.

Rivkah said, "Don't tell him, or anyone. I'll choose when to tell."

"Alright. But why?"

"The mothers have all been sent to Jerusalem." She pulled back from his arms. "I won't leave Massuot Yitzhak."

"Should we talk about this?"

"What is there to talk about?"

Vince pressed his hand behind her head, to pull her tighter to him. "Then we'll stay."

CHAPTER 85

HUGO

January 15

In the parlor, Hugo dropped his pants.

Mrs. Pappel stopped him. "What on earth are you doing?"

He showed her a jar of the concoction he'd made. "I'm going to rub this on my scabs, to keep them from breaking open."

She took the jar to smell. "Dear God, what's in this?"

"Honey and onions."

"Do it outside. I won't have that smell in the house."

On the porch, Hugo stepped out of his trousers to knead the ointment into his thighs. No one walked by in the afternoon; most of the settlers were squatting in a hole or behind sandbags, or resting in bed.

The mixture was his mother's creation. Hugo had burned and mashed many a hand and finger as a plumber in Leipzig. She'd made the oil each time he came home cursing and sucking on some wounded finger or wrist. She would have been miserable here. No corner shops, no vegetable market, no one her age to kibitz with but Mrs. Pappel, though the two would have gotten along. Both women had wisdom won over years. Hugo had no notion of growing old; he couldn't imagine it.

Mrs. Pappel came out on the porch. She sniffed Hugo to be sure she could sit in his company. She brought her tea and worried quietly.

The Etzion bloc was almost out of ammunition. Medical supplies were finished. Radios down to their last batteries. The roads were blocked. If the Arabs returned before supplies arrived, the Gush would be overrun.

Hugo had not pulled up his pants. He said to Mrs. Pappel, "Stop."

"I beg your pardon. Stop what?"

"The way you're sipping your fucking tea. I can hear your thoughts. We're all going to die. Stop it."

"Well." Mrs. Pappel lowered the teacup to her lap, then stood. "I'll get you some tea and you can listen to you own concerns. Pull up your trousers."

She returned with her own tea freshened and a steaming cup for Hugo. Teacups in hand, they let some silence hover over the quiescent hills and the dormant orchards and workshops. The onion and honey, bittersweet on Hugo's hands, conjured his mother and sisters and old Germany. Hugo took a risk and offered the past as a topic to Mrs. Pappel.

To his surprise, she let him recollect. His childhood tales pleased her and in stages evoked her own, of pre-war Austria and Britain. Neither had done this in a long while, remembered and spoken from memory. Mrs. Pappel confided that she'd never reminisced with Rivkah because she didn't want to upset the girl. Hugo seemed impossible to upset. She told him of her young marriage in Vienna, the long time in London with Morrie. On the porch, after the sun fell, they listened to each other. Neither buried anyone, all were alive in their talk. Hugo made no mention of the camps or the Irgun. Mrs. Pappel omitted the Haganah and guns. They spoke as if they'd never left their homes or come to Palestine.

CHAPTER 86

HUGO

January 16

Hugo didn't try to keep up with the running haverim.

Settlers from across the bloc, from Kfar Etzion, Massuot Yitzhak, Revadim, and Ein Tzurim, raced down their hillsides, through the wadis. Vince, Rivkah, and Yakob didn't wait for Hugo but hurried into the blue desert dusk. Mrs. Pappel stayed behind in a wrap against the January chill. She said to Hugo as he left the porch that she was too old to run to or from the dead.

Hugo's scars gnawed if he pushed too hard. He walked as briskly as he could past the quarry, then up the unpaved road to Kfar Etzion, to arrive with the last stragglers.

Seven British army vehicles were stopped outside Neve Ovadia, the library of Kfar Etzion. Three trucks were open cargo haulers with tarps tied across their beds. The other four were armored halftracks. A tall policeman, patrician in a civilian suit, climbed down from the lead truck. It seemed he'd waited for the settlers to gather en masse before speaking, to address them all instead of piecemeal. Three hundred kibbutzniks formed a large semicircle; solemnly he stepped to the center.

"All the women. Please go to your homes. Now."

One hundred women hesitated before departing, Rivkah among them. A few at a time, without a word of protest, they turned away, brave enough to know this was not the time to remark. The rest followed, slowly and mournfully, linking arms.

The British soldiers had no delicate way to unload the bodies. With the trucks' headlamps shut off to do the work in half-light, they handed down corpses to haverim who gripped stiffened arms and legs. On the white ground before the library, the bodies were laid side-by-side. The row grew longer, and with each Jew lifted from a truck, tremors swept through the gathered. Some corpses had limbs cut off; these pieces, too, were handed down.

No one demanded to know how this happened; no one said anything. The settlers only gasped and rapped their stricken hearts. The policeman stood unapproached. Hugo inched through the crowd to stand near the growing row of bodies. Twenty lay in the pale line, like a knocked-down picket fence, then more, another every twenty seconds. When the last body was set down in the failing light, the crowd staggered where they stood or kneeled now that the burden was known. In Hebrew they uttered the number, "*lamed hey*," thirty-five.

Yakob stepped out of the crowd with other commanders of the bloc to speak with the policeman. No one else moved.

Hugo strode into the open, to review the dead. The killing wounds in each fighter were plain. Many hands and arms were gone, noses and ears sliced off. They all wore the uniform of the Haganah, and many bore the patch of the Palmach.

At the dusty boots of one fighter, Hugo eased to the ground. No one told him to get away from the bodies or questioned why he'd stepped forward. It would have made no difference if they had. The dead were shared; they were his. No one could tell him they were not.

Hugo unbuttoned the Haganah fighter's green vest and did not look away from the desecrated face. He dug into pockets and was not gentle, for gentleness served no purpose. Hugo searched for papers, identification, to know who this battered boy was. He found a wallet.

Hugo held up a driver's license to the crowd. "I've done this before."

He laid the license on the fighter's chest, then slid on his knees to the next. Another man emerged from the crowd to help. He was small-framed like Hugo, little in his hands and feet.

By the convoy's headlamps, the leaders learned from the policeman
the story of the lamed hey. Quietly with the other man, Hugo searched
the corpses. After each had his name returned, the men of the Gush
wrapped the bodies in sheets, then lifted them onto stretchers to bear
them into Neve Ovadia.

Inside the library, candles were lit behind each bloodied head, a
guard of honor was posted. The murmur of shovels began in the dark
cemetery. The digging would take the rest of the night to bury the thirty-five. The settlers went back to their homes, or to foxholes and lookouts.

CHAPTER 87

RIVKAH

January 17

On her way to the dining hall, Rivkah found a place to vomit. Mrs. Pappel said she had a few more weeks until she would show.

The child must be healthy to be so demanding. Rivkah spit to clear her mouth; a hand rested on her spine. She straightened against it but did not turn to Vince, her tongue too sour. He handed her a napkin.

"How did you find me?"

"It's not hard. I just never lose you."

Her nausea and constant hunger, the dreadful events of the last few days, Vince's answer, all made Rivkah cry. Vince reached for her, but she felt too queasy to be held, so she pulled her sweater tighter against the evening haze; this kept his arms away. Rain had come during the day and the dusk was damp, tufted and cold.

They returned to the dining hall and joined Hugo, Mrs. Pappel, and Yakob at a table. Fifty rifles leaned against a wall.

In the front of the murals and a hundred haverim, Uzi, the commander of the Haganah company in Gush Etzion, began the meeting. He was sabra, and long-legged like Vince.

"I want to tell you what happened to the lamed hey. After the Arab attack on Gush Etzion three days ago, a convoy of thirty-five Palmach and Field Force students assembled to bring you supplies. The Arabs have blocked the roads, so they had to travel on foot. The night after the attack, the thirty-five left the village of Har-Tuv for the fifteen-mile hike. Each carried a hundred-pound pack of ammo, blood plasma, and batteries. They got a late start, and maybe they should have turned back as soon as it was clear they couldn't make the whole trip during the dark. But they pushed on, knowing how badly the supplies were needed. At dawn, with the bloc three miles away, two Arab women spotted the platoon outside the village of Surif. They spared these women, who then alerted the local militia. An Arab force of eighty attacked the platoon in the valley between Surif and Jab'a. This force grew fast; more villagers joined until the column was facing over two hundred. The British in Bethlehem knew about the attack but did nothing. Six frontal assaults were made on the platoon. All six were repulsed."

Uzi took a wide stance, hands behind his back, a martial posture.

"The surviving fighters carried their wounded to the top of a hill. They battled into the afternoon, until their ammo was gone. They fought with rocks. The Arabs launched a seventh assault. The rest, you know."

The Haganah commander paced in front of the mural.

"When the thirty-five failed to arrive at the bloc on schedule, we alerted the British in Bethlehem. To their credit, they sent out patrols to find the bodies. Arab villagers refused to carry Jews on their camels to the army's trucks. The British carried our dead themselves. We owe them thanks for that."

Uzi lowered his head. Some of the lamed hey were well known and beloved in the bloc, including the man Uzi had replaced as commander.

"Your settlements are on land given to the Arabs by the UN's map. The Arabs claim this land. The Haganah does not have enough soldiers and materiel to guarantee your safety. Right now, Jerusalem is under a massive blockade. But make no mistake, you are not without advantages. The Etzion bloc holds the high ground above the Hebron road. Any Arab force trying to attack Jerusalem out of the south has to go past you. The Haganah will send as many reinforcements as we can spare to help shore up your position, to hold that road. I don't know how many and I don't know when. But you are the southern defense of Jerusalem. Take me at my word. There will be another battle for Gush Etzion."

Pacing, Uzi said, "The force that attacked the lamed hey wasn't just an Arab militia, but a mob that ran from their villages to take part in a bloodbath. The Jewish bodies were disfigured, you saw this for yourselves. The Arabs have made it plain. They will conduct a war of extermination. They won't allow a single Jew to live on land they claim. Consider this when you decide today whether to go or stay."

Uzi stopped walking to face the haverim.

"Once Haganah fighters arrive in Gush Etzion, you will all be given the chance to leave for Jerusalem. You've done your share. There'll be no judgment."

The Haganah commander nodded, a curt gesture, then swept out of the hall.

Red Yakob moved to the front. He called on Hugo.

"When will the landing strip be done?"

"Two or three days."

"Make it two."

Hugo grabbed his rifle from the wall and left for the bulldozer in the valley.

The first to stand was Shmuel, one of the quarrymen, chiseled into a muscular figure. "You all know I've got no family. Most of you don't, either. But if you've got a wife in Jerusalem, a child, then go. I won't think anything bad about you. Like Uzi said. No one will." Shmuel bent to take his seat, then straightened. "I'm done being a refugee. I'm staying."

The big lad sat. A second pioneer stood, the carpenter Meir, a lean boy in round glasses. He grabbed one of the rifles from against the wall. "I'd never held a gun before. Last month I shot a man. I don't want to do it again. No one here does. But I will."

At Meir's table, Orli, who worked in the fields and with Rivkah in the clinic, rose. "It doesn't seem right for strangers to defend our homes without us. It doesn't feel moral."

More stood to speak quickly, then sit. No one addressed the gathering in long or passionate ways but chose their words carefully; what they said would affect the lives of everyone in Massuot Yitzhak.

Yakob reminded the haverim that the war would eventually end. When it did, Gush Etzion would be inside an Arab state. No one believed that was going to change. Unless they held their lands now, they'd have little hope of staying on them after peace was restored.

A few voices in favor of evacuation made themselves heard.

Natan, a shop worker, one of the first settlers of Massuot Yitzhak three years ago with Rivkah and Mrs. Pappel, said, "I came to Palestine to be a citizen of a Jewish State. Life under the Arabs will be living in a new diaspora. We'll always be in danger, always in exile. It's not what I hoped for."

At the same table, his brother Ehud, one of the boys who'd defended the orchard with Vince, got to his feet.

"I've planted a whole orchard here. If we can't hold onto it, I want to go plant a new one where I can watch it grow."

Aharon stood. "I've got the strength left to defend my home. Not for starting over on another hilltop. You all need to know, I'll be the last one to leave."

The discussion struck a lull. Rivkah patted Mrs. Pappel's hand, to rise as the elder.

Mrs. Pappel got to her feet. "I understand. Every bit of this place is precious. But sentiment won't defend it. We need to ask ourselves, are we being too brave? The Haganah will defend these hills, they'll turn your homes and fields into a fortress. The thirty-five died trying to bring us guns and ammunition, not seeds. Ehud is right. The planting is done. Massuot Yitzhak is now a bunker for the defense of Jerusalem."

She indicated Meir, resting her hand over her heart.

"I've never killed anyone either. I'm sorry for you."

Mrs. Pappel stepped into the center of the hall.

"If anyone is considering leaving, if you have any doubt, you need to go. Go to your families. It's been said already, no one will blame you. We may even envy you. If you're unsure, you won't add enough to the defense of our land to risk your lives. You're farmers. Can a soldier plant a field, can a soldier turn salt into soil? No. You can. Palestine will need you when this is over. Think before you answer. Because if you stay, you stay as soldiers."

Yisakhar, a burly welder, asked, "What about that Arab attack? A thousand. And we held them off."

"A miracle. A miracle that was denied to the convoy of ten. Denied to the lamed hey. It might be withheld from us next time."

Shmuel spoke again. "Mrs. Pappel, what will you do?"

She wended through the tables. Everyone hushed as she passed on her way to Shmuel, one of her first students three years ago. Mrs. Pappel bussed his cheek.

"I'm old. I'm like the dead in the cemetery. They're old, too, you see? No one gets older than that. I'll stay with them."

Vince pressed Rivkah's hand. "Tell them now."

"Are you sure?"

"Go ahead."

Rivkah stood before the settlers of Massuot Yitzhak.

"My father was too brave. He stayed in Vienna when I asked him to go. If he had not been, he would have a grocery store today in Tel Aviv. My mother was too brave, she believed in my father. But Austria was not our home. Europe was not your home. Palestine was. For all of us, always. This was our homeland before we were born."

Rivkah stepped behind Vince. She lay one hand across her belly, the other rested on Vince's shoulder.

"Palestine is the homeland of my child, before it is born. We will stay."

CHAPTER 88

VINCE

February 8
Massuot Yitzhak

Hugo finished bulldozing the airstrip. Then he set about making landmines.

With a team of metal workers, Hugo welded them by the hundreds. He and his boys worked at night because that was when the generators ran, to power the perimeter lights and search beacon. They adapted tools and materials already in Massuot Yitzhak: unused TNT and ammonal from the quarry, empty tins, rifle cartridges, nails, and scrap iron.

The Haganah's airplanes brought him detonators. Hugo designed a firing mechanism from a sharpened nail and a steel spring. His team made blast mines and fragmentation mines.

Vince's team buried them.

With a squad of diggers and armed guards, Vince burrowed in the tough soil. The earth made him and his helpers work as hard to lay a mine as to plant a tree. He took meticulous notes on the location of every minefield, badly scared with his boys as they lay mines, set the primers, and moved on.

Under a lowering sky, in a wind the bare hills did nothing to hinder, Vince drove a shovel into the dirt and left it. He sent his team up the slope to rest. He'd fetch them in two hours.

The young workers trudged away, already tired from night patrols, guard duty, training, and digging defense works. They were hungry, for though three convoys had reached Gush Etzion this month and planes were landing on Hugo's runway, the bloc's food, barely enough for two hundred settlers, now had to be shared with one hundred and fifty Haganah reinforcements.

Vince's eight boys reached the crest of the hill. None went on to the kibbutz but stayed in the orchard. Setting up ladders and handing out shears, they set to pruning the branches. They were farmers, too.

Vince shuddered in the wind made cooler by his sweat. Instead of climbing the incline with his team, he walked the wadi to Massuot Yitzhak's southern slope, where he would sit and take his rest admiring Rivkah.

He passed foxholes and trenches of boys he couldn't name, the Haganah fighters from Jerusalem. They were as young as the kibbutzniks, university students. Vince exchanged waves and walked on.

Across the hillside, a phalanx of pickaxes rose and fell to extend a trench to the base of Rock Hill. Vince found a rock and took a seat unnoticed by Rivkah and the haverim laboring beside her.

She worked stroke-for-stroke, one piston in the long machine of them. On the crest of Rock Hill, a half-dozen Palmachniks kept an eye out.

Vince closed his eyes and found rhythm in the picks. Soon, a different sound arose, an engine. Vince watched a Piper Cub line up its approach to the landing strip. The diggers paused, too; this was a pretty sight.

The plane touched down cleanly, even in the wind. A mule cart left Kfar Etzion to come unload the cargo.

The pilot emerged, pulling on a leather jacket, then a heavyset man stepped out. He wasn't dressed for the raw weather of the highlands. The pilot peeled off his jacket for him, then turned to dragging boxes out of the plane. The big visitor threw a carrier bag over his shoulder and followed where the pilot pointed, up toward Massuot Yitzhak.

He walked with his head down, straining on the incline. Vince didn't recognize him until he was much closer.

The reporter waved at the line of diggers, affable. The leather jacket was too small.

Vince stood to shout, "You're looking for me."

The reporter stopped. "Haas?"

The man made his way across the slope. Vince called out, "What are you doing here?"

The reporter lifted an arm to signal they should wait until they were close enough to speak normally. Once in front of Vince, he put his hands on wide hips and said, "Whew."

"Still sitting at my desk?"

"Not for a few months. I've been working out of Jerusalem. How are you, Haas? You look good."

The reporter, fists on his waist like a sugar bowl, did a slow pan to take in his surroundings, the Hebron hills, trenches and barbed wire, Jews digging, Jews on guard, guns on top of Rock Hill, Yellow Hill, Lone Tree Hill.

"You ready to go home?"

"What?"

"Dennis sent me to come get you. Once the plane's unloaded, we're gone."

Rivkah climbed the hill. The reporter read Vince's darting eyes.

"Look, you don't have to leave altogether. If you don't want to go back to New York, Dennis said you can work out of Tel Aviv. Haas, everybody knows about the attacks on the convoys. The big attack on the bloc. I've talked to the cops, the army; I've talked to everybody. You're surrounded by Arabs. They're coming back for this place. Dennis doesn't want you here for that. I don't think you want to be here for that." He looked around again. "I sure as hell wouldn't."

Rivkah skirted the big reporter to stand with Vince. The reporter said "Hello," but was ignored.

He said to Vince, "You've done your bit."

Rivkah asked, "Who are you?"

"I'm from his newspaper."

"New York."

"Yes, ma'am."

"What do you want?"

Vince put a hand into the reporter's chest, a small shove. "Give us a minute."

"Okay. But…." The reporter motioned at his wrist, as if to a watch. The plane wouldn't stay much longer, nor would he. The reporter galumphed down the hill.

Rivkah asked, "Is he your friend?"

"No."

"Has he come to take you away?"

"He mentioned it."

"What did you say?"

Vince spread his hands. "What do you think I said?"

She walked across the slope, away from the trench, Vince on her heels. She mopped her brow with a kerchief. He doffed his jacket to drape it over her shoulders; she'd taken hers off while digging. Rivkah shrugged it away.

Vince said, "Come on," appealing. She let him cover her against the wind.

Rivkah did not speak until they reached the quarry road. She stopped on the path. From here, Vince could turn one way to the airplane, the other to Massuot Yitzhak.

"You should go."

"Are you serious?"

"Your life has come to fetch you. Did you think it wouldn't?"

"It's not just my life anymore. Listen. We can go together. To Tel Aviv. You and the baby will be safe."

Rivkah slipped his jacket from around her shoulders. She held it out to him, to say, take this with you to Tel Aviv.

Vince said, "The other mothers left. Why not you?"

"Their children were sent away. The women chose to go with them."

"Do you think I want you standing in that trench shooting at another thousand Arabs? They're coming back. They'll be ready next time."

Rivkah pointed with Vince's jacket at the diggers downhill. "Tell me who you want in that trench instead of me. Aharon? Yakob? Hugo? Missus Pappel?"

Again, she wrapped Vince's coat around herself, accepting that it was cold.

He said, "I'm not wrong to be afraid for you." Vince stepped close to have his arms around her. Rivkah lay her head against his chest.

Downhill, the reporter watched. With no signal from Vince but seeing them embrace, he figured the deal was done, the goodbye said. He headed for the landing strip.

Vince looked over the top of Rivkah's head, to the blocked Jerusalem road. In the Wadi Shahid, the mule cart had been loaded. The pilot cranked his aircraft back to life.

Vince took his coat. Rivkah returned to the trench to help it reach the defenders of Rock Hill. He walked up the slope with no glance back at the plane. Vince was going to go lay down on Mrs. Pappel's sofa for two hours, to rest.

CHAPTER 89

HUGO

March 10
Massuot Yitzhak

Red Yakob hadn't grown up on a farm any more than Hugo. Both were the sons of teachers. Yakob was a sabra soldier, but this morning he marched happily into the apple orchard with a stepladder on his shoulder. Beside him, Hugo carried a rifle.

The rains had done well over Gush Etzion, and some snows. Massuot Yitzhak's swollen rivulet burbled, a glossy thread down the hillside. On some mornings the spring air unveiled the faraway sands of the coast, or on the opposite horizon the blue sprawl of the Dead Sea. The land sparkled. Beside the paths grew wild narcissi, cyclamens, and anemones; in the orchards the seedlings fattened. At breakfast, Yakob said he wanted to make something grow, to feel what that was like. He asked to join the orchard crew for the day and assigned Hugo to guard.

On the ladder, trimming the top of an apple tree, Yakob talked.

"You've got to make room in the tree, that's what they said. Too many branches and the leaves will shade each other. It takes sun to make fruit, so you cut, here, see, and here. This one. Look here, Hugo."

Snipped twigs fell. Yakob narrated each cut for an hour of barbering the trees. Hugo picked up some twigs; they bled fragrance and would have blossomed had they not been cut. He stopped listening to Yakob and walked far enough from the orchard not to hear the shears of the others working the trees. Hugo fixed on the hillside below, the minefield, the wadi, and the Arab-held hills three miles off.

He'd not stood there long when the small crump of an explosion drew his attention. On the rumpled plain to the south, across the Abu Rish, a powdery cloud boiled in the breezeless day. The dust hid the cause. Hugo edged onto the incline, careful to stay above the minefield. One mile away, a few tiny figures scurried, then disappeared.

✳ ✳ ✳

Vince had laid the mines; Hugo had built them. Yakob took both to go see what had happened.

In the sharp noon light, red Yakob, Hugo, and ten Palmachniks followed Vince through the minefields. Yakob became a different man as a leader; he clamped his jaw and moved with a predator's grace and hush. Hugo took long strides to stay in Vince's footsteps.

The southern rim of the Abu Rish rose to a low plateau, called the Mukhtar's Saddle. A plum orchard grew on the tableland with views of Kfar Etzion and Massuot Yitzhak. The stand of fruit trees hadn't been pruned, too far from either kibbutz, too dangerous to guard. At the base of the slope up to the Saddle, Vince stepped in front of Yakob and the patrol.

"Careful." He checked his notebook. "There."

Vince approached with caution, Hugo close on his heels.

Three shallow craters marked where a string of mines had blown. Scorch marks stained the bottom of one of the holes, damp enough to tack Hugo's fingertips. Someone, at least one, had been hurt here, maybe killed.

Hugo asked Vince, "Was it the pliers?"

"Yes."

Hugo had taught Vince how to lay a boobytrap. An Arab reconnaissance squad must have been lurking around the base of the Saddle, creeping close to the settlements. A pair of pliers left in plain view, picked off the ground, would trip a wire attached to three mines set to blow in sequence. The bloc's settlers and Haganah fighters knew to stay on certain paths and touch nothing unfamiliar. This was why. A blood trail trickled westward.

Yakob said, "They're scouting."

The Palmachniks patted Hugo on the shoulder for the boobytrap, not Vince, then pivoted with Yakob to return to Massuot Yitzhak. Vince hung back. Hugo stayed with him.

Hugo asked, "What are you thinking?"

"I meant to ask you. Why pliers?"

"They have a special significance for me."

Hugo wiped his wet fingertips in the dust. Vince didn't look up from the blotches.

"It's been a long time since I've written anything."

"I don't think you could get this into eight hundred words. I've meant to ask you something, too. You don't carry a gun. Why not?"

"So I can go on telling myself I'm a reporter."

Vince kicked dust over the bloody crater. Hugo let him determine how long to stare. When he turned away, Hugo followed at a distance. He wanted no more judgments on killing from Vince, who'd seen a great deal but done little of it himself. They returned to Massuot Yitzhak, dodging the mines.

✳ ✳ ✳

Hugo didn't want to sit on Mrs. Pappel's porch and rehash the day with her over tea. Vince needed tending, and Hugo left the women to it. His scars itched; he needed to walk. The evening stayed pleasant. With candles flickering in the settlement's windows, the stars pulled Hugo into the open. On his own, he strolled for an hour.

Mrs. Pappel found him overlooking the southern slope, gazing at Kfar Etzion on its hill a mile away. The big kibbutz looked spectral, candlelit too.

From behind, she said his name. Hugo invited her to sit. They both wore pistols.

"You missed the news on the Jerusalem radio tonight. They were talking about you."

"Really? What did they say?"

"A group of Arabs was attacked today near Hebron. One was killed, two wounded."

"That would be me."

"Have I told you? You're about the age of my son."

"You don't talk about him."

"He's in America, with a couple million other Jews."

A sparkle arched above the Mukhtar's Saddle, too close to be a shooting star. A second flash left a similar trail. Both flamed out in the valley.

Mrs. Pappel said, "Tracers."

More burning rounds sailed at dark Massuot Yitzhak but fell short on the slope. The bullets came out of the tiny village of Khirbat Safa a half-mile from the Saddle. Perhaps they were fired by mourners, or a mother with a rifle.

More blazing bullets hit nothing. Hugo lay facing the real stars to make himself a smaller target. Mrs. Pappel did the same. He expected someone to ring the alarm, but no one did.

The shooting from sad little Safa ended after ten minutes. Mrs. Pappel and Hugo went back to the porch. Rivkah and Vince greeted them with tea.

In the starry quiet, neighbors passed the word from house to house. A massive convoy was scheduled to arrive from Jerusalem tomorrow, a column of fifty trucks. A low alert was in place; every fighter and kibbutznik was ordered to sleep in their clothes tonight. Vince grabbed a blanket, kissed Rivkah, and disappeared to the orchard, putting himself on duty. Rivkah went to her room. Hugo stayed on the porch with Mrs. Pappel so long that he dozed. When he stood to go to the guest house, the old woman was still sitting with him. He bussed her cheek and told her to go inside, that everything was fine. A giant convoy of soldiers and supplies was coming tomorrow to save them, and her son and the millions were safe in America.

CHAPTER 90

HUGO

March 27

Before daybreak, Yakob entered Hugo's room. Hugo hadn't time to sit up in bed, still in his clothes, before Yakob tossed his coat on top of him. Yakob found Hugo's boots and arranged them for him to step into. Yawning on the edge of his mattress, Hugo tugged up his suspenders.

"Do you sleep? Ever?"

"I do. In my mother's house. I'll take you some day. You've never had latkes like hers."

"What are we doing?"

"Going to the highway."

"What for?"

"Sabotage."

Hugo laced up his boots sleepily, no match for Yakob's wakefulness. Outside, five Field Force students waited with rifles and two ladders. The last dewy bits of night left them grey but still very young.

"Why do I have to come?"

"You're Irgun. You're Kharda. This is right up your alley. You'll see."

With Yakob's hand at his spine, Hugo fell in with the students. Once he had Hugo walking, Yakob patted his back. "We're going to cut the phone lines between Hebron and Jerusalem. The big convoy's coming. We don't want the Arabs talking."

Hugo tramped down the road out of Massuot Yitzhak. Two students each carried the ladders; one walked with a coil of rope. The morning pinked as they passed the airstrip and set out overland below Yellow Hill.

He worried about mines, how ironic it would be if he stepped on one and did himself in with his own handiwork. Yakob led the patrol like he knew where he was going. They passed foxholes and strongpoints in the Wadi Shahid and the bunkered houses of Hirbet Sawir; hunkered-down settlers and soldiers greeted the patrol keenly, excited for the arrival of today's convoy. Fifty-one vehicles, with food, weapons, fuel, timber, concrete, reinforcements, enough to last Gush Etzion for two months.

The walk to the highway took thirty minutes. Hugo's legs held up well. The telephone poles beside the road were too tall for a single ladder. The students used the rope to lash the two together, making one twenty-foot span that sagged in the middle when they stood it on end.

"You want me to go up that?"

"You're Kharda."

"Stop that. I'll fall and break my neck."

"You won't. It'll hold you."

"That's why you came and got me. I'm small."

"Well. You are."

"Sonofabitch."

A pair of wire cutters appeared in the redhead's hand. "Latkes. The best in Jerusalem."

The conjoined ladders bowed worse when leaned against the pole. The Hebron highway was empty, but they had no guarantee that a truck-load of Arabs wouldn't race past at any moment. Hugo snatched the cutters.

The students held the ladder. Hugo shinnied up the first rungs, climbed another ten, then hopped over the knotted joint, making the whole assembly sway frightfully.

Reaching the top, he clung to the pole with one hand and tried to snip the wire with the other. The thick phone line called for both hands on the cutters. The ladder wobbled, an unconfident thing.

Hugo called down to Yakob, "This is high enough to kill me. Just so you know."

Yakob rested his elbow on a shoulder of one of the Palmachniks, like men joshing.

"A Nazi camp didn't kill you. A British noose didn't. The Arabs have tried it. You're Kharda. Cut the fucking wire."

Using both hands, Hugo extended the cutters to the phone line. Yakob was wrong. Hugo was alive just as the warden had said he would be, as Pinchus had showed him, because he did not matter much.

Squeezing hard, Hugo severed the wire. The black line recoiled from his clippers, springing away to collapse satisfyingly dead in the road.

✳ ✳ ✳

They cut the phone line in two more places to be sure the Arabs couldn't repair it. Hugo pocketed the wire cutters; he might want them later for a boobytrap.

Yakob led his saboteurs up Lone Tree Hill. From there, they'd be among the first to see the convoy.

On the hilltop, ten Palmachniks huddled in a warren of holes and trenches. A lean-to kept the wind and moisture off them. A massive oak stood sentinel here, the tallest thing in all of Gush Etzion.

Hugo found Gabbi on the hill. He'd not seen her in two months, since the funeral of the lamed hey. She seemed hungrier than before. The sinews in her neck stood out; a dusky tinge circled her eyes. The girl had slept too little, seen too much.

After a cursory greeting, Gabbi gave Hugo her frank opinion on Rivkah. Her pregnant sister should be elsewhere, but Gabbi didn't say Jerusalem. She said America, with Vince. She wanted to see her family sprout there, where it would flourish. In America, her papa and mama, and Gabbi herself, would always survive. Or else why had Rivkah left them in the first place?

She asked Hugo not to tell Rivkah she'd said this; she was tired and shouldn't have spoken. Hugo rested a hand on the rifle she held, the thing that never left the girl's side and might keep her safe in Palestine. Hugo left Gabbi to her vigil.

The first sign of the convoy came not on the road but in the air, an Auster scouting ahead. The little plane's racket filled the morning valley, then it touched down on Hugo's landing strip.

The Jerusalem road came down from a high bend at Dheisheh into the valley of the patriarchs. Little Ein Tzurim, with a better view of the road than Lone Tree Hill, cheered first.

An armored car of the Haganah led the way. Behind it lumbered a rolling behemoth, a roadblock-buster with a bulldozer plow affixed to its grille. Behind the battering ram rolled a procession of trucks, armored buses, and vehicles so lengthy Hugo and Yakob couldn't see its end, even from atop the ladders the boys leaned against the great single oak.

CHAPTER 91

RIVKAH

A carnival mood arrived with the convoy. The settlers' travails were banished, hunger forgotten, the graves put out of mind. Even without their children, Massuot Yitzhak danced and whistled at each laden truck.

Rivkah waited with Vince beside the road. Eight supply trucks stopped on squealing brakes in Massuot Yitzhak, twenty transports powered up Kfar Etzion's hill, three each went to the two smaller kibbutzim. Rivkah had no shyness over her glee, nor did Vince; both clapped and cupped hands to shout. Rivkah needed nutrition for the child; the settlement needed fighters and guns and concrete. This was a day of deliverance.

In the wadi below, armored cars and buses disgorged a fresh company of reinforcements. One hundred and thirty-six fighters stepped off the buses; eighty-five swapped places to return to Jerusalem.

In Massuot Yitzhak, the settlers reached for crates and boxes, an excited clatter. Planks were used as ramps to roll fuel drums to the ground. Vince joined Rivkah in line to carry supplies off a truck.

The Haganah man handing down supplies swung a box to him, then to her. Vince turned away first, then froze looking over Rivkah's shoulder.

"I know you."

Rivkah pivoted, too. A tall Haganah captain knit his brows at her. A scar traced his jawline from behind one ear.

Vince said, "You were Aliyah Bet. In Germany."

The captain nodded, not to Vince but to Rivkah.

"Éva."

She set her box on the ground as if it were on fire and jumped at him, crossing wrists behind his neck. Rivkah laughed into the captain's chest.

"Oh my God."

In eight years he'd grown and broadened, been hurt and changed. Even so, she had her arms around the boy who'd pulled her out of the water.

Rivkah left a hand around his waist. In German, she said, "Vince. This is Emile."

She'd never mentioned Emile to Vince, who set down his carton and took Emile's hand. With them, he switched to German.

"The Fulda train station. I was with the Buchenwald group."

"I remember. We put you on the *Katznelson.*"

"You told us you'd make it back to Palestine one day. Here you are."

Vince and Emile, incredibly, had met before, even for a moment in all the world.

Emile poked Rivkah. "The last time I saw you, you had no clothes on. You were running from the guards at Atlit."

"You, too." Rivkah said to Vince, "Emile saved my life."

Here was Emile, returned. The long scar down his jaw warned her not to celebrate him just yet.

"Where have you been?"

"Let's get the trucks unloaded. We can talk while we work."

Vince hefted his box. He eyed Rivkah with open curiosity, to hear more about how another man had saved her life, how the two of them were once running naked.

Emile took a carton off the truck; Rivkah lifted hers off the ground. They joined the flow of settlers ferrying supplies to the dining hall and storage sheds, the fuel depot and shops. Massuot Yitzhak's portion of the convoy was forty tons.

Walking through the kibbutz, Rivkah pointed out her house, the front door she'd patched from bullets fired by British police. Quickly she gave Emile the highlights of her last eight years. She'd adopted the name Rivkah, left her by a woman who'd died in Atlit. Mrs. Pappel had taken her in. Rivkah showed the orchards and terraces; she tried to describe the work.

They set their boxes outside the dining hall, then turned emptyhand-
ed for the walk back to the trucks. Vince shadowed them, gracefully taking the rear. "Now you," she said to Emile.

From Atlit, he'd been sent to the internment camp on Cyprus. In
1943, after three years behind wire, he volunteered with five thousand
others for the Jewish Brigade. He fought in the Italian campaign under the
British Eighth Army. The scar was nothing special. A gift from a German.

At war's end, the Haganah assigned him to the Aliyah Bet. Emile
stayed in Europe visiting Displaced Persons camps, recruiting able-bod-
ied men and women to build, plant, and defend a Jewish homeland.

When the civil war with the Arabs broke out, he was summoned to
Palestine. Emile became Palmach and was given command of a unit defending convoys between Tel Aviv and Jerusalem. The Arabs challenged
every column, blocking the highways with debris, firing at them from
the high ground.

Emile said to Vince, "You made it here, as well. I heard the Royal
Navy boarded the *Katznelson* with no time to spare."

"It was close. The last few had to jump."

"Were you one of them?"

"No. I was caught."

"Ahh." Emile liked an adventure story. "Were you in Cyprus, too?"

"No. I stayed in Palestine for about a year. Then I went home.
And I came back."

"Home? Where is home?"

"I'm an American. A journalist."

"An American?" Emile's smile struggled to remain. "Are you Jewish?"

"I'm not."

"Why do you speak German?"

"My parents are from Munich."

"What were you doing at Fulda?"

"Press Corps, with Patton's Third. I arranged the train you put us on."

Emile stopped walking. Rivkah and Vince halted with him; she
reached for Vince and stood in front of him.

"Emile?"

"I should like to know your friend's last name."

Vince answered, "Haas."

"The American reporter."

"I already said that."

"The *Herald Tribune*."

"You got it."

"You are quite well known, Mister Haas."

"In some places."

"May I ask, what are you doing in Gush Etzion? Are you reporting?"

"I was."

"You were. And now?"

Rivkah said, "Emile, stop."

"I mean to ask Mister Haas if his presence here is because of his newspaper? I haven't read any of your writing in a while. Since last year, I think."

"I've been busy."

"Doing what?"

Rivkah couldn't fathom what was going wrong. Emile had turned rigid and guarded. This couldn't be jealousy, not after eight years. Around them, settlers lugged boxes; some sang Hebrew fieldwork songs. Vince hooked a thumb at the hastening settlers, for Emile to see that he'd been doing the same as them.

"Defending this place."

"This place." Emile pointed to a machinegun behind a sandbag wall and the two young men behind it. "This place is not yours to defend."

"That's not yours to decide."

"When I leave, you will leave with me."

Vince retreated a step, out of Rivkah's reach. "No, I won't."

"You will. On my authority. And my authority is ample."

Rivkah asked, "Why?"

"In Germany, in France, even Italy, the local papers sometimes print-ed articles by Vincent Haas. We admired the American who rode an illegal ship to Palestine. Who wrote about the hangings, the bombings, the set-tlements. We were admirers, Mister Haas. I am. May I ask one question?"

"Go ahead."

"I recall you wrote beautifully about the *Exodus 1947*. Billy Bern-stein. The American second mate. He was beaten to death by the British."

"He was."

"Two other Jews were killed on that ship. They were not Americans. Tell me their names."

"I don't know them."

"That is my point. Zvi Yakubovich, a seventeen-year-old orphan, and Mordechai Baumstein, twenty-three, a survivor of the German camps. I won't have an American die in Gush Etzion. Especially a famous American. Yours will be the one name everyone remembers."

Rivkah reached to Emile. She put both hands against his tunic as if she might push him. He gripped her wrists to see that she didn't. Emile, gentle, let her loose.

She said, "I'm pregnant."

"Don't," Vince spoke behind her. "Don't beg him."

Emile beheld her, amazed for the moment. She nodded that it was true.

"Then you should come, too."

"No." She answered quickly for him to understand there would be no argument. "He's done nothing wrong. He's a part of the kibbutz."

Emile beckoned two of his Haganah soldiers to come.

"A moment ago, when I asked if he'd been sent to Cyprus. What did he say?"

"He'd gone home."

"Home to America."

"Emile, it's his child."

"His child is a Jew." To Vince, he said, "Do you think others aren't away from their loved ones? Their children? These people were sent here by history, not their newspapers. This is their struggle. It's just your story. I can't let your name mean more than theirs."

Emile turned again to Rivkah. He aimed a finger at the ground.

"You have no other home. Not in America, not in the world. The same for your child. You may stay here if you want, you and your baby. Defend your home." Emile positioned his two guards to flank Vince. "We leave in ten minutes. If you resist, I'll put you in handcuffs. Give me your word."

Before Vince could reply, Rivkah said to Emile, "You have his word."

CHAPTER 92

VINCE

Vince held Rivkah the way he had on a blanket at the concert in Ein Harod. In his memory of that field, it felt like he'd never let go. He held Rivkah like that now, with ten minutes left.

She asked, "Where will you go?"

"Jerusalem."

"Will you write from there? For your newspaper?"

"I suppose."

"Palestine needs that from you."

"What do you need?"

She pulled back her head, the first step toward releasing him. "To know you are safe. To see you again soon. To put your child in your arms."

Fifty replacement fighters tramped up the hill from the wadi. More made their way to Kfar Etzion. Each carried a gun and an unyielding manner. The bloc had braced itself with cement defenses, fortified positions, minefields, barbed wire, rifles and mortars, two hundred Haganah, and three hundred farmers.

"Tell Missus Pappel goodbye. And Yakob."

"What about Hugo?"

Vince could tell Hugo himself. The little man strode their way.

Rivkah said, "He has a knack for showing up."

"He does."

"I love you."

Vince kissed her. He wanted to lift Rivkah off the ground.

Hugo spoke as he approached. "People are watching."

The barrel of Hugo's rifle bobbed over his shoulder, always there. He halted, hands on hips, pretending to complain.

"Tired of unloading trucks?"

In the valley, the Auster fired up its propeller to lead the column away. The metal gates of the vehicles slammed shut, drivers and Emile's troops climbed into the cabs. Engines awoke.

Vince said, "I have to go."

"Go where?"

"Jerusalem. With the convoy."

"For how long?"

"I don't know."

Hugo looked to Rivkah to make sense.

"Vince is going to write for his paper again. He's needed. He'll stay until the war is over. It won't be long."

"I'll go with you." Hugo hoisted a hand before they could ask. "I think I'm done. Yes. To tell you the truth, I'm done."

From his back pocket, Hugo handed Rivkah a pair of wire cutters. He pecked her cheek.

"I'll see you again. Tell Missus Pappel. And red Yakob."

He handed his rifle to the first settler who passed. A Haganah man pointed Hugo to the lead truck. Nimbly, he hopped on the bumper, over the gate, and vanished.

Rivkah smiled as though she'd just witnessed something good.

She said, "It won't be long."

"If there's any way to get back to you, I will, as fast as I can."

The eight trucks revved, ready to roll. The Auster took to the air and banked north. Emile's pair of guards moved toward Vince.

She said, "I'll be here."

Vince rubbed the back of her hand with his long thumb. With guards on either side, he left Rivkah.

CHAPTER 93

HUGO

Massuot Yitzhak's white days and sparkling nights were not so sooth-ing. Hugo admired the stars no less than the next fellow, but kibbutz life was not loud enough to quiet him. He needed a city. Hugo would go to Tel Aviv.

He was finished with guns, making them and firing them. He'd fought enough Britons and Arabs; he could sit in any company and tell his own tales. Hugo had no medals; he had scars. He would accept work as a plumber until he could start his own company and hire others. He'd get rich in this new country by its water and its shit and be glad of it.

Hugo took a seat on the open floor of the first transport's bed. He breathed exhaust while the engine idled; he rattled his head at himself. He was leaving the bloc exactly as he'd arrived, in the back of a truck, empty pockets, wearing the clothes he'd been arrested in.

Vince swung over the tailgate, to fold beside Hugo on the wooden deck. Vince dropped his head into his crossed arms, hiding his face. The vehicle jolted forward; the column followed.

Hugo patted Vince's knee. "What happened?"

"I got thrown out."

"Did you fight with Rivkah?"

"No. The captain in charge of the convoy. You remember Fulda? The Aliyah Bet man?"

"With the scar."

"He's an old friend of Rivkah's. He didn't want me there. Said if anything happened to an American in the Etzion bloc, it might take attention away from the settlers."

"Did he say settlers or Jews?"

"Jews."

"Ah. That's a Zionist. Pinchus is like that. And you may not like to hear it, but he's right."

Hugo got to his feet to watch Massuot Yitzhak disappear. The column crossed Hugo's air strip, then rolled between Yellow Hill and Lone Tree Hill. In the Wadi Shahid, the armored buses of the departing fighters joined the emptied trucks and the Haganah's armored escorts. All got in line behind the goliath roadblock-buster. A thousand feet up, the buzzing Auster lazed above the Jerusalem road.

Entering the highway, the convoy picked up speed. In minutes, the hilltops of Gush Etzion fell miles behind, four emerald perches against an unblemished sky.

On the bouncing deck, Vince curled up in his scarecrow way. Over the wind and motor, Hugo asked, "What are you going to do?"

"Go back. First chance I get."

"Really?"

"Rivkah. The child. I have to."

Hugo sat again beside Vince. "What's it like? To feel like that?"

"It's probably like being a Zionist."

"You don't care."

"I don't fucking care."

✳ ✳ ✳

Among sere foothills, the convoy continued north on the slow rise to Bethlehem. Weeds, shrubs and wildflowers dotted the rocky slopes on both sides of the road. The Haganah's column stretched more than a mile with the Auster circling above. No other traffic was out, not even fellahin and mules.

Ten minutes outside Gush Etzion, the column halted. Hugo knocked on the cab wall. The driver's assistant slid back the rear window.

"What's going on?"

"No radio. You know what I know."

Hugo climbed the slat wall of the truck bed. The blockbuster had left the convoy to charge up the hill alone.

A hundred yards ahead, the truck rammed something. Dust and white bits splattered off the plow and the giant bulled through. The column surged on behind it.

Hugo's truck flew past rocks littering the road. Two hundred yards further, the blockbuster collided with another roadblock. Again, the column hurtled through the breach.

Ahead on the winding road lay Solomon's Pools. The brushy slopes, bareknuckle ridges, crevices, and patchy wildflowers; this was the spot where Hugo had been attacked before.

CHAPTER 94

VINCE

The Jerusalem Road

The blockbuster smashed through a third rockpile. The truck where Vince and Hugo rode raced into the gap even before the dust settled. Three trucks back, one speeding vehicle failed to negotiate the opening, glanced the debris and careered off the road to trip on the rocky slope. The truck tipped on its side and skidded sparking down the hill. The rest of the transports plunged through. An armored car pulled over to rescue the scrambling driver and assistant.

Near Vince's truck, the first bullet zinged off the asphalt; a hidden rifle snapped. Arabs in the crannies of the hills aimed at the convoy's tires. Beside Vince, Hugo gripped the cab roof and faced the wind.

The blockbuster plowed through a fourth roadblock, then a fifth and sixth, all in the span of a half mile. Every collision rang like a smith's anvil. Emile and his men inside the buster were taking a harsh beating out front of the convoy.

More gunplay clapped from the hillside. The truck right behind Vince shrieked and jolted; a tire had been hit and blown out. The driver didn't slow but ran hellbent on the rim to get out of range of the Arabs' rifles.

The road rounded a rising bend. The scout car and blockbuster disappeared behind a slope. When Vince's truck cleared the hillside, his driver braked hard: one hundred yards ahead, the buster and scout car had stopped in the roadway, stymied by a rock pile too big to be butted aside.

Dozens of stones, each larger than a steamer trunk, barred the path. This blockade, the seventh, had been the labor of a hundred men. The convoy ground to a halt and bunched up. From the hills, the Arabs opened fire.

The first barrage was aimed at the tires. Down the long column, the armored cars and buses returned fire. The road rippled with flying bullets. Vince and Hugo had no guns, nor did their driver and his assistant. Vince jumped out of the bed to hide behind the truck; the drivers joined him, then Hugo, cursing.

The buster set to work against the roadblock. It swung a steel crane into play to lift the boulders out of the road one by one. Some rocks it managed to nudge aside with the plow. The Arabs poured a torrent of gunfire against Emile and his crew. The convoy fought back to hold the Arabs in the hills.

Hugo put his back against the rear tire. Vince pressed close, trying to share the cover of the wheel. The driver and assistant did the same behind the front tire. Over Hugo's head, a bullet splintered a plank of the sidewall and showered him with shards. Hugo grumbled again that he was done.

In the convoy were two hundred armed fighters. Their firepower roared back with rifles, Stens, and Spandau and Bren machine guns, an awesome response. If the blockbuster could free the column in time, they might survive.

Vince ducked under the truck to watch Emile's buster struggle to clear the roadblock. The giant mashed against one of the biggest stones, too large for the crane, to shunt it out of the road. The rear tires burned against the tarmac; the rock gave way only inches. The driver shifted into a higher gear for more push, but the plow slipped off the stone. Before he could back off the throttle, the truck shot forward, glancing the rock and turning the truck sideways. The wheels spun too fast, the boulder no longer held it back, and the blockbuster surged across the road before the driver could hit the brakes. The great truck slammed into a ditch.

The buster tried to regain the road, but its front tires and plow were mired deep. The rear wheels fumed and screeched, but the truck only bucked.

The scout car reversed and raced back to the tightly packed convoy. Gunfire swelled as Arabs descended on the trapped column, shooting as they came. Rounds pattered the road, the air zipped over Vince's head. Hugo leaped into the truck's driver's seat shouting "Get in!" The driver and assistant had no quarrel with Hugo firing up the engine and crammed into the cab. Vince scrambled into the truck bed.

The scout car whizzed past. The Haganah officer driving yelled at every truck: "Turn around, turn around!" With lightning hands, Hugo backed the truck, butting into the fender of the vehicle behind still limping on its flapping tire.

Hugo had little room to maneuver; ditches bracketed the road. He wheeled the truck south and belted out the window to Vince, "Back to Rivkah!"

Vince thumped on the cab roof. "Go!"

The scout car raced down the convoy's length ordering retreat. In moments, the column was reduced to bedlam. Trucks swerved into one another, several slipped or were shoved into the ditch. Armored cars and buses bumped the supply trucks out of their way. Drivers tried to make sharp turns on flat tires or bare rims, a few jackknifed and tipped over. Chaos squirmed down the long line, every vehicle under fire. The convoy became a squealing, tightening snarl. At the tail end a half-mile away, the scout car burst free; five trucks and five armored escorts followed south. The rest of the forty trucks stayed gridlocked, and the Arabs crept closer.

CHAPTER 95

HUGO

Hugo leaned on the horn, so did others while the column scrambled in disarray. Vehicles that could still move blocked each other and honked in panic. Armored trucks and buses blazed guns at the hills and ledges where the Arabs fired down. Hugo shifted madly, looking for any path through the maze, but only made matters worse with others trying the same.

He struck the steering wheel. Beside him, the driver moaned, "We're stuck."

At the front of the convoy, the Arabs focused on the blockbuster. Bullets plinked armored sides and bounced off the road as if the truck stood in a rain. The crew had to stay inside or die.

Vince shouted, "What do we do?"

Hugo muttered, "Shit," before he climbed out. Vince jumped down with him. A bullet whizzed over their heads. "We can't stay here."

Vince ducked behind the truck. One more time, they kneeled shoulder-to-shoulder behind the rear wheels.

Hugo asked, "What would we be doing right now? If I'd taken your advice and gone to America. Where would we be?"

"In a café. Eating lunch."

"What would we eat?"

"Hamburgers."

"Could we have beers?"

"You go ahead. I have to work."

"I'd like a beer, then. May I pay? Am I rich in America?"

"Sure."

"Good." The driver tumbled out of the cab. Hugo called to him, "A beer, please."

The driver dove for cover behind the front tire. A Haganah man sprinted their way, bellowing to every truck, dodging through the wrecks and stymied vehicles. In his wake, drivers leaped out of their cabs.

"Leave the trucks! There's a building next to the road! Head there now!"

Hugo pointed at the stranded blockbuster. "What about them?" The Haganah man made a helpless gesture before he dashed away.

Arab voices in English spilled from the hills, "We will soon cut your throats."

Hugo shouted over the truck. "Do shut up." To Vince, he asked, "Do we die today?"

"No."

"I agree. Stay with me."

With Hugo in the lead, they lit out for the stone house beside the road.

CHAPTER 96

VINCE

Hugo and Vince ran in fits and starts. Under fire, they took cover behind buses and armored vehicles, hugged close to trucks that were deserted in the ditch, tipped over, or crippled on puddles of flat tires.

A dozen drivers and Haganah fighters scurried with them. One at a time they galloped into the open; the Arabs shot at everyone. Bullets drummed on the immobile column; some armored cars still returned fire.

Hugo, smaller than Vince, had an easier time of it. He drew little fire, but bullets scalded the tarmac every time Vince's lanky frame popped up. He had several close calls; Hugo, who always went first, watched and rooted for him.

Five armored cars formed a protective barrier at the approach to the stone house. Vince, Hugo, and the drivers bolted the final distance.

The building was old and thick-walled. A staircase divided two large first-floor rooms; the weathered floors felt solid. Half the convoy, a hundred men and women, crowded inside. In a corner, a nurse bandaged the wounded.

Old, cheap furnishings littered the place; a few cots and a desk, forgotten clothing, crumpled papers, and rusted tins hinted at poverty.

Hugo asked one of the drivers, "What is this place?"

Still panting from the run, the man said, "In the summers, laborers pick the grapes and oranges. This is Nebi Daniel, one of their squatter homes."

As soon as Haganah fighters hustled inside, they manned the attic, roof, and windows. A radio was brought in, the battery to run it salvaged from a truck. Vince and Hugo hurried up the rickety stairs. On the roof, a dozen defenders set up Bren guns and a Spandau to cover all four directions. South of Nebi Daniel, Arab snipers looked down from a rocky ledge and the rooftops of homes left and right two hundred yards away. North, villagers flowed through the brushlands from the hamlets of Dheisheh and Beit Jalla. Five hundred Arab guns surrounded the stone house, a number that seemed to grow by the minute.

The convoy was too gnarled; it could not resurrect. A few armored trucks tightroped the shoulder of the road to gather up guns and trapped drivers. Outside the front door, fifteen fighters with a machine gun took position in a ditch. Another squad dug in behind a rock fence bordering an apple orchard. Six armored cars girdled Nebi Daniel. More drivers staggered through the door.

Three hundred yards away, stuck at the head of the dead column, Emile and the blockbuster's crew fired from every portal. Arabs crept down the slopes.

One armored car wove through the column to reach the blockbuster. Arabs targeted the wheels; a front tire popped, then the other. The vehicle tried to reverse but couldn't steer on rims. Six fighters bailed out and ran the hundred yards for the stone house. All made it through the front door which slammed shut behind them.

✷ ✷ ✷

By sundown, a thousand villagers and guns teemed in the hills and neighboring buildings. They kept up a desultory fire, pinging the stone house, trading shots with the armored cars. Arabs snuck close enough to call out cutthroat threats. Three times, Haganah vehicles tried to reach the blockbuster. Two overturned under the drumbeat of Arab bullets and needed rescue themselves; the third gave up and rushed back to Nebi Daniel.

A hundred Palmach and Field Force fighters manned the fortress, the perimeter, and the roof. Eighty unarmed drivers and assistants huddled inside, frightened and hungry; a medical team treated a dozen wounded. A Haganah officer called for volunteers to relieve the gunners for a few hours. Hugo went outside to the dark ditch; Vince joined seven fighters on another attempt to reach the blockbuster.

The Palmach leader of the team asked him, "Why do you want to go?"

"I have a friend in there."

"Do you know how to shoot?"

"It's been a while. But yes."

"Who's your friend?"

"Emile."

The Palmachnik whistled. "He hasn't got many friends. Come on, then."

The young officer took a rifle from one of the window guardians. He gave this to Vince with six ammo clips. Vince worked the bolt and dry-fired the rifle. An armored truck idled outside. He climbed in with the team.

The truck pulled away; the men muttered, "Go, go," and held on while the driver snaked through the ruins of the convoy. In the light-less, badly ventilated interior, every round fired through the slits cuffed Vince's ears.

The truck dipped and dashed down the knotted road. Bullets beat on the armor. Vince slid his rifle into a firing portal to shoot at an Arab sitting on a large rock. The Arab didn't jump; Vince missed him badly.

The truck passed the last abandoned vehicle of the convoy. Speeding into the open, Arab rounds drubbed the truck's sides; a cataract pummeled the roof, and they came fast and many on the road near the tires. The driver stopped suddenly, jarring the fighters. The hillside blinked with hundreds of flashes; in rapid fire, Vince spent his first five-round clip.

The driver held his ground, enduring the barrage. The armored truck had stopped fifty yards from the blockbuster, close enough for the crew to run to them, though under intense fire. Vince reloaded. Everyone in the armored car opened up at shadows and sparkles. The interior of the armored truck grew deafening.

In the darkness, near the blockbuster, a flame flickered. An Arab had skulked close and lit the rag fuse of a Molotov cocktail. He hurled the burning bottle against the cab; instantly, fire spread with the splashed fuel. A second Arab flung another firebomb at the rear wheels.

The blockbuster ignited front and back. Bullets clobbered Vince's truck, waiting for Emile and his team to emerge. Vince emptied another clip by the glow of the rising fire; the others did the same while their own truck rocked from bullets pecking at their armor.

Flames engulfed the blockbuster. Vince's driver backed away, quitting the rescue. The faces of the fighters around Vince flickered through the portals. "Get out," they yelled, "get out of there."

Vince's truck spun around to race back to the stone house. Vince lost sight of the blockbuster, but the explosion rocked him off his feet. He scrambled up for a portal. A second explosion blew the blockbuster's gas tank. The great truck reared to stand on the V-plow in the ditch, then fell back on flaming tires.

Vince said, "Emile." The name would be Emile's only remains; the burning blockbuster would leave nothing else. Vince charged the bolt of his rifle.

The driver accelerated for the cover of the dead convoy. Every Arab in range turned on Vince's fleeing, lit-up truck.

He no longer heard his own gun or the guns around him, nor the pelting against the armor. Vince fired at black shapes and scarlet twinkles; he grew mute and breathed cordite and lost himself through the hot barrel of his rifle.

A bullet broke through the wall, the first to puncture the metal plating. A fighter screamed, "AP!" Armor-piercing rounds.

Another hole opened over Vince's head. All the fighters froze. They looked to each other as if there was something the next man could do. Their best defense was speed, away from the firelight of the burning buster. If they could reach the tangled column, they might hide. The next armor-piercing bullet hit Vince in the shoulder.

CHAPTER 97

HUGO

The landscape of broken trucks, the stone building, the scrub on the hillside, everything shivered under the orange flash of the fireball. As it faded, Hugo and the fighters in the ditch returned their eyes to their guns.

The armored truck that had attempted the rescue skidded up to the stone house. Arab snipers took potshots; the gunners on the roof answered. Men hurried from the truck, carrying one wounded.

Hugo learned the names of all fourteen in the ditch, everyone a student and smarter than him. They were sabra; to them he was a survivor of Europe. They didn't ask about the camps because they faced people who would, if they could, kill them.

With midnight, the Arabs came closer. They didn't sneak up but announced themselves in Arabic, Hebrew, English, even German, calling for the Jews to lay down their arms and surrender. The Arabs set fire to some abandoned vehicles near the stone building, then a silence descended. In the glow of these flames, the Arabs began their assault.

They raked the stone building with Brens and rifles. Palmachniks in the armored trucks responded. The night jittered with fires and sparking guns. The boys in the ditch and Hugo made a firing line but held back on their triggers. Hugo had seen this before, these Arab charges. He said, "Make everything count."

Wild shrubs flecked the slope, and each flicker of the blazes made a shadow shift on the hill like a running man. Then, with a high-pitched battle cry, a horde of Arabs rushed forward, firelit. They came as they had at Massuot Yitzhak in waves of hundreds, relying on numbers. Not all had weapons, yet they advanced as though they might swarm over the defenders of Nebi Daniel. Hugo and the boys in the ditch mowed them down with one machine gun and thirteen rifles. The bravest villagers made it near enough to die by grenades the boys lobbed. Hugo was unsure that he hit anyone with his bullets and didn't care. The Arabs dove for the ground when he shot, and that was enough.

One boy in the ditch took a wound, yelped, but held his post. Hugo measured the assault not in minutes but bodies. The shooting howled from the roof, from the ditch, from behind the orchard wall, and from the armored cars around the stone house; the fight peaked, then slowed. Hugo had the chance to shoot a man stumbling away but didn't. The attack was done. Hugo and the boys lowered their hot guns, with no more grenades at their feet.

The trucks burned to the axles. In the waning flames, the Arabs took away their many dead and wounded.

Hugo stood for the first time in hours. He ached in his legs from pent-up nerves. Leaving the rifle and ammo behind, he walked the length of the ditch saying each boy's name. Hugo took the arm of the wounded boy to help him back to the stone house.

CHAPTER 98

HUGO

"It hurts, doesn't it?" Hugo asked this not out of sympathy but to say, see?

A nurse said, "He's in shock. Keep him still." She left to attend to more of the injured.

Vince asked, "How many did we lose?

"Twenty wounded. Six dead. Let me see it." He peeled apart the sheaves of Vince's cut-open shirt.

Vince said, "I passed out in the truck."

"I imagine so."

"I woke up on the floor in here. I passed out again when someone shoved gauze into the hole. I was awake for the attack."

"Stop talking. Roll over." Hugo helped Vince lift his right shoulder enough to see the exit wound.

"I can move my fingers."

"Good. You're still a reporter."

"Emile's dead."

Hugo rested a hand in the center of Vince's chest, the place where a lily would be if he were dead, too. "I know."

"How do I tell Rivkah?"

Hugo patted his palm over Vince's heart. "I'll tell her." He smoothed Vince's hair. Hugo wagged a finger. "Remember. You're not allowed to die among the Jews."

✳ ✳ ✳

The wounded groaned terribly, too many for the medicine. Eighty drivers and the wounded had to look on the bodies brought inside. Hugo went to the roof.

Up there the fighters granted him a spot and a shared canteen. One offered him a rifle, but Hugo passed. "I can't hit anything."

Only stars broke the spring night; no one lit a cigarette, no Jew on the roof or the perimeter, not among the thousand Arabs skulking about the stone house. The fires on the jumbled road had all burned low, the blockbuster reduced to embers. Every few minutes some villager on the hillside or in the orchard fired off a round to keep the pulse of the battle beating.

Two miles off, Bethlehem did not sleep. Behind it, Jerusalem brooded. The men on the roof whispered guesses how this would end. Hugo rolled on his back to see the highest stars, the ones not blotted out by the cities.

The splutter of airplanes stirred the men on the roof. Arabs racked rounds in the night, so many they sounded like crickets. The sounds of the Austers grew closer and circled the road. A Palmachnik next to Hugo worried about having things dropped on him. One engine climbed in pitch; the plane zoomed down unseen to roar across Nebi Daniel at a hundred feet. The Palmachnik wrapped arms over his head. The dark Auster dropped sacks just beyond the armored trucks ringing the house, where the Arabs would get to them first. The plane climbed, chased by gunfire. Muzzle flashes dazzled the hill and road; Hugo refigured the number of Arabs surrounding him to two thousand.

✳ ✳ ✳

March 28

Throughout the night, a string of Jewish planes dropped food, water, and ammo to the Arabs.

Every attempt out of Nebi Daniel to retrieve the supplies looked like suicide. The Arabs had so many guns around the building that no Jew, not the bravest, could venture more than ten yards before calling down a hail of bullets. By sunup, the Arabs had claimed almost all the sacks and crates. The Austers quit dropping supplies and switched to bombs.

In the dawn light they flew higher, away from the Arabs' gunfire. The pilots dropped grenades into the orchard and on the slope. Sometimes the planes flew in low and quick with a Bren gunner in the passenger seat to pepper the Arab positions. The planes were more accurate with weapons than they were with boxes.

At ten o'clock, the Arabs launched another assault, out of the north from Beit Jalla and Dheisheh. Two hundred villagers tried advancing through the fruit trees behind a smoke screen, but the roof gunners, the boys behind the stone fence, and a pair of strafing Austers beat them back. Hugo spent the attack feeding ammo belts into the Spandau.

By noon, the battle for Nebi Daniel settled again into siege. Random rounds were exchanged; the Arabs kept shouting promises of either fair treatment or murder. Hugo left the roof with a quarter-full canteen.

Vince lay among the wounded, now numbering forty. He'd grown pale and sweaty. The doors were shut, windows blocked, so the first floor had no ventilation. Blood and the airless heat added to the misery. Every so often, a bullet pierced the front door, so it had to be avoided.

Hugo eased a hand under Vince to bring him upright to the canteen. Vince looked drained; he needed food, blood, stitches. Raspy, he asked, "How bad is it?"

"You, or the situation?"

Vince coughed; the wracking almost collapsed him. "Jesus. I hope the situation's doing better than me."

"Barely. We're almost out of bullets. You just drank the last of the water. We're outgunned twenty to one. Still, and I'm not a betting man, I think you'll go first."

"That's not funny."

"It's a matter of taste."

Vince was already half ghost. "Anyone coming to get us out of here?"

"Other than the Arabs?"

"Yeah."

"Jerusalem's trying to put together a strike force. But we've got most of their trucks."

"How about the British?"

"There's an Army convoy two miles north."

"Doing what?"

"Negotiating."

Vince coughed again. "Fuck. My life depends on Jews, Arabs, and the British arguing."

Holding his right arm, white and weak, Vince lay back on the floor.

Hugo said, "I'm going to rejoin the Irgun."

Even for this, Vince didn't open his eyes.

"I thought you were done."

"It seems I'm not."

"Why?"

"What I am done with is others making bargains over my life. Someone else's conditions for me to live. Let them bargain with me."

Vince nodded against the floor, his only motion. "They shot me, Hugo."

"That was a factor in my decision."

He sat with Vince a while. When Vince appeared to sleep, Hugo went back to the roof of Nebi Daniel where the air, at least, was clear.

CHAPTER 99

HUGO

Into the afternoon, swooping Austers strafed the trees and hillside; Arabs fired at the planes and sniped at the stone building but did not mount another all-out assault. Hugo stayed with the fighters on the roof, listening to them carp about hunger.

In the late day, finally, a gunshot off the hill was not followed by another or answered from Nebi Daniel. The Haganah's planes banked away toward Jerusalem. Quiet gained a foothold around the stone house.

Hundreds of Arabs, with an unnerving shuffle, began to emerge from their hiding places. They came down the long hill, black robes and weapons, and flowed through the orchard like floodwaters. Hugo gaped at their number; they were a horde, more thousands on every side than anyone had guessed.

Out of the north, a British armored car slipped past the remains of the blockbuster. The vehicle picked through the convoy's tangle and burnt hulks. Behind it came a column of trucks and half-tracks.

A Palmachnik on the roof stood up; no one had done that in thirty hours. Hugo and the other young fighters joined him to peer down on the gathering Arab host. They arrayed themselves side-by-side to let the Arabs see them up there, the small band of defenders. The boys lapped arms on each other's shoulders, Hugo's too. Below, in the ditch, the ones Hugo had fought alongside last night did the same, to have the Arabs approach them as if to a wall.

On the roof, the boys who'd manned the Spandau walked to their weapon and set to dismantling it. The rest beat their weapons with rocks, threw pieces down the chimney and off the roof. They mangled their guns joylessly. Hugo left them to it and went down to Vince.

On the first floor, a Haganah man smashed the radio against a wall. An officer strode out to meet the arriving British. Two nurses lifted the dead off stretchers and replaced them with wounded who could not walk. The rest of the injured, sixty in bloodied clothes, were helped to their feet.

Vince was ghastly pale, and his shoulder was a mess. Hugo put him on his feet. Vince buckled once but gathered his legs under him.

With Vince's arm yoked across his shoulders, Hugo walked into the late day. Some color returned to Vince's cheeks now that he was upright and moving. He staggered again when he saw the sea of Arabs surrounding the stone building.

Down the length of the abandoned convoy, Arabs scavenged the forty trucks. They pried at metal cladding, rolled away tires and wheels, yanked at motors for parts, and carried off windshields and seats. Two doctors, an Arab and a Briton, refused to let any of the attackers inside Nebi Daniel until all the wounded and dead were evacuated. Haganah fighters handed over those weapons they'd lacked the time to ruin.

British soldiers searched the defenders before putting them onto the waiting trucks. The wounded were helped on first. Vince moved with Hugo out of step; he seemed like he might crumple at every stride.

Arabs stepped between the line of wounded and the British trucks. They began their own search, patting the clothes of the departing Jews, men and women alike. They pulled back blankets on the stretchers. The Haganah protested to the British who did nothing.

One Arab stepped in front of Hugo and Vince. The man stood tall in a drab brown waistcoat. He held up an arm to stop Hugo and Vince. In English, he said, "We will search you."

Hugo said, "He's hurt."

"That will not change. But you, my friend, are not."

The Arab reached for Hugo. With his good hand, Vince slapped the Arab's arm away.

Others closed in; a spark had been lit. Vince and Hugo were cut off from the wounded in line and the British soldiers. The Arab wrapped a fist around Hugo's collar as if to pull him away. Vince would not let go of him.

The Arab doctor elbowed through the crowd, howling in Arabic at every villager in his way. The British doctor stayed on his coattails, straining his own voice. The mob let them through, but before they could reach Hugo and Vince, the tall Arab fighter whispered to Hugo.

"Where is your mother, Jew?"

The doctors tried to peel the Arab's hand away. Hugo didn't want to be let go, not yet.

He said, "She's dead." Hugo gripped the Arab's lapel in return and tugged him so close he spoke up into the Arab's beard. "But I, my friend, am not."

Hugo let the Arab loose him with a small shove, then helped Vince into the truck.

The defenders of Nebi Daniel rode away. The British convoy rolled through Bethlehem, then sped for Jerusalem. Hugo held Vince's good hand until the column stopped at a hospital, and Vince was taken away by medics.

CHAPTER 100

RIVKAH

April 4
Massuot Yitzhak

At sunup, a *sharav* wind blew out of the east, carrying heat and sand
from the Sahara.

The wind whipped across Gush Etzion. The temperature soared;
inside her house Rivkah perspired while hot sand rattled the windows.
The air turned yellow and the sun, robbed of its gold, became white,
a daytime moon.

The sandstorm raged until noon. When it passed, a layer of grit covered everything. Settlers took brooms to the street and walkways. Guards
who never left their posts stood still for a good sweeping. The flowers of
Massuot Yitzhak, the first of spring, shrank from the dust and the spiking
heat. In the orchards, the fruit blossoms were not so brittle and drank up
the warmth. Orchard workers had predicted a bumper crop that would
ease the supply problems of the bloc. Rivkah went with them to brush
the leaves clean.

The men working alongside her asked Rivkah to go easy, find some
shade; they pointed at her belly, all knew she was pregnant. She answered
that if one of them was pregnant, he would be in the shade.

That evening, Rivkah couldn't sleep. She'd had Vince in her bed
long enough to conjure him at night: his feet hung off the end of the mat-

tress, and when on his side he tucked a hand under his cheek. For a skinny man he cast off a lot of warmth. Rivkah awoke confused and reached an arm to the sheet next to her. She found him gone, only the heat there.

Rivkah lay a long time wondering if she were awake with him in Jerusalem. Was he there in pain, or spreading his fingers on the empty side of his own bed? She felt selfish to have Vince keep her company. Let him sleep and heal. She sat up to break the link. Rivkah lit a candle on her bedside table to read again the radioed message from Hugo that Yakob had brought that afternoon: *Vince wounded, will live. Emile dead.* She took the candle with her out to the porch.

Night in Massuot Yitzhak had no peace left. Lights glimmered on perimeter fences, the generators ran, and the mine makers toiled in the barn. Haganah and settlers walked patrol or manned guns behind sandbags. The stars did little to hide or soothe any of this.

Mrs. Pappel shuffled out to keep her company. "It's too hot for tea."

"I've never heard you say that."

"I suppose I'm not in the mood."

"Why can't you sleep?"

"The same as you."

Mrs. Pappel took stock of the early morning. Settlers and soldiers guarded every corner, lights shimmered in the valley and on each slope. All of Massuot Yitzhak slumbered with one eye open and a weapon at hand. Even Jerusalem's glow to the north was turned down like a lantern.

Mrs. Pappel said, "My father's brother was a rabbi. He came every Sunday for dinner. Before the meal, my mother would ask him for a prayer. Every Sunday, he recited Psalm 144."

She recited from memory, "'Blessed be the Lord my strength, which teaches my hands to war and my fingers to fight and subdues peoples under me. Part your heavens, Lord, and come down. Touch the mountains so that they smoke.' After dinner, my mother would ask him if maybe he could recite something more pleasant next time. But this was the one my uncle chose, every Sunday. He made sure my brothers and I heard. In Vienna, fifty years ago. This war was being fought at our dinner table."

Mrs. Pappel sighed and fell into reverie. Rivkah asked her nothing more; memory was a luxury and each of them could decide for themselves how much of it to share.

The swelter did not break. The bombmakers welded in their shop, and the lights glowed on the perimeter.

CHAPTER 101

HUGO

April 7
YMCA hotel
Jerusalem

Hugo skipped down the stairwell from his sixth-floor room. His thighs did not hurt. He had little hunger first thing in the morning, a rare gift from the camps, a facileness with starving.

He nodded to the desk clerk and a maid; neither looked comfortable with his genial mood. Their own hunger must have soured them, or perhaps they were aware that Hugo never paid for his lodgings or his meals. Pay with what? They knew who he had been: Irgun.

Hugo stepped out into the sunshine, then under the umbrellas of the patio. Because of the Arab blockade, the waiters had few patrons and only eggs and flatbread to serve. They smiled back at Hugo, less annoyed than the other staff because the waiters snuck bites and stole coffee.

Across Julian's Way, the King David Hotel stood sun-drenched and stolid. The building was renewed but empty. The British had gone and no tourists came to Palestine. The hotel would be grand again, but not today.

Pinchus waited at Hugo's table. Crossing the patio, overly pleased, Hugo waved. Pinchus did not.

Hugo sat across from him. "Thank you for coming."

"Hello, Kharda."

"I'd prefer it if we could leave Kharda behind."

"If you wish. Hugo."

Hugo motioned at the tabletop without even a glass of water on it. "Did you just get here?"

"I waited a bit."

"I've waited my share for you."

Pinchus broke a small grin. "That's fair."

"Did you send my message to Massuot Yitzhak?"

"I did. I was concerned to see Vince Haas has been hurt. Badly?"

"A bullet in the shoulder. He'll be in hospital a while. Then a sling."

"And this Emile?"

"A fighter. A good one."

"Was Nebi Daniel awful?"

"Not the worst."

Pinchus pushed up his thick glasses. Had he asked what the worst was, Hugo would have said death row, waiting for you.

Pinchus steepled his fingers. "What have you been up to?"

"I've been here a week. Mornings I sit on the patio, signaling for you. I nibble at what the staff can spare, stare at the King David, and am reminded that I am a pauper. I take my afternoons with Vince at the hospital. How have you been?"

"I'm sorry to no longer call you Kharda. It suits you better."

The waiter arrived with unasked-for coffee. He would return with eggs and pita, the only meal he could bring.

Hugo said to Pinchus, "Please pay my bill here."

"Of course. What else do you want from me?"

"I want to come back to the Irgun."

The little church made by Pinchus's fingers opened and closed.

"Why would you want that?"

Before Hugo could respond, Pinchus pointed across the street to the King David.

"We knocked that building down. Plumbers were needed to replace it. Do you know how much money they made? You knocked down Goldschmidt House. The Arabs blew up Ben Yehuda Street. There's a war coming, Hugo. A thousand buildings are going to be wrecked all over

Palestine. Why would you want to be one of the destroyers if you could be one of the builders?"

"This is one of your trick questions."

"It's not." Pinchus admired the King David. "Do you think I don't wish sometimes for a different trade? Can you believe I often envy you? Your choices? Walk away, Hugo."

"No."

"Why?"

"I thought for a moment that I was finished. But the Arabs haven't stopped trying to kill me or my friends."

"I understand you better and better, Hugo."

A waiter approached with two plates. Pinchus raised a palm to back him away.

He said to Hugo, "Personally, I should like a path other than violence."

Hugo waved the waiter onward, contradicting Pinchus. "And I should like a breakfast other than eggs and bread." The waiter set down the plates, then withdrew. Hugo took up a knife and fork. "Until then, I'll eat what's in front of me."

Hugo dug in before Pinchus touched his cutlery. The first taste of bread sopped in yolk reminded him that he'd been in a good mood. With the tip of his knife, he indicated the meal in front of Pinchus and said, as if he were the host, "Go ahead."

Pinchus's better humor returned, too. He picked up the utensils. "I suppose you do not wish to be a driver."

"I do not."

"One of our fighters, then."

Hugo spread his hands to present himself for the job, at last.

A mile to the east, on the Mount of Olives, an Arab artillery piece boomed. The shell landed somewhere in the Jewish Quarter. The explosion echoed off the King David.

Pinchus cut into his eggs. "As it turns out, your timing is excellent. We are at war now."

"No one's calling it that."

"Ah, but it is. It's the war for the road to Jerusalem. The blockade has brought the city almost to collapse. Empty shelves in grocery stores, hoarding and black marketeers. Food riots. The Arabs cut the water pipe-line. Jerusalem is very hungry. I'm enjoying these eggs."

"How about the convoys? Why can't the Haganah keep the city supplied?"

Pinchus shook his fork at Hugo, as if Hugo were responsible.

"That debacle at Nebi Daniel. The Haganah lost fifty trucks. That's more than half of what they had. The Arabs hold all the high ground along the road to Tel Aviv. We've lost a hundred fighters defending those convoys. The Arabs have desecrated many of the bodies." Pinchus set down his knife and fork. "This is a terrible thing."

He left a few mouthfuls on the plate as though he felt it unfair that he should be full in Jerusalem. Pinchus paused to consider the re-maining egg and bread, then finished. Had he not, Hugo would have reached for them.

Pinchus sat back, hands laced. The man could not look satisfied.

"The columns into Jerusalem can no longer be protected. The loss of life and materiel is unsustainable."

Pinchus peered over the edge of his coffee cup, into the dregs. He drank the last, then set down the cup with a ring of the saucer. A bird sang in a springtime tree, and for a moment, with the King David shining across the street, Hugo could imagine, if he could not recall, peace.

Pinchus continued, "The Haganah is going to secure a corridor from Tel Aviv to Jerusalem."

"That's forty miles. Ten thousand Arabs."

"Twenty thousand."

"Impossible."

"Yes."

"Can they do it?"

"The Haganah is committing fifteen hundred fighters, three times bigger than any force they've ever assembled. All other operations have been cancelled to free up the weapons and soldiers. They're calling it Operation Nachshon."

"How's the Haganah going to open up the road?"

"By pacifying every village that operates against the convoys."

"You mean eliminate."

"In some cases. Those villages which agree not to attack our convoys will be spared."

"If they keep their word."

"Of course."

"If they don't?"

"The Haganah will not distinguish between individuals and locations. If one bullet comes from an Arab village, they will not go looking for the shooter. The entire village will be held responsible."

"That sounds harsh."

"It is calculated to be so. There is an added advantage to Nachshon."

"Most of the area along the road has been set aside by the UN for an Arab state."

"Very good, Hugo."

"This is conquest."

Pinchus spread his hands, the way Malik might have done to reveal the knives in his sleeves.

"That has always been the intention. Nachshon is simply part of a wider campaign, to expel as many Arabs as possible from what will become the new Jewish state."

Pinchus showed his teeth, the gap in the middle, one of the many places something was missing in the man.

Hugo asked, "Won't the British stop it?"

"Two-thirds of their army has already left. More sail to England every day. They won't interfere."

"When does the operation start?"

"Yesterday."

Twenty feet away, the waiter held his ground with the bill in hand. Hugo beckoned the man to come. The waiter laid the bill on the table. Pinchus asked, "Is there more coffee?"

"I'm afraid not, sir."

The waiter's deference indicated he knew who he was speaking to. He almost bowed as he retreated. Still, there was no more coffee. Hugo slid the check to Pinchus.

"Where does the Irgun fit into this?"

"We don't, really. So, we are seeing that we do." Pinchus extended a hand, as though giving Hugo something.

"Tell me."

"We are going to win this war. Once it's done, it cannot be allowed that the Jewish Agency and their Haganah are viewed as the lone saviors of Jewish Palestine. Not after what the Irgun has done. Not after what we have suffered."

"What did you do?"

"We have demanded a piece of Nachshon."

"Where?"

"The opening of the operation has gone very well. Just outside Jerusalem, the village of al-Qastal fell quietly on the first night of Nachshon, with no Haganah casualties. The next day, the Haganah silenced two more villages, Khulda and Deir Muheizin. But the Arabs are attempting to re-take al-Qastal. The Haganah has asked us to reinforce their unit there. We have, of course, refused. Al-Qastal is their victory, not ours. Let them hold it. The Haganah has offered us other targets, villages off from the highway, less pivotal. These, too, were turned down. We have our eye on a village of our own."

"Which one?"

"The last hilltop before Jerusalem. Seven hundred Arabs live there, mostly stone cutters. The *mukhtars* have signed a pact to stay neutral. But in the last few days, Iraqi irregulars have moved in. They've fired at traffic and taken part in the fighting for al-Qastal. We have informed the Haganah this is our target. They have agreed. We'll join forces with the Lehi for the assault."

"The Stern Gang? You're letting them in on this? They're assassins."

"Our little brothers in the Lehi take a harder stance than we do, I accept that."

"Are you sure about this?"

"They'll bring forty fighters. We need their numbers. I want the village depopulated, but not destroyed entirely."

"Tell the Lehi that."

"I expect you will."

"Does that mean you're sending me?"

"If it's your wish."

"It is."

"Then welcome back to the Irgun."

"When?"

"In three days. I will let you know where to report. We'll have a weapon for you."

"A Sten."

"Of course, Kharda. One last time, if I may."

Pinchus raised the napkin from his lap to his lips. Hugo had never heard him say thank you or conclude a meeting with any sort of manners. Pinchus simply signaled that he was done. Hugo stood; Pinchus kept his seat.

"Be aware. Once the war is over, the Jewish Agency will look to sideline the Irgun in the matters of statehood. They've taken to calling us dissidents and terrorists. The Haganah have given us this chance. We must behave above reproach. Obey your better angels, Hugo."

The magnified eyes blinking at Hugo believed angels, even the better ones, could still kill.

Before walking away, Hugo asked, "What's the name of the village?"

Pinchus got to his feet and tugged down his vest. "A little place no one will remember. Deir Yassin."

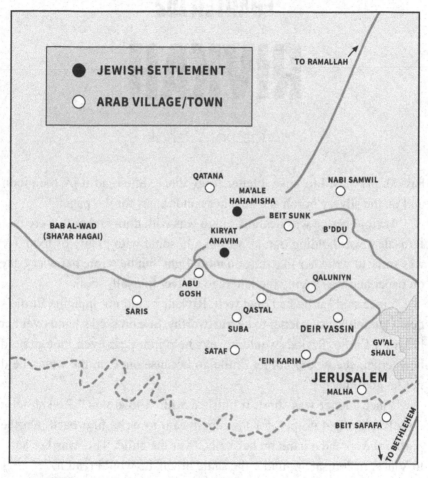

OPERATION NACHSHON / DEIR YASSIN / JERUSALEM

CHAPTER 102

RIVKAH

Massuot Yitzhak

Rivkah pretended to have a letter from Vince. She read it by the moon, and on the silvery porch she held her hands apart for the page.

He told her he was healing. Hugo was with him, and both were fine. Jerusalem was holding out; he was in a hospital with plenty of food. He was sorry to write her like this, on moonlight, but he wrote her every day on paper and was saving the letters to deliver himself, soon.

Vince said Emile had died well. Rivkah would not imagine Emile's death but felt Vince's letter to be trustworthy. She pressed a hand over her heart for Emile. Rivkah would always hold him dear even though he'd been cruel; she would not let Emile go because once, in the water, he'd not let go of her.

Vince's letter was short. It finished with "I love you." Rivkah let it dissolve; she had no pen for the moonbeam to write him back. On the porch, she spread a hand on her belly, over the child. This was her letter to Vince. In Jerusalem, under the same moon, he would read it.

CHAPTER 103

VINCE

April 8
Bikur Cholim Hospital
Jerusalem

The sun inched across the floor. By midday, Hugo still hadn't come.

The old nurse arrived to change Vince's bandages. She indicated the apple on his bedside table. "Where's your little friend? The one who eats your apple every day?"

"You take it."

"He's not coming? He's been here all week."

"Take it."

"I will. Let's have a look."

The nurse peeled back his dressing. She kneaded the exposed mouths of the tunnel, front and back. With forceps, she plucked out the packing that let the channel heal gradually. Vince bit his lower lip and looked away.

The nurse said, "No infection. Good."

Sepsis was a concern throughout the hospital; penicillin had grown scarce under the siege. The nurse re-stuffed the wound, then wrapped his shoulder. Vince didn't draw a full breath until she pocketed the apple.

He asked, "Did you talk to the doctor?"

"I did. You'll be here another week."

"I have to leave sooner."

"You won't. That shoulder needs to knit and be kept clean."

"I'll speak to the doctor myself."

"Will you, now? What will you tell him?"

"That I'm needed."

"In Gush Etzion."

"Yes."

Whatever the old nurse had lived in Palestine, hardships or joys, made her manner kindly.

"You just came from there, dear."

"And I need to go back."

"You won't. The Arabs have blocked the road."

"I'll fly in."

"Perhaps you could. You have connections. But let me tell you what will happen if you leave this hospital too soon. We'll have no painkillers for you, no penicillin. What little we have stays here. You'll need a great deal of care, if you want to keep that arm. Whoever's waiting for you in Gush Etzion will have to provide it. Your medication will come from their thin supplies. Even if you stay here another two weeks, you'll leave in a sling which you'll wear for a month, or risk reopening your wound. So, tell me. Why would anyone want you in Gush Etzion, of all places, if you cannot fight?"

"Because my child is there."

She patted his good arm. "There are children in Jerusalem. And grandchildren. Gush Etzion stands between them and the Arabs. If you want to protect children, especially your own, let a soldier fly there instead of you. Let weapons go, and ammunition. I'll check on you later, Mister Haas."

The old nurse put the apple back on the table and left Vince alone with the sun creeping up the wall.

CHAPTER 104

HUGO

April 9
Beit HaKerem

Every Irgunist was younger than Hugo. They sat in clusters or paced the wooden floors of the abandoned factory. They played cards, wrote letters they tucked inside their tunics, hid their fear, or wore it like a breastplate as if it might protect them.

Hugo tried to sleep, his back against a steel beam. He had a Sten across his lap, extra magazines tucked in his belt. Like the others, he was battle-dressed in Haganah hand-me-down khakis and a green waistcoat. A British steel helmet from World War I lay against his leg.

Three boys edged over. One asked if his name was Kharda. Hugo admitted to it and let them call him that. Soon, forty or more, half the force, gathered around as word spread that Kharda was among them. The other Irgunists kept to themselves, asleep or in surly silence.

Kharda. The driver at Goldschmidt House. Smuggler of oranges to Barazani and Feinstein. Judge kidnapper. Survivor of Europe, and death row.

Where did he go after prison?

Gush Etzion.

Did he know about the convoy of Ten?

He had been on it.

Had he seen the Lamed Hey?

He'd shoveled dirt on their graves.

What of the Arab attack on the Etzion bloc? A thousand, wasn't it?

He'd been the first to sound the alarm.

Nebi Daniel?

Five thousand Arabs.

With every answer, Kharda became living proof that a man could dodge the reaper.

He asked them questions. What has been their training, their experience? None had been in a real battle. Yesterday they'd practiced inside a vacant building, thrown stones as grenades into rooms, then rushed in behind unloaded guns. Their commanders had passed a course in combat leadership. A quarter of the boys had no weapons; their plan was to pick up the guns of fallen Arabs.

Hugo asked, "You sound confident. Are you?"

Oh, yes. The Arabs were going to flee in their nightclothes at the first sounds of the attack. A loudspeaker just before the assault would alert the villagers and send them running. The Irgunists and Lehi would enter an almost empty town. Mopping up, they called it. That's all they would have to do, Kharda. Mop up.

Hugo said, "Fewer than you think will run from Deir Yassin. A lot are going to fight. Do you know what to do?"

One Irgun boy answered softly, "Fight back."

Hugo said, "Kill them."

He slouched against the girder and closed his eyes, with nothing more to say.

CHAPTER 105

HUGO

Deir Yassin

A misty pall blanketed the Irgunists creeping through an orchard. The trees and ground were damp and spooky. Beyond the trees, across a clearing, Deir Yassin slumbered behind shuttered windows and iron doors.

The fighters skirted a quarry among the trees. Hugo glanced into the depths. Stone cutting was tough labor. This was the work of the village.

The company halted a hundred yards south of the first houses. Every structure looked solid, built from the quarries, a hundred fifty homes on a dozen unpaved streets. Every Irgunist found a bush or a fruit tree's shadow to hide inside. The dark would dissolve in the next hour. Hugo lay on his chest in the breathing hush of the fighters.

The commander of Hugo's unit hissed to call him forward. Hugo inched his way through the squad to kneel beside the young man, a long-necked sort, balding early, with the look of a constant student.

"Kharda."

"Yes."

"I saw the men talking with you in the factory."

"They were."

The young officer had a pistol in hand though they were out of range from the village. It seemed to reassure him.

"You showed up last night out of nowhere."

"I wish it had been nowhere."

"The men know who you are."

"Do you?"

"I do."

"Then what can I do for you?"

"I may ask your help."

"With what?"

"You've been in combat before."

"I have."

"I may ask you to help me keep order in the village. So that we don't...."

The officer stopped there; he didn't describe what he feared because he'd not seen it before, and Hugo had. The young man had no nightmares and didn't want them.

Hugo said, "I understand."

"Will you help?"

"No."

✳ ✳ ✳

With a dozen Irgunists, Hugo stole to within twenty yards of the first stone houses. It would be safest to lead the charge into the village, to be the first ones shooting before the Arabs could lift themselves out of confusion and shoot back.

One- and two-story homes lined a street parallel to the orchard. A slow, open incline ran from the trees and quarries up to the front doors. Hugo lay on the pebbly ground, the Sten under him. The submachine gun was bare metal and silver, a nice bit of handiwork. He covered it to keep the faint light from glinting off it and the three Arabs smoking in the road from seeing it.

Hugo lay close enough to hear their voices. The moon was down; the last, blackest hour ticked by. These three Arab guards, starred by their cigarettes, might be the first killed.

The young officer scuttled forward. With him came two Bren light machine gunners. While the gunners set up their tripods, the officer whispered to the forward squad. He had a dislike for Hugo now and didn't look directly at him.

"We go in five." The officer tapped one of the Bren triggermen on the back. "When you hear the loudspeaker, send a tracer burst over the village." The gunner was smaller than Hugo; it was curious, to give the big Bren to this little fellow.

The officer rose to his knees to see ahead better, but he kicked free a small stone which skittered away and clacked against a larger rock. The officer froze, then flattened to the ground.

Out of the dark, an unseen voice called to the three guards. "*Ya, Muhammad.*"

The young officer whispered to Hugo, "Was that the password?"

"No." The password was *Ahdut Lohemet*. Unity in battle.

"He said *Ahdut*. I heard it."

"No, you didn't."

"It's the Lehi."

"Those are Arab voices."

Despite Hugo's warning, the officer cupped a hand to his mouth to utter into the night, just loud enough, the response, "*Lohemet.*"

Hugo rolled to his side to pull out the Sten.

The young officer smacked the Bren gunner on the back.

"Fire."

The Bren sent a white-hot stream of tracers arching over Deir Yassin.

Hugo and the forward squad mowed down the three Arab guards before they could jump. Three spilled cigarettes glowed on the ground when Hugo ran past. The fourth Arab, the anonymous voice, had disappeared. Hugo heard nothing from the loudspeaker that would warn the villagers to surrender or flee.

Gunshots erupted. In eight-man squads, the Irgunists split off to assault their first targets. Hugo followed the young officer whose mistake had sprung the attack.

A large, two-story home anchored the center of the block. No lantern or candles burned inside. With his team, Hugo approached, the Sten at his hip. The big, dark house brooded with guns trained on it.

A slam startled Hugo. One of the Irgunists unleashed a burst against the stone façade as if to shoot the building for scaring him. Out a side door, into a weedy alley, ten Arabs emerged to dash uphill into the village. Hugo swung his Sten to shoot them in the backs and missed them all. Bare feet flickered away into the shadows.

At another, smaller house, the Irgunists used a grenade to blow the front door off its hinges. Before the smoke cleared, they tossed in two more grenades; the stone walls muffled the blasts. The Irgunists rushed inside, firing as they went.

From deeper down the dirt lanes of Deir Yassin came the crack of gunplay and the crump of grenades. Arab men and women screamed the alarm from house to house and the first wails of children reached Hugo. The young officer ran ahead; the battle called him onward.

With a smothered thud, a bullet struck the officer. A rifle report clapped as the officer fell over on a deadened leg. Hugo roared, "In the window!"

Volleys from the Irgunists forced a dark figure on the second floor to recoil; bullets smoked the wall around him. Two fighters dragged the bleeding officer out of the street. The squad raced back toward the dark orchard, shooting at the building over their shoulders. Without intending it, Hugo became the only one left in the street. He could run beneath the sniper back to the trees or dash the shorter distance, straight at the house. Movement in the murky window sent him speeding at the building.

Hugo arrived full tilt, ramming the wall to stop himself. A small overhang put him out of sight from the sniper. The front door was metal and decorative. A grenade would barely dent it.

Bawling voices came from inside, furious, perhaps panicked, but they were many. This building couldn't be left in the rear. Hugo yelled, "Gelignite!"

From behind the orchard trees, his squad sparred with the shooter on the second floor. A second sniper joined from the roof. Hugo's call for explosives was relayed; a sapper was found. Courageous and nimble, under covering fire from the orchard, the man sprinted to the porch. He skidded on his knees beside Hugo and doffed his backpack.

He pulled from the satchel a paper-wrapped sausage, four ounces of blasting gel, made in England, labeled *Dangerous*. A half-meter fuse trailed from one end. Hugo snapped his fingers, then held out his palm.

"Two more."

The sapper hooked a thumb at the metal door. "One will open it."

"I don't want to go in there. Do you?"

Behind the door, voices scampered up and down stairs. The sapper licked his lips, then pressed a hand against the stone wall as if measuring it. Hugo peered with him into the opened satchel, at a hundred sticks.

The sapper said, "No, Kharda." He pulled out three more.

With a steel wire, the explosives expert wrapped together the four tubes. He laid the bundle at the base of the door. "Fifteen seconds. Ready?"

He scratched a match down the stones and lowered the flame to the fuse. The white sparks held the same glittering beauty as the tracers. Then the sapper and Hugo ran.

✳ ✳ ✳

Hugo and his squad scurried from house to house.

The Irgunists kicked in or blew down every door they came to, even the quiet homes. They tossed in grenades, then rushed behind the blasts into roiling, blinding dust. Foyers first, then room after room, they sprayed bullets at stunned and downed Arab fighters, shot at shifting shadows without determining what made them shift. The Irgunists emerged from the buildings shouting, "Secure," and moved on.

Wherever snipers were met, if the resistance was too stout, sappers reduced the houses to rubble, collapsing stone walls on Arab shooters and whoever else might be inside.

Through the morning, the battle clawed uphill. The Arabs answered the Irgunists from windows with Stens, rifles, and pistols. Women hurried under fire out of embattled homes to gather guns from fallen fighters of either side. With the sun climbing into morning and the wounded and killed mounting on both sides, Arab resistance began to stiffen; as the Irgun's supplies of explosives ran low, the attack began to bog down.

Two hours after dawn, the Irgunists had made little progress penetrating Deir Yassin. Few had the experience of soldiers; Hugo watched the young fighters fail to protect each other with covering fire or advance using the terrain, not like the Palmach, Haganah, and Field Force he'd fought alongside. Most of the Irgunists had been trained as saboteurs. Pinchus had sent them into the village knowing this.

The wounded needed to be evacuated, but no one could be spared to carry them out. Platoons complained about the dwindling stores of ammo and gelignite. Several fighters stayed behind in houses they'd taken, the ones not obliterated, to stop the Arabs from returning. The rest pressed on, storming house after house, tedious and perilous.

At nine o'clock, Hugo came to a tall stone dwelling where a sniper was being engaged. Irgunists lifted a bleeding comrade onto a door and hustled him off to the collection point near the village entrance. Three more kneeled at the building's doorway, waiting for a sapper to come blow the door in so they could rush inside. All three looked unsure. Hugo darted into the open; the Arab sniper ignored him running to the wall.

One boy said, "Kharda."

Hugo did not ask his name. "Have you done this before?"

"This is my first."

"What have you been doing all morning? Never mind. Tell me what you will do."

The young Irgunist held out a grenade. "Throw this inside when the door opens."

Hugo indicated the pin. "Pull that first."

"I will."

"Then shoot everything but me and those two. Got it?"

The squad surrounding the house opened fire to cover the arrival of the sapper. He brought only one gelignite stick, laid it down, lit the fuse, and took off again. The Irgun boys moved back on the marble porch, hands over their ears.

The blast blew down the door. Two Irgunists tossed their grenades across the smoking threshold; the young one pulled the pin and added his. One, two, then three blasts flashed, shrapnel buzzed out the opened portal. Hugo yanked the boy to his feet and with a hand in his back shoved him inside, the other two followed Hugo closely.

Instantly, the boy fired into the grey boiling cloud; screeches came from the staircase. Hugo pushed the boy's gun down; women were screaming. The pair of Irgunists rushed past them to go deal with the sniper on the second floor.

Three Arab women cowered on the staircase. Two were young like the Irgun boy; the third was an elder, perhaps their grandmother.

"Take them outside." Hugo pushed the boy again to make him move. The lad leveled his gun at the three. He spoke Hebrew, gently, for them to go outside or he would kill them. They hurried ahead of the boy's rifle.

On the second floor, another grenade went off. Two shots snapped.

Hugo crept into the still-hazy den off the main hall. Furniture lay overturned and split open, curtains were mangled and much chinaware was in shards. In the debris lay two men, both in khaki uniforms, one in a red-checkered keffiyeh. Hugo advanced with the muzzle of his Sten in their stunned eyes.

"Up."

The Arabs staggered to their feet without their weapons, barely conscious. Both bled from their ears. The two Irgunists clomped down the stairs; one disappeared to clear the rest of the house. The other spoke Arabic.

He asked the Arabs who they were. Dust-coated and woozy, they produced papers. These were not stonecutters of Deir Yassin: one was Iraqi, the other Syrian, come to fight the Jews. Hugo's Sten pointed for them to head for the door.

On the porch, the boy waited behind the women. With the house pacified, the squad stepped from cover. The two Irgunists trudged off, job done. Hugo walked out guarding his two shuffling prisoners; ahead, the boy prodded the three women into the open.

"Move aside."

Hugo did not see who'd called out. The Iraqi and Syrian halted, arms high, the women, too. The elder woman looked back to Hugo as if he were her protector.

Twenty yards away, the barrel of a light machine gun was leveled at Hugo. Behind the Bren was the little gunner who'd fired the first tracers to open the battle.

"Walk away, Kharda. You, too."

No one seemed to know the Irgun boy's name. The Bren gunner lowered his cheek to the stock. On the verge of tears, he said, "For my brother Bobby."

The Irgun boy said, "No." Hugo shoved him hard.

The Bren gunner let Hugo leap clear before slaughtering the Iraqi, the Syrian, and the three women. No one stopped him. The Bren still had tracer rounds in the magazine. The silk wrap of the old woman caught fire, and on the ground her clothes ignited. Hugo turned the Irgun boy away to move deeper into Deir Yassin.

✳ ✳ ✳

At noon, the assault reached the village center. There, the Irgunists joined the smaller Lehi force. Neither group would answer to the other's commanders. The Lehi, too, were low on ammunition and explosives. The assault had stalled.

Arab women were pressed into carrying Jewish wounded to the rear. Snipers shot at them, dropping some. Getting the hurt and dead to safety became almost impossible.

No one knew how many Arabs were killed. Corpses by the dozens lay in the dirt lanes and alleys, many more inside the stone homes, killed by grenades, bullets, or entombed in rubble. At least a hundred villagers had been killed, half were women and children.

Twice that many prisoners had been taken. The Irgun gave them the choice of being trucked to the Jerusalem's Moslem Quarter or to a neighboring village.

With the sun high, Hugo rested his back against a shaded wall. Six fighters did the same, helmets in their hands and rifles on their laps. Around the corner, the last Arabs fighting in Deir Yassin had turned a big house into a fortress. From windows and parapets, they shot at any

Jew who showed his head. The Irgun and Lehi mounted several assaults together; all failed.

Fifteen Palmach arrived to ask about the wounded and how they might assist in the evacuation. When they saw the attack had bogged down and the wounded couldn't be moved, the Palmachniks said they would enter the fight.

Hugo had three full magazines for his Sten. Donning his helmet, he got to his feet and approached the Palmach commander.

"My name is Kharda."

CHAPTER 106

HUGO

Hugo strapped his empty Sten across his back.

He strode through areas of the village controlled by the Irgun, where every window was shattered and every home gutted behind its stone face. Hugo walked by spring blossoms and gardens in the yards.

Potshots spurted out of the western part of Deir Yassin from the mukhtar's house where several Arabs had barricaded themselves; the mukhtar's house might not fall until tomorrow.

Jewish fighters denuded Arab corpses of valuables, money, and jewelry. No one prevented this. Those homes still standing were rummaged for clocks, silver, lamps, and pots. Irgun and Lehi sat not far from the dead to eat their first meal of the day.

An order came down from the Haganah to dispose of the Arab bodies. The fighters combed through the wreckage they'd made, but the effort was halfhearted. The debris of the stonecutters' village was heavy; recovering crushed corpses proved too much for the exhausted boys. The stench of defecation, blood, and putrefaction in the rubble overwhelmed them. The recovery effort soon stopped, left for others who had not fought in Deir Yassin.

Burning the corpses seemed the easiest way of disposal. Everywhere in the village, bodies smoldered but would not catch fire. The clothes burned, but wool and cotton made poor kindling, and no one had gasoline; the bodies only charred. The smoke they made was filthy from fat. When the fires burned out, the corpses were not ash but uglier things,

things Hugo had seen before. Hugo and every Jew wore a bandana across their face which made them appear like thieves.

Until dusk, Hugo walked all of Deir Yassin. He didn't eat nor loot, did not search through the rubble, did nothing anyone told him to do. He gave away his Sten.

With the sun disappearing, Hugo stood in front of eight solid homes, all captured by him and the Palmach at the end of the fighting. Hugo didn't recall what he'd done inside these houses, only the rattle of his Sten and the dust on his tongue. The Palmachniks had dragged bodies into the street to warn the Arabs defending the next house to come out. The Arabs had not.

Hugo finished his long walk around Deir Yassin where he began this morning, outside the orchard, standing over the first three Arabs to die. He was numb, and comfortable with the numbness.

After dark, disobeying orders, Hugo left Deir Yassin.

CHAPTER 107

VINCE

April 11
Jerusalem

Hugo arrived by bicycle.

He pedaled up Chancellor Avenue and rang the handlebar bell when he saw Vince standing in the hospital courtyard.

Chancellor and Jaffa Streets were quiet; Jerusalem under siege kept its voice down.

No traffic rolled through the intersection, just bikes and military vehicles. Days ago, a sixty-truck convoy had reached Jerusalem, the first in weeks, bringing food, fuel, and ammo, enough to keep the city surviving. In a window of his ward, Vince and his nurse cheered the column. None of the other wounded could join them but raised their voices from their beds.

Hugo dismounted the bike beside an elm shading the patio. When he leaned the bike on its kickstand, the thing keeled over, taking two parked bikes with it. The tangle of wheels and frames frustrated Hugo, and he left them jumbled.

He climbed the steps. Vince greeted him with a lefthanded clasp.

"Why did you ride a bicycle?"

"The taxis aren't running. Besides, I still don't have any money."

"Where did you get it?"

"I don't know. I just took it."

"You stole it?"

"They're everywhere, like cats. I don't think anybody actually owns a bicycle." Hugo peered down on the heap he'd left. "How are you?"

"They let me outside today." Vince wiggled the fingers of his right hand hanging from the sling. "My arm hurts. But it works. What about you? You okay?"

Hugo shrugged. The question wasn't adequate.

"Did he come?"

"Over there."

Across the patio, on a bench under another elm, the *Herald Tribune* reporter got heavily to his feet.

Hugo said, "He's fat. No one should be fat in a starving city."

"I think he knows some shady people."

"So do you."

"Listen." Vince put a hand on Hugo to stop him walking across the patio. "Before you talk to him. Tell me quick. What happened?"

"What have you heard?"

"That there was a massacre. Is it true?"

"Some of it."

"How much?"

"How much has to be true before all of it is?"

Hugo strode across the sunny flagstones, Vince followed. Beneath the elm, the reporter and Hugo shook hands.

"Thank you for talking with me. Mister...?"

"Kharda."

"Is here okay?"

The reporter gestured to the shaded bench. Hugo remained standing, and Vince took the seat. The reporter sat to flip open his notebook.

"You were at Deir Yassin. With the Irgun."

"I was."

"May I ask a question first?"

"Yes."

"Why are you talking to me?"

"I've been instructed to."

Vince raised his good hand. "Normally, he'd talk to me."

The reporter waggled his pencil between himself and Vince. "I get it, I'm second place. Guess what? I don't care. Now, Mister Kharda."

"Yes."

"The Irgun has made a statement that two hundred and fifty-four Arabs were killed. That's a very specific number. Does that sound accurate to you?"

"It's impossible to know an exact count. Corpses were everywhere. In the streets and alleys, inside the houses, in the quarries. Parts of bodies."

"You were there. Is it a proper figure or not?"

"It is the number the Irgun wishes to report."

"Why?"

"Because it is a very big number."

"I see. Alright. Tell me about the battle."

Hugo paced, hands behind his back like a man talking to himself in a cell.

The battle was to start with a pre-dawn warning to Deir Yassin from a loudspeaker in an armored car. The car was found abandoned, stuck in a ditch far from the village. Hugo never heard the warning. Seventy-two Irgun attacked from the south, an uphill fight. Lehi attacked out of the north, downhill. Lehi made better progress with half the fighters.

"The fighting was fierce, mostly in the first few hours. We blew up dozens of buildings. The rest we cleared with grenades and guns. In all the smoke, shooting in tight quarters, no one could be sure who or how many died in each house. Any Arab who stayed in Deir Yassin was captured or killed." Without remorse, Hugo repeated, "Any Arab."

"Did the Irgun and Lehi fight well?"

"Why do you ask me that?"

"You're not trained as soldiers. You're not Haganah. You're terrorists."

"Two hundred and fifty-four. Draw from that what you wish."

The reporter raised a palm, the point taken. "What time did the battle end?"

"Two o'clock."

"Then what?"

"We told the Haganah, here is the village, we're done. You take it; we don't want to stay."

"Why not?"

"You understand. The British are leaving Palestine. But they hate the Irgun and Lehi. We've given them good reason. In Deir Yassin, a hundred of us were in one place, a blasted-out village with no Arabs left. We were afraid the British might bomb us or attack us. We wanted to go. But the Haganah said no."

"Why?"

"They told us to clean it up before the Red Cross arrived."

"Clean it up?"

"The bodies."

The reporter looked up from his scribbles. "Did you bury them?"

"After a day of combat, to ask us to lift cement blocks and Jerusalem stone to uncover the remains? No. We did not dig graves."

"What did you do?"

"We threw the Arabs into the wells and the quarries. We made piles and tried to burn them. Are you judging me?"

"Professionally, no. Personally? Of course I am. I think you should get used to it, Mister Kharda."

The reporter scratched in his notebook. "You burned piles of bodies."

"They were not the first I have seen. Would you like to ask me about that?"

Vince wanted to stop the interview. He regretted bringing this callous man to do the job that should be his. But his arm was in a sling, and this ape was Dennis's reporter in Jerusalem now. Vince stood from the bench, because Hugo needed to see him stand.

Hugo waved him back down to the bench. The reporter remained aloof and asked more.

"I heard there was looting. Jewelry and money were taken off the dead."

"That is so."

"What about rape?"

"Have you been told there was rape?"

"It's in the wind."

"I saw no instances."

"What about the Arabs who surrendered?"

"Again, what have you heard?"

"Prisoners, mostly women, children, and elderly got trucked into the Old City. Driven around. Crowds spit at them. Then they were driven back to Deir Yassin and executed in a quarry."

"You've been told this?"

"Why would I make it up, Mister Kharda?"

Birds in the elm caught Hugo's attention. He gazed into the lightly swaying branches.

"What is your name?" Before the reporter could reply, Hugo faced Vince, "What is his name?" Hugo waved off both questions. "I don't care."

He walked away, hands in his pockets. In the sunlit center of the courtyard, Hugo halted, then returned under the elm. The reporter addressed him straightaway.

"Was this a slaughter, Mister Kharda? You said you were instructed to talk to me. Is that what I'm supposed to hear? Deir Yassin was a slaughter?"

Hugo's hands stayed jammed in his pockets. Vince got to his feet. "That's enough."

Hugo rattled his head. He'd been told to do Pinchus's bidding, and he would do it one more time.

"The Arabs have committed atrocities. Every Jew knows what they are. Yesterday, in Deir Yassin, we ran out of Arabs to kill. Write that."

Hugo swung his small shoulders sideways like a door opened to usher the reporter out.

The reporter shut his notebook and stood beside Vince. "I hope your shoulder heals up."

Without a word to Hugo, the man walked off. Hugo took the reporter's place on the bench. Vince sat beside him, softly, as though one of the birds had landed.

"Why did you do that?"

"Because it's true."

"Not all of it. You said not all."

"No."

"Was it two hundred and fifty?"

"No."

"How many?"

"Maybe a hundred."

"What about the prisoners on the trucks? Were they shot in the quarries?"

"I didn't see it. But there were excesses. There was brutality. It was war."

"Then why the hell did you let him walk out of here thinking it was a massacre? He's going to print that."

"Pinchus wants him to."

"Why would Pinchus want that? What's in it for him?"

"What's in it for everyone? Pinchus boasts about the number of Arabs we killed; it adds to our prestige. The Haganah gets to label us terrorists one more time, which helps their narrative that we don't belong in the government. The Arabs slander all Jews as savages. The British add this to our crimes. Everyone profits from a massacre at Deir Yassin."

"Hugo, this is dangerous."

"Is it? Are you keeping up with the news? Today, three more villages were deserted. Three thousand Arabs, gone, without a shot fired. The Arabs are terrified. A hundred thousand will leave Palestine on their own, just because they're afraid Deir Yassin will happen to them."

Vince let moments go by. More birds sang overhead.

Hugo said, "You should know. I would have."

"Would have what?"

"Kept killing. I did run out." Hugo strode off. "I'll see you tomorrow."

He went down the patio stairs to the mangle of bicycles. Hugo didn't know which one he'd ridden, so he abandoned them all. He turned to Vince at the courtyard railing.

Hugo said, "The Arabs won't let this go. There will be reprisals."

"I've got to let Rivkah know."

"She knows."

"I need to get her out of there."

"If you do, if you even try, you'll lose her. You understand that."

"She's hardheaded."

"She's a Jew of Massuot Yitzhak. Who among them is not? It's your bad luck to have one for a lover. And soon a child."

Hugo strode away. Vince's shoulder ached; the morning pain shot had worn off.

CHAPTER 108

RIVKAH

April 23
Gush Etzion

Gabbi fanned a timid flame under the cauldron. The top of Yellow Hill had little to burn, only sticks. The winds had blown away the dry leaves, and the spring scrub was still green. Gabbi was losing patience. She told Rivkah, "Go find more."

Rivkah went to forage down the slope. She picked her way through spring thorns, away from the Palmach's lean-to shelters and hasty cabin, sandbags, trenches, and guns. Every part of the bloc lay in sight from the crest of Yellow Hill, with a clear view of the Hebron road.

Rivkah wandered far until she found a dead tree; she filled her arms with twigs, sure this would please Gabbi. She returned to the hilltop before the flame petered out and dropped the sticks at her sister's feet. They built a crackling fire.

Finally, the water boiled. The fire made a comfortable glow in the warm dusk, and the sisters held hands in the unneeded warmth outside the Palmach cabin. They exchanged quiet moments like gifts.

Rivkah said, "Happy Passover."

"*Pesach sameach.*"

Into the boiling water, Gabbi lowered a cheesecloth wrapped around the utensils for the meal. The knives and forks went in *terefah*, then came out *kasher*.

Rivkah held the door for Gabbi into the busy cabin, then followed. She stayed on the threshold to see her sister disappear among the ten Palmachniks, her brothers, making preparations for the Seder.

Weapons were leaned against one wall; they, too, seemed present for the ceremony. Rivkah was seated at the far end of the table from the new commander of the Haganah's force in Gush Etzion. A glass of red wine waited at each place. The commander reached first for his glass, the others joined and, before drinking, all leaned to the left; in Egypt, when the Jews were slaves, only the free were allowed to recline while eating.

Water was drizzled over each pair of hands. Herbs were eaten, then a matzoh broken, for the parting of the Red Sea. The cabin hushed to its bare rafters and the little snaps of the campfire outside. The young commander nodded at Gabbi, the youngest commando at the table. She asked the question of the child.

"Why is this night different from all other nights?"

The commander said, "If we were in our homes tonight, our fathers would read us the *Haggadah*. We do not have a Haggadah on Yellow Hill. What we have is twelve around this table, five at their posts outside. We are all of the same blood, with a shared story that our people around the world will tell this night. But you and I, around this table, on these hills between Hebron and Jerusalem, we have a story only we share. Only us. So, let us have our own Haggadah tonight."

The fighters took each other's hands and Rivkah's, then held them high, a passion for one another and the circle they made. By lantern light, the commander spoke.

"We thank God for taking us out of Egypt. For the ten plagues that set us free. For dividing the waters that let us cross into our own lands. For bringing us here. When I say this, I mean you and me, to this place, to this hill. We are the defenders of Jerusalem tonight. We are the plagues."

The commander squeezed the hands he held, then let them go. The rest followed.

"A great war is coming. The Arabs expect it will take a matter of days. They are leaving their homes thinking to be back to water their gardens."

The commander took up one of the broken pieces of matzoh. He snapped it to hand the pieces around the table. "The Arabs intend to conquer Jerusalem. Gush Etzion has a role to play to prevent that. To reach the city from the south, they must go past us. For that, we are thankful to God."

The commander chewed the bit of matzoh and closed his Passover story. He raised his wine and, with the company of free men and women, leaned to drink.

✳ ✳ ✳

The young fighters took their weapons and departed from the cabin. In the newness of night they filled their bunkered positions on Yellow Hill. The campfire had burned out. Before taking her post, Gabbi said goodnight to Rivkah. The commander hung back, as well. The young fighters argued from their positions over the ten plagues, who would be the frog, who the gnat, who the fly, who the angel of death. In the darkness, Gabbi shouted out that she would be the angel.

The commander asked Rivkah, "Will you walk with me? You and your sister?"

After nightfall, the view of Gush Etzion from the top of Yellow Hill was beautiful and strategic. Perimeter lights glowed around each settlement, and Jews on guard were hidden in the starry landscape. The commander said to Rivkah, "Thank you for coming."

"Thank you for inviting me."

"I was told about you on the day I arrived."

"Told what?"

"You're pregnant. In Gush Etzion, that's a brave thing. The father is in Jerusalem?"

"Vince."

"The American newspaperman."

"He was wounded at Nebi Daniel."

"I'm sorry. I trust he's healing."

"We don't know. I haven't heard in three weeks. The planes are taking off from Tel Aviv now, so there's no mail from Jerusalem."

"I'll see what we can do. Perhaps we can arrange a short radio chat."

"That would be wonderful. Thank you."

He walked them across uneven ground, north over the hillcrest.

"This place would make a fine orchard. I'm amazed at what you settlers can do."

Gabbi held an open hand to Rivkah for the credit. Gabbi had never wielded a tool; she became a soldier days after arriving.

The commander said, "I was a farmer in Galilee. I can't imagine planting anything in this." He kicked a rock. "I can understand your attachment to the place."

They walked further, to Yellow Hill's northern slope. Rivkah didn't ask where they were headed as the commander led them down the incline.

Gabbi cut through the hush with long strides. The commander admired the stars and the mild air, hands in his pockets.

"I wanted you to come with me because you've been asked for. Both of you."

Gabbi and Rivkah slowed, the commander strolled backwards.

"Come on, then." The commander turned and walked on.

Rivkah asked, "By who?"

The incline eased as they entered the flats below Revadim.

"I think this is far enough." He raised his chin to listen into the dark wadi. He appeared boyish in this mystery of his; it occurred to Rivkah that, away from the table of his Palmachniks, the commander was younger than she.

In the notch between Massuot Yitzhak and Revadim, not far into the night, a camel barked.

✳ ✳ ✳

Malik swirled out of the night. His robes kicked and his great hands reached for Rivkah. He pressed her against his chest, smelling of sweat, leather, and herbs. Malik reeled Gabbi in, too. Rivkah stayed encircled by his arm and heart, until Malik pushed the girls back and reached for the commander's hand.

"Commander."

"Malik of the Tarabin. I'm glad to meet you."

"Thank you for bringing my friends." Malik beheld Gabbi. "I could turn three circles and each time I faced this young woman she would become more fearsome. Look at you."

Malik faced Rivkah. He stroked his beard as if composing a poem on the spot. He wore Mrs. Pappel's pinky ring.

"You're with child."

"How did you know?"

"Do you not own a mirror?" Malik asked the commander, "Do you not see?"

"I do."

Malik smoothed the rough backs of his fingers against her cheek. "It is strange. I have never been able to lie to a woman. I have never known when they lie to me. But this." He extended both hands. "*Wallah*. This is a great truth from God." Malik folded his arms. "Vince?"

"Yes."

He pretended a grave displeasure. "I will speak with him."

"Malik, what are you doing here?"

Somewhere in the dark, his camel bleated, perhaps to say we should not stay long. Malik kneeled, weighed a pebble, then tossed it away.

"I sent word to your commander. I wanted to see you both. I cannot bring guns, so I bring him what I have in trade."

Gabbi said, "You're an informer."

Malik answered without looking up at her. "At the moment."

The commander kneeled with him. "I thank you."

Something in Gabbi's unsympathetic tone, in the commander's kind crouch, made Rivkah say, "We've known Malik for two years. He believes we can all live together. He's never wanted bloodshed."

Malik selected another stone. He didn't toss this one away but closed it in his fist. "I cannot stop it, child."

He rose to his full height and slid his hands inside the sleeves of his robe, his fighting posture, not to fight but to be seen as a man who has.

"I am no traitor."

The commander stood with Malik. "Of course not."

"But I know this. If Arabs take Jerusalem, this will become a war of forever."

"I agree."

Malik turned to Gabbi. "You will forgive me."

She laid a hand softly on Malik's arm. "I spoke without thinking."

Malik nodded. "The British no longer control Hebron. It is under the Arab Legion now. Five hundred fighters from Jericho have arrived. These are not villagers or Bedu, but trained in Trans-Jordan, with good weapons. They have British tanks. They have the armored vehicles they took from you at Nebi Daniel. Five thousand villagers have ridden their mules to Hebron to take part in an attack. The Legionnaires held a parade. Their leader said they must open the road to Jerusalem, and they must do it soon. If Gush Etzion continues to block them from the south, Jerusalem cannot be taken. If Jerusalem does not fall, the courage of the entire Legion will fail."

The commander made a short bow. "I'm pleased they've noticed."

Out in the night, the camel woofed. Malik's time inside Gush Etzion was short. He took a backward step; in this small distance he began to fade into the dark.

"Hear me. Right now there is no intention in the Arab Legion to eliminate your settlements. They want to move forces to Jerusalem, that is all. The British also want the road open so they can bring their troops up from the south to leave Palestine, and to transfer others down to Egypt. With every convoy you attack, every hole you blow in the road, and every mine you lay, you place a bigger target on your backs."

Gabbi said, "And Jerusalem lives another day."

Malik retreated another eclipsing stride. "Goodbye, Gabbi."

"Goodbye, Malik."

"Commander. Hebron will turn their attention to you soon. Be advised."

The commander said, "Malik of the Tarabin."

To Rivkah, Malik said, "Stay a moment."

Gabbi and the commander walked off. Malik waited for their footsteps to rise up Yellow Hill. He retreated again, became an outline.

"I inform only this once. So he would bring you to me."

"I believe you."

"Child, in Hebron there is madness. They scream Deir Yassin. Deir Yassin. If they can, they will visit the same on you. Beware. Do you hear me?"

"I do. Will you see Mrs. Pappel?"

"I cannot." He backed again, shedding more light. "I cannot. Tell her something for me."

"Yes."

"I am her friend. I will always be her friend."

"I will. Is there more?"

Malik's eyes were too dark and his beard too black to shine in the stars. "Yes."

His next step away made him vanish.

CHAPTER 109

HUGO

May 1
Jerusalem

She rolled to her side, reaching for the cigarette pack on the nightstand. "Do you want one?"

From behind, Hugo touched her bare shoulder. "No."

"Did you ever smoke?"

"I did."

"When?"

"In Leipzig. I quit."

"Why?"

"They were hard to get in the ghetto. Impossible in the camps."

She put the cigarette to her lips for a grey breath and lay back. "True."

"Why do you smoke?"

"My husband did. I picked it up from him. I might stop now."

"I'm sorry."

Hugo propped his head on his palm. She gazed up into her own cloud.

"What were the odds of us seeing each other again?"

"Very good, apparently."

Hugo's window was slid up. Jerusalem lay quiet this warming noon, with little traffic on Julian's Way. Birds twittered; a bicycle bell far below sounded just like them.

With a deft flick she sent the cigarette butt spinning out the window. She rolled to her front, elbows on the sheets. "I'm glad you recognized me this morning. I didn't see you."

"You were wearing green."

She ran a finger in the furrow between two of his ribs. Hugo said, "Please don't."

She withdrew her touch. They looked at each other with too much understanding. Her camp eyes were gone; she'd gained weight, married for a while.

She asked, "When was the last time for you?"

"A few years ago."

"Where?"

"We were trucked to a village after a bombing. Some women were brought from the Gotha camp to work. One woman and I found a spot in the rubble. I don't remember it as sex. Not really."

"What was it?"

"I think defiance."

She blinked, something melancholy behind her eyes. "Do you go to synagogue?"

"No."

"I didn't either, not for a long time. A month after you and I jumped off that ship, I married the Palmach who rowed me to shore. We made a home in Jerusalem, that was enough. I slept most nights. He was killed on one of the convoys. After that, I couldn't sleep by myself. Nightmares. Sometimes about my husband, though I didn't know him very long. Mostly I dreamt about the Nazis. Them I knew."

She swung her legs off the bed to shake another cigarette from the pack. Hugo walked fingertips up the knobs of her spine. He asked, "Do you pray?"

"No. But I go to synagogue anyway. Can I ask you something else?"

"What."

She struck a match for the cigarette. The open window seemed reluctant to pull the haze from the room.

"Are you lonely?"

Hugo rolled away on his side of the bed. His pants lay on the floor. He stepped into them, then searched for his shirt and socks. In the mirror, he buttoned up his shirt, covered his reedy chest, then pulled up the suspenders. Hugo found his socks and shoes and moved to the chair to put them on.

He stood. Everything he owned, he wore.

She said nothing as he left the room. Hugo took the many stairs down from the YMCA tower.

On the patio, the sun, the umbrellas, and the waiters greeted him. Hugo's table was vacant. He let a lunch come to him that he would not pay for, that he felt he'd already paid for. If she came down in her green dress to join him, Hugo would have them serve her, for she had purchased it long before, too.

CHAPTER 110

RIVKAH

May 4
Massuot Yitzhak

Rivkah had never before seen tanks.

She stood on the quarry path to watch three climb the rocky heights rising from the Hebron Road. Even at two miles off, the tanks were clanking leviathans. In the road, three dozen armored trucks disgorged a thousand Arabs. This time they were not villagers but Arab Legionnaires. Malik had forewarned this day, exactly this.

With a booming smoke ring, a tank fired the opening salvo. The round struck a stone wall of the old monastery on Russian Hill, built in the last century to house Russian Christians in the Holy Land. The monastery commanded a view of the Brakha Valley and the road. When the dust cleared, the wall had held. The blast sent all the settlers watching with Rivkah sprinting to their sandbag bunkers, to trenches and foxholes, to the orchard hill, to Yellow Hill and Lone Tree Hill. Rivkah dashed up to her house, to tell Mrs. Pappel the fighting had started and she was headed to it.

Mrs. Pappel sat at the table. She slid a sealed and addressed envelope to the center of the tabletop, so anyone entering would see it.

"It's a letter to my son."

Rivkah darted to her bedroom for her canvas bag of medical supplies. Before leaving, she embraced Mrs. Pappel. "You'll write another one tonight. We'll mail it tomorrow."

"Where are you going?"

"The monastery. There's going to be wounded."

"I'll come with you."

"Stay here. The kitchen will need to prepare food. It's going to be a long day."

Mrs. Pappel took hold of Rivkah. "All this time. I never told you something."

"What."

"I hate cooking. Morrie had to get rich so we could hire someone to feed him."

Rivkah stroked her thumb down Mrs. Pappel's cheek. Shouldering her medical bag, she rushed down the quarry road, running between Rock Hill and Yellow Hill where Gabbi was at her post. She hurried across the airstrip, into the Wadi Shahid. In the flats, dashing for the embattled monastery, Rivkah was joined by a medical team from Kfar Etzion, two women and two men carrying folded stretchers.

Near the rear of the monastery, they entered a minefield. Placards marked the path through the mines; in case of an attack, the signs would come down. All the signs were in Vince's hand. Rivkah led the way.

Before she and the medics reached the rear of the stone building, the sky whistled. One of the medics dragged Rivkah to the ground. The whistle became a screech, the earth shuddered, and a shockwave roared over Rivkah and the medics. Had she been standing she would have been swept away. One explosion followed another as the mortar shell set off a series of mines. When the eruptions stopped, they leaped up to run into the monastery.

A Haganah fighter met them in a courtyard, then hurried them inside. The monastery was the Haganah's headquarters in the Gush, the ideal spot for disrupting the Hebron Road; this was why the Arabs made the monastery their opening target. The structure was thick, two stories tall; inside was the natural chill of high archways and stone floors. Casualties were being collected in the dining hall. Tapestries and candelabra decorated the room. Three bleeding soldiers lay on a table that could seat fifty.

The four medics tended to the wounded. Another shell rocked the walls; dust spilled from the ceiling. The medics lay themselves across the wounded soldiers.

A fighter ran into the hall, blood on his young face. "Bring a stretcher."

Behind this soldier Rivkah and a medic took the stairs two at a time. A balcony above the main gate had an unfettered view of the Hebron road, the firing line of tanks, and the tide of Legionnaire fighters rising in the Brakha Valley. On the balcony stood a Vickers machine gun on a tripod, covered in bricks and stones knocked out of the monastery's façade. The weapon was unscathed, barely dusty, but slumped behind it lay a broken young fighter.

The boy moaned. One shoulder appeared out of joint. Coughed blood stained his chin. Rivkah eased him away from the ruined wall; bricks and concussion had caved the boy's ribs. He'd dived across the machinegun to save it.

A half mile away, the trio of tanks idled on the slope. Their British commanders stood in the turrets, but the tanks fired no more. The British wanted only to make their point. Open the road.

Rivkah and the medic lifted the wounded boy onto the stretcher. Before they could lift, the medic shouted, "Down!"

Another shell whooshed from above, not from the tanks but from a mortar on the road. The Arabs had come to Gush Etzion with a different purpose than the British. They wanted not the road but the land.

Rivkah protected the boy on the stretcher. The mortar shell landed short of the monastery, to explode in the trenches and barbed wire defenses on Russian Hill. Haganah fighters down there shouted, "First aid!"

The medic bellowed, "Wait!"

He and Rivkah hustled the wounded machine gunner down the stairs and hoisted the stretcher onto the dining hall table. The boy screamed to be lain on his torn back.

The medic told Rivkah, "The trenches. Go."

She ran out the monastery's main door, into sunlight and battle haze, into the trenches to the calls for help.

She pushed her way to a downed officer, brushing aside his worried squad. Without a word, the officer gave Rivkah his combat knife to cut away his pants leg. Quickly she poured sulfa into a shrapnel gash. Rivkah wrapped his leg, left his squad a tourniquet in case the bleeding didn't stop, and kept the knife.

The Arabs kept up a steady fire of rifles and mortars on the defenders of the monastery. Rivkah stayed in the trenches while medics darted back and forth to carry the wounded out. Mortar shells crashed around the Haganah boys; machine gun rounds and sniper bullets ricocheted off the stones or drilled into the dirt. In the Brakha Valley the Arab thousand smoked cigarettes while the monastery and defense posts were walloped.

Rivkah chased calls for help in the trenches; she ran through the earthworks and across a cratered field to reach wounded near the barbed wire perimeter. Twice she ran back to the monastery to refill her medical bag. One of the young fighters recognized her, and word spread of the pregnant angel in the trenches.

By midmorning, the shelling slowed. The British tanks lumbered west to lay siege to the Mukhtar's Saddle. The fighters in the ditch lay grenades and full magazines at their knees, sorry to see the shelling end; now the ground attack would begin.

The Arab thousand roused themselves. Legionnaires tossed away cigarettes, and the villagers unleashed a single-throated roar. The armored trucks opened machine gun fire, engaging the monastery's few automatic weapons. In the trenches, every Haganah gun fired. Rivkah could no longer hear cries for help.

Five hundred Legionnaires advanced in a broad front up Russian Hill. The monastery responded with all its firepower. The officer whose leg Rivkah had tended to shouted to her, "Get out!"

Rivkah hadn't the voice to answer though the gunfire, but she shook her head.

✳ ✳ ✳

The Haganah prepared to evacuate the monastery. The defenders spoiled every weapon they couldn't carry away. Rivkah was with the last group to leave, into the Brakha Valley, making for Kfar Etzion. The last fighter through the minefield yanked down Vince's warning signs.

CHAPTER 111

RIVKAH

The Arabs captured the Mukhtar's Saddle in the afternoon. The three tanks rumbled onto the plateau and crushed the orchard there, then began a duel with Gabbi's mortars on Yellow Hill. The western side of the kibbutz, the rows of homes, the dairy barn, and the library, took a beating.

After an hour of tanks and mortars swapping shells with the defenders, two hundred Arab villagers grew impatient, wanting their own piece of victory. They charged at Kfar Etzion's rifles. The dug-in settlers and Haganah laid them low, casting dead and wounded across the Wadi Abu Rish and down in the cemetery. Legion troops stayed back to let the bombardment do its work, as they had at the monastery.

Kfar Etzion's children's house had been turned into a post-surgery ward. While the battle raged, Rivkah worked there, holding hands with patients to distract their pain. She sat for some time with the officer who took the leg wound in the trench. Fuzzy from anesthesia, he asked about her child as if it were born. Rivkah let this be, gave herself a daughter, and told him the girl was safe in Jerusalem with her father.

✳ ✳ ✳

At dusk, Rivkah joined a squad of Palmach as their medic on Kfar Etzion's south slope. Twenty-five fighters took cover in the damaged houses. Jewish snipers rested rifles on sandbags.

A mile off, haze poured from the monastery's windows; flames flashed inside them. The Arabs would burn it down to keep the Haganah out. Below the Mukhtar's Saddle, a hundred Legionnaires advanced. They walked into a minefield and suffered. The guns of the Palmach added to their misery.

With the monastery ablaze, mines in their path, and the unsilenced guns of Kfar Etzion ahead, the Legion troops retreated to the Saddle, to brood over their next move.

In the failing light, the tanks withdrew. When the British turned away, the Legion and Arab villagers lost their appetite for pushing deeper into the bloc. As night touched down, the Legionnaires loaded onto the trucks that had brought them from Hebron; the villagers who'd come for plunder walked away home. No cheers went up while the Arabs scoured the battlefield for their dead and wounded.

There seemed little point to the assault. It was punitive, not much more. The settlers and Haganah remained on their hilltops; the Jerusalem road was still blocked. Palmachniks made their way through the dimming Brakha Valley to put out the monastery fire and reoccupy the remains. Another unit headed for the Saddle.

The fight had been costly on both sides. Twelve bodies lay in Neveh Ovadia, candleflames at their crowns. Forty Haganah and eight settlers had taken wounds. The Arabs lost over a hundred killed and injured.

Rivkah ate her evening meal in Kfar Etzion. They had won the day, but it did not show. The defenders finished their plates quickly, to ready for more guard duty, for the vigil and the *Kaddish* over their dead.

In the dark, Rivkah walked to Massuot Yitzhak. Below the quarry road, the sighs of shovels rose from the cemetery under the glow of gravediggers' lanterns.

✳ ✳ ✳

Arriving home in the night, Rivkah dropped her medical bag on the porch and sat. She wanted to listen to nothing, no cannons or gunfire. She tried to stop the day from replaying in her head. Rivkah expected

Mrs. Pappel to come with tea and the story of her own day. No lanterns were lit inside.

"Mrs. Pappel?"

She went inside to light a lamp. She checked Mrs. Pappel's room, then sat at the kitchen table. The letter was gone.

Rivkah tore from the house to the dining hall where Mrs. Pappel had been assigned. In the kitchen eight young settlers prepared for the morning meal. No one had seen Mrs. Pappel since the afternoon. One said, "She wasn't much help."

Another said, "She packed a sack of food and left."

"Where was she going?"

"To Yellow Hill. That's what she said."

"During the battle?"

"Yes, of course."

Rivkah flew out under the stars, to rush to Yellow Hill and ask Gabbi what she knew. But Yellow Hill was a half-mile away, through darkness and mines. The Palmachniks and the sentries would not know she was coming. Rivkah changed direction, murmuring "No, no, no."

She ran through the settlement to the last place she wanted to look, the clinic.

✳ ✳ ✳

"She's alright." The nurse spread her arms the instant Rivkah burst in. "She's alright." Rivkah fought her off and flung open the door into the little ward.

Six beds were poorly lit by one kerosene lamp. An open window ushered out the fumes and the smells of bandaged boys and let in the trill of insects from the orchard. Rivkah inched down the row of wounded fighters. They eyed her without greeting.

Mrs. Pappel lay in the last bed. Rivkah stifled a gasp. Only one of Mrs. Pappel's feet, the right, lifted the blanket. Rivkah braced herself on the mattress.

Mrs. Pappel said, "I'm so glad you're safe. Now go find a chair, dear." Rivkah hesitated to leave her bedside. "Go on. We can't have you falling around in here."

One of the soldiers called for Rivkah to take the chair beside him.

Rivkah sat, and Mrs. Pappel reached for her, a way to tell her to stay contained. Her skin had the pallor of the limestone hills. Mrs. Pappel's teeth gritted when she moved and spoke, showing how wracked she was despiteher effort to hide it from Rivkah.

Mrs. Pappel said, "Look at you. Such a hero. You smell like blood."

"What happened?"

Mrs. Pappel looked down at herself. She tried to shift her left leg to display it under the covers but caught her breath at some stab and left the leg still. The blanket should not have lain flat.

"I stepped on a mine."

"My God. How? Where?"

"I told you, I hate cooking. By noon, I figured, enough. The one place I didn't want to die was a kitchen. You were at the monastery. I was scared for you, but even from a mile away I could tell that was no place anyone should be delivering lunch. So I filled a bag for Gabbi and the boys on Yellow Hill. Halfway there, shells started to fly in and out, explosions all over the place. I didn't know it, but I ran right into a minefield."

Mrs. Pappel pointed. "Right below the knee."

"I'm so sorry."

"I think the mine was one of Hugo's. Its heart wasn't in it. Two lovely young men came down the hill with a stretcher. They carried me all the way to Kfar Etzion. The doctor did what he had to."

"I was in the clinic. I didn't see you."

"I saw you, Liebling. Fearless. After the surgery, I asked to be brought back here. You were busy with others, and that's as it should be."

"No."

"Yes. And I don't want you slouching around here with me, either. You have work out there. The Arabs will come back. Stop in. Bring tea. Enough for these boys, too."

Mrs. Pappel twisted the gemmed, silver band on her left hand.

"Do you think Malik will mind?"

Rivkah lost hold of her tears.

"Malik will put you on that mean camel and ride you to the sea."

"We can swim."

"You can swim."

Rivkah laid her cheek on Mrs. Pappel's good right leg. Against the blanket, she cried more. Mrs. Pappel lay her hand on Rivkah's crown; a tremble in the fingers did not mask how much pain she was in.

"Go home. You had a day."

"So did you."

"But I've had a bath. Go. I'll be here tomorrow."

She kissed the grey top of Mrs. Pappel's head. "Where is your letter?"

Mrs. Pappel patted her gown. "Yakob brought it to me. I'll keep it for a while. How's the baby?"

"Fine."

"Then everything else is fine. Goodnight, Liebling. Give the young man back his chair."

The night outside was different, deeper and blacker, perhaps colder. Rivkah did not go home but to the barn where the Field Force kept its radio. She asked the operators there to locate the Haganah commander, so he could keep his word and let her radio Jerusalem.

CHAPTER 112

VINCE

May 10
Jerusalem

The radio room had space for one person at a time; Vince stood on the threshold. The basement of the Jewish Agency was quiet, just ten Haganah men and women on the late shift monitoring the radio frequencies of posts around Palestine.

At one minute past eleven, Vince grew concerned the call would not come through. Before he could lay a hand on the radioman's shoulder, the soldier spoke into his headphone mic. "Jerusalem here. Just a moment." He left the headphones on the table for Vince.

"Five minutes."

"I need more."

The radioman shook out a cigarette and did not offer one to Vince. They swapped places; he stood in the doorway. His black hair was slicked down; he seemed debonair, in no hurry.

Vince said, "Please."

"I know who you are. The American reporter who took a bullet at Nebi Daniel. Do you know who I am?"

"I'm sorry, I don't."

"I'm a Jew with a brother at Kfar Etzion. I work this radio eight hours a day. I haven't spoken with him in a month. That's your time. Those are my orders." The radioman closed the door.

Vince put on the headphones, aware of every second. He pressed the talk button.

"Rivkah?"

"How are you? We only heard you were wounded."

"I'm fine. A bullet through my shoulder; it's healed up. Got out of the hospital three days ago."

"What happened?"

"Emile was in the blockbuster truck. They were taking fire. I tried to get to him."

"I'm sorry. Thank you."

"How's everything there?"

"Mrs. Pappel was hurt. She stepped on a landmine during the attack. It took off her right foot. I'm trying to get her on a plane to Tel Aviv. You'll go see her?"

"Of course. She'll be alright?"

"Yes. Yakob and Gabbi send their regards. How is Jerusalem?"

"The Arabs are mostly gone. There's an invasion coming. They'll be back."

"Hugo?"

"He was with the Irgun at Deir Yassin."

"My God. Was it a massacre like they say?"

"Hugo says no. Either way, it was bad. Rivkah."

"Yes?"

"Can we stop?"

The moments of humming silence were costly. "Alright."

"I love you. You called to hear me say that."

"I did."

"I've been doing everything I can to find a way in. But there's no traffic out of Jerusalem going south. There are no planes out. I pulled every string I could. I even asked Hugo to check with Pinchus. There's nothing. I can't get to you. Can you get out?"

"No."

Two minutes were gone.

"How's the baby?"

"She kicks."

"She?"

"I think a boy would be quieter."

"Not my boy."

"Then perhaps he. Malik says he wants a word with you."

"You saw him?"

"He snuck in for a moment. Are you writing?"

"No."

"Start. Hear me. We share this child. But we have different fights. Mine is not yours, so you cannot come here."

"What do you want me to do?"

"I want you to report on the birth of our child into a free Jewish state. Tell me you understand."

"I'm trying."

"Please."

"I miss you."

"We're not apart, Vince. In this, we are never apart. I will go now."

"We've still got two minutes."

"Let's leave those minutes ahead of us, and know they're there. Goodbye. I love you."

"Don't go."

Vince listened to the static until the radio man opened the door.

CHAPTER 113

VINCE

May 12
Jerusalem

In the morning shadow of the King David Hotel, the passenger door of a
green Škoda opened.

"Climb in."

Vince asked, "You're my driver?"

Behind the wheel, Hugo looked around the old car. "One last
joke from Pinchus."

Vince tossed his duffel into the back, then squeezed in. Traffic was
light on Julian's Way, but the taxis were running again.

The morning shined under a Mediterranean sky. Hugo honked at a
bicyclist for no reason other than to scare him, then waved jovially. The
trip to the Jewish Agency took under a minute. A sabra woman with
black ringlets of hair, Sten at her waist, waved them into the convoy.

The sidewalks teemed with dignitaries loading into armored vehicles and heavy sedans. Wizened men and women who'd brought Jewish
Palestine to this day paused to kiss each other's grey cheeks to say well
done, we have made a new world, or goodbye, should the convoy be
attacked. Their entourages herded them to the vehicles.

The beat-up Škoda seemed an interloper in the convoy. Hugo hung
an arm out the window to pat the side of his little car, to say it belonged.

Vince said, "I spoke with Rivkah."

Hugo raised a finger between them. "Before you say anything more, let me speak. I'm going to stay in Tel Aviv after we get there. I'm going to go talk to an old Czech who will give me a flat in exchange for work. I'll do his plumbing, and when I'm done, I'll sit on my veranda and listen for the sea. And I'm going to keep Pinchus's car."

Hugo faced Vince fully. Like the old Jews on the sidewalk kissing each other, his manner was farewell.

"Before you tell me how heartbroken you are that Rivkah is staying in Massuot Yitzhak, listen to me. Gush Etzion has saved Jerusalem. They've blocked the Hebron Road, and that bought the Haganah enough time to take the rest of the city. If not for them, Jerusalem would not be Jewish anymore. The farmers and soldiers, you and me, Rivkah, Missus Pappel, Yakob, every one of us bought that time. One day, I will say to your child that he was a Jewish hero before he was born."

"Rivkah says it's a girl."

"So much the better." Hugo pressed his palms together. "I have one more thing, my friend."

"Sure."

"Don't tell me who's hurt. Who's dead. I ask God to let me be a plumber. That's all."

Vince patted Hugo's narrow shoulder. Laying a hand on him brought back memories. Vince opened the passenger door and stepped into the street. He circled the Škoda's grill to the driver's side.

"Get out. Let me drive you."

CHAPTER 114

RIVKAH

Massuot Yitzhak

Mrs. Pappel hopped to each bedside to kiss the five fighters. They called for her to get moving. On Gabbi's arm, Mrs. Pappel left the room. Passing through the door, Rivkah thanked the boys for letting her be the one to fly out of Gush Etzion.

The stonemason's cart waited. Zipp was the last animal left in Massuot Yitzhak, a warrior herself. She'd helped build the strongpoints, collected the wounded and dead, and carried bodies to Abu Rish at a stately pace. Rivkah took the old mule by the reins to head down to the airstrip.

Gabbi rode in the cart with Mrs. Pappel. In the valley, the pilot let his engine idle while the supplies were unloaded, to be sure his Auster could take off quickly.

The morning sky seemed as deep blue as a vein; Rivkah was glad to send Mrs. Pappel off into it. Rivkah tucked her into the passenger seat of the rattling plane and leaned in to hug her goodbye. Mrs. Pappel slid off Malik's silver ring and put it on Rivkah's index finger. She clutched Rivkah's hands as if to blend them into her own. The pilot waited no more and leaned across to close the door.

CHAPTER 115

HUGO

Tel Aviv Road

The long convoy rushed out of Jerusalem, down through the gorge between looming limestone cliffs. The long column passed beneath the ruins of Deir Yassin without slowing and, like that, with speed, Deir Yassin was behind Hugo.

The wind rushed in through the Škoda's open windows. The convoy approached Latrun where the gorge ended, opening up the first view of the sea twenty miles west.

Hugo said, "Thank you for driving."

"The least I could do."

"We've reached that point, you and me. There's not much more we can do for each other."

"Maybe so." Vince pointed far ahead, to the water. "You're lucky."

"Am I? What do I have?"

"Whatever you want. And this great car. Think Pinchus will ever come for it?"

"I hope so. I'd like to see him again."

Soon, the column slowed on the outskirts of Tel Aviv. The salt breeze smelled stronger here. People on the sidewalks clapped for the soldiers and important people of the convoy. Traffic pulled over to let them go past to the northern edge of the city.

One by one, the armored trucks and sedans stopped before the Jewish National Fund building, an impressive structure set off by palm trees and manicured grounds.

In his turn, Vince pulled the Škoda to the curb. He got out to retrieve his duffel from the back. Hugo slid behind the wheel. Vince laid an elbow in the windowsill.

"I can get you a press pass. Stay a few days. Watch your nation be born."

Hugo gestured at the sunny building and notables filing inside.

"I've seen this nation born. This is just the birth certificate."

Vince set down his bag to shake Hugo's hand. Hugo had no luggage.

"You were right, Hugo. About everything."

"Write it, Vince. I'll read it. Call me if your pipes back up."

Hugo drove off, to find work and an apartment high enough that when the wind was wild, he might hear the sea.

CHAPTER 116

RIVKAH

Gush Etzion

Inside the burnt monastery, some Haganah boy played jolly tunes on an accordion, dancing numbers that sounded like a carnival or wedding. The music swam through the mist, through holes and busted windows in the monastery's face, out to Rivkah in a trench.

The mood in the trench was somber. Rivkah and a dozen fighters were close enough to the Arabs to hear them talking.

She rested her head on her medical bag. She must have napped, for when she opened her eyes, the fog and the deep night remained, but the accordion had stopped.

The voices of the Arabs were gone, too. Rivkah sat up to the grinding of machines, the growl of armored trucks, and the squeal of tanks. She could not see through the fog and the predawn dark, but the sounds were warlike.

An hour later, the charcoal light of sunrise revealed five hundred Legion soldiers and an equal number of villagers below Russian Hill, all squared off against the monastery. A second Arab force marched through the Brakha Valley toward the Saddle; a third flooded into the Wadi Shahid. For this attack, the Arabs brought two thousand. Three Legion tanks bided their time in the Hebron road.

The sun peeked above the hills, then a bugle tweeted. From the beds of twenty armored trucks, mortars cut loose against the monastery. The opening barrage had little effect; the defenders were well dug in. A bunker protecting a Spandau took a direct hit, but the crew shook off the timbers to right their machinegun.

The bombardment lasted only a quarter of what the Arabs had thrown at the monastery last week. With double the attacking force, they were surer. A last salvo descended, smoke rounds. Another bugle called from behind the boiling smoke. Shouts followed: "*Udrub! Wahad al wahad!*" Strike. One after the other.

The guns of the Haganah, the Brens, the Spandau, the fighters in the trenches and monastery, all held their fire.

Ten armored cars rolled onto the battlefield, shooting as they came at Rivkah's forward trench. The boys had no answer, no armor-piercing rounds.

From the monastery and Yellow Hill, the Haganah's mortars entered the fray. The fusillade destroyed an armored truck and forced another to drive over a mine. Behind their armored vehicles, to the call of bugles, Legion infantry advanced through the smoke.

The Haganah held the high ground; now it came into play. Automatic fire from the monastery hacked at the Arabs' front ranks. Mortars from Lone Tree Hill and Yellow Hill set off landmines under the assault. The Spandau cranked up a murderous crossfire along with the boys in the trench.

Wounded and dead began to reduce the Arabs' numbers; still, the Legionnaires pressed the attack with discipline, moving behind covering fire that drove down the heads of the Haganah and Field Force. Arab villagers crept across the cratered ground that the Legion took for them.

The boys in the trench made the Arabs pay for every inch they gained. Rivkah clutched her medical bag, ready to jump at the first howl. The fighters tucked their cheeks to their guns, and none were wounded in the first minutes.

The Legionnaires battled to within three hundred yards of the trench. The fighting paused; the trench and monastery, the Spandau in the wrecked bunker, all waited for the Arabs to take another step.

The sun cleared the hills behind the Hebron road. Under a truce flag, two armored cars climbed the slope to collect casualties in the valley.

The boys with Rivkah counted ammunition and shared with those who were short. The Spandau crew called over that they had a half-dozen fifty-round belts left. In every window of the monastery, a Haganah fighter kneeled beneath a brow of soot from last week's fire.

The boys passed canteens. Some slumped to steal some rest.

The second assault began when the three Legion tanks rolled off the Hebron road.

In the trench, the Haganah boys muttered, "Hold your fire. Hold your ground."

No one pulled a trigger against the Arab armor. The boys continued to say "Hold," strapping themselves down with the word.

At two hundred yards, the armored trucks opened fire. Bullets raked the trench, zinged off stones, and sizzled the air. The Haganah boys ducked and waited.

The lead tank thundered. A shell struck the monastery with enough force to shake the raw ground under Rivkah. A cry went up for first aid.

Rivkah scurried to the end of the trench. The fighter calling out had run under fire from the monastery, then jumped into the ditch. Blood trickled between his fingers clapped over his forehead. The berm of the trench perked with incoming bullets.

Rivkah lowered the man's hand to examine his wound. Through a squint beneath his bleeding brow, the Haganah commander said, "Hello, Rivkah."

"Let me see."

The bullet had sliced a groove over the commander's eye but only that. Rivkah slapped a bandage on the gash, then circled his head with gauze.

"How is my sister?"

"Armor's moving into the valley. We had to abandon Yellow Hill. I sent her unit to Kfar Etzion."

"I'll see her tonight. What are you doing here?"

The commander reached past Rivkah to grip the leg of a kneeling Haganah boy.

"Tell everyone to get back to the monastery. Now."

"Yes, sir." The young fighter leaped away to spread the retreat order.
He ran off with bullets scalding the rim of the trench. The commander
said to Rivkah, "Please hurry."

She cut the gauze, then tied off the bandage. Three fighters stayed in
the trench to cover the commander and Rivkah. He asked her, "Ready?"

She jumped out with him. The Spandau laid down fire; running past
the machinegun crew the commander yelled, "Retreat!"

With Rivkah he bolted into the blackened, battered building. Behind
Rivkah, the Spandau crew ran in, hauling their heavy weapon.

The commander touched his bandaged head. He said to Rivkah,
"Go back to Kfar Etzion."

"I'm needed here."

"We're not going to hold out long." The commander called a fighter
to him. "Take her bag. You're the medic now."

The boy did as he was told, then hustled back to his jagged
hole in the wall.

Before Rivkah could protest, the commander said, "It's not going to
matter where you are. Go to your sister."

Another shell shook the monastery, sprinkling cinders and dust
over the defenders. Rivkah and the commander nodded, then sent
each other off.

CHAPTER 117

VINCE

Tel Aviv

The press wasn't allowed inside during deliberations. Vince milled with reporters and photographers he didn't know.

In their cars under seacoast palms, some listened to the news. A dawn attack led by the Arab Legion was underway in Gush Etzion.

Several officials recognized Vince as they arrived or exited. He heard many times, "Vince Haas. We thought you were dead." A few asked where he'd been. When he said the Etzion bloc, they patted his shoulder. No one knew more than what was on the radio. All figured the assault was a sample of what the Yishuv could expect soon when the Arab nations attacked together.

In the afternoon, the journalists pitched in to send for food and beer. Vince ignored his hunger and stalked the doors of the Jewish Fund building. Soon a Haganah officer came out, a mustachioed and narrow man with hair parted in the middle. Vince walked alongside him.

"Vince Haas, *Herald Tribune*."

"Of course, Mister Haas."

"Do you have a minute?"

"I'm afraid I do not."

"I'd like to know what's going on."

"As would we all. Thank you."

Vince stopped. At the officer's back, he said, "I was at Buchenwald. The King David. Nebi Daniel. In Gush Etzion. Stop fucking walking away."

The Haganah officer dragged his feet. "Come inside. I will speak only with you. You will not quote me by name."

He led Vince into a building quieter than it ought to be. He found a small office with a potted tree in a corner. The officer settled onto the edge of the desk.

He began. "I was at Nebi Daniel, as well. What would you like to know?"

Vince shook the Haganah man's hand. "What's happening at Gush Etzion?"

"May I ask, what is your connection to the bloc?"

"I lived there the last four months. I've got friends there. A child coming."

"I see. Mister Haas?"

"Yeah."

"I need to return to Haganah headquarters. To monitor this exact situation. You have my sympathies." This officer, too, laid a hand on Vince's shoulder. "Now please ask me questions about Palestine."

"Did you know Emile?'

"I did."

"Because of him, I'm not in Gush Etzion."

"I was not aware of that."

"I belong there."

"Report what I tell you, Mister Haas." Vince pulled out his notepad and pencil. "The council has asked me if we can win the upcoming war."

"What did you tell them?"

"The Arabs have conventional weapons and equipment. A greater number of troops. Many have been trained by the British. Some will even be led by the British."

"Who will invade?"

"We are preparing for the entire Arab League. Syria, Egypt, Trans-Jordan, Lebanon, and Iraq. If they all come at once, they will have an advantage."

"But?"

For the first time, the Haganah officer smiled.

"Very good. But. War is not mathematical. It cannot be predicted unit against unit, weapon against weapon. Morale must be considered. Our forces are steadfast, the Yishuv is mobilized. We are trained, we have a plan, and we are stubborn. The Arabs, you have noted, can be somewhat disjointed. If I wanted to be cautious, I'd say our chances are even. If I were honest, I'd say the Arabs have an edge. For now."

"For now?"

"A mass conscription of Jewish youth has started. We have weapons coming. Many weapons."

"Such as?"

"Get this down. I think I should like it read in America."

Vince scribbled to keep up: In Czechoslovakia, the Haganah had purchased ten German fighter planes, thousands of Mauser rifles, machine guns, and millions of rounds. In the United States, decommissioned B-17 bombers and transport aircraft waited to take off. In France and Italy, mortars and mountain guns, light tanks and half-tracks filled the holds of cargo ships at anchor. All of it counted down until a Jewish state was declared and Britain's embargo on Palestine's harbors and skies was lifted, in two days.

"Will it get here in time?"

"It must. It does us little good to have a nation and no one to live in it."

Vince stood to shake hands again, for Nebi Daniel, Gush Etzion, and what was coming. The officer stepped into the hall with a hand up to pause Vince. He would go first, by himself.

"I have one more thing for you. Please tell no one. Let this be announced by the Jews."

"Sure. And thank you."

"By a vote of seven to two, the council decided on a name for the new Jewish nation."

"What is it?"

"We will be Israel."

CHAPTER 118

RIVKAH

May 13
Kfar Etzion

The windows of the recovery ward had been sheeted over to block the lantern light, so the Arabs would not have it as a target in the night. The air inside stank from kerosene and gauze, swabs and sweat, stirred by the comings and goings of orderlies who lifted the wounded from beds to stretchers.

Rivkah stood over the last fighter to be evacuated. She helped move him to a stretcher, supporting his head. When he was settled on his back and biting his lip, Rivkah set a hand over his bandaged chest but did not pat.

"You're going to be fine."

The boy's wound whittled his voice into rasps. "When this is over."

"Yes?"

"Will you go to dinner with me?"

"Of course."

She'd gotten many such proposals since sundown. Some hurt boys reached for her hand on their way into surgery, some when they woke and took stock of themselves. The appeals ranged from a meeting in Jerusalem to marriage: the worse the wound, the more dear the request. Rivkah said yes to all the hurt boys—and was a widow several times.

Two orderlies raised the young man's stretcher. Rivkah followed outside.

Beneath the hospital's pitted wall, only half could walk. The surgeon divided the thirty patients into three groups and assigned stretcher bearers.

Out of the darkness, a dozen Jews arrived, led by Gabbi.

Rivkah stood aside while her sister assigned four guards to each group. Gabbi alone was Palmach, the rest were settlers with guns. She beckoned Rivkah to join her group.

The sisters hugged, then looked each other over. Gabbi said, "I heard you were at the monastery. I was afraid for you."

"You were right. You were on Yellow Hill."

"We almost melted our mortars. It's good to see you, sister."

Gabbi shrugged her rifle into her hands. She turned to her group. "Let's move."

✳✳✳

So no one would stumble, Gabbi set a slow pace into the Abu Rish. She led the seventy settlers, stretcher bearers, and wounded through thorns, over loose rocks. The guards held their rifles tight to keep them from rattling; the wounded tried not to moan. Out front, Rivkah and Gabbi could not whisper. The Arabs on Yellow Hill would have patrols out.

A mile away, Massuot Yitzhak was lit only by starlight, like the procession. Rivkah stroked the back of her stern sister's head.

Before they arrived at the quarry road, the night sky buzzed. A plane, one of the small Austers, appeared out of the west. Gabbi halted the troupe to let the stretcher bearers and the wounded rest.

The Auster, the only plane of the day, banked in a far echoing arc around Gush Etzion, getting its bearings. The drone of the engine dropped closer to earth, over Revadim in the north, then barreled for Yellow Hill.

From the Mukhtar's Saddle, from the monastery, Lone Tree, and the Hebron road, all in Arab hands, tracers streaked to find the plane. Hundreds of bright-burning bullets bathed every part of the bloc in their glow. The plane appeared inside the white web of them. The Auster held its course, then it dropped a bomb on the Arabs who'd taken Yellow Hill.

A fireball flashed on the crest. The plane climbed for another run. More tracers scratched the blackness reaching for it.

Rivkah, Gabbi, and the seventy were all crouched in the open wadi, every face and bandage whitened by the tracers. In her full voice, Gabbi called down the file, "Can we run?"

Litters were lifted. She told Rivkah, "You know the way. Go."

Rivkah took off for the quarry road. The Auster and the gunfire of angered Arabs masked the commotion the seventy made.

Red Yakob and a dozen others waited at the foot of Massuot Yitzhak's hill. They relieved the exhausted stretcher bearers and ran up the slope on fresh legs. Rivkah patted Yakob's matchstick cheek, then pushed him onward.

Gabbi's orderlies and settlers followed. The Auster stopped circling, finished with bombing. The pilot had done what he could and flew west. The Arabs settled down.

Alone with her sister, Rivkah said, "I'm going back to Kfar Etzion. They'll need help. I want you to stay in Massuot Yitzhak."

"No. I go with you."

"You can't."

Gabbi folded her arms. "A long time ago, you did this to papa. You left him because you didn't think he could protect you. I can."

"That isn't why."

"Then what is it?"

"Vince and Mrs. Pappel are in Tel Aviv. I need you, my blood, to be away from me, like them, for a little while. If we're apart, we can survive. Like an orchard. Some trees will live."

"What about the child?"

"If I could choose, the child would be far away, too."

Rivkah stepped back, fading like Malik, but she was not so dark as him. She held out both hands to leave Gabbi, a strong young warrior Jew, and to say to her, there you are.

CHAPTER 119

RIVKAH

May 14
Kfar Etzion

Rivkah used a bale of straw for a pillow. No one rushed past her; every defender of Kfar Etzion was in place. She had no gun and lay on the open ground.

Rarely had the stars winked this brightly. They'd dazzled once on the sea and again in the first days of Massuot Yitzhak. And with Vince after the Bernstein concert. Perhaps never so brightly as with Vince.

She didn't close her eyes; she had more need of the minutes. Rivkah tried to think of others, Mrs. Pappel and Hugo, red Yakob, the young families in Jerusalem, even Pinchus. Each led Rivkah back to herself and Vince and the child under her hand.

She sat up to the cry of bugles. The night had little left to it. Rivkah wished it would end, to get on with things.

She shouldered her medical bag. The bugles didn't stop but were overmatched by the rumble of machines.

The sky shrieked. Mortar shells rocked homes and farm buildings, orchards and terraces, bare earth catapulted on the concussions, the straw shed caught fire. The Haganah answered, and gunfire rang all around the kibbutz. On the shaking earth, Rivkah had no safe place; she could not be still, so she ran to the fight.

✳ ✳ ✳

At midmorning, two hundred Arab villagers attacked the main gate into Kfar Etzion.

They massed first in the Wadi Shahid, then advanced like a spear, the boldest in front, the rest fanning out. Bugles spurred them on.

From behind sandbags and inside Neve Ovadia, thirty Jews defended the gate, armed with rifles, Stens, machine guns, and Molotov cocktails.

A Haganah fighter pulled Rivkah behind the wall of a greenhouse. He said, "Stay," then ran off to a better position for his rifle.

The attackers entered a fig orchard beside the road. When they emerged, they came under fire on their flank from a handful of Palmach who'd snuck into the crevices of Rock Hill.

Suddenly taking rounds from an unexpected direction shocked the Arabs. Some dashed back to the fig orchard; many, confused, ran straight at Rock Hill and fell there. The fighters behind the gate poured it on then, and the Arabs' first surge at the gate fell apart.

An armored car bustled into the wadi and fig orchard. A dozen wounded called to be found. The handful of dead waited their turn.

Rivkah rested her back against the greenhouse wall. The seeding tables had nothing on them; hoes and rakes lay in piles unused for months, but there were no pickaxes, which had all gone to digging the trenches for this day.

Ordnance men ran forward to distribute ammunition and repair weapons. Rivkah hustled her medical bag to the defenders. None had been hurt yet, and their morale was high.

On the road beyond the fig trees, a motorcyclist puttered among the Arabs. The rider seemed to be delivering orders. A dozen armored cars began to line up on the road; behind them, hundreds of Legion soldiers joined the irregulars for a second push at the gate. Rivkah hurried back to the cover of the greenhouse.

Among the Jews, someone yelled, "For Jerusalem." The call was taken up. Some raised voices for Kfar Etzion, or Revadim, Ein Tzurim, or Massuot Yitzhak, for wives and children. Rivkah stood to call out, "For Mrs. Pappel."

On the road, the armored cars surged forward. The first in line was a colossal steel truck. At high speed, it disappeared into the orchard; the rest followed. When the great vehicle broke out of the trees, it powered across broken ground, staying off the road to thwart the mines laid there. The other trucks hung back to lay down blankets of covering fire.

Around the main gate, the defenders racked weapons and readied Molotov cocktails. Bullets pelted their sandbags and the library walls. The Haganah and haverim waited, heads down, with no way to stop the giant charging their way.

At full speed, the truck crashed the gate. Poles cracked out of the ground, barbed wire snarled across the grill. The truck thrust deep into the farmyard, dragging the remains of the gate.

The defenders rose up to fire at the vehicle with every weapon available. Bullets sparked and pinged off the truck's armored hide; a woman fighter was the first to rush forward and break a burning Molotov cocktail against it. Flames licked over the armored car's flanks, bullets puffed in the dirt around the tires to flatten them.

Tangled and flaming, the great truck backed out of the farmyard. The gate had been shattered. Kfar Etzion stood wide open.

✳ ✳ ✳

The defenders of Kfar Etzion's gate fell back to Neve Ovadia.

The library had taken a beating in yesterday's bombardment. One pitted wall teetered near collapse; holes were blown in the roof. Debris lay everywhere; all the window frames were empty of their windows. Haganah and haverim spread through the building to tip up tables in every opening.

Rivkah bandaged an officer's neck wound. Others fired at the armored cars and Legion soldiers streaming into the settlement. The officer thanked Rivkah, then called a fighter to him. He handed over his Sten.

Rivkah asked, "What's going to happen?"

"I'm going outside to negotiate our surrender."

"It's over?"

"This part is."

"Is there nothing else we can do?"

"There is. But I see no need for it. How much gauze do you have? May I see?"

She showed him. The officer said, "Find a broom. A stick, anything. Go up on the roof and make a white flag. Put it up as fast as you can. I'll wait. Not long."

Rivkah spun away for the staircase, over plaster and stone litter. In the wreckage of a second-floor room, she found a bare curtain rod and ran with it for the stairwell to the roof.

Outside, she tied strips of gauze to the rod until she'd made a banner. Rivkah stood in full view of the Legion troops, all hurrying to find their own cover. Six armored cars and the scorched giant with wire stuck in its grill took positions in the center of the yard.

She hoisted the white streamers. Weapons tilted up at her, making her step back. She retraced the step, then the bandaged officer exited the library, hands raised. He looked to see Rivkah was there, then strode into the open. The Legionnaires trained a hundred guns on him.

She waved the surrender flag while the Haganah officer called to the Arabs, "*Halas.*" It is finished. One Arab walked toward him. The Haganah man dropped his hands. The Arab raised a pistol.

At the report, Rivkah almost lost her grip on the flag. The officer staggered backwards, struck in the stomach. The Arab fired again. The officer backpedaled into the shrubs of the library where he tripped and fell, gutshot.

In the library under Rivkah's feet, the defenders' guns erupted. Rivkah lowered the white flag. Below, Arabs scattered; a few were hit and went down. The one who'd shot the officer got away.

She crouched to observe the end. The Legionnaires and the defenders exchanged a terrific fire. The library took so many rounds from the armored cars Rivkah feared the wall might collapse beneath her.

In the bowels of Neve Ovadia, the cry slowly took hold. One by one, the weapons of the Jews went quiet. As each silenced, the call could be heard more distinctly.

"Cease fire. Cease fire."

CHAPTER 120

RIVKAH

The settlers and Haganah beat their weapons on the floor and walls. They crushed two machineguns with concrete chunks and scattered bullets into the rubble. A radio was wrecked. The white flag in Rivkah's hands was left intact.

Another officer gathered the defenders; they came dusty and down-hearted. From the farmyard, Arabs shouted for the Jews to come out.

The officer said, "Everyone's head up. You fought well. You've done everything asked of you. You know this." He raised an arm to Rivkah. "Give me the flag. I'll go first. All of you stay here until it's safe."

Rivkah was among the many who said no. The defenders of the gate would surrender together. She held the white banner back from the officer. He smeared a hand over his lips to bite back emotion.

He led the way out of Neve Ovadia. Rivkah came next with the flag; the rest followed empty-handed past the Haganah officer dead in the bushes.

In the workshops and farm buildings, the mob was already looting. Arabs pushed past the defenders into the library to strip it.

Sporadic shooting continued around Kfar Etzion. Some reports rang from the homes among the looters. Dozens more haverim and Haganah drifted to the farmyard, hands high, with Arabs herding them at gunpoint.

Rivkah stood in the sun with the defenders, all battle-weary. Many had wounds, but she could not bind them. Armored trucks and half-tracks rumbled through the kibbutz to snuff out the last Jewish resistance. An

Arab grabbed the flag from Rivkah to toss it into the shrubs beside the officer's body.

When the last of the hundred defenders shuffled into the farmyard, Legionnaires and irregulars gathered to see them. Ten Arab fighters walked forward. One screamed at the Jews, snatched a grenade from his vest, and made furious gestures. A second Arab leveled a Tommy gun. The defenders recoiled, Rivkah at their center.

Out of the Arab crowd strode a small man in a white keffiyeh and a European suit. A camera hung about his neck. He commanded the two red-faced Arabs to walk away. They stomped off, consoled by their armed comrades. The cameraman raised apologetic palms to the defenders.

With gestures, he ordered them to sit, then measured the scene through his camera. He retrieved the white flag from the bushes but changed his mind and told the Jews to stand without it, hands in the air.

The photographer snapped several pictures. Finished, he lowered his camera to remember the defenders of Kfar Etzion with his eye, then turned away. The hands of the Jews came down.

On every side, the fellahin ransacked Kfar Etzion. They danced out of homes holding up clocks and pots as if the things they stole were the heads of their enemies. The Legionnaires showed no interest in plunder but gazed hard at the Jews who'd surrendered to them.

An armored car shunted through the Legionnaire's ranks. At fifty yards, the vehicle turned broadside to Rivkah and the fighters. Guns stuck out from firing slits. The defenders packed in denser, raising hands as if they might fend off bullets. Rivkah covered her belly.

The first automatic fire cut down those closest to the armored truck. Rivkah's legs failed, or she was knocked over, but she was not hit. The Jews screamed, Rivkah, too, on the ground. Bullets whisked over her head, mowing down settlers and Haganah, toppling them onto each other; still, many scrambled to their feet. Rivkah's world became two choices, lie down or run.

In panic, heart pounding in hammerblows, she pushed off the dirt, unaware if she was wounded, only that she was in motion. Some Jews rushed right at their slaughterers, dying or managing to wrestle away a few guns. The ones who survived this sprinted away, firing behind them.

Legion soldiers and Arab villagers together shrieked "Deir Yassin" as they gave chase or fell on the surviving Haganah and haverim. Horror drove Rivkah's legs; she might have followed the boys galloping away, but she was too far behind and alone. She dreaded a bullet in the back as she bolted, madly searching for a hiding place. Rivkah took the first chance at concealment and jumped into a trench, to gather her exploding heart and think how to escape.

She lay face-down, panting into her arms, too frightened to look back at the farmyard where gunfire and wailing wore on. She begged the child not to kick, not to know. If Rivkah lay unmoving in the ditch, she might be thought dead, be passed over. Her breathing betrayed her; she could not silence her lungs. The end of a rifle prodded her ribs.

In English, a voice demanded Rivkah get up. A second voice echoed, "Get up, Jew."

By her arms, she was hauled to her feet. Two Legionnaires with beards and bandoliers yanked her out of the ditch. Locking her arms at her sides, they steered her back to the farmyard.

Bodies spoilt the ground, eighty, ninety defenders, and a few dead Arabs. The blood reeked. The two Legionnaires forced Rivkah through the carnage, past wrenched faces and akimbo limbs.

They marched her past milling troops stunned by the butchery they had done. The two shoved Rivkah behind the looted barns, under a copse of trees. They did not speak, and their hands were vice-grips. She had nowhere to look for help, no one to hear her. Kfar Etzion lay murdered.

With no hope, she said, "Please don't do this."

The two halted her among the shade trees, trying to be hidden. They turned Rivkah loose. One hefted his rifle to warn her from running. The other spit and grabbed a fistful of her white sleeve. Until now, Rivkah had not noticed the spattered blood on her. She knocked the Arab's arm away.

The soldier with the gun grinned; the other did not. He raised a finger as if it were a knife, another weapon to warn her. He stepped forward.

Rivkah swung, but the Arab dodged her fist.

He leaned in as if he would pounce. She readied to leap and meet him; they would spring at each other.

The hands of the other Arab, the one watching, flew off his weapon, the gun fell at his backpedaling boots. A roar in the trees had kicked him over. The Legionnaire reaching for Rivkah had a moment to shift his eyes away before more bullets pinned him backwards against a tree trunk where he slinked down dead. The first Arab tried to crawl away, but Malik walked from behind cover with a Thompson submachine gun, black robes unfurled, stood over him, and killed him.

One of Rivkah's knees buckled, the other held. She braced against the ground and stood.

Malik approached, one hand out as if to ward her off. "I am sorry. I am so sorry."

Rivkah tried to fly into his arms but Malik held her away.

"You cannot. Others are watching. Are you hurt?"

She shook her head.

He muttered, "I cannot believe you are alive." He indicated her hand where Rivkah wore his ring. "Mrs. Pappel?"

She searched for her voice, panting, void of words. Malik patted the air to quell her wildness.

She said, "Jerusalem."

Both of Malik's hands returned to the smoking Thompson.

"Girl, you must listen to me."

Despite his caution, Rivkah touched Malik's arm to make him real. He nodded, a small gesture for a giant.

"You are my friend."

"I am."

Through the trees, he eyed the horde swarming into Kfar Etzion.

"Those are my clan. My cousins. The day has come when there is no choice for me. You understand?"

"I understand." She showed Malik the Jewish blood on her. "It's the same."

"This I know. Walk."

With the muzzle of the Thompson, he gestured to the farmyard. Rivkah turned, sickened to go back there.

Over her shoulder, Malik said, "I am going to put you into an armored car. You will be taken away to Hebron. I will come as soon as I can. Right now, you are my prisoner. Act like it, or there is nothing I can do. Where is your sister?"

"Massuot Yitzhak."

"Good. There's been shelling but no full attack."

"Will they be allowed to surrender? Or another massacre?"

"Don't be clever with me. Today was not the start. Did you hear them screaming Deir Yassin? This is what I feared. Exactly this."

Hundreds of Arabs watched them come. Malik lapped a great hand over Rivkah's shoulder. He steered her through the Legionnaires, parted their anger and plunder with his girth and the barrel of his gun.

In the farmyard, Arabs with pistols dispatched the wounded haverim and Haganah still alive in the piles. Behind her, Malik said, "Look away."

Rivkah should be dead, the child with her. Hugo had said this; how powerful it was to be alive beyond your own death. She did not avert her eyes.

CHAPTER 121

MAY 15
KIBBUTZ SAMAKH
STATE OF ISRAEL
By Vincent Haas
Herald Tribune News Service

YESTERDAY, AT 4 P.M., the declaration for the establishment of a free Jewish nation was read aloud to the world.

The event was broadcast live from the Tel Aviv Museum. The Palestine Philharmonic played the national anthem, *Hatikvah*, The Hope. Hundreds of dignitaries in the hall stood to sing. Around the earth, I suspect, millions did the same.

The opening words were stirring like any good declaration of independence: *The land of Israel was the birthplace of the Jewish people. Here their spiritual, religious, and national identity was formed. Here they achieved independence and created a culture of national and universal significance. Here they wrote and gave the Bible to the world...*

I heard nothing else.

I am not in Tel Aviv. I was there for a day, but I left. I'm in a little kibbutz in the Jezreel Valley, hard by the River Jordan where it flows into the Galilee. I'm covering a unit of Haganah fighters on the front line of a war that started at 4 p.m. yesterday. Syrian tanks are coming for them. One of the soldiers in the bunker with me, trying to get some sleep, called for the broadcast of the ceremony in Tel Aviv to be cut off. "We'll listen to the fine words another time." And that was it.

Another time, indeed. To have such a thing would be considered a luxury in Palestine. It's been years since this land has rested. When has there been another time for the Jews or the Arabs here, not just an always dangerous, urgent, now?

On May 8th, 1945, the war in Europe ended. The very next day began the Jews' revolt to throw the British out of Palestine.

On November 29th, 1947, the United Nations announced the end of Britain's Mandate and the partition of Palestine into two states. Inside hours, the first blood was spilled in a six-month civil war that claimed three thousand Arab and Jewish lives and sent hundreds of thousands of Arabs into exile.

Last night, on the first midnight in the nation of Israel, the last British warships sailed beyond the territorial waters of a place they no longer controlled. At sunup, the war machines of five Arab nations invaded to wrest away that control.

Once again, I'm a war correspondent. To be honest, I never stopped.

I left New York three years ago, first to Germany, then to this suffering land. In that time, I've reported on, even taken part in, the constant struggle for Palestine. I took my own bullet, fired a few. I've tried to see myself reflected in the flames of the struggle, tried to understand what sort of man I am. I've witnessed and measured myself in the fighting. But there has been no understanding for me there. I'm neither Jew nor Arab, and though I have participated, I stand nothing to lose in Palestine but my safety and life, and these are by my choice. There's nothing for me to learn from violence; it's just too abhorrent. The lessons are only about violence itself.

I made a friend in Germany. I came to Palestine with him on an illegal ship. I watched the war change him, then change him back. I didn't understand.

I met a woman. The land had changed her, and as I fell in love with her I fell for the land, too. I didn't understand.

The friend is safe. The woman is not. She stayed behind in a kibbutz bloc south of Jerusalem in Arab-controlled territory. Gush Etzion is a place you'll hear about. In the same hours Israel was being born, Arabs massacred a hundred Jewish farmers and soldiers there, and took another three hundred prisoner. This brutality was done in reprisal for a similar act by the Jews against the Arabs, in another small place called Deir Yassin.

I don't know the woman's fate or that of our unborn child. She'd asked me to go to Tel Aviv to see her new nation enter the world. When I learned I wouldn't be able to do the same for my own child, I left Tel Aviv for the front line. This is where the violence will be. And this is where I have discovered I've been wrong.

Loss has been the creed of the Jews and Arabs for millennia, never more so than over the last several years, in Europe, and now in the land newly called Israel. Until yesterday, before Gush Etzion, I'd lost pretty much nothing on the scale of these paired peoples. Now, I understand. Now, in that terrible way, I'm a Jew. I'm an Arab.

I will stay here. I will know what happened in Gush Etzion, to her, my child, my friends, this land. I will see you all again, another time. Reporting from Kibbutz Samakh, Israel.

Finis

ACKNOWLEDGMENTS

The great historical novels of Wouk, Uris, and Clavell set the template for epic historical fiction. I read them as a young man; as a writer in my own fashion, I want nothing more than to have my work stand near theirs.

This book took a few years. Along the long way, several hands grabbed an oar. My friend, first editor, and frequent muse Rachel Landsee demanded this work be my best. If I think it is, it's because Rachel said so.

My best friend Lindy Bumgarner has kept me fed and buoyant throughout, and for the decade before.

David and Shiu Mien Block provided respite, company, and a loving place to have a scotch and dumplings.

Katharine Sands, other people's remarkable literary agent, is a dear pal and irreplaceable advisor. She thinks too highly of me.

My agent Doug Grad, beneath an easy laugh and flowing manner, is a fierce negotiator. Doug is regular people in an irregular profession.

Adam Bellow is the publisher and editor I needed. Adam understands not only what I have written but what I wanted to write. Imagine being published by the son of your all-time favorite novelist.

I want to thank the many veterans of the Mighty Pen Project for their loyalty and affection to me and the writing program. They show courage in the stories they create for our class, no less than what they displayed in uniform. The Virginia War Memorial, my partner in the Mighty Pen, has done everything and more to support the veteran writers and me.

If you wish to read an archive of powerful Mighty Pen works, please go to *scholarscompass.vcu.edu/mighty_pen*.

Lastly, I want to appreciate my brother Barry's service in Vietnam. Agent Orange caught up with him this year. Safe travels to high ground, Barry.

ABOUT THE AUTHOR

New York Times bestselling author David L. Robbins has published fifteen novels. He is also an award-winning playwright, screenwriter, and essayist. The Virginia Commission for the Arts has named David one of Virginia's the two "Most Influential Literary Artists" for the last fifty years.